Thine is the Kingdom

Eileen Townsend is the author of the bestselling novels *Of Woman Born*, *In Love and War*, *The Love Child*, *The Other Woman*, *Child of Fire* and *Dreamtime*. With her husband, Professor Colin Townsend, she compiled *War Wives*, the widely acclaimed story of women in the Second World War. Of Scottish birth, she is an MA graduate in Modern History and Political Science. Eileen Townsend now lives on the banks of Lough Derg in the west of Ireland.

D0716417

Eileen Townsend

THINE IS THE KINGDOM

HarperCollinsPublishers

HarperCollins*Publishers*
77–85 Fulham Palace Road,
Hammersmith, London W6 8JB

This paperback edition 1996
1 3 5 7 9 8 6 4 2

First published in Great Britain by
HarperCollins*Publishers* 1995

ISBN 0 00 647991 X

Typeset in Linotron Meridien
at The Spartan Press Limited,
Lymington, Hampshire

Printed in Great Britain by
HarperCollinsManufacturing Glasgow

This book is dedicated to 'my ain folk', the people of Dundee, whose own turbulent past is writ large in the annals of Scottish history, and by the sweat of whose brows the 'golden fleece' was spun that made others rich and gave their city more millionaires per mile than any other in the British Empire.

CONTENTS

Book One   This Fair Mansion   9

Book Two   A Land of Dreams   251

BOOK ONE

This Fair Mansion

Myself and what is mine to you and yours
Is now converted. But now I was the lord
Of this fair mansion, master of my servants,
Queen o'er myself; and even now, but now,
This house, these servants and this same myself,
Are yours – my lord's.

SHAKESPEARE: *The Merchant of Venice, III, ii*

Chapter One

Dundee, Scotland.
31 December, 1820

'A Guid New Year to ane an' a',
An' mony may ye see!
An' durin' a' the years to come,
O happy may ye be!
And may ye ne'er hae cause to mourn,
To sigh or shed a tear!
To ane an' a', baith great an' sma',
A hearty, Guid New Year!'

The child's eyes grew wider in her pinched face as the fear in her heart grew. Her back was pressed so hard against the damp wall of the room that she could feel the icy cold of the plaster in the very marrow of her bones. She was sitting on the floor, her thin arms clasped around her knees, and for most of the past ten minutes she had had her face buried in the coarse linen of the shift that covered her frail body.

It was the prolonged screaming she could not stand. She had never heard Peggy in a state like this before. Not ever. Peggy was not the sort. Of all their family, her elder sister Margaret McMahon, known to all as Peg, was too gentle a character ever to raise her voice, however sorely she was tried. But tonight it was a different Peggy altogether. Tonight, as the child watched silently from the darkest corner of the cramped back room, Peggy McMahon thrashed about as if demented on the straw mattress, and the entreaties to heaven that came from her lips were matched only by the bitterness of the tears that spilled from her eyes.

'Help me! Please, dear Mother of God . . . Mam . . . Somebody . . . Help me!' Peggy's voice was hoarse with tears and beads of sweat stood out on the pallid skin of her brow as a long, agonizing groan greeted another spasm of the pain that racked her lower body.

The child cowering in the corner hid her face once more and pressed her hands over her ears, unable to bear her sister's agony. Then, all of a sudden, there was a different kind of scream: a high-pitched sort of cry, then a gasp, as a moaning sob was emitted from Peggy's dry lips.

Their mother, who was ministering to her elder daughter's needs, turned and barked at the younger one, 'Kathleen, get me a clean towel off the dresser there!'

The nine-year-old scrambled up and hurried to obey, grabbing the newly washed linen square and thrusting it into her mother's outstretched hand.

'It'll not be long now, so it won't . . .' Bel McMahon's voice was hoarse with hours of pacifying and coaxing as she stretched out a towel and held it in place between her daughter's bent knees. ''Tis coming, Peggy *aroon* . . . Sure and one more push should do it. Come away now . . .'

But Peggy had barely enough energy left for the last shuddering effort. As she struggled to half raise herself on the bed, she took a deep breath and pressed down with all her might, then a gasp that was a mixture of shock and relief burst from her lips and she slumped back on to the pillow. Into her mother's waiting hands, the cause of all her suffering slithered, bawling its indignation to the world.

The relief was enormous. 'What is it, Ma?' Peggy whispered. 'Is it a laddie or a lassie?' Her eyes were closed and she could not even summon enough energy to open them and glance down at the foot of the bed.

'Never you mind,' the older woman said, wrapping the tiny creature in the waiting towel. 'Just you lie still there. I'll be back in a tick.'

The child was still watching silently from her dark corner as the bent figure of her mother sighed deeply, straightened up and half turned towards the door. In her arms was the swaddled body of the infant; its wrinkled face was the colour of Peg's red flannel petticoat and a high-pitched wailing sound was coming from its lips.

The child gasped. A baby! Peggy had laid a baby! The knowledge stunned the watching child. So Mamie had been right! Mamie Moran, one of her friends who lived in the next close, had told her that Peggy was going to have a baby, but Katie hadn't believed a word of it. 'You're just plain daft, Mamie Moran!' she had declared at the sheer preposterousness of it.

But Mamie had been adamant, nodding her carroty head emphatically as she assured her friend, 'My mammy said so, so it must be the God's truth, so it must.' And none knew more about babies than Mamie's Mammy, for Rose Moran had brought thirteen mouths into the world to feed in as many years and Mamie herself had borne witness to the delivery of most of them.

But Katie was not half as worldly-wise as her friend. She knew nothing of the facts of life, having experienced no such happenings within her own family. Her sister Peggy was nine years her senior and their two brothers, Seamus and Noel, were even older than that. She had been more than sceptical of Mamie's information at first, but her friend seemed to know all about such matters. 'It's in there,' she had stated emphatically, prodding somewhere around Katie's midriff. 'Your Peggy growing one in there and it'll come out one day. She'll lay it in the bed or on the floor just like one o' Auld Geordie's hens laying an egg.'

Katie had pondered long and hard on the information, and there was no denying she had been curious about the growing size of her sister's stomach as an increasingly weary Peggy climbed into bed beside her each night.

'My but you're getting awful fat, Peggy,' she had uttered on more than one occasion, and poor Peggy had merely given that wan smile of hers and agreed with a sigh, 'Aye, lass, I'm getting fat all right.'

But learning that Peggy might actually have a baby inside her was truly mystifying, and eventually she had pressed Mamie further on the matter as they sat together on the front step of the close. 'If it's true – and I'm no' saying I believe it, mind – but if she really does have a bairnie inside her then it must be awful sore. And how does it come out? What do you mean it's just like one o' Auld Geordie's hens laying an egg?' What on earth had the pullets that scratched in the dirt in front of the old man's croft across the road from their tenement have to do with poor Peggy?

Mamie had shrugged and tossed her mane of fiery red hair. 'Och, you've seen a hen lay an egg afore now. It's just like that.'

Then she had grinned and jumped up from the step to squat in the dirt, making a cluck-clucking sound as she waddled about, flapping her elbows.

Katie was even more mystified. 'Does it hurt?'

Mamie stopped clucking and frowned as she considered the question. 'Well, maybe it's a wee bit sore, for Mammy always squawks a bit, so she does.' And her frown deepened as she remembered her mother squatting in front of the kitchen fire and calling on the Holy Mother of God to relieve her of the pain, as yet one more Moran battled its way into the world.

It seemed incredible to Mamie that her friend should be so ignorant of such things. 'Did you think your Peggy had just been eating an awful lot to get so fat?'

'Och no!' Katie had been shocked at the suggestion, for she knew fine that Peggy would often go to bed hungry to make sure her little sister had a decent bite at suppertime. Food was never in such plentiful supply on the Hawkhill that folk like themselves could actually have the luxury of getting fat.

Many of their neighbours were, like themselves, of Irish

stock, originally enticed across the sea a decade or so earlier by the boom in the flax-spinning trade, producing supplies for the army and navy in the war against the French. But things had been very different over the past five years; the end of the war had brought the fighting men back in their thousands to towns and villages all over the country that were unable to support them. Their city of Dundee was going through hard times, and the word was that things would get worse before they got better. Hunger was a constant companion to all who walked these mean streets.

But the state of employment in the town was the last thing on young Katie McMahon's mind as she realized that her friend Mamie had been right. Peggy had indeed laid a baby, and her eyes were on stalks as she watched her mother head for the small wretched room that doubled as both kitchen and parlour. Bel McMahon was holding the newborn child in front of her like some bloodied sacrifice.

With an anxious glance towards her sister on the bed, Katie stood up and sidled across the room. Then the palpitations in her breast grew stronger as she stopped in her tracks at the door.

Her mother's voice broke the silence. Mam was never a great one for religion, but here she was praying out loud.

'Dear God, may Ye who understands all that is in a mother's heart, forgive me this day! Dear Father in heaven, I beg Ye understand and forgive this sin, if sin it be!' Bel McMahon's voice was hoarse and imploring in the darkness as she placed the child on the rag rug in front of the dying fire.

As the child watched, her mother took a spill and lit a candle from the remaining embers in the grate and, placing it on the hearth beside her, in its flickering glow she knelt over the whimpering, flailing body of the infant. Then, taking the end of the towel in which the child was loosely wrapped, she held it tightly over the nose and open mouth of her grandchild.

Katie's heart lurched and she wanted to cry out loud as the palm of her mother's hand pressed down firmly over the infant's puce face.

Her mother was staring into space; her finely wrought features had a strange, vacant expression, and from her lips came a strained, halting version of the Lord's Prayer as she waited for the tiny lungs to breathe their last. '. . . Thy will be done on earth as it is in heaven . . .'

'*NO!*' Katie could bear it no longer. She rushed forwards and pulled at her mother's bent shoulders. 'Stop it, Mam! Stop it! You're hurting the bairn!'

The face that turned to glare at her was full of pain. '*As ucht Dé bailigh leat!*' the response came in Gaelic, for Bel McMahon never failed to revert to her native Irish when deeply upset. 'Get out o' here, Kathleen! This is no place for the likes of you.'

'But . . .' Katie gazed down in despair and confusion at the hand still so firmly pressed over the mouth and nose of the child. Her mother's knuckles were showing white beneath the skin, and veins, like knotted blue threads, were visible as Bel McMahon strained to keep the life-giving air from her grandchild's lungs. From the room behind, Katie could hear the sound of muffled sobbing coming from the bed. 'You canna kill it, Mam,' she pleaded, keeping her voice as low as possible so her sister would not hear. 'You canna kill it.' Tears were welling in her eyes. 'You canna kill oor Peggy's bairn.'

'Our Peggy's and the divil's,' was Bel McMahon's response. 'Declare to God, there's no place for the divil's child in this house – even if we could feed it! Sure, and I'd ask Auld Nick himself to make black puddings out o' the blood o' the miserable bastard that fathered this poor craetur, but it would be too watery! God rot him and all his future childer, be they bastards or no!'

Whoever she was speaking about was obviously a sad case. 'Can – can ye no' pray for him, Ma?'

'Pray for him? God love ye, child, the very idea! The

only praying I'll be doing for the young bugger is that a cack-handed cobbler castrate him on a red-hot last so he canna defile another innocent young lass like our Peg!'

Katie shrank back, stunned by the venom of the outburst. A shiver ran through her. Something awful was happening here tonight and the bitterness of her mother's words only added to her misery and confusion.

Several seconds passed. Katie wished whatever was going on would stop. She longed for the scant warmth and security of her bed. The two rooms she knew as home were bitterly cold. It was a freezing dank cold that froze the very marrow of the bones. The creeping black mould that clung like a dark green and black fuzz to the walls around the skirting boards brought an unpleasant fusty odour to the nostrils. Katie could smell it now as she remained motionless and silent, save for the chattering of her teeth. She was shivering from both cold and fear as her mother continued to kneel over the infant on the rug, muttering in that strange tongue that was Irish Gaelic. The child hated the language, for she could not understand it and it made her a stranger in her own home.

Finally, Bel McMahon removed her hand from the baby's face and sat up with a grimace and a sigh that seemed to say it had been a bad job well done. *'Dia liom!'* Before her lay the motionless body of her newly born grandchild. Beneath her breath she muttered a few more words in her mother tongue. Despite her child's fear of it, the old language seemed to bring the most comfort in times of greatest stress.

Perplexed and fearful now, Katie stood staring down at the immobile features of the tiny creature as her mother met her younger daughter's eyes. Bel McMahon's mouth was in that grim line the child knew so well. No one argued with her when she had that look, not even her da.

The young girl took a deep, shuddering breath. 'It has stopped greeting, Mam.'

'Sure and it has stopped its greetin' all right.' Bel

17

McMahon wiped a weary hand across her forehead as she sat back on her heels.

'It – it's not dead, is it?'

Her mother glanced down at the mite on the rug. Her thin lips parted and twisted slightly and for a moment no words came. 'Aye, it's dead,' she said at last. Then before the child could protest, or query further, her voice took on a harder edge that brooked no argument. 'What had to be done is done,' she said bitterly. 'And there'll be no more said on the matter in this house or outside it. Do you understand that, Kathleen?'

Bel's eyes burned into those of her daughter and Katie nodded mutely.

With that, Bel McMahon sighed and turned back to the task in hand. Deftly she wrapped the small body tightly in the towel that was now its shroud. Clutching the dead child to her breast, she got to her feet a trifle shakily and headed for the door that led to the outside. 'I'll be after coming back in two minutes,' she said, over her shoulder. 'See that your sister's all right.'

When she had gone, Katie edged slowly towards the bedroom door. In the guttering candlelight she could just make out the haunted face of Peggy gazing at her from the bed. 'Was it a laddie or a lassie?' the young woman whispered.

But Katie could only shake her head. She had no idea.

As she lingered in the doorway, from the street below came laughter and the sound of revelry; it was Hogmanay, the last day of the old year. Tomorrow would be the first day of 1821. Half the city was out there now, gathering in the Overgate and round the Old Kirk steeple to celebrate the ancient festival. All the old songs would be sung and bottles of 'the craetur' handed round, and Robbie Burns's 'Auld Lang Syne' would resound from every house in the country. But not theirs. Not tonight. There had been murder here tonight. Committed by their own mother.

'Your bairn's dead, Peggy.'

'I know,' Peggy answered faintly, and turned her face to the wall.

'Can I get you anything?'

There was no reply.

In the distance they could hear the sound of church bells pealing. Katie turned and left the bedroom to walk to the kitchen window to look down on the street below.

> 'Should auld acquaintance be forgot,
> And never brought to mind?
> Should auld acquaintance be forgot
> And the days o' auld lang syne?'

Chapter Two

If Katie hoped the watery sunlight that greeted New Year's Day might shed some light on what had taken place the night before, she was to be disappointed. Not even her father, when he rolled in drunk in the early hours of New Year's morning, or wakened sober and sore-headed later in the day, ever referred to what had happened on the rug in front of the fire that Hogmanay. The word 'baby' was never mentioned in their house.

Not even Peggy herself, who simply lay in bed and got weaker and weaker with each passing day, ever referred to the happenings of that night. In the days and weeks that followed, she seemed to simply fade away. Childbed fever, the doctor called it, aggravated by the consumption that was the scourge of all who lived in these dank, airless dwellings that characterized so much of the city.

The day Peggy died was a cold Sunday morning several weeks into the new year. It was a miracle she lasted so long, they said. Dr McPherson had not expected her to see the week out after the birth. 'The lassie seems to have given up on life,' he told Bel, her mother.

'Aye, well it's not much o' a life to hang on to, is it?' had been the reply, and Katie, listening in the next room, had felt a shiver run through her.

They laid Peggy out in her best linen nightgown, in the same bed she died in. She had never looked bonnier, everyone agreed. 'The fairest of the fair in looks, mind and deed,' the minister said on his first visit to enquire if it would be a proper Church of Scotland Christian burial or a Papist one.

Bel McMahon had been quick to enlighten him. 'I'm

sure the good Lord won't mind if she's sent on her way wi' the chunterings o' either or none,' she said, ushering him to the door. 'You lads could do little for her in life so I doubt if you'll be able to make up for it now she's dead.'

A makeshift bed was made up for Katie in the kitchen until after the funeral.

'You'll miss her more than most, Kathleen,' Bel said quietly, as calloused hands tucked in the blanket around the small frame of the child curled up for the night in the old armchair. '*Go bhfoire Dia orainn* . . . I just wish Seamus and Noel were here to say Cheerio. They were grand lads, the pair o' them, and they thought the world o' Peggy, so they did. Aye, and she o' them . . .'

It was not often that Bel could bring herself to mention her two sons, and Katie was aware of the pain in her mother's eyes and voice as she spoke. The child shivered beneath the prickly fibres of the blanket. Her life seemed changed in so many ways since Peggy's death. In truth things had never been the same since that night the baby was born. A dark curtain had come down on their lives that cold Hogmanay, as the bells of the Old Kirk rang the new year in. It was as if in the days and weeks that followed they had all been waiting for Peggy to die. There had been an inevitability about it that even Peggy herself seemed to accept.

'You will get better, Peg, won't you?' Katie had continued to ask.

But her big sister would just shake her head and smile. 'What for, bairn?' she would sigh. And the child had no answer.

'In the midst of life we are in death,' Father Connolly, the parish priest, had kept repeating by way of solace when he called to pay his respects, and it was true, for death was a frequent visitor to every household in the town. There was not a family in the close that had not had a funeral go from their door in the past year.

And now it was their turn. It was all over. Peggy really

had gone. 'She will go to heaven, Ma, won't she? Peggy will go to Jesus?' the child asked fearfully from the depths of the armchair as her mother straightened up and rubbed absentmindedly at the ache in the small of her back.

'Sure and there's no doubt about that.' Then Bel McMahon's lips hardened into the thin line her daughter knew so well. 'But the one that put her there won't be joining her, that's for sure. That young divil – for all his airs and graces – will burn in the fires o' hell for what he's done. And the sooner the better is all I can say.'

Katie looked puzzled. Who exactly was this young devil with airs and graces, and what on earth had he done to deserve such a fate? Her curiosity was aroused. 'Why should somebody else burn in hell, Ma, just because poor Peggy's dead?'

But Bel McMahon merely shook her grey head. 'One day, when you're older, you'll understand, child. And one day, God willing, that redheaded divil'll get what's due to him. An eye for an eye, the good book says, and as sure as there's a God in heaven the family that sired such a creature will be made to pay for the sorrow they have brought to this poor family of ours. I have never wished ill on another human being in all my born days, but I hope the good Lord strikes that animal dead for what he's done to us!' Then, as if death itself was not enough punishment for the young man in question, she continued bitterly, 'Aye, and may his obituary be written in weasel's piss, the sleekit young bugger that he is!'

Word had it that he had even got a young housemaid into trouble when still a pupil at the grammar school on School Wynd. 'Castration would be too good for the likes o' him!' Bel declared to her husband. 'Sure and wouldn't I like to hang the young bugger up by the testicles until they dropped off and then choke him to death wi' them?'

Rob McMahon's pale face had turned even paler at the thought. He knew if his wife lived to be a hundred she would never forgive that young man for the death of her favourite child. By making her pregnant, that lad had killed Peggy as sure as if he had placed a gun to her head. As long as there was breath in her body, Bel would hold him responsible.

But what was as clear as day to the mother seemed dark and mysterious to the child. Katie felt as if there was a great black cloud hanging over their lives, with people – wicked people like the young man with airs and graces, whatever they were exactly – lurking in the shadows, waiting to do them even more harm.

But as she snuggled down further in the armchair on the night before Peggy's funeral, she could tell from her mother's tone of voice that it would do no good asking any more questions. 'Don't you worry, Mam, I'll pray that Peggy goes to heaven,' she whispered reassuringly.

'You do that, lass.'

Katie waited until her mother and father were fast asleep in the box-bed by the side of the fire that night before stealing out of the chair and creeping into the bedroom where her sister's body lay. It was dark in the back room and she made her way to the window at the foot of the bed. There was a full moon and, after opening the curtains, she turned to gaze upon her sister. Peggy had never looked more beautiful. With her long fair hair combed out over her shoulders and her hands clasped as if in prayer on her breast, it was hard to believe she was not going to wake up any moment and cast this darkness from their home.

They buried her the following day, and the child shed bitter tears when the black-draped horse and cart came to take her beloved sister away. It was as if they were cutting the heart out of the family. Everybody had loved Peggy, for Peggy was that kind of a person. A slip of a girl, some said of her, for she had been no taller than five feet, and weighed next to nothing. But she had been blessed with the fair good looks of the Fitzgeralds, her mother's side of the family, and she had been a gentle soul, better suited to

23

pursuits of the mind than the soul-destroying work in the biggest of the Falcon Mills, where she had headed before daylight each morning to work as a spinner alongside her mother.

Young Katie hated the very sight of the Falcon Mill. Its great red sandstone bulk had loomed large in her family's life since the day she was born, and long before. With its magnificent carved falcon, wings outstretched and talons clinging to the family crest above the main door, it stood proudly at the foot of their road – the Hawkhill – the straggle of stone buildings that rose from almost the heart of the city to a point several hundred feet above sea-level, from where you could see the whole blue-grey expanse of the Firth of Tay spread out in the distance.

The Hawkhill had not always been built over like this. Once it had been a green and pleasant place. They had flown hawks from here, so the old folk said. But that was long ago, when the thriving seaport of Dundee was little more than a huddle of small cottages around the mouth of the river. And it was long, long before people began to give way to machines. Nowadays generations of handloom weavers were being cast aside in favour of the great clanking monsters of the factory looms that were being employed in the spinning of the golden fleece they called flax.

The first flax-spinning mill had opened in Dundee in 1792 and now, twenty-nine years later, there were eighteen, with more opening all the time, despite the recession the country was going through. New and improved machinery was being introduced by mill-owners hungry for profit. There was money to be made – big money – and the local men who had first invested their capital into the mills at the end of the last century were determined to see it grow.

In Broughty Ferry, the fishing village to the north of the city, at the mouth of the River Tay, the mill-owners were busy building their mansions. Great stone fantasies they were, with gracious green lawns, tree-lined drives and baronial turrets, and inside only the finest French furniture that money could buy. Every day one heard tell of painters and other craftsmen being brought over from the Continent to decorate these palaces. Money was no object, and rumour had it there were already more millionaires per mile in that part of the city than anywhere else on earth.

But that was a world away from the Hawkhill and the people who lived there, such as the McMahons. Theirs was a different lot entirely, for the ending of the war with France in 1815 had seen harsh times indeed for the majority of the townsfolk who had made their living as handloom weavers in their own homes. Since Waterloo there had no longer been the constant need for cloth such as the tough osnaburg web that provided the sails for Nelson's navy, and the unemployment that resulted had brought many families close to the point of starvation.

That the war had brought prosperity while it lasted there was little doubt, and it was hearing tell of how weavers in Dundee were being paid twenty shillings for working a hundred and fifty yards of osnaburg that had brought men like Rob McMahon and his young family over from County Tipperary in search of such riches. By the end of the war, however, when he had been no more than four years in the city, the need for such quantities of cloth had dried up and the price had fallen to only five shillings; most fathers could no longer feed their children.

For a time Rob had obtained work as a stamper in one of the last handloom weaving shops left on the Hawkhill, and as a small child Katie would visit him at his task of hammering the damp yarn with a heavy wooden mallet on a large flat stone positioned at the door of the shop. It was hard, sweaty work, but for a few years at least Rob was happy; he could keep the wolf from the door. Then their world fell apart when the shop finally closed on New Year's Eve, 1815, when Katie was barely five years old. Like so many others, he was surplus to requirements.

Special yarn-beating machines were being installed all over the city, and far fewer stampers were needed.

Young as she had been, Katie could still remember her father's last day at work. He had sat in front of the fire and wept that night, and when she had crept out of bed to ask why, he had simply shaken his head and said quietly, ''Tis the machines, Katie *aroon*. The machines and the men who own them have done for the likes o' us.'

She had not understood what he had meant by that, but he had been strangely quiet when two years later his own wife and daughter were taken on to tend one of those new-fangled machines in the great red sandstone monstrosity they called the Falcon Mill, that Augustus Falconer had built at the foot of the Hawkhill.

Since then her mother's and sister's lives had revolved around that strange, noisy place, with its tales of children falling asleep at their task of bobbin-shifting, to be hideously mangled by the machinery that clanked on regardless. But for Rob McMahon there was to be no pay-packet at the end of the week. The owners of the relentless rattling factory looms that were now taking the place of the hand-machines wanted no truck with men like him. Not when they could get their wives and children at half the price.

But despite the male unemployment, still they came, landing at the West Tide harbour, or trekking overland, the starving of Ireland and the Highlands and islands of Scotland; whole families, huddled beneath their plaids, shivering on the dockside or taking shelter in the doorways of the Overgate. Mothers, fathers and children, with often not one word of English between them. Gaelic, both Scotch and Irish, was still as common a tongue as English as booted feet clattered down the stairs and out of the closes of the stone tenements, as the women and older children emerged in the early hours of the morning for one more day of toil.

Katie avoided even passing the door of their personal prison. The Falcon Mill — even the very name made her shiver. It was a place to be feared, a strange, alien world, with its enormous stone bird ready for flight, its beady eyes on the far horizon. The falcon was looking far out to sea, where her brothers had headed as soon as they were old enough. But that was an impossible dream if you happened to be born a girl. Instead she made do with climbing away up past the ranks of steeply stacked tenements that were home, to the very top of the Hawkhill itself, or even higher, up to the great green mound they called the Law Hill. From there, far above the smoke-blackened chimneys, you could see the masts of the great sailing ships jostling one another along the dockside before heading out to the turbulent expanse of the German Ocean.

From the window of the back room she had shared with Peggy, she could just make out the glint of the sea; she knew it was not always as grey as it appeared on that cold March day they buried her sister. As winter turned to spring, it would begin to sparkle blue in the sunlight, and the raucous cries of the seagulls as they swooped and soared over the rooftops would once more be like a siren call to the young girl as she stood at the small window gazing out and longing with all her heart for that same freedom to fly away, as far away as possible from these two dingy rooms. If only she had the wings, she too would head for the open sea, to do as both her brothers had done and sail away to the ends of the earth to breathe fresh air and live – really live – not just exist until an early grave claimed you, as had happened to Peggy and so many others around here.

But whilst she had loved her sister, Katie could barely remember her brothers. No one knew if Bel and Rob McMahon's two sons would ever come back. They had been gone a good few years now. Rumour had it that Seamus's boat had gone down with all hands during a squall in the Southern Ocean, and that Noel had jumped ship in Boston to be with an American lass he had met on shore.

Whatever the reasons for their absence, if they were missed at home then Bel McMahon and her husband had never let their feelings show. Decent folk did not show their emotions. Apart from the time of Peggy's funeral, only once had their mother let her guard slip, and that was one cold Sunday morning in February, on the day that should have been Seamus's twenty-first birthday. As she lifted down the polished wooden spill-holder he had carved for her on his first voyage to set light to the fire, she had said softly to her youngest child, ''Tis hard the good Lord is on mothers, Kathleen. We suffer in their coming and in their going. God's truth, how we suffer . . .'

Now, as Katie stood at the head of their close one Sunday evening in early spring, shortly after her sister Peggy's funeral, she remembered those words and wondered how much her mother had suffered in Peggy's going, and if Peggy herself had suffered in her own child's death. Certainly neither had ever really made their feelings known. In fact, with the baby's birth and sudden death, followed by Peggy's own death several weeks later, and barely a word of explanation about either, the whole episode had left the child feeling both confused and unhappy. She still had nightmares about her mother putting her hand over the baby's mouth. And sometimes she dreamt that she too was being suffocated and would wake up screaming in the middle of the night. But she dared not tell her mother the reason for her night terrors. Somehow she knew that terrible episode must never be spoken of again.

She was standing on the front step musing on the turn her life had taken when Davey Lorimer, her special friend from down the road, passed by. Katie adored Davey. He was a few months older than her and, at ten years old, with brown curly hair and a pugnacious expression, he was small for his age but tough. He could, and often did, take on any lad on the Hawkhill, or from the Overgate gang down the road. His family were not Irish like her own, but came of local fisher stock, from the village of Broughty Ferry, four miles to the north. What became of his father, Katie never knew, but in the last year of the war with France, with four fatherless children to feed, his mother Betty had walked into the city to work alongside Bel McMahon and her daughter Peggy in the Hawkhill's Falcon Mill.

Davey stopped uncertainly by the front of the Mc Mahons' close and wondered what to say for the best. It was the first time he had spoken to his friend since they buried her sister in a pauper's grave.

His booted feet shuffled uncomfortably in the dust and he surveyed the ground for a moment or two before squinting up into the dying light of the afternoon sun. Katie's dark head was silhouetted against a shaft of light and, young as he was, his heart missed a beat. She had been his favourite of all the lasses on the close as far back as he could remember. 'I'm right sorry about your sister.' The words were blurted out.

'Aye. So am I.'

Their eyes met and he gave an embarrassed half-grin as he dug a wedge of sticky brown toffee from his trouser pocket and, after picking off most of the fluff, held it out to his friend. 'Go on, you can have a sook.'

Katie accepted the offering gratefully and poked the sticky mass into the corner of her cheek. She sucked hard on the lump for a moment or two, savouring its sweetness.

'That's lang enough.'

Reluctantly she handed it back.

Davey slipped it into his own mouth and moved it around on his tongue as Katie licked her fingers and implored him for another few seconds of heaven.

'Go on, Wee Davey – just one more lick.'

'No, why should I?' It felt great to be in possession of something so coveted by someone else. In a minute or two she would be begging him, imploring him to give in. 'Why should I? Tell me that.'

''Cause I asked you nicely, that's why!' The answer was as indignant as her feelings as she watched with her mouth watering.

He made no reply, but the delicious sucking noises that were being emitted from his lips made patience an impossible virtue. Katie took a deep breath. She could feel her hands forming fists at her side. He was being deliberately provocative. There was only one thing for it. 'If asking nicely doesn't work, I'll batter ye!'

He looked startled, then merely grinned and shook his head. She'd have to do better than that. She was only a lassie. She didn't frighten him.

With that Katie sprang into action and aimed a flailing punch in the direction of her friend's right ear.

The suddenness of the jab made Davey jolt back, half swallow, then choke on the wedge of toffee. He doubled up at the side of the road, going alarmingly red in the face as he coughed and spluttered in his fight for breath.

Shocked at the result of her action, an alarmed Katie dashed over and began to thump him on the back, then when that produced no result, she looked around her frantically for help. A well-dressed young man was passing on the other side of the road and she ran towards him shouting, 'Hey, stop, Mister! Stop!'

Grabbing her prey by the arm, she hauled him over to where the choking boy was now on his knees at the mouth of the close.

'Help him, Mister, please! He's got a lump o' toffee stuck in his throat!' she implored, jumping up and down in her concern.

The young man took one look at the gasping child, whose eyes were now streaming, his face puce, and, clutching Davey by the shoulders, he jerked him to his feet, then turned him upside down before giving him an almighty thump in the back. Davey's head was between the young man's knees and at the second thump the offending lump shot out to land on the dirt at Katie's feet.

'That'll teach you not to steal from sweetie shops!' Davey's saviour admonished as he lowered the gasping boy to his feet once more. It was only this morning that Mattie Mutch who ran the little shop on the corner by the mill had complained to him about children pilfering from the open counter behind her back. And this scruffy pair certainly didn't have the spare halfpenny required to buy a lump of toffee, that was for sure.

Then turning to Katie, the young man said sternly, 'Your brother could have died. That'll teach you bairns not to pinch what doesn't belong to you.' He had absolutely no doubt that the sweet was filched.

'He's no' my brother!' Katie protested in indignation. 'Seamus and Noel are my brothers and they could beat you in a fight any day, Mister! They would, too, for you saying nasty things about us like that.' She took great exception to the young man's supercilious manner and his total certainty that the sweet must be stolen.

At the sound of the two names, the young man turned back to look curiously at the girl. Bells were ringing in his head. His brow puckered beneath the quiff of red hair. 'And what might *your* name be?' he asked.

'Dinna tell him, Katie!' Davey protested, wiping the tears with the back of his hand. Almost recovered now, he was on his knees retrieving his sticky treasure from the dirt at the side of the road.

'Katie, eh?' Along with the names of Seamus and Noel, those bells in his head were deafening him now. He folded his arms, his hazel eyes taking in the slight frame and long dark hair. She certainly didn't look much like her sister, that was for sure. 'Your surname wouldn't be McMahon by any chance?'

Katie glanced nervously at Davey, who was standing up now and wiping the toffee on the sleeve of his jacket.

'She's no' telling you anything!' he shouted at the young man. 'So you needna ask!'

The young man stood for a moment longer, looking

from one to the other. 'I'll wager you're Katie McMahon or I'm a Dutchman!' he declared, shaking his head and looking again from one to the other for a moment or two before continuing on his way.

'You're a Dutchman! You're a Dutchman!' Davey shouted after him, determined to have the last word, even if it meant telling a lie.

'You were awful rude to that mannie,' Katie said, turning to her friend once the young man was out of earshot.

'He deserved it,' Davey said defensively. 'My ma says he should be hanged and not allowed to walk the streets like this.'

'Wh – what do you mean?'

Davey looked at her in scorn. 'Do you no' ken who that is, then?'

Katie shook her head, feeling very foolish indeed.

'He's Willie Falconer, that's who. Your Peggy's murderer!'

Katie's jaw dropped open. 'I – I don't know what you mean,' she said at last, her eyes peering after the figure disappearing into the distance.

Davey shrugged his shoulders and sucked hard on the sweet. He had only heard part of the story, and was not that sure he understood it all himself. But one thing was for certain: his mother Betty was convinced that young Willie Falconer was responsible for Peggy McMahon's death; and so he must be, for his mother was never wrong.

He sat down with a sigh on the stone step at the end of the close and squinted up at Katie as he moved the toffee from cheek to cheek. 'My mam says they should try Willie Falconer for murder. Hanged he should be.'

Katie's brow furrowed as she peered down at him in the growing twilight. Then in the back of her mind she could recall her own mother saying something about a young man with airs and graces and the devil in connection with poor Peggy. 'Does yon Willie Falconer have airs and graces, Wee Davey?' Surely if he did, that would clinch it.

He would indeed be the devil her mother referred to so bitterly.

She gazed into the distance, but there was now no sign of the tall eighteen-year-old with reddish hair who was Augustus Falconer's only child. Young though he was, the heir to the Falcon Mill was spoken of with some awe around here, both for his temper and his brains. They said he had been Dux Medallist at the grammar school in both Latin and Greek – a feat not even his father had accomplished. And he had recently completed his last year of schooling and the rector had been quite insistent that he should be enrolled at Edinburgh University, or at the very least at St Andrews, just ten miles across the Tay, but his father would have none of it. There was only one place for his only son as far as old Augustus Falconer was concerned, and that was at his father's side, helping run the mills.

But the two children knew nothing of the young man's educational prowess or his father's hopes for him as they pondered on the situation.

It was Davey who spoke first. 'Airs and graces? Well, I'm no' rightly sure.' Then, quick to cover his ignorance as to the meaning of those fine-sounding attributes, he added vehemently, 'But he'll still go to hell, that's for sure.'

Katie eyed her friend curiously. 'You're daft, Davey Lorimer. Why should Willie Falconer go to hell?'

'For what he did to your Peggy, that's what for.' Davey's blue eyes narrowed. 'Didn't they tell you that Willie Falconer was the father of her bairn?'

33

Chapter Three

In the weeks that followed her sister's death, Katie felt both confused and lonely in the two rooms that the McMahons called home. Peggy had been more than a sister, she had been her best friend, someone to confide in and cuddle up to in bed at night when the world seemed a cold and hostile place. She longed to talk to her parents about Peggy's death, but something told her it was still not the right time to raise the subject. It would never be the right time, for in their family Peggy had become a non-person. Like Seamus and Noel, it was as if she had never existed.

Ignoring her youngest child's torment, Bel McMahon simply turned her grief inward, picking up her Bible and heading for the Catholic church at the end of their road whenever her own pain became too much to bear. She had never bothered much with religion in the past, but more and more she was turning to the Almighty for support. Certainly she got little of that from Rob, her husband.

Robert McMahon, or Lang Rob as he was better known to his friends, had always been a man of few words. Robert McMahon and Isabella Fitzgerald had been childhood sweethearts in the small Tipperary town of Nenagh, before they had left Ireland as young marrieds in search of work in the new mills on the mainland.

A tall, thin man with the consumptive's grey pallor and hollow-eyed gaze, Rob was more easy-going but much weaker in character than his wife. According to Bel he would happily gamble his last ha'penny on two raindrops running down a windowpane, and any money he made from the bet would be down his throat as fast as it took him to walk the twenty yards to the nearest public house.

It was not easy for a man in this city. Mill-owners preferred to employ women and children who cost them much less in wages. Those husbands and fathers not still eking out a living from working the handlooms from home, or fortunate enough to be in other trades, were relegated to hanging around the street corners. Even temporary work was hard to come by and, as their frustration grew, many turned to drink. For those men who still had a shred of self-respect left, it was not easy to watch your wife and small children rising before dawn to face yet one more exhausting day on the mill floor, while you were forced to wait at home. ''Tis a kept man, so I am!' Rob McMahon's children had often heard him declare in despair. 'A kept man, and that's the God's truth.' And the sad thing was, nobody could deny it.

By the end of the second decade of the century, there were more children than fathers at work in the city. From as young as eight they were employed as shifters, replacing bobbins on spindles, amid the incessant noise and the swirling dust of the flax-spinning mills. For fourteen hours from Monday to Friday and twelve hours on a Saturday, the mill would be their prison. The doors were locked during working hours and what went on within was often little short of murder. Sitting down was strictly forbidden and even their one meal – usually a cold potato – was eaten as they worked. Forced into standing for so long, growing limbs quickly became deformed and those who could stand upright no longer and fell into unconsciousness would have buckets of cold water poured over their heads to revive them. Their only holiday was two days off at New Year.

'It's damned I'll be if another child of mine will go into that hell-hole,' Lang Rob told his wife shortly after Peggy's death, and Bel McMahon had not demurred. One way or another the Falcon Mill had killed poor Peggy and both were determined their youngest child would not meet the same fate. But in front of Katie herself there was never any discussion as to whether she would follow in Peggy's footsteps and go into the mill come her tenth birthday.

It was an unsettling time for the child, and in the whole world there was only one person she could confide in. Davey Lorimer might be only a laddie, but he would listen as she told him of her loathing for the great red sandstone building with that awful bird on top. The two of them would clamber up to the very summit of the Law Hill and lie there in the long grass, looking down on the smoking chimneys of the city that was their home.

'I wish I was a laddie like you,' Katie would tell her friend. 'Then I'd no' have to go into that awful place. I could go to sea like Seamus and Noel and never come back again.'

And Davey would nod his curly head and agree that to go into the mill would indeed be a fate worse than death. 'I'm going to be a politician,' he would tell her. 'Then I can make laws so folk like my ma and yours, and lassies like you wouldn't have to work in places like that.'

And Katie would laugh at such a high-faluting idea. 'Ordinary folk like you canna become politicians,' she would tell him. 'You have to be a mannie wi' money and a lum hat before you can do that.'

And he would look back at her with those eyes the colour of the slate roofs far below them and solemnly swear, 'Then I'll be a mannie wi' money and a lum hat some day, you wait and see.'

But waiting till Davey grew into a mannie with money and a top hat was too far off a prospect to help with the present, so, as the year wore on, Katie did her best to put all thoughts of what the future might bring out of her mind. Mamie Moran and several others of their friends were already working alongside their mothers and elder sisters, so she presumed she too would join the early morning trek to the mill when the time came. It was a fearful thought.

As her tenth birthday grew ever closer, her waking fears became nightmares which would find her screaming and alone amid a cacophony of clanking machines, with metal teeth that grinned in the most evil way. She made a few attempts to raise the subject of the mill with her mother, but Bel McMahon would simply dismiss the matter with an irritable, 'It's talking about that we'll be when the time comes, Kathleen, not before.'

But when the time eventually did come, no one talked about anything with the child, the decision to put her into service instead was simply announced the day before her tenth birthday.

'It's hard work in service, mind, and long hours, but it's better off you'll be, there's no doubt about that.' Then, with a sideways glance at her husband, Bel added, 'And I'd say, 'tis safer you'll be into the bargain, in more ways than one.'

There had been word of Willie Falconer getting yet one more young girl in the family way. 'May the good Lord strike me dead on the spot if I tell a word of a lie,' Rose Moran had declared to Bel on the way to work the week before. 'The dirty young bugger has got the Millan lass into trouble and old Augustus has tried to hush it up by offering the family ten quid to move to Edinburgh.'

Rose Moran had not been struck down and Bel was convinced the story must be true, especially as the Millans, who were being provocatively mysterious about it all, were making suspicious noises about moving down south. No doubt the dust would barely have settled from their coach wheels when young Master Willie would be on the lookout for his next prey. And both her parents knew that, young though she was, they would be well advised to keep young Katie out of that particular fine gentleman's clutches.

Bel McMahon looked up from her darning and rested her eyes on her youngest child sitting practising her letters in the chair on the opposite side of the hearth. Tomorrow she would be all of ten years old and a child no longer; certainly old enough to be taken on by her own employer. Unlike some of his competitors who turned a blind eye to under-age labour, Augustus Falconer actually preferred his child workers to have reached their tenth birthday.

There were many who lied about their offsprings' age to get them taken on earlier, but Bel was determined her remaining child would go nowhere near a spinning-frame. One by one over the years she had lost all her children. Only Katie remained, but if anyone could make it in this hard world, this one could. Of all the McMahon children, she had been the first to walk and the first to talk and through long hours spent at Sunday school she could read fluently from the old King James Bible by the time she was eight years old. There were not many on the Hawkhill who could claim that feat.

Bel sighed as she pulled her needle through the heel of the sock. It had not been easy being a mother. She wished she could have cared more for her offspring, but working in the mill from dawn to dusk left little time for such luxuries as affection. There had been no rejoicing when she realized she was expecting her youngest child. On the contrary, her despair had known no bounds. 'I swear to God I'll throw myself into the Tay if it's true!' she had promised her despairing husband, and she probably would have, had she not been feeling so ill and the river not been such a long walk from their two-roomed home.

Bel McMahon's thin lips twisted into a bitter smile as she thought back to those black days, for Katie would never know how close she came to sharing the fate of Peggy's infant. Yet, Bel felt no shame. For those who failed to get rid of an unwanted mouth before birth, there was little difference in getting rid of it afterwards. It happened all the time. 'Overlaying', the doctors usually called it round here, and nobody turned a hair. What choice was there? Were overworked and under-nourished mothers to starve their existing families by bringing other unwanted mouths into the world that they couldn't possibly feed?

Poor, gentle Peggy had never been one for arguing, and had quietly accepted the fact they could not afford either the shame or the luxury of another mouth at the table – and a bastard one at that. Or had she accepted it, Bel wondered? Could it perhaps have been that the childbed fever her daughter suffered immediately afterwards was not the only factor in her death a few weeks later? That possibility had cast a shadow over Bel's heart. It was something she would never know, but the mere possibility made her determine not to expose her youngest child to the horrors – mechanical and human – of a life in the mill.

'Was Peggy excited before she started work, Mam?'

Her daughter's question brought Bel McMahon back to reality and she gave a weak smile as she drew a length of wool through the heel of the sock. 'Excited? . . . Well now, I suppose you could be saying that,' she answered haltingly, then added tersely, 'but it's a nosy little devil you are, and no mistake. Just you finish up your letters there and never mind about other folk.' The very thought of Peggy as an eager young ten-year-old was pain enough.

'Will I get to wear a maid's uniform when I go into service?'

'You will, to be sure.'

Katie sucked on a lock of hair as a shiver of excitement ran through her. She had seen such young girls answering the doors of the big houses down the town and right smart they looked with their white aprons and starched white caps. She ran a hand through her hair and wished with all her heart it was as sleek and fair as her sister's had been. Gleaming fair hair brushed back in a bun was exactly the right sort for a white frilled maid's cap. 'Did you never think of letting Peggy be a maidie, Mam?'

'Holy Mary and Joseph, what sort of question is that?'

'I just wondered, that's all . . . She would have looked right bonnie in a uniform.'

Bel McMahon closed her eyes and rested her head on the back of her chair. If she had had the good sense to put Peggy into service, she would probably still be alive today.

Slowly she opened her eyes and looked at her younger daughter. 'Sure and Peg would have looked grand in a uniform, I have no doubt. She was a bonnie lass, all right.'

'Bonnier than me.' It was a statement of fact.

Bel gave a weary nod in agreement. Then, seeing the downcast look on her daughter's face, she added quickly, 'But only a wee bit, mind.'

Young Katie had not Peggy's fair, rather genteel good looks, it was true, but she had the makings of a good-looker, nevertheless. She was a McMahon through and through. There was Irish tinker blood in her husband's family, and certainly when she had married him there had been something of the wild gypsy rover about the dark-haired, dark-eyed, handsome young man that Rob had been then. They said his father had met and married his mother at the annual horse fair at Ballinasloe in County Galway, and she had been as dark as he had been. And those same dark good looks were now coming out in Rob's youngest child. As dark as Peg's had been fair, Katie's hair was as black as the raven and already hung down past her waist, making a dramatic frame for her lively green eyes and well-marked brows.

But the young girl curled up in the chair in the Dundee tenement knew nothing of the horse fair at Ballinasloe, or of the young couple who had met there who were her grandparents. As she tucked her bare feet beneath her skirts for warmth and snuggled down further in the chair, she suddenly had another quite disturbing thought. 'I'll not see that much of you and Da when I'm away in service, will I?'

'I hear you should be getting one Sunday afternoon off a month.'

'That's not very much.'

''Tis a damned sight more than you'd be getting off in the mill . . . It's a big girl you are now, Kathleen, and you'll have to learn to stand on your own feet — dirty though they may well be!'

Katie gave a sheepish grin as she stuck a few grimy toes out from beneath her skirts and wiggled them. 'Stand on my own feet,' she murmured. It sounded good.

She remembered those words when, two weeks later, she buttoned up her new black shiny leather boots and prepared to set off to take up residence as under-housemaid in the Reverend Herbert Mooney's comfortable old Georgian house in Grey Street, Broughty Ferry. 'I'll stand fine on my own feet in these, Ma,' she assured her mother, as she gazed down at the finest footwear she had ever possessed. Then she added gravely, 'Are you sure you and Dad will be all right when I'm gone?'

'God help us, and why shouldn't we be?'

'Och, I thought you might miss me, that's all.'

'To be sure we'll miss you all right, but you're going to a far better life than this, and don't you ever forget it. Work hard and keep your head up but your feet on the ground and you'll not go far wrong.'

Bel McMahon even allowed herself a faint surge of mother's pride as she waved her child goodbye from the end of the close a few minutes later. She was a bright spark and should do all right, she told herself, and in the Reverend Mooney's Church of Scotland manse she would be safe from all manner of dangers, especially marauding young men who would not think twice about ruining a poor girl's life.

Although not a Catholic (and to be sure you couldn't have everything in this life), the minister himself was a highly regarded man who had neither wife nor offspring of his own. A bit of a jessie, some called him, with his slight lisp and auld wifie ways, but a kindly fellow nevertheless, and he would make a considerate employer. Bel had first heard from Betty Lorimer, who worked the next loom, that a Broughty Ferry minister was looking for a young housemaid, and that had been all the information necessary for her to take herself down there to plead her daughter's case.

Herbert Mooney had answered the door himself, and had appeared quite impressed by the initiative shown by the tired-looking, grey-haired woman on the step. 'I declare I haven't even advertised the post, my good woman, but come you in nevertheless!'

The minister had appeared to live a quiet, frugal and suitably pious life. The Church of Scotland was not known either for its gaiety or its love of luxury. He informed her he had a local woman, Mrs Gall, who arrived on the dot of eight every morning to keep house, and who left at ten in the evening, and a local girl by the name of Chrissie Cargill who kept much the same hours and acted as a general housemaid. Chrissie, like the housekeeper, went home to her own bed every night.

'That will leave your Katie with the attic bedroom on the top floor all to herself,' Herbert Mooney informed Bel, whose pulse quickened at the thought her own daughter could be the recipient of such a luxury in service.

He had shown Bel the room in question and she was able to describe it in great detail to a wide-eyed Katie the next day. 'You'll have an iron bedstead, with a chair and small washstand, a pine kist, and there are hooks on the wall for your outdoor clothes, and there's a view of the river from the wee window above the bed.'

A view of the river. Katie felt at home already. 'I'll hear the gulls from my bedroom,' she had declared, the excitement already mounting in her breast. All her young life she had longed to live nearer the sea, and now she would be heading for a house within a stone's throw of the mouth of the River Tay itself. She had long heard of the fishing village of Broughty Ferry from Davey Lorimer whose mother came from there, and it was a real thrill to inform her friend she would actually have the good fortune to be living in a place he had always described as the next thing to heaven.

The minister and his two servants made the nervous young girl very welcome when she at last arrived to begin work, and Katie very soon began to feel at home in the fine old house, with its ivy-covered walls and wood panelling.

At first she was overwhelmed by what seemed to her the sheer magnificence of it all. There were damask curtains at the windows, etchings of Dundee and Edinburgh in thin black frames on the walls, a red chenille cloth and fresh flowers on the dining-room table and, best of all, clean cotton sheets on her bed at night. There were rugs on the floor and constant fires in the grate, and Herbert Mooney even gave her leave to borrow what books she cared to choose from his library on the condition she did not remove a second until the first was back in place. This was a privilege she treasured above all others, and from the second week after her arrival there was always a volume gracing the small washtable by the side of her bed. She was also allowed two candles a week for her own use and quickly got into the habit of dressing and undressing in semi-darkness to save her precious light for reading.

Village life was also much to her liking. Broughty Ferry was a lively place full of friendly folk who always had a cheery word in the passing. They even looked different down here, she decided. People had colour in their cheeks and you heard far less of that dry hacking cough caused by the fibrous dust that was so common amongst mill-workers back in the city.

To her delight, she even saw her old friend Davey every so often, for his grandmother still lived in one of the cottages on the shore and he walked down from the Hawkhill to visit her at least once a fortnight. Davey's continued presence in her life was a great comfort, for it meant she had someone she trusted to confide in about her new life in the minister's household.

One fact she was careful not to confide, however, was that she was seeing much more of 'the devil' Willie Falconer and his family than she had ever imagined. The Falconers were the owners of one of the grandest houses on Camphill Road, the long thoroughfare of mansions at the top of the hill, and Herbert Mooney was minister of the local kirk where the Falconer family worshipped each Sunday. Barely a week passed but one or other of them would stop by at the manse for a chat.

Young Willie's first sight of the minister's new maid-servant caused his brows to rise a good half-inch. 'So you're the McMahon girl, right enough,' he observed over his cup of tea in the parlour one Sunday afternoon in early May, 1822. He looked Katie up and down, his eyes taking in the mop of thick dark hair and the furrowed, well-marked brows above the green eyes that now viewed him with not a little suspicion. 'It's a pity you're not as good-looking a lass as your sister was.'

'Aye, and it's a pity you're not as well-mannered a man as your father,' Katie retorted, earning a burst of laughter from the elderly man sitting on the chaise-longue by the window.

It did old Augustus Falconer's heart good to see that young whipper-snapper son of his get his come-uppance now and again. Far too ready with his tongue, young Willie was, but by God this bit of a lass was fit for him. 'What was your name again, hen?' he asked the defiant-eyed child, as she stood with the tea-tray in her hands.

'Katie, sir. Katie McMahon.'

'Well, Katie McMahon, if your mind turns out to be half as quick as that tongue of yours, you'll go far in this world. Tell me, do you like working as a serving-maid?'

'Well, sir,' Katie answered truthfully, 'I reckon it's better than life in the mill.'

Augustus Falconer's florid features took on a look of surprise at such candour, then a broad smile spread across his face. 'Well now, you're probably right there, lass. You're probably right there.'

As he was leaving the manse that afternoon, he leant across to his old friend Herbert Mooney and said quietly, 'If you ever think of getting rid of that young lass, let me know, Bertie, will you?' In his household he could do with some light relief, and he had the idea that that young miss could certainly supply it.

Chapter Four

Over the next few years, as Katie settled into life below stairs in the minister's household, so her confidence and interest in the world around her grew. She no longer had that caged-bird feeling she had suffered from as a small child in the heart of the city. But her ties with her early life were not completely severed; on her one Sunday afternoon off a month, she normally walked into Dundee and up the long climb of the Hawkhill to see her parents.

Bel and Rob McMahon seemed to have settled into some sort of a verbally armed truce now they were bereft of family around them. Rob's drinking was no better. 'Sure, and he'd have me heartbroken if I had such a thing as a heart left!' Bel would declare when her daughter was hardly over the doorstep, and Katie would listen wearily to another litany on the evils of gambling and drink.

Only once did she tackle her father about his habits. It was one Sunday in late autumn, shortly before her sixteenth birthday, as he walked her part of the way down the hill to set off on her return journey to Broughty Ferry. 'I know fine she can be a trial at times, but I just wish you'd listen to Mammy now and again. It does you no good, you know, Dad. I worry about you sometimes. All that drinking . . .'

Her father had looked genuinely surprised. 'Well now, there's a fine thing! To be sure and nobody's given a traneen about me health in the past, why should you start worrying now?'

'Because I'm not a bairn any more and I can see what it's doing to you. And I listen to what Mam says . . .'

'Ach your mother! God give me strength!' Bel would be

the death of him long before the drink was. He cleared his throat and aimed a dart of spittle into a puddle at the side of the road. 'Don't let her kid you. Your mother doesn't give a tuppenny fart about me health. Her only worry is the money.'

'That's not true.'

Rob McMahon stopped in his tracks and turned to his daughter. 'Kathleen, *aroon*, I know that woman back there better than anyone alive, and may all the goats in Gorey chase me down this hill if I tell you a lie. Your mother has her good and bad points like the rest of us, but concern for others is not one of her virtues. Never has been as long as I've known her. She doesn't give a tuppenny-ha'penny damn about me or anyone else. Never has, I tell ye.'

Katie flushed beneath the brim of her Sunday bonnet. She had never heard her father utter such thoughts before. It was as if for the first time he was talking to her like another human being, not just an innocent child. How was she supposed to respond? Somehow it seemed wrong to argue with him. He was confiding in her, after all, yet it seemed equally wrong to agree with him. 'You chose her. Nobody forced you to marry her.' She allowed herself the hint of a smile. 'You must have been a good-looking lad in your day, and if I'm not far wrong you must have had the pick of the bunch as far as the lasses were concerned.'

At that Rob McMahon's dark eyes took on a faraway look as the ghost of a smile played around the corners of his mouth. 'Oh aye, you're right there, Katie girl. At one time I had all the red petticoats between Nenagh and Limerick panting after me . . .'

Then he sighed. ''Tis a pity I didn't marry one of yon red-cheeked farming lasses and settle for life in the ould country. Sure and it couldn't have been much worse than this. And at least I'd still have me family around me.'

'You still miss her, don't you, Da?' She had no doubt he was referring to her sister. Peggy had been the favourite, and rightly so.

Rob McMahon hitched his trousers above the hemp belt that girded his spare frame and he grunted. 'Let's just say if I ever had a chance to do a dirty trick on Augustus Falconer or that son of his, I'd happily swing for it. Folk like that don't deserve to walk God's earth wi' the rest o' us . . . May they all go to hell wi' not a drop o' porter to quench their eternal thirst!'

They had reached the bottom of the hill, and with that he raised his hand and placed it on his daughter's shoulder. 'Aye, well, we can but dream . . . Look after yourself now, lass. Work hard and keep your nose clean. Mighty proud of you we are. Remember that.'

Katie watched with a mixture of affection and sympathy as he turned and made his way slowly back up the hill, a thin, stooped figure, much older in appearance than his fifty-five years. Poverty of a kind she could barely imagine had driven him from his home as a young man, and he must have arrived here with such high hopes all those years ago. But poverty travelled with you. It was an ever-present companion on the road of life, be it here in Scotland or back in Ireland. It broke the spirit and it numbed the soul. It was little wonder that men such as her father turned to drink as the only solace for a life barely worth living.

Her thoughts dwelt on that conversation as she walked the four miles back to the manse. Even after all these years her father still had a festering bitterness towards the Falconers, of that there was no doubt, and she felt a pang of guilt in the knowledge that, since they were Reverend Mooney's friends, she was obliged to entertain them whenever they turned up at the door of the manse. On her visits home she had never mentioned the fact that she was forced into regular contact with her mother's employers, for even after all these years it could only cause pain.

Although, given the choice, she would have no truck with Willie, who was a clever but bumptious and opinionated young man, she could not bring it in herself to

48

dislike his father. The elderly man could not be blamed for the sins of his son, and Augustus Falconer had always been a perfect gentleman as far as she was concerned. In fact, it was hard to reconcile the good-natured, white-haired, rather striking-looking individual who seemed to have a kind word for everyone with the stories she had heard back in Dundee about life in his mills. When she tackled Mrs Gall, the housekeeper, on the subject once, the elderly woman had declared, 'There are two sides to every story, Kathleen, and you must not sit in judgement on any man, or woman, until you have heard both.'

Katie had no doubt what her mother told her of life in the Falcon Mills was true, but the housekeeper's words proved of some comfort as she opened the door to the gentleman in question every other weekend. The elderly man would now drop by as regular as clockwork every second Sunday to take tea with the minister, and would never leave without sharing a joke with the youngest maidservant.

'Mr Falconer thinks very highly of you, Kathleen,' the Reverend Mooney told her as they stood together by the drawing-room window and watched the corpulent figure of Augustus head back up the hill towards Falcon Ridge, his family home, the week following Katie's conversation with her father. 'He reckons you should go far in life.'

Katie eyed the man of God with an ironic half-smile as she bent to lift the empty tea-cups and saucers from the side-table next to him. 'Oh aye, is that so? Then I might even reach the giddy height of parlour-maid, if I'm lucky.'

Herbert Mooney had given a cough and forced a smile to his lips. He could never be quite sure with young Kate if she was being insubordinate or simply telling the truth. That she was a bright young thing there was no doubt, but sometimes he felt she was almost a bit too bright for her own good. 'We all have our allotted stations in this life, Kathleen,' he reminded her. 'We are born into them and must make the best of it. Some folk the good Lord has

49

seen fit to place above us, and to them we must give the respect they are due. You do understand that?'

'Oh, aye, Mr Mooney. But how can you tell? Is it simply that some folk have more money than others? Does that make them better?'

The minister took his pipe from his mouth as Katie headed for the door with the tray of used crockery. 'Good heavens, no, girl!' The very idea went against all his Calvinist principles.

'Then what is it? How can I tell who is better than me and so must always be given this proper respect?'

There was a long silence as Herbert Mooney thought for a moment or two, then he shook his head. 'Get on with your work, lassie,' he commanded. 'Sunday teatime's no time for standing around gossiping about such stupid things.'

But to Katie it was not a stupid thing. Since arriving into the Mooney household she had spent long hours pondering on just such questions. And the more she thought about it, the more unfair life seemed. She even felt guilty about going to bed on a satisfied stomach each night, knowing that her parents back in Dundee would have no such comfort. Even saving her own food to make sure she had a full basket to take them on the last Sunday afternoon of each month was little comfort.

She shared her musings on the subject with her old friend Davey Lorimer, and the two had many a heated argument on their occasional Sunday evening walks around the harbour. Davey was apprenticed to a ships' chandler with a shop on the Seagate, but all his spare time was spent in studying and discussing the political situation with like-minded, usually much older men. To him, admiring France was no longer an act of treachery. On the contrary, the French had shown the rest of the world the way to overthrow injustice and make way for a fairer world. He was all for the common man rising up and claiming his rightful place in society by force.

'"*L'homme est né libre, et partout il est dans les fers,*"' he told her.

She had looked at him askance. 'What language is that?'

'It's French,' he told her proudly. 'I've been learning it at night classes. All the best revolutionary writings are in French. That was said by a man called Rousseau: Man is born free but everywhere he is in chains . . . And it's so true, Kate! You only have to look at this city to see it! Both our mothers are nothing more than cogs in the wheel of what they are calling this great industrial revolution of ours. Human beings are worth more than that.'

He slammed his right fist into the palm of his left hand in frustration as he declared passionately, 'The rich will never give up the reins of power by choice. If there is ever to be equality in this world, then folk like me will have to fight for it. There must be an armed struggle if necessary.'

But Kate was not so sure about that. 'They're not all bad,' she would tell him, thinking of the likes of the Reverend Mooney and his old friend Augustus Falconer. 'Most of the toffs are just misguided. I'm sure they could be persuaded to see the error of their ways if it was explained to them like you've explained it to me.' She had a real horror of the thought of bloodshed, and the very idea of Davey taking up arms against the minister and his friends was so grotesque it was almost laughable.

But Davey was not laughing. 'You're one of life's innocents, Kate. One day the poor man will rise up and cast off his chains, and when that day comes the world will tremble. The French have shown us the way. The revolution will come, and in our lifetime, you mark my words.'

And after such a discussion she would go back to the manse and try out the new ideas she had heard on Mrs Gall, the housekeeper.

The elderly woman, like the Reverend Mooney himself, knew nothing of Kate's meetings with Davey, and she was perplexed as to where all this revolutionary zeal was coming from. 'You think too much for your own good, my lass,' she warned Kate as they sat in the kitchen mending the linen one Saturday evening in late September, 1828, at the end of Kate's seventh year in the post. 'I don't know where you're getting those ideas from but they're not healthy. A young lassie like you shouldn't be bothering her head about such things. We should all know our place in this life, and be happy in it. There's them up there on Camphill Road, such as the Falconers and their like, and there's us down here, and it's no good wishing it otherwise.' Then her blue eyes twinkled behind the *pince-nez* as she added, 'You know what wishing did, don't you? Planted a feather and wished it would grow into a hen . . . It never did of course.'

Kate had given a polite smile. While she did not agree with everything Davey said, Mrs Gall was not the deepest thinker she had come across, and that was a silly, blinkered attitude to take. If no one ever wished for things to improve, then nothing ever would. It was as simple as that. She never could convince Mrs Gall though, and when the housekeeper died of an asthmatic attack some three months later, she felt sorry that they had never been able to see eye to eye on things that really mattered.

Katie was seventeen when the housekeeper passed away, and it came as a terrible blow to the whole household. Mr Mooney took it particularly badly, for Mrs Gall had been with him for over twenty years. He even paid her the ultimate tribute of incorporating a eulogy to her in his sermon that weekend.

Although born a Catholic, and still possessing a lingering fear of ending her days in purgatory for forsaking the Mother Church, Katie was not as regular an attender at the Church of Scotland kirk where her employer preached as the Reverend Mooney would have liked. But she was there that day to hear the man of God guarantee eternal life for his deceased servant by declaring that, in the words of the New Testament: '"In a moment, in the twinkling of an eye, at the last trump: for the trumpet shall sound, and the dead shall be raised incorruptible, and we shall be changed . . ."' Then his voice had risen an octave higher as he cried, 'And, friends, our dear departed servant Mrs Iris Gall shall be amongst them. She will sit at the table of the saints, enthroned in glory . . .' And Katie had been forced to suppress a smile, for she had no doubt that poor Mrs Gall would most decidedly be sitting below the salt. Even in death one was surely expected to know one's place.

The household's grief at the housekeeper's passing was also tempered by a good degree of anxiety. For the past year or so there had been widespread terror and indignation aroused by a pair of Edinburgh-based Irishmen named Burke and Hare who, not content with robbing graves of dead bodies, had taken to murder to increase the number of corpses they could sell to the medical schools.

Professor Robert Knox, the illustrious Edinburgh University anatomist who had purchased most of the cadavers, had even become the subject of a children's street song: *'Burke the murderer, Hare the thief, and Knox the man who buys the beef . . .'*

It was to be heard on every street corner in Scotland, and the exploits of the pair were being talked about and – even more terrifyingly – emulated in most of the big cities in the land. Only recently a group of men had been caught red-handed robbing graves of their newly buried occupants in Dundee's Howff churchyard, and now watches were having to be kept on every fresh grave. It was with great relief that Kate learned that the Reverend Mooney was paying out a considerable sum to have Mrs Gall's last resting-place watched for as long as was deemed necessary.

This information was relayed to her after the funeral service as she served tea to Mr Mooney in his study.

'I'm sure Mrs Gall will rest easy in her grave knowing that,' Kate said, bending to pick up the tea-tray.

The minister gave a grunt of agreement and gestured for Kate to sit down. Puzzled, she obeyed.

'There's one more matter to be addressed, Kathleen,' he said, a trifle formally as he spread his napkin on his lap. 'And it's a matter that would most certainly give rise to a great deal of anxiety on the part of our dear departed housekeeper, I have no doubt about that.' His face was serious as he regarded Kate over the top of his spectacles. 'You probably have a good idea to what I am referring.'

'Indeed I have not,' Katie replied in all honesty as she folded her hands neatly in her lap and perched on the edge of a wing chair. By the look on his face it must be something very serious indeed.

'You mean you haven't discussed taking over the post of housekeeper with Chrissie?'

Katie looked puzzled. Chrissie Cargill, the parlour-maid, had been in quite an emotional state since Mrs Gall's death, and the two had barely had a coherent conversation. 'I – I don't understand . . . Chrissie will be taking over as housekeeper, won't she?'

'I'm sorry to say she will not,' Herbert Mooney replied a trifle testily. 'Chrissie informs me her young man won't stand for it – the long hours, if you please!' He shook his head at the sheer preposterousness of it as he took another sip of the tea. 'They're to be married next summer and – well, not to put too fine a point on it, she doesn't want the job. So you'll have to do it. It's as simple as that.'

Katie looked at him in amazement. 'I'm to be housekeeper?' It was hard to keep her voice level.

'That seems to be the conclusion I've been forced to arrive at.' He looked at her quizzically over the top of his tea-cup. 'You have no objections, I take it?'

'No . . . None at all.' Her heart was singing. She was on her way. Exactly where to, she could not be sure, but one thing was for certain: she was on her way.

The next two years proved to be the happiest of her young life. Not only did she prove to be up to the job, but the minister was fulsome in his praise for the marked improvement in his daily life. Not only was his robe drawer full of clean linen, so he never had to spend time delving in the dirty linen basket to make a soiled stock do one more day, but the quality of the cakes and teabread that appeared on his table had improved considerably. Left to her own devices, Katie revelled in experimenting with the different flours and dried fruit to be found in the local victualler's, and so well known did her baking become that she was regularly requested to make special batches for sale in aid of the church funds.

Her biggest assignment, however, she was asked to do as a special favour for the Reverend Mooney in aid of his oldest friend. It was one cold January morning in 1830, and the nineteen-year-old Kate was ironing in the kitchen when the minister put his head around the door. His face was grave.

He came into the room and stood in his favourite position with his back to the range, lifting up the tails of his coat to warm his posterior as he said quietly, 'I fear our good friend Mrs Falconer will not last the day, Kathleen. My heart goes out to her good man, for Augustus has already suffered more than most during the past few years.'

Kate looked up from pressing the front of one of his dress shirts and laid the iron back on the hot-plate for a moment. 'You mean Mrs Falconer's dying?' She had seldom passed more than a few words with the lady in question over the years, for the mill-owner's wife did not keep well and rarely left the family home. Emily Falconer suffered badly from the ague and severe palpitations and was known to rely heavily on laudanum to get her through the day. They said the thirteen-week hacklers' strike of three years ago had considerably added to her nervous condition, and only the return of her husband's workers at their old rates had prevented a complete collapse. She had been practically bedridden ever since. 'I'm truly sorry to hear that, Mr Mooney,' Kate replied truthfully. 'Poor Mr Falconer.'

'Aye, poor Mr Falconer indeed. He deserves all the help we can give, both now and in the future, for it will be bleak indeed without his beloved wife. And God only knows what the poor soul will do with a funeral on his hands this week, for his housekeeper's gone down with this awful 'flu. He'll need our practical help as well as our prayers, that's for sure.'

His words were to prove prophetic, for Emily Falconer did not last the night. The clock high up on the bell-tower of the kirk had not yet struck midnight when the last breath passed her bloodless lips. But her grieving husband got his help. His friend Herbert Mooney offered up the ultimate sacrifice and insisted that Kate go to Falcon Ridge on loan until at least the funeral was over and Augustus's own housekeeper was well on the way to recovery.

Kate entered the wide stone gates of the Falconer family home on the twenty-ninth day of January, 1830, two days after Emily's death and one day before the funeral, to be met at the door by none other than Willie. The young man who had won all the prizes at the grammar school as a youth, and was now a strapping six-footer and built in proportion, had been his mother's pride and joy. Willie's hazel eyes were bloodshot from tears, and his pale brows furrowed at the sight of Kate standing there with her case in her hand.

'Dear God, who sent you?'

'Mr Mooney did. Your father's expecting me.' She expected no more from Willie. Even as a grown man, well into his twenties, civility was still not one of his strong points. 'Aren't you going to ask me in?'

'You should have gone to the servants' entrance.'

'Oh, should I now?'

'That's what you are, after all. You can't come in here.' His tall frame stood full-square in the doorway, and the two were locked in eye-to-eye combat as his father appeared in the hall beyond.

'Willie, is that the McMahon lassie? What's she standing there on the doorstep for? Ask her in, man!'

Willie glared at Kate, but stood aside. 'You'd better come in,' he muttered.

Kate swept past him into a wide entrance hall. It was the first time she had ever been inside Falcon Ridge and the sheer grandeur of it took her breath away. Above the marble floor, two marble pillars soared from the foot of the stairs to support a minstrels' gallery, from which long black drapes fluttered in the draught.

'Come away in, lass,' Augustus Falconer said, taking her case and leading the way through the hall and on downstairs into the largest kitchen Kate had ever seen.

'It's very noble of Bertie to lend you to me like this,' the elderly man said. 'I swear, with Emily gone and the house-keeper down with God-knows-what, I don't know where I'm at.'

'I'm really sorry about your wife.'

'Aye . . . Well, it was not unexpected, but a shock never-theless, as they say.' Augustus cleared his throat. There was not a great deal to say about Emily's death. He had been preparing himself for it for over twenty years. She herself swore she would never see the age of thirty, but had in fact been over fifty when she died. She had all but taken permanently to her bed after Willie's birth twenty-eight years previously, and their marriage had ceased in all but name from almost the day their son was conceived.

Augustus put down Kate's case and looked around him with a lost air. He never failed to feel out of place down here.

'You look like you could do with a cup of tea,' Kate said. There was a kettle on the side of the range and she walked across briskly to fill it from a pitcher sitting on a marble slab by the back door.

Augustus Falconer watched her with ill-disguised admiration. She might only be a bit of a lassie, but she had her head screwed on all right. 'Your father must be right proud of you, lass. Is he a local man?' The mill-owner prided himself in knowing the background of all his employees, temporary or otherwise.

Kate turned from filling the kettle. 'My father's from Tipperary.'

Augustus's white brows rose. 'Well, I'll be damned. And your mother, she's Irish too?'

'That she is.'

Augustus gave a quiet smile to himself. That might explain the spirit of the lass. They said the Irish families who had swarmed into the town during the French wars were a boisterous lot, and, God help him, he had had to put up with a fair bit from them himself over the years, for he reckoned that more than a third of his workforce were Paddies. 'Do they live hereabouts?'

Kate lifted the full kettle and placed it in the centre of the fire as she shook her head. 'No, they live in town. My mother's still working her guts out in your mill at the foot o' the Hawkhill.'

Augustus Falconer sat down heavily on the nearest chair and avoided her eyes. For once in his life he was at a loss for words. It was a thought that had never occurred to him. Somehow he had imagined that Bertie Mooney's young maid was from the village here, or maybe even a country lass from up around Lintrathen. She was too fresh, too bonnie by half, to be one of the mill crowd. 'I'm sorry about that,' he said. Somehow, with this young lady, he could do no less than tell the truth. 'It's a hard life for a woman.' This was neither the time nor the place to play the caring employer; he was only too aware of conditions in the mills.

'Not half as sorry as I am,' Kate replied briskly. There was no real rancour in her voice, simply an acceptance of how things were.

Augustus Falconer looked up at the proud tilt of the head and the clear-eyed gaze of the young woman in front of him. 'Aye, well, I'm right grateful you've thought fit to come and help me out. You didn't have to, you know. You could have said to Bertie that you'd rather not.'

'I ken that fine,' Kate replied. 'But I'm glad to be here.'
And to her surprise she realized she was telling the truth.

Chapter Five

Emily Falconer was laid to rest in the magnificent marble and granite family vault in the local cemetery. A stone falcon identical to the one which guarded the main door of the Falcon Mill stood on top of the tomb, marking it out from the neighbouring graves with their stone obelisks, open Bibles, Celtic crosses or winged angels. Augustus Falconer and his son Willie led the funeral procession to the graveyard; it was all of half a mile long and contained every local dignitary from the city of Dundee and far beyond. Even the lord provost attended, although he and the mill-owner had been at loggerheads for months over plans for a new Falcon Mill in the Wellgate area of the city.

The Reverend Herbert Mooney presided over the service and was fulsome in his praise for the deceased. He and Emily had always got on well, seeing eye to eye on everything from the latest Walter Scott novel to the shared belief that the Pope was indeed the anti-Christ in human form.

In true Church of Scotland tradition, women did not attend the funeral, so it was to a purely male gathering that Kate found herself ministering after the kirk service and burial. Cold chicken and a selection of cooked meats were on offer, alongside plates piled high with Dundee cake baked specially for the occasion. On the sideboard next to the food stood twenty bottles of malt whisky; there was not a drop left in any one of them by the time the last man had departed.

When at last they had all gone, a sombre silence seemed to fill the house; only the ticking of the French ormolu clock on the drawing-room mantelpiece broke the quietude as Augustus Falconer stood by the big bay-window gazing out into the distance at the grey expanse of the Firth of Tay. A soft rain was falling, causing rivulets to trickle down the windowpane and obscure a view already blurred by tears that misted the pale blue of his eyes. At first he did not hear Kate as she opened the drawing-room door to stand uncertainly on the threshold.

She cleared her throat. 'Is there anything I can get you? A wee drop of laudanum, maybe?' He had complained of a headache earlier in the day.

The elderly man turned abruptly and, seeing the young woman in the doorway, he pulled a large handkerchief from his pocket and blew his nose noisily into it, then dabbed at his eyes. 'Ah, Kate . . .'

He gestured to a chair by the side of the fire. 'Sit down, lassie. You've worked hard today.'

Kate hesitated, then did as requested, as Augustus himself turned back to the window. 'I'll miss her, you know,' he said at last. 'Nearly thirty years we were married. A long time by anybody's reckoning.' No matter what differences there had been between himself and his wife, they seemed of little significance at a time like this. A difficult woman though Emily had undoubtedly been, the house would be the poorer without her.

He turned back to the young woman sitting motionless on the chair beside him. 'How old are you, lass?'

'Nineteen,' Kate replied.

He shook his head. A mere bairn. 'Have ye a lad yet?'

Momentarily Davey Lorimer's face flashed before her, but she shook her head as she gave an embarrassed half-laugh. 'And what time would I have to spend on courting?'

'If it was down to finding time, the whole human race would grind to a halt.'

'Well, be that as it may, the thought doesn't interest me. I'm far better off as I am.'

'As Bertie's housekeeper, you mean?'

'Reverend Mooney's been more than good to me.'

Augustus looked thoughtful. 'How much does he pay ye?'

'That's none of your business,' Kate said, colouring, then added quickly, 'begging your pardon, Mr Falconer.'

Augustus laughed. 'No need to apologize. I'm a nosy auld bugger, but you never learn anything if you don't ask. How much is it exactly? Knowing him it'll barely be enough to keep body and soul together.' He paused, then came right out with it. 'Anyhow, that's neither here nor there, for whatever it is, I'll double it.'

Kate looked at him aghast. 'You want me to come and work for you? But that's poaching!'

'Nah, nah, lass,' he corrected. 'That's no' poaching, that's business. I didn't get where I am today by being sentimental o'er business decisions. If you see something that's good for you or your business in this world, you go after it. That's the philosophy I've lived by for the past thirty years and, by God, it's never let me down yet. It's no good pussyfooting around or the next man'll be in there . . . Now, will ye come or no'?'

Kate was flabbergasted. Augustus Falconer was asking her to leave Reverend Mooney and come and work for him. So much for friendship. He was a businessman to his fingertips. But she could not help feeling flattered nevertheless. 'As your housekeeper, you mean?'

'What else?'

'I . . . I . . .'

'Look,' he said gruffly, sensing her discomfort, 'there's no need to make a decision right away. Bertie's no' expecting you back till the end o' the week anyhow. Think about it. That's all I ask. Just think about it. I've heard from her sister that my ain housekeeper will not be back. They're keeping pretty quiet about it, but I gather it's no' the 'flu but consumption . . . I should have guessed, for that cough o' hers had had her barking far too long to be just a common cold . . . But that's neither here nor there. It's a big decision you've to make, so I'll not press you for an answer right away. You take your time and think about it, that's all I ask.'

And think about it she did. In fact Kate could think of little else over the next few days as she went about her task of overseeing the running of the Falconer household. Falcon Ridge was like no other house she had ever been in. There was an excellent part-time cook, a Mrs Watt from the village, and a staff of twenty-two in all, including grooms and coachmen. In truth, the house seemed to run itself. Everything went like clockwork, so there really was very little for her to do other than the jobs she chose for herself.

It was the evening before she was due to return to the manse when the call came to go up to the drawing room where Augustus was waiting for her. He had just returned from the mill and still had on his outdoor clothes. A log fire was roaring in the hearth, and the oil-lamps were all lit. The room had a warm, welcoming feel to it as Kate hesitated on the threshold.

Augustus beckoned her in. 'And close the door behind you. I canna bear a draught.'

His greatcoat was undone and he had already loosened his cravat. He had a glass of his finest malt whisky in his hand, and his face was flushed as he gestured for her to take a seat.

'I'd rather stand, if you don't mind,' Kate said, smoothing her apron with her hands. She had made up her mind to reluctantly turn down his offer, and did not want to prolong the embarrassment any longer than was necessary.

'As ye wish.'

Their eyes met and held. 'Well?' he said, coming straight to the point. 'Are ye staying or no'?'

'I'm sorry, I can't,' Kate answered, then paused, searching for the right words so as not to give offence.

'Can't or won't?'

She gave an embarrassed shrug of her shoulders. She hoped he would not make this difficult for her. She liked the old man and did not want to offend him more than necessary.

'Is it the money? Is that it? I told you I'd double it, but I'll triple it if that'll make a difference.' He set his glass on the mantelpiece and took three golden sovereigns from his waistcoat pocket and laid them on the table in front of her. 'That'll be two for yourself in advance and one for your folk back in Dundee.' Surely no young woman in her right mind could refuse an offer like that?

'Are you trying to buy me, then, is that it?'

He had been too long in the game to be offended. 'If I have to . . . I told ye before, lassie, this is business. I'm a businessman, not a charitable institution. If I offer you that kind o' money, it's because I think you're worth it.'

Kate could only respect his candour. She glanced down at the three golden coins glinting in the lamplight. With just a fraction of one of those a week her mother could give up work in the mill. 'I – I'll have to think about it,' she said, hesitantly. Then added quickly, 'I'll need to ask my mother.' Somehow her father didn't seem to come into it.

'Get your mantle.'

'What?'

'Get your shawl, or whatever. I'll take you into town. You can ask her now.'

Kate could scarcely believe what was happening when just over half an hour later the Falconer carriage pulled up in front of the close where her parents still lived on the Hawkhill. She thanked God it was a dark and rainy evening and there were few people about, for she prayed the neighbours would not see who was left sitting inside the coach as she rose to get out.

'Are you sure you don't want me to come in with you?'

'Good God, no!' She could just imagine her mother's face if she was to walk in with old Augustus Falconer himself in tow.

Bel McMahon had been back from work less than an hour, and was sitting slumped in front of a dismal fire when her daughter opened the door and walked straight into the small kitchen. 'Holy Mary and Joseph, and what brings you here this time of night, Kathleen? There's nothing wrong, is there?'

'No, Mam, there's nothing wrong. Is Dad in?'

Bel jerked her head in the direction of the back room. 'He's through there, but it's a job you'll have wakening him. He's been at the porter already. Shit-marak he is.'

Kate received the news in silence, her fingers nervously toying with the gloves in her hand. Bel looked quizzically at her daughter as she rose to put the kettle on. 'Well, go on then, out with it.' There was no way it could be a purely social call at this time of night. She had to be in some sort of trouble. 'You're not in the family way, are you?'

'Heavens, no!'

The relief on Bel's face was obvious. 'Well, thank the Lord for that. What is it, then? What's after bringing you all the way back up here at a time like this?'

'I've been offered a new job,' Kate began. Then she paused, but there was no way round it. 'It's as housekeeper in Falcon Ridge.'

Her mother let the kettle down with an almighty clatter on the side of the fire as she turned to stare at her daughter. Surely she had to be hearing things? 'Falcon Ridge, you say?'

'Aye, Mam.'

'But that's the Falconers' place.'

Kate made no reply. None was required.

'Well, I'll be damned. 'Tis hearing things I am. Tell me I'm hearing things.'

'You are hearing things, Mam. But they're quite true. Augustus Falconer has offered me three guineas a week to take over as his housekeeper. Look . . .'

She took out the three coins he had insisted she take with her and attempted to hand them to her mother, but Bel McMahon would have none of it. She knocked them from her daughter's hand with one fell swoop and sent them flying across the room to rattle off the far wall and disappear under the table.

'Blood money!' she cried, her face distorting with distaste at the very idea. 'Blood money, that's what it is!'

'Don't be stupid, Mam,' Kate protested, her voice rising in indignation. 'With money like that you could give up work. Just think of it, no more early rising to flog your guts out every day in that mill.'

'Sure, and I'll think of it all right, my girl. Just as I think every day of that poor daughter of mine lying dead in her grave thanks to that same family you're now offering me money from.'

'But that's daft talk, Mam. You work for the Falconers yourself.'

'Not by choice. By God, not by choice!' If there had been another mill that could have taken her on she would have left that cursed place years ago, but nobody gave up a paying job in this town. Nobody. Work was as hard to come by as gold-dust on these streets. 'I have no option in the matter at all, so I don't. But you have a choice, Kathleen. You already have a decent job in a fine household. He may be a Protestant – and, God love him, he can't help that – but the Reverend Mooney is a fine man – a decent man – not like yon tinks the Falconers.' The thought that her daughter could even be contemplating working under that family's roof of her own free will was almost too much to take.

'You're being stupid and shortsighted, Mam,' Kate protested. 'You're getting on, you know. Soon you might not be able to rise at four every morning and do a full day's work in the mill. And what then?'

'Then it's joining your sister in the paupers' plot in the

Howff I'll be,' Bel replied bitterly. 'And I'll be a bloody sight better off there than living off poor Peggy's murderer's money.'

'Augustus Falconer did not murder my sister,' Kate said, fighting to keep her voice even. 'You know that as well as I do. As for Willie – well, I will have as little to do with him as possible.'

'As little to do with him as possible, is it?' her mother mimicked. 'Well now, 'tis a real comfort to know that, to be sure.' She pushed a hand through her straggle of grey hair and shook her head. 'I swear I'd never be after holding my head up in this road again if folk got to know that you were living under that man's roof. God rot him and that divil o' a son of his! You take that job, Kathleen McMahon, and you'll never be able to walk down this street again, for there's not a man or woman in the whole of the Hawkhill who doesn't know that that family was the cause of poor Peggy's death. 'Tis blood money that's being offered to you – pure blood money!'

The words were being spat in Kate's face, and she could feel the anger boiling inside her mother's breast, but she could not share it. Augustus Falconer was not a bad man and, even if Willie had been the father of Peggy's bairn, he did not kill her. Even he, for all his many faults, could not have wished her dead. 'I'll see what Dad says,' she said, making for the back room.

Rob McMahon was already awake and sitting on the bed, with his legs dangling over the side of the mattress as Kate entered the small room. 'Katie, I thought it must be you . . . All that bloody noise.'

He looked bleary-eyed at his daughter. 'What's wrong? What's she been saying to you?'

'It's what I've been saying to her, Dad. I've been offered a new job, as a housekeeper. It's good money. Excellent money, and . . .'

She got no further.

'Take it!' her father commanded, waving his arm in a

theatrical gesture of agreement. 'Take it and in your great good fortune take pity on us poor paupers from time to time.'

'But it's with Augustus Falconer, Dad. It's at Falcon Ridge.'

Her father peered at her through the darkness. 'Wi' the Falconers, you say?'

'I'm afraid so. Mam doesn't approve.'

Rob McMahon waved a shaky finger at his daughter. 'There's a helluva lot your mother doesn't approve of in this life, but that shouldn't affect your decisions. Take the job, lass, and take the bugger for every last penny you can.'

Kate gave an embarrassed smile. It wasn't exactly what she wanted to hear, but it would do. At least one of her parents wasn't wholly against her. 'Thanks, Dad,' she said, bending down to place an appreciative hand on his shoulder, before turning back to the kitchen to face her mother.

Her mind was made up. 'I'm going to take that job, Mam,' she said, surprising herself at the resolve in her voice. 'I'm going to become housekeeper at Falcon Ridge.'

'Then you'll never set foot in this house again.'

'That'll be your choice, not mine.'

The two women looked at one another across the few feet of bare floorboards, then Kate half turned to go. 'You'll know where to find me if you need me,' she said quietly.

'In the divil's place! God give you sense, lassie, for you'll live to regret it if you ever break bread at that man's table.' There was a pause, then: 'Have ye no shame? You will be supping with the divil himself in that man's house!'

The words rang in Kate's ears as she walked quietly from the room and closed the door behind her.

Old Augustus was waiting impatiently in the carriage down below. He moved his great bulk over in the seat to make room for Kate as she got back into the coach. 'Well?' he asked expectantly. 'What did your mother say?'

'She said I'd be supping with the devil himself if I ever broke bread at your table.'

The old man sighed. It was no more than he expected. 'She could be right, lass,' he sighed. 'God help her, she could be right. But if I'm Auld Nick then I still pay a damned sight better than Bertie Mooney or any of his Holy Willie cronies.'

He gave a wheezy chuckle and reached out and gave her hand a comforting squeeze, and Kate had little option but to smile back in return.

Chapter Six

'Begging your pardon, Miss McMahon, but there's a young man insisting on speaking to you. I've told him you're busy but he won't take no for an answer.'

Kate looked up impatiently from the household provisions' list and sighed. 'Send him away, Maisie.' There was hardly a day went by without some young lad coming up from the village looking for work around the house or in the gardens. Heaven only knew why they always asked for the housekeeper. Maybe they thought she would be more sympathetic to their plight than the Master.

'I'm sorry, Kate, but I'll not be sent away.'

At the sound of the familiar husky voice, Kate's heart skipped a beat. She whirled round to stare straight into the slate-blue eyes of Davey Lorimer. He stood uncertainly just inside the kitchen door, and his face was grave as it looked back into hers.

'That'll be all, Maisie,' Kate said quickly to the parlour-maid. 'I'll send for you if I need you.'

She could feel her face flushing and she put down her pen as a hand went automatically to her head to smooth her hair. It had been several weeks since she had last seen him, for after her acceptance of Augustus's post she had not had the courage to carry on with her usual Sunday evening walk around the harbour, the time of the week when she was most likely to run into her old friend.

'What brings you here, Davey?' she asked in some confusion as she rose from her seat and adjusted her skirts. She feared she already knew the answer, for news travelled fast in these parts. Whatever the reason he was here, it must rank as serious in his mind, for she had never known him venture up near Camphill Road before. In fact, knowing his opinion of the mill-owners, he was the last person she expected to find in the kitchen of Falcon Ridge.

It was strange to be facing him across the kitchen table like this, and she could feel her heart beating faster as she looked at him. Long gone was the Wee Davey of her childhood, for at twenty he now stood a good five feet nine inches tall, and with his brown curly hair and candid grey-blue eyes he had the makings of a fine-looking young man. That round pugnacious face had lost its puppy fat, and had squared up into more of a young prize-fighter's countenance. Kate was conscious of a faint dampness on the palms of her hands as she adjusted the belt of the apron and enquired anxiously, 'Has Mam sent you?'

It was a month now since she made her decision to accept Augustus's offer and she had been half expecting some sort of reaction from home, even if only a message via the Reverend Mooney that her mother was still very upset about the whole thing. A visit from Davey she had not expected. 'Mam – she's not ill, is she?'

'Sick at heart, that's all.'

'Oh God!' Kate groaned and looked heavenwards, as if for celestial help. It was badly needed. 'I might have known. You've come to preach at me. Well, save your sermons for Sunday, Davey lad. I'm not a bairn any longer. I can make my own decisions about what I want to do with my life.'

'How could you do it, Kate? How could you do this to your ain folk – to us?'

'To you? What do you mean to you? What have I done for pity's sake? Taken a decent job that's all. Given myself a leg up the employment tree.'

'But that's not all, Kate. You've . . .'

'I know, I know,' she interrupted impatiently. 'I've supped with the devil, is that it?' she asked, mimicking her mother's words. 'God, you Dundee folk have some lurid turns of phrase!'

'Oh, it's us Dundee folk now, is it? It's you and us. You've become a creature apart?' His lips curled in derision. 'Actually, I wasn't going to pass comment on whom you choose to sup with these days, I was simply going to say, after what a certain member of this family did to your sister Peggy, you have not only let your mother and father down, but yourself most of all.'

Kate gave a hollow laugh at the words so piously spoken. It was no more than she expected, but she bridled at having Peggy's death thrown in her face after all these years. Peggy would be the last person to register disapproval at her wee sister trying to improve her lot.

'I'll thank you not to bring Peg into this, Davey Lorimer. My sister had more charity in her than any of that lot who are pointing the finger at me now. As for letting myself down, well, I'll tell you this, I don't regret it – taking this job – not one whit! Don't forget I grew up back there in the town with the rest of you. I know what it's like. Neither you nor anyone else can convince me I'm doing wrong working here for a decent wage. I know as well as you do what it's like to go to bed hungry at night and have chilblains the size of pullets' eggs on my toes in the winter because my folk couldn't afford a pair of boots.'

She waved a hand around her at the comfortable kitchen, with the blue and white crockery on the tall dresser gleaming in the dancing flames from the range. Morning or night, there was a fire burning in the grate. She would never be cold again. 'Take a look at this and tell me working here doesn't beat slaving half frozen to death in the mill any day!'

The young man's expression gave nothing away as he deliberately avoided looking around him. He had not wanted to believe it when he heard from Bel that Kate was working in the Falconer household, but he had certainly wondered why she no longer took her regular Sunday night walks along the shore around Broughty harbour. She had been too ashamed, that was the top and bottom of it. Every waking hour he was not working in the chandler's shop he was agitating – speaking out in local halls all

72

around the district — against old Augustus and his like. Now one of his best friends was kicking him in the teeth by taking the old devil's shilling. And, if they were both honest with one another, Kate was far more than a friend, and they both knew it. There was something real between them. There always had been and always would be. Only now was not the time to go down that particular path. He had come to reason with her as a friend, nothing else. 'I can understand why you've done it, Kate,' he said slowly, choosing his words carefully, for he had not come here to cause a row. 'Yes, I can understand it but I can't condone it.'

'Well now, Wee Davey, my heart is really breaking at that news,' Kate replied sarcastically, deliberately using his old diminutive to annoy him. 'My goodness, haven't we gone sanctimonious in our old age?'

Davey shrugged. 'Make a fool of me if you like. I didn't come here to fall out with you. You're my best friend, you know that. I just thought you should know it's not just your ma who disapproves of what you've done. We all do.'

'So now I know — if I hadn't already guessed. I've been officially told. Thank you very much. That was really big of you, coming all the way down here to tell me that.'

'I didn't come all the way down just to tell you that.'

'Oh?'

He toyed with the cap in his hands and avoided her eyes. 'I wondered if you'd care to come along to one of the reformist meetings with me on your next Sunday off.'

Kate raised a quizzical eyebrow. 'Oh really?' She could feel her pulse quicken. He couldn't be that angry with her if he was inviting her out, even if only to a political meeting.

'Aye, we could have a sup o' ale in the Blue Bonnet afterwards, then I'd walk you back here to the Ferry . . .' Their eyes met and his had that old familiar twinkle once more as he pleaded, 'You will come, won't you?'

He couldn't be that mad at her. She was beginning to feel better already. 'I might just at that, Wee Davey. I might just at that.'

He looked relieved. 'Right then. When's your next Sunday off?'

At that her face fell. 'I've just had one,' she said. 'I'll not be off again till the end of the first week in April.'

'That sounds fine by me.' As League organizer he could schedule a meeting for whatever day he liked. 'You're sure you'd not mind coming?'

'I'll look forward to it.'

He put out his hand and with an embarrassed smile she took it. 'Thanks, Katie,' he said. 'I appreciate that.'

She had not touched him physically for a long time, and could feel that same tingle run through her as she had felt when she first caught sight of him in the doorway. 'The first week in April, then,' she said softly.

What she did not reckon with was the almost blind hostility her new employer felt about such goings-on. It seemed that the Dundee Political Reform League was making quite a name for itself in the locality, and there was barely a day went past without some mention of its activities in the local newspaper. Every dispute and agitation in the mills was being laid at its door, and over the next few weeks she had to listen to Augustus and Willie complaining loudly about 'those damned revolutionaries'.

Kate was in the drawing room three weeks later, waiting to go over the following week's menus with Augustus on the morning of her Sunday afternoon off, when he glanced up from a copy of Saturday's *Dundee Advertiser*. He had been in an irascible mood ever since breakfast; he had been suffering from shortness of breath and a tightness across the chest of late and his laboured breathing was painfully audible as the scowl on his face deepened. His eyes were fixed firmly on a notice inviting the public to a Sunday meeting on Magdalen Green to protest against working conditions and the long hours in the mills. 'It's those damned agitators!' he exploded, stabbing a forefinger at the offending piece. 'They're at it again. They should be locked up, every last one o' them – aye, and the key thrown away!'

Kate said nothing. She already knew better than to argue with him when his health was playing him up.

'Take a look!' He thrust the paper into her hand.

She glanced down at the notice and blanched. The intimation inviting citizens to attend the meeting was signed by David Lorimer, Secretary, the Dundee Political Reform League. It was the first time she had actually seen Davey's name in print in connection with the League.

'Well, don't you agree a stand should be taken against that lot before it gets out of hand? God only knows what we'll be in for next! Another batch of machinery-smashing, I'd say. Troublemakers like them have done it before and, by God, they'll do it again if they're not stopped. Folk have been transported for less. They ought to be identified and dealt with right away. Weeded out before it goes any further. Wouldn't you agree?'

'I – I dare say they're sincere in what they're doing – in what they believe in,' Kate ventured, handing him back the newspaper.

'Sincere!' Augustus bellowed. 'Och aye, they're sincere all right. Sincere in wanting the likes o' me to go out of business, for that's where it would end, ye ken. All these reforms they shout about – who's to pay for them, that's what I'd like to know? The only way I could afford to make the improvements they demand and give folk shorter working hours is by paying them less, and do you think they'd stand for that? Would they hell! God's truth, lassie, I'd have the biggest riot on my hands this town has seen in years!'

Sucking in another painful breath, he eased his considerable bulk out of the chair and walked to the window to look out in the direction of the city. 'We've had machinery-smashing and the like before, you know. When I first started out in this game I had hundreds of pounds' worth of new looms wrecked by a gang o' hot-heads from Lochee way. Handloom weavers they were. Blamed me for putting them out o' business, so they came down to the Hawkhill determined to put me out of mine.'

He shook his head at the memory of the worst time of his young life. Willie had been a babe in arms and Emily not yet recovered from the birth when the worst of the trouble had been caused. At one point he feared his little family might end up on the street, and he had vowed then never to allow such a situation to develop again. He had worked too hard to risk everything at the hands of scum like that. 'It worries me, all this agitation, I don't mind telling you, Kate. They're a bunch of hot-heads, the lads who are stirring up all this trouble. They get a mob behind them and God only knows what can happen. What I need is some hard information on what exactly's going on.'

He was silent for a moment or two, twirling the ends of his moustache as he contemplated the best course of action, then he turned to her. 'It's your afternoon off today, isn't it?'

Kate nodded a trifle apprehensively.

'Well, what would you say to doing a wee observation job for me, lass? Attending that meeting on the Green, I mean. Would you do that for me? Would you go along and see exactly what's been said – what's being planned? And more importantly who's in charge. I'd go myself, only they'd no' say a damned thing with me around – or young Willie, come to that. Either that or they'd blether a lot o' nonsense to put us off the scent. No, it needs somebody like yourself – one of their own – to see what's going on, to really find out what they're up to.'

'You mean you want me to spy for you?'

'Well now, I'd no' put it like that exactly. And I'd make it up to you. I'll get Charlie to take you there and back in the best carriage and you'd get another afternoon off to compensate.'

Kate picked up the sheet of paper with the week's menus written on it and smiled. 'The carriage won't be necessary,' she said. 'Anyway, I rather think the family crest on the doors would give the game away, don't you?' There was no more familiar emblem in the city than the bird that distinguished almost all Falconer property, from the mills to their personal linen and their very undergarments.

Augustus looked sheepish. 'I dare say you're right. You'll go, though. You'll do me this favour?'

Silence reigned for several seconds as Kate contemplated the idea of spying for her employer at an event about which she knew Davey felt so passionately. She felt momentarily sick at the thought of deceiving him as to the dual nature of her presence there when they met, as meet they surely would. Seeing him again was something she was looking forward to so much. But what excuse could she give to Augustus if she were to refuse? She would only upset him and make things awkward for herself into the bargain.

'Well, lass, what do you say to it? Will ye do an old man a favour? Will ye go?'

'Aye, I'll go,' Kate replied, with a sinking heart. And there was nothing but confusion in her mind as she took her leave and returned to the kitchen.

Chapter Seven

The April sun was still high in the sky when Kate finally reached the wide expanse of grassland bordering the River Tay that was known as Magdalen Green. It was a typical East Coast blustery spring day, but luckily the rain that had been threatening all morning had kept off and a welcome sun had consented to make its presence felt in full measure.

To her surprise she was accompanied most of the four miles into town by straggling groups of chattering people all headed in the same direction. There was much laughter and larking around from the younger element, and there was a definite feeling of festivity in the air. It seemed that news of the meeting had spread throughout the town and into the surrounding villages, so that both the genuinely interested and the merely curious were gathering to 'see the fun', as one young lad put it.

The words 'reform' and 'revolution' were on everyone's lips these days, both in the British Isles and on the Continent. People were demanding rights unheard of before, and most of the agitation was coming from the industrial cities such as Manchester, Glasgow and Dundee. The Dundee Political Reform League was still something of an unknown quantity where the majority of the population was concerned, and this afternoon would prove an ideal opportunity to see one or two of the members in action. Were they really the wild revolutionaries that the newspapers were making out, folk wanted to know?

Several hundred citizens were already gathered along the grassy riverside area when Kate arrived. They made a colourful sight, for most were in their Sunday best, the women clad in either a bright scarlet mankay or a tartan plaid, pinned at the neck to spread gracefully over the skirts of their brightly coloured dresses. There were also a good number of Easter bonnets to be seen as members of the female sex took advantage of the sunshine to show off the latest in fashionable millinery.

Although there was quite a rough element to the crowd, from what Kate could make out there also seemed to be a fair number of well-to-do gentlemen present. She even spotted old Dr McPherson, who had attended Peggy all those years before. The average age-group seemed to be twenty to thirty, however, and Kate recognized a fair number of Willie Falconer's drinking cronies among the crowd; she breathed an inward sigh of relief, however, that her employer's son himself was nowhere to be seen. She had had no idea the afternoon was to be such a well-attended affair, and it was a great enough trial having to combine a meeting with Davey in this carnival atmosphere with what was tantamount to a spying mission for Augustus.

She caught sight of Davey immediately, for he was in the middle of the Green aloft a makeshift stage; a rickety-looking contraption made of four barrels with a board on top. Flanked on all sides by several serious-looking young men and one or two women carrying banners bearing the words, 'Dundee Political Reform League', he was already in full flow as she made her way closer to the centre of the proceedings.

As she came within earshot and gazed up at his gesticulating figure, she was surprised by the fluency and passion with which the words were delivered. This was a side to him she had never seen before, and a feeling of pride welled within her as she was carried forward by the surging wave of onlookers converging on the platform. Every so often he would pause, his thumbs hooked into the sides of his waistcoat, and look around him as he waited for the merits of a particular point to sink in, then he would beam in appreciation at the ensuing cheers and shouts of, 'Hear, hear! Well said there, lad!' He was milking the crowd for all it was worth and, there was no doubt about it, he was winning them over to his side. Wee Davey had grown up, Kate thought proudly.

An indication of the professionalism with which the speech was delivered was the fact that, when he finally spotted her, to her embarrassment, he doffed his cap with a flourish in her direction, whilst not interrupting for one second the torrent of words raining down on the assembled crowd.

Blushing, she raised a hand in return, as the elderly woman next to her said, 'Yon's a fine-looking young man, but he'll no' last long up there. Tak' a look at they lads.' She gestured with her head towards a small knot of militiamen lurking not twenty yards away. Normally the peace of the town was guaranteed by six elderly gentlemen known as the 'town guard', all of whom were long retired from army service and a familiar sight in their blue cloth dress-coats and three-cornered lace-trimmed hats; these peace-keepers, however, with their clutch of ex-army weapons, were another matter altogether. They looked as if they meant business.

'They'll hae him doon off that thing and will be reading the Riot Act to him afore he's got much further, you mark my words. It'll be the tolbooth for him and the rest o' his cronies afore this day's oot.'

Kate glanced again, more anxiously this time, at the group in question. They were lounging against a cart, with two fine-looking horses between the shanks. Since a massacre by the militia of innocent people gathered to hear the great reformer, 'Orator' Henry Hunt, at St Peter's Fields in Manchester some eleven years previously, the government had attempted to prevent such a thing happening again by passing several public order acts. Although the most restrictive elements of these acts had been repealed over the past few years, the organizing of any type of meeting that might be seen as seditious and inciting revolution was not only foolhardy, it was downright dangerous. Kate had no doubt that the woman was right and that Davey and his friends were running a severe risk of being locked up, and perhaps worse, for organizing this meeting today and preaching rebellion to the masses. More important men in the community than them had suffered just such a fate. The local Unitarian minister, Thomas Fysche Palmer, and George Mealmaker, a leading figure in the Society of the Friends of Liberty, had both been transported to Australia, and it was no secret that many more were spending years locked up in the town's tolbooth for political protest. Heaven only knew how many were lying in its cells right now for exactly the type of thing Davey and his pals were up to. To be standing here on Magdalen Green and calling for such things as better conditions in the mills, repeal of the Corn Laws, and even parliamentary reform to give the common man a voice, was a dangerous thing and no mistake.

'. . . And so, friends, I beg you to rouse yourselves. Take some control back into your own hands. When you see wrongs being done, either by your employer or by the government, then remain silent no longer. Protest . . .!' Davey's impassioned voice rang out over the heads of the crowd, most of whom were still giving him a fair hearing, although a group of newly arrived young men appeared to have no interest at all in politics and were intent on having sport by taking pot-shots at the speaker with whatever missiles came to hand.

A pebble whistled over the heads of those nearest the platform and caught the edge of Davey's bonnet, knocking it sideways on his head. He turned to shake his fist at the stone-thrower when, amid the cheers and jeers of the crowd, another voice assailed Kate's ears.

'Well, well, well, if it's not Miss McMahon . . .'

Kate whirled round to look straight into the face of Willie Falconer. Augustus's son was dressed in his Sunday best and was quite a dandy. A dark blue frock-coat was set off by a chamois-leather waistcoat, pale beige pantaloons and brown buckskin leather boots. A kid-gloved hand touched the brim of his hat, but there was little respect in the eyes that looked her up and down. 'Back among your own folk, are you?'

He threw a scathing glance around him. Most of the onlookers in their particular vicinity were quite obviously from the poorer part of the town and, no doubt, quite a few were from his own father's mills. 'Are you here to sympathize or to thank the good Lord that you have managed to claw your way out of all this?'

'Neither actually. I came because your father asked me to.'

Willie's eyebrows shot up as his hackles rose. 'Is that so?' It should have been no more than he expected. He had been adamantly against his father taking on the McMahon girl as housekeeper and had made no secret of his disapproval. 'And you do everything my father asks of you, do you?'

'He's my employer.'

Willie twirled his cane between his fingers. There was something about this young woman that unsettled him. For a start she was Peggy McMahon's sister, and he had no wish to be reminded of that fact. His affection for the McMahons' elder daughter had been genuine, if misplaced. In his mind, he had not forced himself on her as he suspected her family believed. On the contrary, they had been meeting secretly for a good month before he had his way with her, and when she had eventually given herself to him on the leather cushions of his father's reserve carriage, she had seemed every bit as carried away by the moment as he had been.

For several weeks he had been picking her up from a designated spot on a Sunday afternoon, and they would drive out on the Perth road and stop in a quiet byway to share a bite to eat and a bottle of wine from his father's well-stocked supplies. Peggy had never tasted wine before, and after two glasses her natural reserve would dissolve into affectionate giggles and embraces as they snuggled down in the back of the carriage, with the curtains tightly closed.

He could not tell if she was really fond of him or merely dazzled by the prospect of such a weekly treat, but they had got on well together and, for his part, he was certainly physically attracted to the girl. With her long fair hair, comely figure and gentle manner, she was a cut above any other female in his father's employ. He had had his eye on her for a good year before he finally persuaded her to join him in their first clandestine meeting, his first tentative suggestions being met with a blushing, 'Oh Mister Willie, I think not! The very idea!'

Unlike her sister, Peggy McMahon had always been one to know her place. Demure in both manner and speech, had she been born into his own sector of society she would have been regarded as quite a lady. He had been as shocked as she was to learn of her pregnancy. He knew there could never be any question of marriage; society, let alone his mother, would never stand for it. So he had deliberately avoided any contact with her after learning of the expected child, even going to the extent of asking his father to transfer him to the Falcon Mill on Dens Road so he would not have to face the mute reproach in her eyes whenever they caught sight of one another on the factory floor.

He had not seen her for over three months when he learned of her death. The news had depressed him for days, and to make matters worse he had had several accusations of murder hurled at him in the streets around the McMahons' home after the funeral. That had upset him more than anything. He had been petrified his mother would get to hear of the baby that had been born and had died, or of the death of its mother several weeks afterwards. She had never been a well woman, and such an

83

unfortunate affair coming to light would undoubtedly have hastened her death.

'I'll be honest with you,' he found himself saying to Kate. 'I never wanted Pa to take you on in the first place.'

She bridled at that. 'And why, may I ask?'

'I don't see that it's any of your business.'

She nodded knowingly. 'I wouldn't expect you to admit it, but it's because I'm Peggy's sister, isn't it?'

Now it was Willie's turn to flinch. 'It had nothing to do with your sister. I – I hardly knew the girl.'

He was lying. She could tell by the furtive way he avoided her eyes as he spoke. 'Some would say different,' she informed him. 'Some would say you knew her only too well.'

Willie's normally fair complexion went quite pink, but he chose to ignore the jibe. 'I had my own very good reasons for not wishing you to be part of our household,' he said stiffly. 'For one thing you're far too young for the post of housekeeper, and for another, in my opinion, you're nothing more than a little gold-digger.'

'A gold-digger!' Kate exploded, causing heads to turn around them. 'Take that back this minute, Willie Falconer! Take that back or you'll regret it!'

'I will take nothing back that's the truth,' Willie replied piously.

The two glared at one another, then Kate let out an indignant gasp at the sheer cheek of it. She had had quite enough. Casting aside her role as a would-be lady, she drew back her umbrella to take a swipe in the direction of his midriff.

Willie grabbed hold of her arm and twisted it quite painfully as he steered her away from the watching eyes and listening ears to the privacy and shade of an old rowan tree. 'We'll have no scene, if you don't mind. The gentlemen of the Press are here in number and the last thing the family needs is for one of their employees to feature in a scandal.'

Kate jerked herself free from his grip and fixed him with a stare that did nothing to disguise the contempt she felt. 'The Press!' she scoffed. 'You mean that boring old jessie Jockie Henderson from the *Advertiser* over there?' She threw a scathing glance in the direction of a portly, elderly gentleman sharing a hip-flask with a young spotty youth who was scribbling furiously into a notebook as Davey addressed the crowd. 'They wouldn't know a scandal if they fell over it!' She shook her head and gave a contemptuous laugh. 'It never fails to amaze me that such a gentleman as your father could have sired such a gutless worm as you, Willie Falconer.'

A smile quirked the corner of Willie's mouth. A worm now, was it? Even that was an improvement on murderer, the charge usually thrown at him by her kith and kin. And he had to hand it to her, she had guts – even if she did accuse him of lacking them. Not many young women in her position would give as good as they took. 'Have you eaten since breakfast?' he asked.

'Eaten since breakfast?' Kate's amazement at this astonishing change of tack was obvious.

Willie glanced sideways at the few heads still turned curiously in their direction. 'I thought, rather than remain the focus of needless gossip around here – and even risk "that boring old jessie" Jock Henderson's attentions – we might partake of a glass of something and a bite to eat at the Exchange Coffee House.'

Kate had never been inside Dundee society's most popular meeting place, but she most certainly was not going to be tempted by the young man beside her. 'There's nothing I'd like less,' she said truthfully, forcing a smile to her lips. 'Now, if you'll excuse me.'

The tip of her umbrella bit into the toe of his shoe as she dug it in the general direction of the ground and whirled on her heel.

Willie winced and took a step back as she sailed past him. His eyes followed her and, despite himself, he felt a distinct pang of disappointment. She might look nothing like her sister, but there was an almost animal magnetism about the young Miss McMahon. With that dark, gypsy-like hair, her neat figure and quick tongue, he could certainly see what his father saw in her. Augustus had always had an eye for the ladies, and there was no faulting his taste where this one was concerned, even if her motives *were* suspect. 'Blast you, Kate McMahon,' he muttered under his breath. He was not used to being turned down by young women, and it was not a happy feeling.

Disconsolate, he melted into the crowd, jostling around the foot of the platform, glancing across every so often at Kate who seemed to be paying rapt attention to the inflammatory rantings of the young man on top of the makeshift stage.

A fight broke out a few yards away from where he was standing, and somebody threw a rotten potato at the speaker. The vegetable caught Davey at the side of the head and sent him staggering backwards, his booted feet slipping on the scattering of small objects and rotten fruit already littering the planks beneath him. With a yell he toppled backwards from the stage to land sprawled on top of two elderly men at the foot of the contraption.

'Davey!'

To Willie's astonishment, Kate rushed forwards, pushing her way through the crowd towards the young man.

'Oh Davey . . . Davey!'

'Katie! Stay out of this!' Davey struggled to get up, apologizing profusely to the two onlookers now lying on the ground beside him. He could sense things beginning to get dirty. Names and oaths were being hurled in his direction by several youths in the crowd surrounding him.

'Bloody Papist scum!' With the likes of the Irishman Daniel O'Connell's success in pushing for Catholic emancipation in Parliament, every radical who attempted to stir things up these days was tarred with the Papal brush, whatever his religious persuasion.

The youth who yelled the insult followed it with a well-aimed kick at the side of Davey's head. The booted foot caught him on the right temple, grazing the flesh, and at this Davey pushed aside the concerned hands assisting him and staggered to his feet, making a rush for his assailant.

Kate screamed as the two of them met head on and tumbled to the ground in a twisted heap of flailing arms and legs.

Impulsively she threw her umbrella aside and launched herself on top of Davey's attacker. 'Let go of him! Let go of him, you pig!' Quite irate now at the injustice of it, she was tugging at her friend's assailant's shoulders in a vain attempt to make him release his grip.

A cheering crowd was quickly gathering in a ring around the three of them, with cries of, 'That's it, lass! Give him one! You get stuck in there, hen!'

Willie, who was watching in a mixture of horror and fascination from the sidelines, could scarcely believe his eyes as Kate's ladylike skirts flew up above her knees and her neat booted feet lashed out at the hind-quarters of the tow-headed youth on top of the other curly-headed fellow.

The sport was shortlived, however, as within a couple of minutes a pair of militiamen appeared, pushing their way through the cheering crowd of onlookers.

'That's it, then! Break it up, you lot!'

Strong arms dived into the fray and separated the tangled limbs, to emerge a minute or so later with both Davey and his attacker held firmly by the scruff of their necks, whilst the taller of the two guards had Kate securely by the wrist.

'It'll be the tolbooth for the three of you. You can sort out your quarrels in there!'

Davey looked despairingly at Kate. So much for the perfect afternoon he had had planned. It had been a grand idea all right: she would hear him speak and, hopefully, be cheered to the echo, then the two of them would retire to the Blue Bonnet for a quiet jug of ale and a good old chat, something they hadn't had for long enough. 'I told you to keep out of it!' he gasped, wiping the blood from the side of his face. 'Oh, Katie, I told you!'

'How could I?' she began, but was cut short in her protestation by the tall figure of Willie Falconer striding purposefully through the crowd to place himself firmly in front of the man holding both Davey and Kate.

'Mr Falconer, sir!' Willie stood a good half-head taller than the militiaman, and there was not a town guard, regular or irregular, who was not acquainted with Augustus Falconer's son and heir.

'You may release your hold on the young lady,' Willie said, with all the authority acquired through a lifetime's observing his father at work. 'She is an employee of ours and I will be personally responsible for her behaviour from now on.' He glanced at Kate. 'Her involvement in this little spat was purely accidental, as you can imagine.'

The guard frowned for a moment, then let go Kate's wrist which she rubbed in relief as he said sullenly, 'Aye, well, if you say so, Mr Falconer, I expect that'll be in order . . . We'll no' be handing over these twa young buggers, though. It's the doghouse for them, where they can scrap to their hearts' content like the mongrels they are.'

'You can't do that!' Kate protested. 'You can't lock Davey up! Mr Lorimer here was attacked by this character!' She stabbed a finger in the direction of the tow-headed youth, who was now nursing a bloodied nose. 'None of this was Davey's doing. You have no right to arrest him!'

'Well now, that's something that can be decided by the judge, young lady. It's not up to you – or me, come to that. You just think yourself lucky you've got a fine gentleman like Mr Falconer here to speak up for you or you'd be joining them in their ride to the tolbooth.'

At that Willie grabbed hold of Kate's arm. 'Let's go!' he said through gritted teeth. 'Let's get out of here before you make more of an exhibition of yourself than you already have.'

Kate opened her mouth to protest further, but Davey's voice intervened. 'Weary Willie's right, Kate. Do as he says.' His tone was resigned and his eyes were serious as they looked into hers. 'This is not quite the afternoon we planned, is it?'

At that, the two guards swung their prisoners round on their heels and began to frog-march them towards the parked cart some fifty yards away.

Kate watched them go until the tug of Willie's hand on her arm forced her to turn back to the man at her side.

'So it was a tryst you had here with that bit of radical scum, was it? I'm sure my father would be interested to hear that.'

'You're not going to tell him, are you?' Kate said, brushing the dirt from her skirts, then adjusting her bonnet which had been knocked sideways in the skirmish.

'Give me one good reason why I shouldn't.'

The two of them stood looking at one another in the middle of the dispersing crowd. Kate's chin tilted that bit higher as she said quietly, 'Because if you did then I wouldn't agree to partake of that cup of coffee with you, would I now?' She hated every word she uttered, but it was by far the lesser of the two evils.

A slow grin spread across Willie's face. 'You're not stupid, Kathleen McMahon, are you?'

'I don't believe you ever thought I was.'

Willie gave a sheepish half-laugh as he held out his arm for her to take. That was just the trouble. She was too bloody clever for her own good – and his.

Chapter Eight

Despite Willie Falconer's attempts at conversation, Kate had little to say on the twenty-minute walk from Magdalen Green to the new Exchange Coffee House on Shore Terrace. Her thoughts were purely on Davey and what would happen to him after his arrest. Come what may, she had to do something to help him, and the young man on whose arm her hand now reluctantly rested might just be in a position to help.

The floor of the Coffee House was thronged with customers when they entered the main salon. It was *the* place to be in town on a Sunday afternoon, and Willie seemed on familiar terms with most of the well-to-do clientele who propped up the long central counter or sat at tables around the room.

'Looks like we're out of luck,' he commented as he removed his hat and glanced around him. 'All the seats seem to be taken.'

'Over there!' Kate pointed to an elderly pair of gentlemen in the process of vacating one of the window tables.

Her companion did not need a second telling, for he sprinted across and laid claim to the two empty chairs immediately. 'This will do champion,' he declared, removing his gloves and placing them on the table beneath his hat before pulling out a chair for Kate. 'Two cups of your best coffee, lad, and a slice or two of seedcake into the bargain.'

A freckle-faced urchin in an oversized apron scuttled away to see to the order as Willie sat himself down and turned to Kate. He could tell from the number of young men glancing curiously in their direction that he was already the object of some speculation as to who exactly was the pretty young woman accompanying him this afternoon. He was also aware that Kate was equally conscious of the interest they had aroused and, by the look on her face, was not enjoying it. 'You're probably wondering if you'll get that cake down you without choking on it – seeing as you're eating it here as my guest.'

She allowed herself a tight smile as she removed her gloves. 'You're quite a mind-reader, Willie Falconer.' There was no way on earth she would be here if she didn't believe he was her only hope of helping Davey.

When she had finished adjusting her skirts, she turned her head to the side with an upward tilt of her chin and deliberately avoided his gaze by concentrating on observing the other guests.

Willie leant back in his chair and watched as she made herself comfortable, noting approvingly the flushed cheeks and worried green eyes beneath their frame of thick dark lashes. There was something about the proud way she held herself that reminded him of Peggy, but that was the only resemblance between the two sisters. He allowed himself a wry smile as he admitted to himself that they obviously did not have the same taste in men, for he had been the only male object of Peg's adoration, while Kate here acted as if she could not bear to be in the same room as him. She also seemed to have a distinct taste for the rougher element in town, if her involvement with that young lout on the soapbox was anything to go by. 'They'll have no mercy on him, you know?'

'I beg your pardon?'

'That ruffian boyfriend of yours. They'll not only read the Riot Act, they'll throw the book at him.'

Kate went cold and he could see from her face that his words had had the desired effect. Incredible though it might seem, she really seemed to care for that lout, and the knowledge gave him a strange sense of power. She must know that in her position she could do nothing to help him. It took someone from his own class to wield any sort of influence in this city. 'Does it upset you to think of him rotting in the tolbooth?'

She gave a strained nod of the head and looked away, unable to bear the mock pity in his eyes and voice.

'It'll be transportation for life at least. In fact, he'll be lucky to get away with that. Other folk have been hanged for far less, as you well know.'

Kate froze at the words so casually spoken, for there was no denying the truth in them. She felt both anger and helplessness and had to resist the impulse to get up and run from this place. How could she sit here so calmly with Davey on his way to God only knew what fate? All around her lounged the other Willie Falconers of this world, well-off young men whose families had the power and influence to buy anything they wanted, including the judiciary.

As if reading her thoughts, Willie's voice intervened. 'You'll want to help him, I have no doubt.'

'You know I do, and you also know that there's nothing the likes of me can do on my own,' she said bitterly. 'I'd give anything to help Davey, but it would do no good. I need help.' Somehow she could not bring herself to ask for it directly.

Willie mused on the words. There was no doubt there was desperation in her voice, a fact that both intrigued and annoyed him. How could she possibly care so much about the fate of such a creature? 'You'd give anything, eh? He really means that much to you?' His auburn brows quirked as he looked across at her.

Kate made no response and he took that as an affirmative. As he sat there, his pulse began to quicken.

'You have an idea?' she said, her hopes rising. Maybe he wasn't such a bastard after all.

All sorts of ideas were filling his head; some made the palms of his hands grow damp just thinking about them. 'Leave it with me,' he mused. 'I'm sure between the two of us we can come up with some sort of solution that's mutually beneficial.'

Kate's spirits rose. He was being infuriatingly enigmatic, but if that was how he wanted to play it, then it was all right with her. She'd go along with anything as long as it helped Davey out of this awful mess. 'I expect you're in here quite a lot with a fair selection of young women,' she said, deliberately changing the subject.

'Well, I . . .'

'In fact, you're quite the young man-about-town, so I believe. I'm surprised that by your age you haven't given up the chase and settled down with some well-connected young lady yet.'

'I have my reasons,' Willie replied, deliberately ignoring the provocative 'at your age' comment. He had privately decided long ago that he would make no move in the marriage direction before the age of thirty, when his father was due to make him a full partner in the business.

'It can't be a shortage of money that's stopping you, that's for sure.'

Willie merely smiled. That much was certainly true. His mother's death had left him very well off indeed, quite independent of his father's fortune. But there was more to life than money. Like the old man, he was inordinately proud of the Falcon Mills and lived for the day he would come into his full inheritance. He was seven years past his majority now, and the fact that he was still being made to wait to assume an equal share of the running of the business irked him more than anything. It was demeaning, as if his father still could not accept him as an adult. 'Money is not everything in life,' he said in a quiet voice.

'Only those who have it could have the luxury of saying that. Having never had it I can only say that, if it isn't everything, then it's as near as damnit.'

Willie made no reply. She had touched on the very topic that had been worrying him in her own regard of late, and now he actually had the opportunity to do something about it, he would be a fool to let the moment pass. He shifted slightly in his chair, so he had his back to the room, then leant forwards across the table to say quietly, 'I think we understand each other pretty well by now, Kate, wouldn't you agree?'

She looked surprised. 'You could say that.'

'You've never really liked me, have you?'

She was taken aback. Did he have to be quite so blunt? 'Well . . .'

'No, be honest.'

She drew in her breath and wondered how to phrase her thoughts without giving too much offence, particularly since she was desperate for his help in freeing Davey. 'I have a great deal of respect for your father,' she began, but got no further as Willie interrupted triumphantly, 'Aye, my father – I knew it!'

'What do you know?'

'Quite apart from my ability to help your loutish friend, you probably think you're having to put yourself through this to avoid me telling tales to my father about this whole sorry mess on the Green this afternoon.' He paused and looked her straight in the eye. 'But what would you say if I told you he would be a damned sight more upset at the thought of you and me taking coffee together here than about what happened back there, or about your friendship with that young ruffian?'

Kate frowned. He wasn't making any sense. 'That's stupid.'

'But it's true.'

The boy returned with the order and Willie took a florin from his pocket to pay for it. When the lad had left he took a sip of his coffee and nodded his head emphatically. 'It's absolutely true. The old man would be livid, and with good reason. We're both young and healthy and I'm reckoned to be a fair catch – by most folk at any rate.'

He gave an almost bashful smile as he looked down into his coffee-cup, then lifted his head. As his eyes found hers he could feel the hairs on the back of his neck begin to prickle as their gaze locked. There was no disputing it, Kate

McMahon was having an effect on him that her sister never did. 'Aye,' he sighed, 'I reckon Pa would be mighty put out if he could see us now.'

Kate sat up on her seat, her fingers tightening on the handle of her cup as she gave a strained smile in return. 'What you're really saying is, you think your father would object to me making eyes at you – should I so desire.' God help me, she thought. Despite his undoubted good looks and money, she wouldn't consider Willie Falconer as a suitor were he the last man on earth. Far too much muddy water had run under the family bridge for that. The very idea was too ludicrous for words. 'He wouldn't approve at all?'

'Approve? He would go bloody wild.'

Kate bridled at that. Was it because old Augustus felt she was unworthy of his precious son? 'And why exactly, may I ask?'

There was a long silence, then Willie took a deep breath. 'Because he's an old man with a young man's craving and he has designs on you for himself, that's why.'

Kate gaped at him. 'I – I don't believe you!' She replaced her cup with a rattle in the saucer. Her heart had lurched at the words and she stared at him in disbelief. 'You really believe your father would be jealous of us being here together?' The very idea was quite preposterous, and it was all she could do to stop herself bursting out laughing. 'Why, he must be almost forty years older than me if he's a day!'

'Aye, that's true. But he's still a full-blooded man, with a real man's feelings and desires. In fact, he's more of a man than most half his age.'

He mused on the truth of his words and nodded in affirmation. 'The passing years don't seem to mean the same to a man as a woman, and in his case it must be in the blood, for his own father had him when he was in his sixties.' He had not meant to divulge that particular piece of personal information, but it was true. His grandfather's first marriage had been childless, and it had only been after his first wife died and he married a woman almost thirty years his junior that Augustus had been born. 'Aye, he's still a real man all right, is Pa, there's no doubt about that. In fact, the old bugger would bed you tomorrow, if – '

'If I gave him any encouragement?'

Willie shifted uncomfortably in his seat. It was important he got his message across without causing too much offence. 'I – I just feel it's up to me to warn you, that's all. I've seen the way the old boy looks at you, and I don't want you raising any false hopes about the situation.'

'False hopes?'

'About him marrying you.'

'I see.'

He could tell from the frozen expression that came over her face that the offence had been taken. 'Oh, it's not that you're not a bonnie enough lass. Far from it. There are few in this town could hold a candle to you for looks. And you're bright with it. Too damned bright for your own good sometimes. You'll make some man a fine wife some day. But not Pa. He may bed you but he'll never wed you. I – I just thought you ought to know that.'

Kate looked him straight in the eye. 'I'm not good enough, is that it? You're telling me I'm not worthy of him? He knows it and you know it. It's the old story: good enough to bed but not good enough to wed.'

Willie looked as uncomfortable as he felt as he shrugged his shoulders and said, 'Well, that's not exactly how I would have put it.'

'But that's what it amounts to.'

He nodded his head and felt a nerve twitch in the side of his jaw. That always happened when he was tense. He was playing for high stakes here, for his impromptu heart-to-heart with Kate might just misfire. 'You must have realized by now he's not had an easy time of it in that department over the years, with my mother being a semi-invalid for so long. He wouldn't be human if he didn't respond to someone like you coming into his life. But desiring and even satisfying that desire is not the same as . . . as . . .'

'As making an honest woman of someone.' Did he realize, she wondered, just how sanctimonious he was being, considering his own shameful past?

'I knew you'd understand.' A look of relief came to his face. With as attractive and spirited a young woman as this, it was not beyond the realms of possibility that she might just persuade the old man to make such a relationship legal, and then where would he be? A fat lot of good it would be being Augustus's only son if when the old man passed on he left a young wife to inherit the lot. 'I – I hope you don't mind me being so honest. It is for your own good, after all.'

Kate's gaze was fixed firmly on the brown liquid in her coffee-cup. What Willie was saying both repelled and excited her. She had no idea if he was speaking the truth or not, but could not imagine why he should bother making such a thing up. Was old Augustus really so enamoured by her? In a strange way it gave her a feeling of power she had never possessed before. Gooseflesh covered the skin of her arms as a tingle of anticipation ran through her. Willie would only tell her this if he was frightened of something. He didn't give a damn if his father bedded her; his only concern was that he didn't wed her. Her pulse raced and she did her best not to let it show as she took another sip of her coffee.

'You're not saying very much.' It was almost a reproach.

'You've taken me aback, that's all.'

'I've given you something to think about, I expect,' Willie said, relaxing somewhat. 'It's not unknown for young women to be taken advantage of by their employers. It happens every day. You don't want to end up like poor Peggy now, do you?'

Kate's breath caught in her throat at the bare-faced

cheek of it. 'You mean with a bastard Falconer bairn?' she said icily.

Willie had the good grace to blush. 'It's a hard world, Kate.'

'You're right, Willie Falconer,' she replied, through tight lips. 'And I certainly don't want to end up like poor Peg.' Far from it, she told herself.

Willie heaved a sigh of relief and sat back in his chair, beaming as he reached for his coffee-cup. 'Then I take it we know where we stand?'

'We certainly do,' Kate replied. 'Nobody is going to take advantage of me, Willie, you can rest your mind easy on that.'

Their eyes met and there was a strangely defiant look in Kate's gaze that made the smile fade on Willie's lips. 'You're a strange one, Kathleen McMahon, and no mistake. I swear to God I can't tell what you're really thinking.'

Kate smiled – a real genuine smile for the first time that afternoon. 'Maybe it's just as well, Willie . . . For both our sakes.'

Chapter Nine

The ill-fated meeting organized by the Dundee Political Reform League made headline news in the local paper the following morning, a fact that Kate was made aware of by Willie who came into the kitchen brandishing a copy as she prepared his father's breakfast tray.

'I see that ruffian of yours got quite a mention,' he said, tossing the paper on to the table in front of her. 'Lorimer's the name and it gives his address as the Hawkhill. Isn't that where your mother lives?'

'Aye, it is.'

It helped explain her agitation yesterday. They were both out of the same sewer. 'Grew up with him, did you? Childhood sweethearts, is that it?' Willie reached over and lifted a piece of buttered toast from the tray Kate was preparing, and took a bite as he regarded her quizzically.

'I grew up with a lot of folk,' she replied noncommittally, buttering another slice to replace the one taken.

Willie shooed one of the house cats off the rocking chair by the side of the range and sat himself down, rocking quietly for a minute or two as he watched Kate busy herself with the breakfast tray. He knew she hated it when he observed her like this, and that was half the pleasure. Whilst it was the height of rudeness for servants to stare at their superiors, no such rule applied the other way round. It was an unspoken affirmation of her inferior status and he knew that was what irked her more than anything. But more than that, he actually enjoyed watching her. Their time together in the Coffee House had led to a sleepless night fantasizing situations between the two of them that would have had the Reverend Mooney frothing at the mouth in consternation.

At last he spoke. 'That friend of yours – the Lorimer creature – I've been making a few enquiries and what I said yesterday was right enough. They reckon he'll definitely get time or transportation, if not worse.'

At that Kate's reserve broke. She paused in the changing of her apron from her working one to the white frilly affair that Augustus liked to see above stairs. 'But you said you'd help him! You promised me, Willie!' Whether he had actually done so, she could not remember, but it had seemed like that to her. Her face was distraught as she looked at him across the table.

'Well now, I can't say I remember making any promise as such,' Willie said slowly. 'As I remember it, we were to come to some sort of agreement – some sort of trade-off, if you like.'

He was playing games with her, playing games with Davey's very life. 'I don't know what you mean,' she said quietly. 'But I'll do anything I can to help Davey, you know that.'

Willie looked at her intently as he bit on his toast. 'That's what I thought you said.' He dabbed at his mouth with a clean napkin from the tabletop. 'And I told you yesterday I was sure we could come to some sort of compromise. You don't get "owt for nowt" in this world, as they say down south, you know, Kate. It's a hard world out there.'

'You don't have to tell me that.'

'No, no, I don't, do I?'

They looked at one another, then she picked up the tray. 'I'd better take this upstairs.'

'Have you seen Pa since you got back from the Green yesterday?'

Kate shook her head. 'No, he was visiting friends in Monifieth till late last night . . .' Her voice tailed off, for her mind was still on Davey. 'You really think there's a risk he'll be transported?'

'Your pal? Bound to be,' Willie assured her. 'They're cracking down hard on that sort of thing at the moment, seeing as all the carrying on there's been in Paddyland of late. Give Papists the vote and they'll have all sorts of undesirables demanding it.'

'Ireland's not Scotland.'

'No, but all this agitation amounts to the same thing. You give the Catholics voting rights and what happens? You get the likes of that Lorimer character shouting his mouth off, that's what. Before you know where you are, the lower orders are up in arms demanding God-knows-what to be upside down with the Catholics. It's certainly got the likes of Pa sweating, I can tell you.'

'But, despite that, you said you'll help him — you'll help Davey?'

'Trust me,' Willie said.

Kate gave a tight smile as she turned to head for the door. That was the last thing she would ever do.

Serving Augustus's breakfast used to be the parlour-maid's job, but since Kate had taken over as housekeeper, the old man had insisted she be the one to bring him his tea, toast and morning newspaper. He liked her to be there to listen and pass comment as he glanced through the news of the day. 'You've a sensible head on your shoulders — for a bit of lass,' he told her on more than one occasion, and she knew he valued her opinion on most things.

'By the way,' Willie called after her as she manoeuvred the tray out of the door. 'You haven't forgotten that other matter we spoke about in the Coffee House?'

'No, I haven't forgotten.' How could she possibly forget? Apart from poor Davey's predicament, she had thought about little else in bed last night. The knowledge that old Augustus might be looking at her as anything other than a first-rate employee had come as a shock to the system. She almost wished Willie had held his tongue on the subject, for she could feel the colour surging to her

101

cheeks just thinking about it as she climbed the stairs from the kitchen to the first floor where his father would be waiting.

She could smell the familiar fug of Augustus's pipe as she opened the breakfast-room door. He was seated in his favourite leather armchair in the bay-window, and his florid face wrinkled in pleasure at the sight of her. 'Kate!' Noticing her flushed cheeks and taking it as a sign of good health, he beamed his approval. 'My, but you're looking bonnie this morning. That walk to the Green must have done you good yesterday. I had hoped to see you when I got home last night, but I must admit I was a wee bit later than I expected.'

Kate put the tray down on the table and set about laying out his breakfast. 'I – I had a bit of a headache when I got back, I'm afraid. I went to bed early. I'm sorry to have disappointed you.'

He waved away her apology as he laid his pipe in the ashtray and prepared to eat. 'There's no need to be sorry. You know I don't expect you to wait up if I'm after midnight.' There was that special twinkle in his eye as he leant forward and said in a confidential tone, 'I was about to say a lass of your age needs her beauty sleep, but with your looks that's hardly necessary.'

She flushed an even deeper pink as she spread the napkin across his knees. What she had previously regarded simply as Augustus's fatherly banter had now taken on quite a different hue.

He watched approvingly as she poured the tea and handed him his cup. He had never been so cosseted in his entire life until she joined his household. 'Thanks, lass.'

The newspaper was neatly folded by his plate and he reached for it, shaking it open as he felt inside his waistcoat pocket for his spectacles before placing them on the end of his nose and glancing at the headlines.

He liked to familiarize himself with the main news items before beginning breakfast and, as he scanned the pages,

Kate stood with her back to him, gazing out over the rooftops that reached right down to the water's edge.

'Mmm . . . Seems there was quite a turn-out for that Reform League nonsense I asked you to take a look at, but from what I see the devils who organized it got their just deserts. They'll probably hang the lot o' them to make an example of them, and a good job too!'

'H – hang them!' Kate gaped at him. Somehow hearing someone of Augustus's age and authority say the dreaded words shocked her to the core.

'Aye, and even that's too good for them, in my opinion. And I've no doubt the sheriff will take the same view.'

Kate began to shake.

The old man looked at her curiously. 'Are you all right, my dear?'

She opened her mouth but no words came. She was staring at Augustus, but all she could see was that hangman's noose and Davey's face swimming in front of her. It was one thing listening to Willie proclaim doom and gloom about Davey's fate, but somehow it bore so much more weight coming from Augustus. He was a wily old bird and there was very little he was ever wrong about when it came to things like this.

'Are you sure you're all right?' Augustus put down his paper and was looking at her in some concern. Had she taken ill, he wondered? She had gone quite white and looked as if she was trembling.

He got out of his chair and came over to her as she turned away, reluctant to let him see the tears that were welling in her eyes.

'Are you feeling all right, lass?' he repeated, taking her arm and gently turning her to face him.

Kate took a shuddering breath and nodded mutely as Augustus regarded her silently, clearly perplexed. He had never seen her as upset as this before. Was it something he had said, or was she simply not feeling well? The pale eyes behind the spectacles were serious as he took both her hands in his. 'Something's bothering you, my dear. Is it anything you can tell me about?'

Kate shook her head. After what he had just said, he was the last person she could tell, and that made it all the worse. All her hopes rested on Willie now, and that was a terrible situation to be in. God help Davey, she thought, as helpless tears began to stream down her face. God help him, for I certainly can't . . .

'Lass . . . Lass . . .' Augustus had never seen her in a state like this. He could feel his own florid cheeks begin to burn as he uncertainly placed his hands on her shoulders, murmuring, 'Now, now, whatever ails you, it canna be as bad as all that.'

His concern was too much for Kate. Suddenly she had had enough of being strong and facing the world on her own. In the face of Davey's awful predicament she felt impotent and alone. He was relying on her, and all she could do was stand here bubbling like a wee lassie.

'Nothing's so bad it can mak' you greet on a bonnie morning like this.'

He was trying so hard to be helpful, but his sympathy was only making things worse.

He reached out and gently wiped away a tear with his fingertips and his tender gesture was too much for Kate, who threw her arms around his neck, burying her head in the soft worsted of his waistcoat as she tried in vain to stifle the sobs that shuddered through her.

Both confused and perplexed and totally at a loss as to what to do or say next, Augustus stroked her hair as he would a small child's, making gruff comforting noises in a vain attempt to stem the flow of tears. Women were like this sometimes, he reasoned. They could burst into tears at the drop of a hat, then be right as rain the next minute. And he felt strangely touched that she should be clinging on to him so helplessly like this.

They were still standing locked in each other's arms a minute or so later when a gasp from the open doorway made them turn with a start to see the tall figure of Willie standing there.

'Good God, what have we here?' Willie gaped at them both in disbelief.

An embarrassed Kate immediately disentangled herself from his father's embrace and made to rush from the room, but Willie barred the way.

'Hang on a minute, I think this requires some explanation, don't you?'

'I – I . . .' Kate looked in confusion towards Augustus.

'I don't see that any explanation is required,' the old man replied stiffly, sitting himself back down in his chair to resume his breakfast. 'And certainly not to you, young Willie.'

He looked up at Kate. 'You can go and get on with your work now, lass. I'll see you later.'

When she had gone and the door closed behind her, Willie marched over to where his father was sitting. 'I don't know what that touching little scene was about,' he said, trying to keep control of his voice. 'And seeing as I'm only your son, I don't suppose it's any of my business.'

'You're right there,' Augustus said, now seated at his breakfast. He had not the faintest idea himself, but he certainly wasn't going to give Willie the satisfaction of knowing that. He gave a wheezy chuckle as he bit into the toast. It amused him to get his son going, for young Willie was well known for his temper, and no one could take the wind out of his sails better than the old man himself.

'You ought to be ashamed of yourself, consorting wi' a little trollop like that. Have you gone daft or something?'

'Na, na, lad, I've no' taken leave of my senses, I can assure you o' that. On the contrary, I've never been more sane in my life.'

He smiled as he lifted his tea-cup to wash down the mouthful of toast. He was really enjoying this. That look on Willie's face was quite something to behold. 'Young Kate is no trollop, and well you know it. On the contrary, she's the most intelligent young woman I've come across in many a long day.'

'You don't know what you're saying!'

'Oh, I know what I'm saying all right.' Life was suddenly worth living with Kate McMahon around. For the first time he actually looked forward to getting up in the morning, as it meant seeing her again. He gave a quiet smile, for God alone knew how happy it would make him to have her there throughout the night as well.

'You've cracked. You've finally cracked,' Willie was saying. 'It's Mother's death that's done it. It's nothing to be ashamed of. I can understand, I can help you, if you'll only admit it.'

'Admit what, lad? Admit that for the first time in my life I feel like a real man in my ain house? Admit that for the first time in God knows how long I'm actually enjoying life again? If it's the truth you're after, then I freely admit to both those things.'

His appetite gone, Augustus pushed the breakfast tray away and reached for his pipe. 'Now what brings you in here to see me at this time o' day, anyway?'

Willie could only gape at him and shake his head. He had quite forgotten. But whatever it was, nothing was more important than getting to the bottom of this.

He turned to a watercolour portrait of his mother on the far wall. 'What would she say?' he demanded. 'What would my mother say if she could have borne witness to the scene I've just walked in on this morning? You with your arms around that — that servant!'

He shook his head at the memory. It was his worst nightmare come true, and far sooner than he had ever anticipated. His poor mother . . . Emily Falconer had always been one for the hired help knowing their place and not getting above it. Mortified, she would be, mortified and disgusted. 'How could you do it, Pa? How could you do it, with your own wife still warm in her grave?'

Augustus looked at his son across the few feet of table and shook his head. 'Willie lad,' he sighed. 'That woman may have been your mother and my wife of thirty years, but tell me this, how the hell could she still be warm in her grave when she was never anything but as cold as charity towards me in her lifetime?'

He looked across at the picture of the stiffly seated woman in the dark blue bombazine dress on the far wall. 'Poor Emily,' he sighed. 'It wasn't a man she should have married, but a bank account on twa legs.' He gave another of his wheezy chortles and shook his head wearily. 'Ye ken, I told old Bertie Mooney twenty-odd years ago, when I learned she was expecting you, that this could be no ordinary pregnancy. It had to be no less than the Second Coming, and I damned near christened you Jesus Christ, for God only knows how you came to be conceived. If it wasn't an immaculate conception, it was as near as damnit!'

'Haud your wheesht! Just shut your mouth, damn you!' There were tears in Willie's eyes now. He had adored his mother, and could not bear to have ill spoken of her by anybody, let alone his own father. It was akin to spitting on her grave. And such personal remarks into the bargain . . . 'Don't you dare defame my mother like this! How could you defile her memory? My mother was . . .' he searched for the right word to do her justice. 'A saint! That's what she was – a saint!'

'Aye,' his father agreed, in a tired voice. 'And the trouble wi' saints, Willie lad, is that they're the devil to live with.' Then, before his son could protest further, he gave a dismissive wave of his hand. 'Get out of here, lad. Away and take your snivelling nonsense out o' here. I've a job of work to do this morning and I'm late already.'

With that, he turned back to the paper on the table beside him and held it up in front of him until he heard the door close and his son's footsteps fade into the distance. 'Silly young bugger,' he muttered to himself. What did he know of life? The trouble with young Willie was he was still wet behind the ears, and was taking far too long to dry out. Maybe it would be no bad thing if he was made to be a wee bit jealous at having someone like Kate around. It might make him grow up a bit and start acting like a man for a change, and not the spoilt bairn that he undoubtedly was.

The following day, Augustus had made arrangements to take the carriage to Forfar to investigate the possibility of opening a flax-weaving mill there. He had been warned that opposition was already mounting from the large number of household weavers in the burgh, and it was important he got as many councillors on his side as possible before he made the formal application. Because the county town was some fifteen miles distant, he intended seeing as many officials as he could in the one trip, and would probably not be back until late. 'I'm meeting some cronies at the King's Arms for supper and will probably stay on for a dram or two afterwards, so why don't you take the evening off?' After that unaccountable tearful scene yesterday morning, Kate had seemed overwrought for the rest of the day. She was probably overdoing things, he thought. An evening to herself would not go amiss.

Kate appeared surprised by the suggestion, but was quick to accept. There would be no question of putting her feet up, however. There were more pressing matters to attend to.

Chapter Ten

It was a good hour's walk to the Hawkhill, so Kate set off just after six in the evening, planning to get there in time for the mills coming out. This time it was not her own mother and father she would be heading for, but Betty Lorimer, Davey's widowed mother. Kate could well imagine how upset the poor woman must be to have her son locked away in the tolbooth; she would be especially glad to know Kate intended seeing Davey himself before heading back for Broughty Ferry, and would be doing everything she could to help him.

It was a typical spring evening and there was a blustery south-westerly wind with rain blowing through as she set off on the four-mile walk into town. She huddled tightly into her tartan plaid as she made her way along the Dundee Road, her bonneted head bowed into the oncoming gusts. How she envied those she saw rattle past, snug and dry in their carriages. How much simpler and more convenient life would be to have such transport at one's disposal, she thought wistfully.

After forty-five minutes' brisk walking she had left the grassy foreshore behind and the teeming area of the harbour with its tall-masted ships, almost blocking the river right across to the Kingdom of Fife on the opposite bank. She was back on her old home territory of winding streets that snaked their way upwards towards the grassy mound of the Law Hill that dominated the city. As she passed the familiar landmark of the Falcon Mill, she gave a wry smile as she glanced up at the stone bird of prey above the front entrance. Its wings were spread ready for take-off, but it would never fly. Unlike the seagulls that still soared overhead, it was firmly embedded in the rock from which it was hewn. Like most of the people who went in and out through that door each day, it was firmly fixed in its place in the scheme of things. Once upon a time she had hated everything it stood for, and in a way she still did, but there was no denying life was very different now. She could see things from the perspective of those above, and had come to realize that not everyone in that elevated position was all bad. She felt almost protective towards old Augustus whenever she heard an outsider pass a detrimental comment about him.

Passing Granny Mutch's sweet-shop, she called in for a bag of pandrops for her father. In times of such great change in the city it was comforting to know the old corner-shop with its window full of ha'penny treats was still in business. Granny Mutch had stood behind that counter for at least a generation and, as Kate began to walk up the steep sloping street that was the Hawkhill, she found her mind going back to the day she had first set eyes on Willie Falconer. He had saved Davey from choking on a lump of toffee from that same sweetie-shop. She wondered if Willie even remembered the incident, and if he did what he would make of it if he knew that the young man he saw being arrested on Magdalen Green was that same little lad whose life he had saved all those years ago.

Davey's mother Betty had barely had time to hang up her shawl on the hook on the back of her front door when Kate's knock had her opening it again to look in astonishment at the well-dressed young woman on the step.

'It's Kate McMahon, Mrs Lorimer. May I come in?'

It took a moment or so for recognition to dawn. 'Good God, Kate lass, I'd never have recognized you! Come away in.' She led the way into the sparsely furnished room that served as both kitchen and parlour. 'Tak' a seat,' she flustered, clearing a space on an old settle that stood against the wall by the fireplace. 'I'm sorry the place is no' as tidy as it might be, but I'm just in.'

The room was cold and bleak, with spores of green and black rot visible along the skirting board. The dampness within the four walls, even at this time of year, chilled the soul as well as the bones. The room contained even less furniture than Kate remembered. The best bits and pieces had probably been sold off over the years to relieve the hardship.

She sat down thankfully on the wooden settle and dug inside her basket to extract the few things she had brought with her. She laid them out beside her on the seat, wishing she had brought more. 'I thought you could use these. They're not much, but they'll help fill a corner in your press.'

'Fill a corner in my press!' Betty gasped, falling on the gifts in delight. 'My, but this is far too good o' ye.'

Betty picked up the items and lovingly stroked each one in turn before cradling them protectively to her breast. 'You'll manage a glass o' something or a bite to eat afore you go.'

Kate knew there was little enough in the house without wasting it on social niceties for the likes of herself. 'It's kind of you, but I can't stop. I just wanted to let you know that I'm doing everything I can to help Davey.'

'Help Davey?' his mother repeated with a scornful laugh. 'The only way anybody's going to help my Davey is by supplying him wi' a new brain, and that's the God's truth.'

As she placed the butter, cheese and sugar in a wallpress by the side of the fire, she threw Kate a despairing glance. 'I've had seven bairns, Kathleen; three are dead, one's in Glasgow, one laddie's at sea, I've a married lassie in Perth, and Davey was my bairn, my last hope.'

She sat down heavily on a chair by the side of the fire and passed a hand over her thinning grey hair, pushing a hairpin back into the meagre bun at the nape of her neck. She looked older and more tired than Kate remembered. The passing years had not been kind, but Betty Lorimer had been a fighter in her day and was not going to give in easily to illness or overwork. What upset her more than anything these days was that her youngest child seemed hell-bent on making life even more difficult for her. 'I've been tellt by the doctor that I canna keep going at the mill for that much longer and what does his lordship, Master Davey, do? He gets himself arrested, that's what. A fat lot of good he's doing for himself or his mother lying rotting there in that tolbooth!'

She chewed nervously at the skin around the nail of her right index finger as she contemplated the worst. 'You know what could happen to him in there, don't you, Kate? He could be stuck there for years or, worse, he could be sent out to Australia. Transported to Botany Bay. Gone for good, he could be, so he might as well be deid.'

Kate sat in an embarrassed silence as Davey's mother's face crumpled before her eyes and she began to cry; strange, dry, tearless sobs that shook her thin body with painful shudders. Kate averted her eyes. She had seen such sobbing before from her own mother. It was easy to be cried out in such an existence.

'I'm sorry, hen,' Betty Lorimer said at last, dabbing ineffectually at her eyes. 'It's good o' you to take an interest. But, if you ask me, only the good Lord himself can help oor Davey now, and he's nobody but himself to blame. It was his choice to get himself involved in politics.' Then her brow furrowed as she looked across at Kate sitting quietly on the settle. 'How can a bit o' a lass like you help him, anyway?'

'Oh, it's not me really,' Kate hastened to assure her, as she stood up to go. 'It's . . . it's . . .' But somehow she could not bring herself to say Willie Falconer's name. After Peggy's death it would be mentioning the unmentionable around here. 'It's Augustus – Mr Falconer, my employer,' she lied, naming the lesser of two evils. 'He promised me he would put in a good word for Davey in the right quarters.'

The older woman stared at her, finding it hard to believe her ears. 'Augustus Falconer's promised to put in a good word for my Davey?'

'That's right,' Kate assured her. 'It was decent of him really.'

'Decent of him?' Betty Lorimer said in incredulity. 'It's a miracle, if it's true.'

As Kate walked towards the door, Davey's mother caught hold of her arm. 'I appreciate you coming to tell me this, Kathleen,' she said quietly. 'I want you to know that. I'm no' like some who claim they are too proud to take help when it's offered, no matter where it comes from. And I stick up for you, lassie. Let nobody say I don't.'

'You stick up for me?'

'Aye, that I do. When others come that shite about you being auld Augustus's whore, I remind them what the Bible says. "Let him who is without sin cast the first stone." I tell them that, and it soon shuts them up. There are no' many saints in this close, or beyond it, I can assure you o' that . . .'

Her voice continued, but Kate had stopped listening at the words, '*Augustus's whore*'. Was that what they really thought of her around here? All those folk she had grown up with – was that what they really believed?

Careful not to let her hurt show, she laid a comforting hand on Davey's mother's arm. 'Look after yourself,' she said quietly. 'And I promise I'll do my best by Davey.'

'God bless you, lass,' the older woman called as Kate disappeared back down the stairs. 'God bless you, hen! It's a pity there's nae mair like you in this world!'

Not more like me, Kate thought bitterly to herself. More mill-owners' whores, does she mean?

It was with a hurrying step that she descended the tenement stairs and made her way through the close and out into the street. The rain was now no more than the odd spot blowing through the gusting breeze. A small knot of barefoot children were huddled round the step, and they looked up at her curiously as she squeezed past. Impulsively she took a silver threepenny bit out of her pocket and thrust it into the biggest girl's hand. 'Get yourselves some ha'penny chews from Granny Mutch's,' she told her. 'And don't forget the wee ones, mind!'

The children looked at her in amazement as she hurried across the road. If she hoped to be allowed to see Davey, she knew she would have to present herself at the prison before darkness. No visitors were allowed after nightfall, so there was no time to lose.

It was only a short ten-minute walk from the Hawkhill to the tolbooth and, happily, there was someone in the outer office of the prison to answer her knock on the heavy oak door.

She waited anxiously, listening to the chilling sounds of the chains being unhooked and the heavy iron bar being lifted. The young man in charge peered out and eyed her suspiciously as she asked to be allowed to see Mr David Lorimer for a few minutes. It was not often such a well-dressed young woman applied to visit a prisoner.

'Aye well, it's getting fairly dark, so you'll better be no more than a couple o' minutes or so.' His voice was grudging as he swung back the door to allow her to enter. He had a thin, consumptive face and a bad crop of boils on his chin which he was trying to disguise by growing a beard.

'Don't worry,' Kate assured him. 'I'll not be long.'

The basement corridor he led her through was dank and gloomy and smelt of urine and excrement to such an extent she almost gagged before she was half-way along. What looked like an indoor open sewer ran down the right-hand side of the passage, and the stench from it was almost unbearable. The guard noticed her holding a hand over her nose and mouth and gave an understanding smile. 'It doesna exactly smell o' roses, does it? But then the buggers we get in here are no' exactly flower-sellers.'

She attempted a weak smile behind her hand. At the sound of their feet, some of the prisoners started to bang on the locked doors of their cells and shout out to them. She could hear raised voices and cursing from beyond almost all the doors as they hurried past, and she wondered about the men, and occasional women, who found their way down here.

At last the warder halted as they reached the end of the passage, lifting one of the heavy keys from his belt to unlock a door. 'Here you are then, Miss.'

Davey was in a narrow cell on his own. It was no more than four feet across and six feet long, and it contained no furniture, save a bucket against the wall that obviously served as a toilet. The place stank just as much as the corridor outside, and she wondered how he could bear it. He was lying on a narrow stone ledge that doubled as a bed, and he let out a gasp of disbelief when he saw Kate standing there behind the guard.

'Kate – in God's name, what brings you here?' He sprang to his feet, his whole face lighting up at the sight of her.

'I'll be back in a few minutes,' the guard warned them. 'No carrying-on or anything now. It's against regulations . . . And I'd better take that basket off you, Miss.'

Kate handed over the basket she had brought and thanked the guard as he locked her into the cell. 'Don't worry, I'll not be long.'

Davey could barely contain his elation at seeing her. 'God but it's good to see you, Kate,' he said, clutching her hands in his as they sat down side by side on the stone ledge.

'I – I had to come,' she said softly, her eyes taking in the painful-looking swelling and grazing at the side of his head. 'Oh Davey, I was so worried when they took you away.'

He gave a dismissive shrug at her concern. 'Aye, well, I'm sorry if you were upset. I wouldn't have asked you to come to the Green if I'd thought that was going to happen. But, for all that, it was a risk worth taking.'

'A risk worth taking?'

Her incredulous tone annoyed him. 'We're not stupid, you know, Kate, we knew what we were doing. Nothing has been granted to the common man without people putting their own lives and liberty at risk. Far better people than me have paid a far bigger price than this.'

Even in the semi-darkness of the cell, she could see his eyes were shining as he spoke. His brown curly hair was tangled above the injury, his cheeks and chin covered in a heavy growth of beard. He was no longer the young devil-may-care Davey she knew. He looked every inch the revolutionary he was now purporting to be. She felt a curious combination of despair, frustration and pride as she looked at him. 'I fear for you, Davey,' she said softly. 'I really do.'

Their eyes met and held as he raised her hands to his lips and kissed each in turn. 'Katie, my Katie,' he said softly. 'Who do you think I'm doing all this for? It's for us – the likes o' us and our bairns, and our bairns' bairns . . .'

Her heart turned over. 'For us and our bairns?' she repeated, her voice a mere whisper, her eyes large and luminous as she gazed at him.

'Who else would I be doing it for? I love you, Katie McMahon,' he said softly. 'You know that. I've loved you ever since you were knee-high to a spuggie. And you love me too.'

The last sentence was said so matter-of-factly that she was forced to smile. He loved her and she loved him too. It was a simple fact. They had both known it all their lives.

'It's important we know that, for choosing a path like this is far from easy. Such luxuries as personal happiness must often be cast aside for the greater good.'

'The greater good?'

'Do you think when they stormed the Bastille in France that they stopped to wonder if they were putting themselves in danger? Of course not. They knew they risked imprisonment, and even death; they risked never seeing their loved ones again, but still they went through with it.

They had right on their side, you see, Kate, and good will always triumph over evil.'

They were fine words. 'You don't mind being stuck in here then – if it's for this greater good that you speak of?'

'Of course I mind,' he said heatedly. 'I mind like hell. Stuck in here I can't do a damned thing for the cause. I'd give anything to be a free man again, but a fat chance there is of that.'

Her heart raced. 'There is a chance,' she told him, her voice shaking. 'And a fine fat one at that.'

'What do you mean?'

'I've asked Augustus Falconer to help you and he's agreed.' Again she could not bring herself to admit it was Willie she had turned to for help.

He stared at her in incomprehension. 'You've done *what?*'

'I – I've asked Aug – '

She got no further, for he let go her hands and broke in with '*Augustus* – so it's *Augustus* now, is it? It's not Mr Falconer any longer – all those auld bitches on the Hawkhill were right.'

'Wh – what exactly do you mean by that?' Kate said, shifting uncomfortably on the hard stone.

'Those who claim you're Augustus's whore: it sounds like they could be right, doesn't it, Kate?'

His eyes bore down into hers, and she could feel her cheeks burning as indignation welled within her. This was not how she had planned it at all. First he tells her he loves her, then he accuses her of being Augustus's whore. 'Is that what you really think?' she asked through tight lips, inching away from him on the hard stone seat.

'Grow up, Kate,' he said wearily. 'Augustus Falconer is one of the richest and most powerful men in this city. You are merely his employee. He hates the likes of me and my pals in the Reform League with a passion, and you come here and tell me he's agreed to speak up for me. What

117

would you make of it? What would you think if you were in my place?'

'You really believe I'm Augustus's whore, then?' Tears burned the surface of her eyes as she stood up to go, and she prayed they would not fall. She had her pride and would leave here with it intact.

'Put it like this, Katie – I'm a grown man and you're a grown woman. You put two and two together in a situation like this and they make four, not five. You must be doing that old bugger some bloody big favour for him to do this one for you!'

'Time's up, ma'm!'

The voice from the doorway made Kate whirl round. The guard was standing there waiting for her to take her leave.

Too choked to speak, she turned to go, but Davey grabbed her arm. 'I just want to say I don't blame you, Kate. Not really. I may have spoken out of turn just now. But I know we all have to make our way in this life as best we can. Just watch yourself, that's all I ask. Remember what the buggers did to the likes of your Peg. Remember what they've done to hundreds of Pegs over the years. Whatever happens to me is in God's hands; just see that you end up on top and not six feet under like your sister . . . Oh, and if he really is going to speak up for me then say, Thanks, would you? I'll take help from the devil himself if it aids the cause.'

Kate could only nod her head and attempt a strained smile. 'Good luck, Davey,' she said, holding out her hand, and he took it, clasping it in both of his. 'It's a hard road you've chosen.'

'And I fear it may be a lonely one into the bargain,' he said, holding on to her hand until the guard intervened.

'That's it. Not one second more.'

She could still feel the pressure of his fingers on hers as she retraced her steps back through the stench of the narrow passage into the outer office.

The young man in the guard's uniform looked at her curiously as he handed back her empty basket. 'I'll see the prisoner gets the stuff that was inside,' he said.

'Thank you. I'd appreciate that.'

'Do you know the prisoner well?' he asked, finding it hard to reconcile her genteel looks with the wild-looking young radical in the cell.

Kate gave a wan smile as she pulled on her gloves. 'Not any more,' she said softly. 'He's a stranger to me now. A beloved stranger.'

What made her say that she had no idea. She was not even sure it was true. She only knew that the Davey she had known and loved as a child was not the young man in that prison cell. He spoke of causes such as the repeal of the Corn Laws and Catholic Emancipation – things that she knew little about and, if the truth be told, cared even less, and her Davey would never have believed she would prostitute herself to Augustus Falconer for any favour – no matter how great.

She paused on the road outside to glance in the direction of where she believed his cell window might be. Her eyes lit on a black hole half-way up the wall that was heavily barred, and she shuddered as she thought of him lying there on that cold stone slab. They had come a long way from the Hawkhill, the two of them. It might only be ten minutes' walk away, but they had both travelled too far down the road of life to ever turn back now. Where it would eventually lead them both, only time would tell.

'Goodbye, Davey,' she whispered, holding the collar of her plaid cloak tighter around her neck. 'Goodbye and good luck.' He was going to need it.

Chapter Eleven

Kate felt physically and mentally drained when she finally arrived back at Falcon Ridge after her visit to Davey in prison. Was she wrong to raise false hopes, both in himself and his mother, about her ability to help? The thought plagued her, but she knew if there was the faintest chance she could help she could not have remained silent. Something had to be said and done to raise their spirits, but she was by no means confident she could trust Willie to keep his promise to her, if promise it had been.

As she walked up the drive, she could see from the open door of the coach-house and the black empty space where Augustus's carriage should be that he was not back from Forfar yet. She felt relieved; she was in no mood for conversation, and half hoped that Willie might still be around with some news for her.

In a few minutes she would be back in the warmth of her kitchen, and perhaps the feeling of deep gloom would lift. Walking back here in the darkness tonight had been akin to walking away from her past. That she loved Davey she had no doubt, and in his own way she knew he loved her, but the paths they had chosen had diverged so much that she could see no way back to the closeness they had once shared. Although he seemed grateful for her attempt to help him, he also appeared resigned to whatever fate awaited him, so great was his belief in the causes he had chosen to fight for. And no matter how much she might wish it otherwise, they were not hers. Although she felt concern and sympathy for her fellow human beings, she believed it was up to the individual to make his or her own way in life. Her personal road was not an easy one, but it was of her own choosing, and whether it led to misery or happiness would depend on no one but herself. That was how she wanted it and that was how it would always be. Her decisions would be her own. She would be no one's pawn, like poor Peg had been, forced to lie there and see her own child murdered.

As she skirted the large bay-window of the drawing room to head for the servants' entrance, through a chink in the curtains she could see a light burning. With his father not returned from Forfar, it had to mean that Willie was still up. Her pulse quickened. Should she risk confronting him about keeping his promise? She decided against it. She had no wish to antagonize him unnecessarily. No doubt if he really was going to do something to help Davey, he would do it in his own good time.

She stifled a yawn as she crossed the gravel path and opened the side door to make her way down to the kitchen. She could not remember feeling so tired and dispirited before. More than anything she wanted a cup of tea. Tea and then bed.

She could hear a faint clattering of pots as she pushed open the kitchen door.

'Helen, is that you?'

A tired-looking, mousy-haired girl appeared from the dark recess of the passage that led to the utility rooms. Her sleeves were rolled to the elbow and she had that steamy, flustered look about her that came from too long a session of pan-scrubbing. 'Miss McMahon? I was just getting worried. I th – '

'There was no need for that,' Kate interrupted the scullery maid, more irritably than she intended. 'I'm back safe and sound, as you can see.'

'Would you like me to get you something – a cup of tea, or a bite to eat?'

'I'm quite capable of making myself a cup, thank you, Helen. There's been no sign of the Master back yet?'

'No, ma'm. I heard Mister Willie tell one of the

gardeners that his father wouldn't be back till after midnight.'

Kate glanced at the clock on the wall. It had just gone eleven. In that case, she doubted very much if Augustus would even have set off from Forfar yet. When he and his business cronies got together, it could be all hours before they rose from the table. 'Aye, well, I'm sure Mister Willie is well informed . . . But there's no need for you to wait around any longer now I'm back. You can take yourself off to bed. I'll see to the fire and lock up down here before I turn in.'

The girl, who was little more than a child, looked relieved. 'Oh thanks, Miss McMahon.'

As Kate removed her plaid and bonnet, the maid took her candlestick from the pantry shelf and lit it from the remaining embers in the range. 'I'll be going up then, ma'm.'

'Goodnight, Helen. Sleep well.' Kate yawned as she lifted the kettle back on to the hook above the fire. By the feel of it there was enough water there for a small pot of tea and, with a bit of luck, she would have the time to drink it and put her feet up for an hour or so before Augustus got back.

Once brewed, she placed the pot on the brass trivet by the side of the fire and, after taking off her boots, she settled down in the rocking chair to enjoy her cup of tea.

From her place by the gleaming black range, her eyes scanned the large room, with the enormous oak dresser at one end, its shelves groaning with the blue and white china that was used for everyday ware. A tall-backed wooden settle stood against the wall on the other side of the range, and the centre of the room was filled with a long, well-scrubbed pine table, with benches at either side, at which the staff took their meals. It was a comfortable existence down here below stairs, she told herself; it was warm and secure and offered a way of life which, although tiring at times, was a good deal better than most could expect in the outside world. But it was a far cry from the world Davey had chosen. His was a hard path indeed, a dangerous path that, God forbid, might even end in death.

After a few minutes she began to feel drowsy. Replacing her empty cup in its saucer, Kate yawned and closed her eyes as the chair rocked gently in the firelight. Her eyelids, now leaden with the events of the day, fluttered then closed. Within seconds she had fallen sound asleep.

She did not hear Willie enter the room a few minutes later, and was not aware of his tall figure standing over her as she drifted into oblivion. He was sure he had seen her slight figure flit past the drawing-room window ten minutes or so ago, and was annoyed to find her asleep so quickly. He leant over and shook her by the shoulder. 'Kate – are you asleep?'

She awoke with a jump and her heart sank to see his face looming above her. 'Willie!'

'I was just wondering if you were asleep.' His checked shirt was open half to the navel, and he had his old leather knee-breeches on. He scratched the mat of curling red hair on his chest as he leant back against the brass rail of the mantelpiece and looked down at her.

'Asleep?' she repeated, fighting a yawn. 'Well, I would have thought that was pretty obvious.' She tried hard to keep the irritation from her voice as she struggled to wake up. The last thing she wanted to do was to antagonize him. 'Do you want a cup of tea? There might be some left in the pot.'

He shook his head impatiently. 'No, thanks. I haven't come down here to drink tea.'

She looked at him curiously. 'Then just why have you come down, may I ask?' He was not exactly a frequent visitor below stairs. 'Is it about your promise to help Davey? Have you managed to speak to the sheriff?' She was sitting up in her chair now, looking up at him expectantly.

For once Willie seemed at a loss for words as he drummed his fingers on the mantelpiece. He seemed distinctly on edge about something. 'I said I'd help your friend and I will,' he said at last. 'But it's not as easy as you seem to think. Asking a favour of someone as important as the sheriff is not something to be done lightly.'

'I never thought it was,' Kate began, but Willie silenced her with a wave of his hand.

He stood there looking down at her with a most peculiar expression on his face, until she could bear it no longer and got up off the chair on the pretext that the fire needed another log.

'I said it would be a compromise, some sort of trade-off, Kate,' she heard him say, in a voice so huskily low that she turned to look at him. 'You did hear me say that?'

'Aye, I heard you say that all right,' she replied, wiping the wood-dust from her hands. What exactly he meant by it, she was not quite sure, but no doubt he would let her know soon enough. 'If it's money you're after . . .' She gave a half-laugh. 'Well, you're welcome to whatever it takes out of my wages each week.'

'Your wages wouldn't buy a favour from a solicitor's clerk, let alone the county sheriff!'

Her face fell. 'Well, what is it then? What can I possibly give you that . . .' She got no further, for suddenly she knew. She knew by the way he was looking at her with that funny expression on his face, and by the strange husky tone his voice had assumed. She knew exactly what was being demanded in return for his helping Davey, and she felt a complete fool that it had never occurred to her before. Her throat went quite dry as she looked at him and took a half-step back.

'What you want of me, it's a lot to ask, Kate, and what you're willing to trade in return will depend on how much you value your friend's life.'

She listened with a sinking heart as he continued in a quiet voice. 'I don't have to tell you what they do to people who incite revolution in this country. Hanged by the neck until dead, is the phrase. Or, if he's lucky, transportation for life. Is that what you want? Is a few moments of pleasure for us both too high a price to pay for your friend's freedom? For that's all it would be, you know . . . Just you and me in front of the fire here, then you could sleep easily in your bed tonight. You'd have kept your side of the bargain and I will keep mine. The sheriff is coming into town for a Freemason meeting tomorrow night. I'd make a point of speaking to him.'

He made it all sound so simple, so very easy, but her insides were quaking as she looked at him.

'Most young women expect nothing in return for making love,' he said softly. 'For them the pleasure is enough . . . But you will gain your friend's life, Kate. Can you deny him that?'

Soundlessly she mouthed the word 'No' as he took a step towards her. She knew what he was saying was true, but that did not make it any easier. No man had ever touched her in that way before, and she was not even sure what to expect. She felt frozen to the spot as his hand went out to the back of her head and, with one deft pull, he had undone her bun and brought her hair tumbling down her back.

'It's a fair compromise. No one can say otherwise. A life for a few minutes of pleasure . . . Tell me you agree, Kate,' he whispered, gathering her to him and murmuring the words into the soft curtain of hair at the nape of her neck. 'Tell me you agree . . .'

'I agree,' she heard herself saying, as she closed her eyes and prayed to God he would forgive her for what was about to happen this night. And that Davey would forgive her. For these days her oldest and dearest friend was not only the brother she had never known, he was a man with principles as strong as the iron bolts that kept him caged like an animal in the town's tolbooth. And more than that – much more – her Wee Davey of the scraped knees and tousled hair had grown into a devilishly attractive young man who brought a flush to her cheeks and set the blood coursing through her veins and a strange mixture of pain and pleasure to her heart whenever she set eyes on him. If only it were his arms enfolding her . . . his lips searching for hers . . . She groaned softly in Willie's arms, but not from pleasure. It was a half-sigh, half-cry of pain that came from her very soul.

The minutes that followed held none of the pleasure he had promised, only a physical and emotional agony of a sort that had her silently screaming inside as she lay there on the rag rug in front of the fire with Willie on top of her and wished with all her heart it was over. Beneath her tightly closed eyelids, it was Davey's face she could see as the features of the young man on top of her contorted with the passion of the moment. Forgive me, Davey . . . Forgive me . . . She was giving the most precious thing she possessed for his sake, but somehow she doubted if he would ever understand.

In her head she began reciting the Lord's Prayer over and over . . . Over and over . . . '. . . *and deliver us from evil, for thine is the Kingdom . . .*' Over and over . . . Oh God, let it stop! Whether it took two minutes or twenty she had no idea, as she kept her eyes tightly shut and fought to mentally distance herself from what was happening to her.

When at last it was all over and she opened her eyes, there was a peculiar expression on Willie's face and, although his voice was gentle, there was the unmistakable glint of triumph in the eyes that looked down into hers as he gave voice to a fact that had both surprised and thrilled him at his moment of conquest. 'You never told me I was the first.'

Kate shook her head as she dragged herself into a sitting position on the rug and pushed a long lock of damp hair back from her eyes. 'Does that surprise you? Does that make you feel even better?' she asked in a defeated voice. 'Does that add to the sweetness of victory?'

'Aye,' he said, speaking the truth. 'Aye, that it does.' For the first time in his life he had beaten his father to the draw. No matter what the old bugger did now, he – Willie, his own son – would have robbed him of the one thing that he knew the old man most desired. He felt nothing but satisfaction as he looked down at her sitting there. His mind had been made up what his repayment would be when he'd found her in his father's arms. The bitch had listened to all he had had to say in the Coffee House on Sunday afternoon and had gone straight back to use the knowledge to her own advantage. She had double-crossed him, but two could play at that game.

A distant rattling sound made them both turn in the direction of the window.

'It must be your father,' Kate said in alarm. 'He might come down here. He may want a cup of tea . . .'

'A cup of tea!' Willie gave a scornful laugh as he reached for his leather belt. 'The state he'll be in, he'll be opening his collar to piss! I wouldn't worry yourself about that.'

'You will remember your promise?' she implored him as she tugged a garter into place. 'You will keep your part of the bargain?'

With a satisfied tug at the buckle round his waist, Willie looked down at her sitting there on the rug in front of him. She had brought nothing but aggravation and worry into his life over the past few years and had wasted no time in making up to the old man as soon as he had tried to warn her off. He felt no guilt at what had just occurred. It was high time she was paid back in kind. 'What bargain?' he asked in all innocence. 'I don't remember any bargain.'

Kate gasped and rocked back on her heels. 'But you . . .!'

'I what, Kate?' he said, picking up her blouse from the floor and tossing it at her. Then he laughed. It was a laugh that resonated in her head as, without so much as a backward glance, he turned on his heel and strode from the room.

The kitchen door slammed behind him and Kate stared at it as her hand went to her naked breast. 'Bastard!' she called after him. 'Lying bastard!' A blind anger rose in her, but it was as much for her own stupidity as for his callousness. She had not only been betrayed, she had been cast aside by an animal who had sated itself on her flesh and then moved on. His victory was complete, both mental and physical. But what choice had she had? If there had been the slightest chance of saving Davey's life, she had had to take it.

In a few short minutes tonight she had lost her innocence, but was now far wiser than she had ever been. She would get even. She didn't know how, but she would get even. He would be made to pay with a vengeance before she was done.

Her lower lip was trembling and tears of frustration welled in her eyes as she felt for the straps of her shift and pulled them back over her naked shoulders, before tying the thin satin thread between her breasts.

She had adjusted her skirts and done up the buttons of her blouse and was about to retie her hair when, to her horror, the unmistakable sound of booted feet could be heard in the stone-flagged passage outside. Her heart began to beat faster as she scrambled to her feet. Was it Willie coming back?

Within seconds the kitchen door was thrown open and Augustus himself appeared on the threshold. He was still in his outdoor clothes and his face lit up at the sight of her. 'Kate lass,' he exclaimed, closing the door behind him. 'I certainly didn't expect to find you still up!'

Kate passed an embarrassed hand over her dishevelled hair and attempted a welcoming smile. She had almost forgotten they had heard his carriage return. 'Mr Falconer! I – I was just about to prepare for bed.'

'I can see that,' Augustus said, gazing at the wayward locks in obvious approval. He had never seen her with her hair loose before and his hands itched to touch it. 'Turn round,' he said in a quiet voice.

Puzzled, Kate obeyed.

'It's down to your waist,' he murmured approvingly. 'And as soft as satin by the looks o' it.' Emily's hair had been too thin to grow to even half that length.

Kate blushed and passed a hand over the object of his admiration. 'I – I let it down thinking I might wash it,' she lied. 'But I changed my mind. It's far too late. Tomorrow night will do.'

'Let me wash it for you,' Augustus said impulsively. 'Tomorrow night, let me wash it.' He had obviously been drinking, but was still in control of his faculties. The thought of running his hands through those long flowing locks, whether wet or dry, was almost too much to bear.

He came towards her and as he got nearer the flickering glow of the fire, he noticed for the first time that her eyelashes were spiked with tears and her cheeks were wet. 'Katie lass!'

He stopped in his tracks, his brow creased with concern. This was the second time in as many days he had seen her upset about something, and his heart went out to her. Something was wrong. He could not bear to see her unhappy.

'Come here, lass.' He put out his hand and suddenly she was in his arms and they were standing together, rocking backwards and forwards in front of the fire, and he was stroking her hair and murmuring words of comfort into the silky softness as her wet cheek pressed against the leather shoulder of his gilet. 'Tell me what it is,' he urged her softly. 'Tell me what's ailing you.'

And suddenly she was doing just that. She was confessing her concern about Davey and telling of how they had grown up together and he had been like a brother to her, and how if anything happened to him it would be like losing her own flesh and blood.

Augustus listened in silence as she poured out her heart, and when she had done he shook his head and said quietly, 'You've been sat here worrying yourself sick about

129

that friend o' yours, while I've been drinking myself stupid back there in Forfar . . . Now, it's a selfish auld bugger I am and no mistake.'

Taking her face in his hands, he looked down at her. 'There's no need to fret any longer, lass,' he told her. 'I haven't got this far in life without gaining a few friends along the way; influential friends who know more about the workings o' this city than you could possibly imagine. You've no need to fret yourself over that Lorimer lad o' yours any longer. He'll get no more than a few weeks or so when his trial comes up, I can promise you that.'

A few weeks! *He'll get no more than a few weeks* . . . Davey would not be hanged, or transported to the other side of the world, or spend the next few years in jail!

It was too much to take in. Kate could feel herself slipping from Augustus's grasp as she slid to her knees on the cold slabs of the floor. She looked up at him, too exhausted to say anything but, 'Thank you . . . Oh, thank you!'

He went down on one knee beside her and put out a hand to touch her cheek. 'You have no need to thank me, Kate,' he told her in a gruff yet gentle voice. 'It's me who should be thanking you, for you've brought me more joy in the wee while that you've been here than I've known in all of my previous three-score years.'

He raised her left hand in his and gazed down at the ringless fingers. He knew he was drunk, but not drunk out of his senses. Certainly not that. He knew exactly what he was saying. And maybe it was as well that he had had a dram or two too many to give him the courage required, for it certainly needed courage. By God it needed courage. He was more than three times her age.

'I'm an auld man, Kate,' he told her quietly. 'An auld man who some may say should know better, but what I have to say to you this night I can swear to you I have never said to another woman . . . Aye, even after thirty years o' marriage, that's true. I love you, Katie lass. I love you more than I've loved any woman, for in the time I have known you, you have made me happier than an auld man like me has any right to be.'

He took her hand in both of his and, raising it to his lips to kiss it, he lowered his voice in a husky whisper. 'Will you marry me, Kate? Will you make me the happiest o' men?'

Kate's head was swimming. He was asking her to marry him. He loved her. Dear God, he really did love her. She began to shake her head in disbelief, then, seeing the look of disappointment that flooded across his face, she knew she could not bear to hurt him. That she loved Davey as she would love no other man, she had no doubt. But, despite his prison cell, Davey had moved beyond her now, as far beyond her as it was possible to get. Davey could never belong to her. He belonged to the world – that great big ungrateful world out there that he was determined to save from itself. Much as she knew he loved her, there would be no place for her in the life he had mapped out for himself. He was a messiah of the New Order, on his own personal crusade against the evils of this world. She could never be more than a camp-follower trailing along in his wake – a hindrance to him in his quest for universal justice for all. That she could not bear.

Her eyes met those of Augustus. The old man's were pleading, imploring her to say Yes. Would it be so awful if she did? If she had no place in the life of the only man she knew she would ever love as a woman should love a man, would it be so very terrible to make another one happy? Despite what they said, Augustus *was* a good man, she had no doubt about that. And he could offer her something Davey never could – something she had never had – security. Real security of the kind that meant you never went to bed hungry at night or spent your days shivering for the want of a log for the fire. It was only when you had come from nothing did you appreciate what it meant to have even the basic necessities of life guaranteed. But here at Falcon Ridge she would have that and more – much more. If she had children, they would never know the agony of hunger that she had known. She had witnessed her own mother kill her own grandchild out of poverty; poverty of a kind that killed the soul and then the body; a shameful scourge kept hidden from the rich who could little guess what sufferings were being borne by their fellow men and women. A shiver ran through her. Davey would say she had sold her soul, but what good was a soul in circumstances like that? Automatically she began to nod her head and, as she did so, something deep inside her died.

'You *will?*' Augustus almost shouted the words, so great was his surprise.

Kate continued to nod as tears blurred her eyes. Somehow she could not bring herself to say the actual word.

'Oh, Kate, my dear, you have made me the happiest man alive!'

Kate took a deep breath. Then she began to laugh and sob at the same time as he took her in his arms.

'Come away, lass,' Augustus said gently, rising to his feet with a creaking of bones. 'It's about time you were abed.'

Then a twinkle came into his eye as he added with a husky chuckle, 'But it'll no' be for much longer that you have to climb those stairs to the top of the house. And it'll no' be for much longer that I'll be needing a warming pan at night!'

Chapter Twelve

Kate McMahon and Augustus Falconer were married one month after his proposal of marriage, on the first Saturday in May, 1830, in a private ceremony carried out by the Reverend Herbert Mooney in the drawing room of his Church of Scotland manse in Grey Street, Broughty Ferry.

Kate was nineteen, her bridegroom in his sixtieth year when he slipped the plain gold ring on his new bride's finger. There were those, they knew, who would make great play of the differences both in age and social standing, and for that reason Kate chose the privacy of the old manse she knew and loved to make her vows. It was far from the wedding she had dreamt of, for there were no friends or relatives there from either side to attend the short Presbyterian ceremony and wish them good luck in their future life together. The only two witnesses were Herbert Mooney's maid Chrissie Cargill, and her young man, Ted Lorimer, a fisherman from the village and a distant cousin of Davey's.

No mention was made before the ceremony of the fact that the bridegroom's son was missing. It would have upset Augustus too much. They had kept the news of their forthcoming marriage from Willie for as long as possible, and while it had come as some relief to Kate to find that he had uptailed and left home immediately on hearing of their plans, his departure and the manner of it had left the old man badly shaken. In the days that followed Augustus had attempted to keep his hurt hidden from his bride-to-be, and had succeeded better than he could have hoped, for Kate never gave Willie's absence a second thought as she stood by her husband's side and took her vows.

She wore a new maroon suit for the occasion and a small feathered hat, topped by a veil which she threw back after the ceremony to watch her husband of five minutes scribble his name with a flourish across the foot of the marriage certificate.

'There we have it, signed and sealed!' Augustus declared, handing the quill pen back to the minister and beaming a smile at Kate, who stood by his side awaiting her turn.

Augustus had been by far the more nervous of the two this afternoon, pacing the floor of Falcon Ridge's main hall for a good half-hour before the carriage arrived to take them the few hundred yards down the hill to the manse door. But now it was almost all over, he was visibly relaxed and looking forward to what followed.

'By Jove, Bertie,' he said to the minister, watching his new wife carefully sign her own name on the fine vellum, 'I trust you've got a cup of tea or preferably something a wee bit stronger at the ready, for I could certainly do with it!'

Chrissie Cargill, who was standing nearby with her young man, waiting to sign their own names to the document, spoke up for her employer. 'Never you fear, Mr Falconer sir, there'll be a cup o' tea on the boil in a couple o' ticks. I have everything prepared.'

'Before the ink's dry on the page, indeed,' Herbert Mooney added, shaking a dusting of fine sand over the first two signatures before handing the pen to his maid. 'You and Ted add your names to this then you can go off and see to the refreshments, Chrissie. I can't wait to get my teeth into that new cake you have ready for us.' He turned and winked at Kate as Chrissie bent to laboriously write her name. Chrissie's attempts at cake-baking had been something of a standing joke between the two of them in the past.

Once all five signatures were on the paper, Ted Lorimer came forward and shook Augustus by the hand. 'You have a rare treasure in Kate, sir,' he said. 'You see you take care of her now.'

'Indeed I will, young man, never fear.' He placed a protective arm around his bride's waist as she, in turn, shook Ted's hand.

'Is it all right to kiss you?' Chrissie asked anxiously, when her turn came to give Kate her good wishes.

'Of course,' Kate replied in some astonishment. 'Why shouldn't it be?'

'Well, seeing as now you're a lady and a' that.'

'Dearie me, Chrissie, it's still me inside!' Kate declared, giving her old colleague an extra special hug.

'So I can still come up the brae to the big house to see you if I need any advice?' Kate's expertise in the kitchen was badly missed in the manse, by Chrissie most of all.

'Goodness me, yes! In fact, I shall look forward to it.' Kate was quite adamant on that. Becoming Mistress of Falcon Ridge did not mean she had to abandon all her old friends.

The Reverend Mooney beamed. 'Right then, now that's settled, if the bride and groom will kindly be seated, Chrissie and her young man here will retire to the kitchen to see to that cup of tea that has been promised us.' Herbert Mooney gestured for Augustus and Kate to take the most comfortable chairs on either side of the drawing-room fire, then he opened the door for Chrissie and Ted to leave the room.

The tea and cake duly appeared on the best silver tray and was deposited on a side-table. Chrissie served each one in turn before returning to the kitchen.

When she had gone, Herbert got up from his chair declaring, 'I think an occasion such as this needs something a wee bit stronger, wouldn't you agree, Augustus? Perhaps we should call on our mutual friend auld Grant to add to the pleasure!'

'Auld Grant, eh?' Augustus's whiskered mouth broke into a wide smile of approval as his friend made straight for the decanter he kept locked in the credence beneath the drawing-room window and a large tot of his prized malt whisky was duly poured into two of the best glasses.

> 'Lord grant gude luck to a' the Grants,
> Likewise eternal bliss;
> For they should sit amang the saints
> That mak' a dram like this!'

After the toast to the makers of the blessed spirit, he raised his glass once more and declared, 'Here's health, wealth and eternal bliss to the pair of you. May the wind always be at your back and the road downhill all the way!'

A beaming Augustus raised his own glass in response. 'Thanks, Bertie man. We appreciate that – and this!' He took a swig of the whisky and breathed an approving sigh. 'Aaah . . . the water of life indeed!'

Kate, who had declined a strong drink, but sipped gratefully on the cup of tea, smiled as she tried a finger of Chrissie's specially baked Dundee cake. 'Very tasty,' she murmured with an approving nod in the minister's direction. 'Our Chrissie is improving greatly, is she not, Mr Mooney?'

'Chrissie is a grand lass and she does her best, but she's not a patch on you, Kate,' Herbert Mooney confessed with a sigh. 'Augustus's gain is my everlasting loss. I doubt if I'll ever find a housekeeper to match your good self.'

'Aye, well, Kate's housekeeping days are over now, Bertie my friend,' Augustus said, still ignoring his cup of tea for the glass in his hand. 'Housekeeping's fine for them that have no choice in the matter, but there'll be no more of that type of work for the Mistress of Falcon Ridge from now on.'

Kate looked across at her husband and her brow creased beneath the veil of her new hat as realization dawned. 'You mean you'll be getting someone else in to do the housekeeping?'

'Indeed I will, my dear. That's no job for a lady.'

Kate was silent as his words sank in. It was something that had never been discussed in the few weeks since he proposed to her. Somehow she had taken it for granted that things would be going on as before. She had thoroughly enjoyed her role in organizing and running the household, but quite clearly her new husband had other ideas. The thought of a perfect stranger coming in and taking over those tasks she had taken such pride in filled her with dismay.

Seeing her worried look, Augustus was quick to reassure her. 'Don't you worry, my dear, you'll have as big a say as you want in whoever takes over your role.'

'Aye, it'll be a big change for you being a lady of leisure, Kate,' the Reverend Mooney mused, gathering up the cake crumbs on his plate with the tip of his index finger and popping them into his mouth. 'It'll do you good to put your feet up for a while. But I doubt if you'll be in that position for long. There'll be several wee Falconers running around to keep you occupied afore you're much older, I'll be bound.'

Kate could feel herself colouring as she glanced across at Augustus, who cleared his throat. 'Aye, well, that's as may be, but to be honest with you, Bertie, it would be no bad thing if a new family took its time in coming along. That's a right sore point in certain quarters at the moment, as you well know.'

'You mean Willie has still not come to terms with the idea of a new wife and bairns around the place?' Even as old a friend as Herbert Mooney had not liked to bring up the subject of Willie's absence.

Augustus shook his head and drained the last of the whisky from his glass. 'Worse than that, man, he's taken himself off to Leeds in high dudgeon. He's biding wi' the Marshalls, mill-owning friends o' the family, and, as far as I ken, he has no intention of coming back in the foreseeable future.'

The old man was putting a brave face on it, for at their

last confrontation less than a week ago, his son had declared bitterly, 'You'll not see me under your roof again, Father, if you go ahead with this damned fool idea of marrying that woman.'

As Augustus's only son and heir, Willie had taken the news of the impending marriage very badly indeed. It was his worst fear come true, and no amount of reassurance on his father's part could persuade him otherwise. Neither could his own pleas and arguments persuade his father that marriage to Kate was anything other than the best thing that could possibly happen to him in his old age.

'But what if anything happens to you?' Willie had demanded. 'Where does that leave me?'

'It leaves you having to work away amicably with Kate,' his father had told him patiently, but in growing irritation. 'Surely that's not too much to ask? She's a clever young woman and will be a real asset to the firm. There's no reason why the pair of you shouldn't get on.'

'But as your wife she will be your next of kin. You know fine what that means. If anything happens to you, the whole damned lot will go to her. She will inherit the mills.' The words almost stuck in Willie's throat.

'She'll be my wife,' Augustus had replied stiffly. 'In all conscience I canna deny her what will be rightly hers, nor would I want to. But that is no reason why you shouldn't continue to play your part to the full.'

Play your part to the full . . . He who should have inherited the lot would be expected to merely play a part. The words fell sourly on Willie's ears and curdled his blood. He had opened his mouth to protest further. He still had one last card to play: the fact that he had slept with the bride.

Sweat broke out on his forehead. The words burned on the tip of his tongue. But the longer he stood there, the harder they became to say. His father was no fool. No one built an empire like Augustus had done without having iron in the soul. And, despite his soft heart, the old man had that all right. Willie knew that to attempt to blacken

Kate's name by such an assertion would merely serve to blacken his own even more. Not only would his father refuse to believe it, he would never forgive him for attempting such a dirty trick as to sully his new bride's honour.

That same day he had packed a case and told his father he was leaving. He would go and stay with the Marshalls in Leeds, in the hope his father would come to his senses before making such a terrible mistake.

'If you need me you'll know where to find me,' he had declared, as he stood at the door, bag in hand. 'But if I don't hear from you, I'll know you've not listened to me and have gone ahead with this madness. And by God, if that's the case, then you'll not see me cross this threshold again in your lifetime. Not as long as that woman is Mistress of my mother's home . . . In heaven's name, Father, you built this place for Mother!'

'Aye, and she's dead, Willie lad. She's dead and I'm alive.'

'More's the pity!' his son had hit back bitterly, for had it been his father who had died, things would have been so different. With his father gone, he would have been his own boss by now; all the Falcon Mills would have been his, and he would have been able to look after his mother into the bargain. It would have been grand with just the two of them. They had idolized each other, and he shuddered to think what she would have said had she imagined such a thing happening after her death. 'Yes, more's the pity it's Ma and not you that's lying there in our family vault,' he said bitterly. 'You will bring nothing but shame on the family name by installing that servant in her place.'

'I'll stand for no more of this,' his father had warned, feeling his blood-pressure rise.

'You'll not have to, I'm leaving!'

And, now as Augustus sat here in his friend Herbert Mooney's drawing room, with his new bride in the chair opposite, he thought of that last painful scene with his son. 'He'll be back,' he said quietly, to no one in particular. 'A week or so away and Willie will soon realize what side his bread is buttered on.'

Kate heard the words and her heart went out to Augustus, for she hated to see him hurt like this. He loved his son and, in his own way, she knew that Willie loved his father, but Augustus was surely fooling himself if he believed his son would be back in a hurry. Willie was a proud and clever young man. If he came back at all it would be on his own terms, and something told her that might not be good news either for his father or for her.

Willie's adamant opposition to the marriage had come as no surprise, nor had the reaction of her own parents when she had finally plucked up the courage to tell them several days after accepting Augustus's proposal. True to form, her mother had been quite vehement in her denunciation of both Augustus and all that his family stood for.

Bel McMahon's voice had risen several octaves as she declared, 'They're bloodsuckers, the lot o' them, trading in human misery. The Tay itself wouldn't hold the sweat that's been shed on those mill floors – and for what? So families like the Falconers can build their fancy mansions along the Camphill Road. And now my own daughter tells me she's to join them. My own flesh and blood is to profit by the sweat of a thousand brows that has gone into the making of that family's fortune. You have the gall to stand there and tell me you are to become part of the very family that killed your own sister!'

'Nobody killed Peggy, Mam,' Kate had countered wearily. It was time they all faced the truth. It had been too easy to blame other people. 'Peggy died of childbed fever. As for her bairn . . .'

The eyes of the two women, mother and daughter, had met in that cramped kitchen on the Hawkhill, and Bel McMahon knew at that moment that she was not only accountable before God for what had happened that night on the very rag rug she was standing on, but she was accountable to the small child who had witnessed the death of her sister's bairn. That small child was now a grown woman and was standing in front of her, only feet from the very spot the infant had breathed its last breath. Was the unspoken truth that had haunted both of them down the years at last to be given voice? For a whole decade they had avoided the subject, but Bel was only too aware that her younger daughter had witnessed everything that awful Hogmanay night all those years ago.

'What exactly are you saying, Kathleen?' The question was asked in a tired but defiant voice as Bel's eyes in their hollow sockets met those of her daughter.

Kate had shaken her head. 'I'm saying nothing,' she told her mother, 'for, thank God, I have never been placed in the position you were that night. And I thank God and Augustus Falconer that now I never will be.' There was no more to be said.

At that she had left the two rooms on the Hawkhill that were her parents' home. Her mother had turned her back as she said goodbye, but her father had walked her to the door, closing it behind them so they could not be overheard as they stood together on the stone steps outside. ''Tis hard for her, Kate,' he had said in a voice weary of it all. 'It's from a different generation you are. How can you know what it has been like for us – for your mother especially? Sure, and how can a young lassie like you, still wet behind the ears, know what she has had to do to survive in this life?'

But Kate did know. She had grown up in these two rooms, she had known the hunger, and had seen the exhaustion caused by working all hours on the mill floor. And she had also seen an infant's life snuffed out, and had seen her own sister die shortly afterwards. Only God in his wisdom knew if the two were connected. 'I could never condemn anyone, Dad,' she said softly. 'Each one of us has our own cross to bear and can never know the true weight of anyone else's. All I ask is that neither of you condemn *me* too harshly either.'

141

Rob McMahon had reached out and touched his daughter's arm. 'As far as I'm concerned, you're still our daughter, Kathleen, so you are.'

It was all Kate wanted to hear.

Now as she sat in the Reverend Mooney's drawing room and fingered the shining gold ring on the third finger of her left hand, she tried hard to blank that other world she had left behind from her mind. This was a day to rejoice about the future, not worry about the past.

'At the risk of repeating myself for the umpteenth time, I wish you both every happiness, you know that,' Herbert Mooney said, shaking hands with the newly-weds at the manse door some ten minutes later, as they left to make their way home.

Augustus took Kate's arm and helped her into the carriage. 'You're a good man, Bertie,' he told his old friend. 'There'll be an extra bawbee or two in the collection plate come next Sunday, you can count on that.' The minister's moral support would be repaid in kind many times over, for it was at a time like this when friends showed their true colours.

He had deliberately avoided telling any of his other friends or acquaintances he was remarrying to a lass a third of his age. Let them find out in their own good time, he thought. Reactions would be mixed, he had no doubt about that. Some would condemn him, that was for sure, but many more would envy him his good fortune, whether they were man enough to admit it or not.

They had agreed to spend their first night at Falcon Ridge and then travel on the next day to Montrose for a short honeymoon in the busy seaport on the German Ocean, with its miles of golden sand and bracing air. Work would not allow more than a couple of days away, but Kate was looking forward to her first real journey out of the city of her birth, even though the town chosen was only twenty miles or so up the coast.

There was a supper of bannocks and butter, with partan

bree, Augustus's favourite soup made with succulent crabmeat and fresh cream, followed by atholl brose, Kate's choice of sweet, conjured up with the finest malt whisky, oatmeal and honey, waiting for them when they got back to Falcon Ridge and, much to Augustus's concern, Kate ate very little of either. Her appetite seemed to have disappeared of late. She would merely pick at what was put in front of her, and it took very little to make her feel nauseous. He put it down to pre-marital nerves and assured her she would feel a great deal better after tonight. 'The first night of a marriage is always a bit o' a trial, lass. You'll be fine come the morn.'

It was after nine by the time the supper dishes were cleared away, and Augustus glanced at the clock on the mantelpiece as he took out his pipe and prepared to light it. 'Would you prefer to go on up first and get ready for bed by yourself? I can follow when I've had a smoke and a look at the newspaper.'

The suggestion so considerately made sent a chill down Kate's spine. Much as she was fond of Augustus, the thought of having the same sort of experience with him that she had had with his son only four short weeks ago filled her with dismay and, if she was really truthful with herself, not a little disgust. Willie was of her own generation, a good-looking young man in the prime of life, but Augustus was older than her own father, overweight, and not in the best of health into the bargain.

She had made her bed, however, and now she must lie on it. It was with a sinking heart that she climbed the curving staircase and for the first time entered the ornate master bedroom of the great house as the wife of the Master himself.

The room had not been touched since Emily died in it and, as well as the dried lavender sachets that hung everywhere, it seemed to reek of the personality of Augustus's late wife. With its sombre grey damask curtains at the enormous bay-window, and its heavy furniture, it had an old-lady feel and smell to it, a depressing air that filled Kate with gloom as she stood and looked around her.

Family portraits of all shapes and sizes hung on the walls. All eyes were looking in her direction. Generations of the Falconer family were to bear witness to what was about to occur. Worse still, an exquisite and very flattering watercolour of a young Emily hung next to the bed; the pale eyes were gazing straight back into hers.

Kate shuddered and looked away, but there was no ignoring the object that dominated the room. She stared in growing apprehension at the great four-poster bed with its canopy of plush red drapes, embroidered with the Falcon emblem in gold thread, and at the new nightgown lying on top of the satin quilt. A complete trousseau had been Augustus's wedding present to her, and he had had the dressmaker send specially to Ireland for the trimmings of finest Limerick lace for the nightgown and its matching dressing robe.

She sighed as she walked over and fingered the fine filigree workmanship of the collar. He had known her parents were from close to the city where this delicate craft was practised, and the thoughtful gesture seemed so typical of the man.

She caught sight of herself in the cheval mirror by the side of the bed. Her face had a haunted look to it as she bent down to slip off her shoes.

Although they were well into spring, Augustus had had the maid light a fire in the grate, and the oak logs crackled merrily in the hearth lending a warm glow to temper the sobriety of the décor but, despite the warmth coming from the flames, Kate found herself shivering as she undressed slowly and slipped into her night attire.

She had never known the feel of such fine lawn next to her skin before, and she walked to the mirror to gaze at her reflection in the firelight as she brushed down her hair. She looked almost beautiful, she thought. How different it would have been if she could have been preparing for someone else. Someone like Davey perhaps.

She had not seen her old friend since that evening in the prison cell. Was he free by now? She had longed to ask his cousin Ted after the wedding ceremony this afternoon, but Augustus had always been within earshot.

Whenever she had thought of getting married as a child, Davey had always been the one by her side, and she could feel her eyes misting as she turned from the mirror and gazed into the flames of the fire. 'Oh Davey . . . Davey, what have I done . . . ?'

But Davey would tell her exactly what she had done. She had sold herself for an old man's gold. She had exchanged the chance of marrying the man of her choice for someone who could give her what he never could. He could give her a lifetime free of the threat of hunger for herself and her children. A lifetime free of having to make decisions such as her mother had had to make, and had spent a lifetime haunted by. What she was about to go through this night was a small price to pay for such freedom.

The bed was much higher off the floor than the ones she was used to, and she had to make use of the footstool to climb in. She lowered herself on to the mattress and gasped involuntarily at the comfort that enveloped her. Her body seemed to float on a sea of soft white linen, while her head sank into a cloud of goose feathers encased in lavender-scented pillowslips, trimmed with lace.

She was still luxuriating in the unexpected comfort when she heard the door-handle turn. She stiffened, then slid over to the far edge of the mattress as the bulky figure of Augustus appeared at the bedroom door. His eyes lit up at the sight of her lying in the double bed.

'My, but you're a bonnie sight!'

Kate made no reply, and could not even manage a faint smile in response. It was as if every nerve in her body had frozen.

Sensing her anxiety, he enquired gently, 'Would you like the curtains drawn?' It was still not quite dark outside.

She nodded mutely and watched as he drew the drapes across the wide bay-windows. The brass rings made a swishing sound that had a peculiar finality about it as the outside world was blotted out, leaving the two of them in their own private world.

The room was now lit only by firelight. 'Would you care for me to light the lamps?' Augustus enquired, anxious that everything should be just to her liking.

Kate shook her head.

She was nervous. He understood that and gave a reassuring smile. 'In that case I'll just go on through and get out of these clothes.'

He disappeared into the adjoining dressing room to prepare for bed.

Kate did not move a muscle during the few minutes he was gone, but her eyes were fixed firmly on the closed door of the ante-room. When at last he reappeared, it was all she could do to stop herself from bursting into either floods of tears or laughter. In his outdoor garments there was no denying he was quite an impressive figure of a man, but devoid of them he was something else entirely. His stomach protruded grotesquely beneath the linen nightgown, and his bare legs and feet appeared unaccountably pale and thin as he padded across the floor.

Augustus was totally unaware of just how comic a figure he cut, and indeed had done his best to put on his best show. He had bought himself a new nightgown and deliberately left off his nightcap, carefully combing the remaining few white hairs across the bald crown of his head before making for the bedroom door. It was important he look his best, for this was the night he had been looking forward to for so long. Despite his age, he felt as nervous as a young man about to discover the secrets of married love for the very first time. He could feel his heart pounding in his chest, and told himself he should not have had that last whisky before coming upstairs; as he crossed the floor and approached the bed, he offered up a silent prayer that he would not disappoint her.

The springs creaked as his considerable weight came down on the opposite side to where Kate was still lying as stiff as a board, and he reached out a comforting hand to touch her. 'It's just you and me at last, Kate lass,' he said, cursing the tightness in his chest that caused his voice to wheeze like an ancient pair of bellows.

She could still feel the numbing tenseness in every nerve as she forced herself to half turn towards him. He was wheezing more loudly now, and she could smell the whisky and tobacco on his breath as he whispered, 'You have made me the happiest o' men this day, Kathleen.'

What happened next took no longer than five minutes as Augustus's great bulk mounted her and groaned and wheezed for what seemed an unbearable length of time and then rolled off her to lie quite still, face up on the bed.

'Are you all right, Augustus?' she eventually asked in some concern, when there was no movement from him for a minute or so. It was only the second time she had used his Christian name, and it still sounded strange on her tongue.

There was no response.

'Augustus . . .' She put out a nervous hand and, to her relief, could feel his chest heaving beneath her touch. But still he did not speak.

'Augustus . . . Please . . . What's wrong?' Her hand moved up to seek his face and, to her surprise, his cheeks were wet.

'I've let you down, Kate lass,' he whispered. 'I've let us both down.'

'No,' she insisted. 'Of course you haven't.'

'But I have!' he said fiercely. 'If an auld bugger like me has the cheek to take a bonnie young lass like you for a wife, then at least he should make sure his wedding tackle is still in good order.'

Then, to her dismay, silent tears began to roll down his cheeks: tears that made no sound in his throat but caused his body to tremble and the bed to shake and creak gently beneath them.

Kate got out of bed and returned with a clean handkerchief which he took gratefully. He blew his nose noisily into it. 'I'm black affronted, that's what I am. Black affronted.' He – Augustus Falconer – who had always prided himself in being a real man's man, could not even perform the most basic of all masculine functions, and on his wedding night at that. 'I'll make it up to you, Kate lass, I swear I will. I'll make it up to you. It'll be different the morn's night. I promise you it will.'

It was a promise he was not to be able to keep. Not the following night, nor the night after that. Not even the bracing air of the thriving seaport of Montrose made the slightest difference to Augustus's ability to perform his marital duties as he thought fit. The act of love between them became a torturous pantomime, during each performance of which Kate genuinely began to fear for her husband's life as his breathing became more laboured and the sweat poured from him, soaking the fine linen of his nightgown.

His failure to do his duty as he saw fit caused a black cloud to hang over their honeymoon, and it was a great relief to both when they finally arrived back at the gates of Falcon Ridge.

Chapter Thirteen

'Chrissie, this is a surprise!'

Nervously clutching the edges of her shawl, Chrissie Cargill dropped an awkward curtsey in deference to Kate's new status as she stood before her old friend in the morning room of Falcon Ridge. Her fair skin was flushed with the walk up the steep hill from the manse, and long strands of brown hair, blown from her bun in the brisk sea-breeze, hung around her face. She was a good-natured young woman, half a head taller than Kate and built in proportion, but there was an embarrassed gawkiness about her this morning that was at odds with her natural poise. 'I — I'm sorry to disturb you, Kate, truly I am. I wouldn't have come up here bothering you like this, only I thought I'd better not leave it too late.'

'Leave what too late?'

'It's about your new housekeeper.'

'Aah . . .' Kate gave a knowing smile. Something had told her it was not the Reverend Mooney's business Chrissie had come on. 'You want to apply for the position.'

'Och no, not me!' Chrissie exclaimed in surprise. 'I'm very happy at the manse . . . But I ken somebody who could do the job well and really needs it.'

Kate's interest was aroused. 'Anybody I know?'

'Oh aye,' Chrissie answered quickly. Then, lowering her voice, she confided, 'It's Betty, Davey's mam.'

'Davey's mam!' Kate burst out, trying hard not to laugh. 'You mean Betty Lorimer wants to come and work here?' It sounded far too implausible.

Chrissie looked uncomfortable at her friend's reaction. 'Aye, she wants the job all right. Ted's been speaking to her about it . . . You ken they're cousins?'

Kate nodded, she had known that Chrissie's intended was some relation to Davey.

'Ted's granny and Davey's were sisters,' Chrissie explained, 'and — well, to cut a long story short — Betty was down here in the Ferry visiting some o' the family over the weekend, and she heard about you marrying old Mr Falconer and him needing a new housekeeper and a' . . .'

Kate listened. It didn't take long for news to get around in these parts. 'But Betty's got a job.' Betty Lorimer had been working as a spinner in the Hawkhill Falcon Mill for as long as Kate could remember.

'She's got to give it up,' Chrissie informed her. 'It's her lungs — the doctor says she won't see another new year in unless she gets out o' that atmosphere. To be honest wi' ye, half the reason she came doon here at the weekend was to see if there were any shop jobs or the like going locally. It was only when we got talking about the wedding that Ted thought o' the housekeeper's job here . . . It's not filled, is it?'

'No, it's not filled,' Kate admitted, as she got up from the desk where she had been sitting going over the household accounts. She had given the matter of the housekeeper's post little thought since returning from honeymoon the previous week. In fact, she had told Augustus over breakfast this very morning that she was in no hurry to interview prospective housekeepers, and, even if they did eventually employ someone else, she would want to keep control of the household accounts herself. He had not demurred and, heartened, she had put the subject to the back of her mind.

'She'd be very good,' Chrissie was at pains to assure her. 'Betty's no' stupid, she has a' her letters and that type o' thing. If she hadn't had to go into the mill, right well she would have done for herself given half a chance, by all accounts.'

Kate did not doubt that. Davey always said he took

what brains he had from his mam. But then he had never known his father.

Davey . . . For a split second Kate's eyes took on a faraway look. She had not seen or heard from him since that evening she had visited him in the tolbooth, but not a day had gone by that she hadn't thought of him. Augustus had kept his promise, and Davey had served only twenty days for the fracas on the Magdalen Green, but, from what she had heard, he had been advised by the sheriff to either give up his politicking or leave the city. She had little doubt which it would be, and the thought saddened her immeasurably. The very idea of having as close a connection as his mother so near at hand made her heart beat just that little bit faster. At least she would get news of her old friend from time to time. Yes, if she had to have someone help with the house-keeping, then Betty Lorimer might not be too bad a choice.

She walked to the window, tickling her chin absent-mindedly with the feathered end of her quill pen as she pondered on the matter. There had to be some snags, but at the moment she could not think of any. 'Tell her to come and see me on Friday morning,' she said, turning back to Chrissie with a smile on her face. 'We'll see what we can work out.'

And so it was that Betty Lorimer came to work at Falcon Ridge. Kate warned her new housekeeper not to mention to Augustus that she was the mother of the young radical he had helped get out of prison, and Betty had been only too glad to comply. 'As God's my judge, Kate, I'll no' say a word. As far as that lad o' mine's concerned, his name will never pass my lips in front o' your good man!'

Davey was to prove the only cloud on his mother's horizon as she prepared to take up her new post. But while Betty could barely contain her excitement at the prospect of the new life that awaited her, her son was quite irate at the idea when she had first mentioned it over a supper of bannocks and broth in their kitchen on the Hawkhill a few days after seeing Kate.

Davey still had not got over the news of Kate's unexpected marriage to old Augustus Falconer, and his mother's news was a double blow he certainly had not expected. He could barely believe his ears. His own mother going to serve the pair of them – the young woman he loved and that lecherous old slave-driver! He shook his head as if to clear his mind of the image of the pair of them together. Kate's action in agreeing to become the old man's bride had been the ultimate betrayal. For days after hearing the news he had not been able to eat a thing; only drink could assuage the pain that still ate at his mind and heart. Such agonies were for lassies, he kept telling himself, not something to be borne by grown men such as himself. And certainly it was not something to be shared with the outside world, least of all with his mother.

'I don't know what's got into you all,' he said bitterly. 'First Kate and now you, both prepared to swallow your consciences and take that auld devil Falconer's shilling.' He hid the real pain behind his brave words as he glowered his disapproval and lifted his spoon to take the first mouthful of the soup his mother had specially prepared.

'The devil's shilling be damned!' his mother declared. 'I'll be doing no more than I'm doing at present in that regard. Don't forget it's Augustus Falconer's money I've been taking home in my pocket every week for long enough. I've been slaving away in that mill o' his since you were a bairn.'

'I ken, Mam, I ken. But working in his own home . . .' He could only shake his head in disgust as he broke a bannock in two and bit into the bigger half.

'At least I'll be back in the Ferry, Davey lad. I'll be breathing good clean air again, and you ken fine that's what the doctor says I need to get rid o' this bother wi' my chest.'

There was no gainsaying that, and after talking themselves hoarse, Davey had the good grace to give in before the meal was finished. He knew better than anyone what his mother was going through with her breathing. Who was he to deny her the only chance that might ever come her way? A change to fresh sea-air and a far less tiring job could do nothing but good, no matter whose house it was in. It might even save her life. The fact that Kate was now her Mistress he must try to regard as one of those weird quirks of fate that sometimes occurred in life. There was no reason he should make her feel bad simply because he was being eaten away inside with a pain that would not let him go.

It was decided that rather than have to climb the stairs to an attic, Betty would have her own room in the annexe; it was a new addition to the main house that had only just been finished and of which Augustus was justly proud. Like the gatehouse at the foot of the drive, it had its own specially designed turrets and miniature battlements. 'Betty really will feel like queen of the castle in here,' Kate declared, as she walked round it with her husband just before the new housekeeper's arrival.

Kate had taken great pleasure in choosing the furnishings herself, and it was with immense pride that she showed her new housekeeper over the room on Betty's first morning at work two weeks later. 'Here we are, then!' she said, throwing open the door. 'I hope everything's to your satisfaction.'

Betty Lorimer could do nothing but shake her head as she gazed around her at the pale cream-coloured walls and flowered curtains at the window. On the far side of the door stood a gleaming brass bed, with crisp white bedding neatly folded on top of the new horsehair mattress. The rest of the furniture comprised a walnut wardrobe, a matching chest and washstand, and a small round tip-top table, with one high-backed wooden chair and one easy chair on either side of the black cast-iron grate. 'I've never had furniture like this in my life,' she cried, running her fingers round the edge of the table as if to make sure it was all quite real. 'I can't wait for Davey to see it!'

At the sound of her son's name, Kate's heart lurched. 'He'll be dropping in to see you soon, will he?'

'Och aye, I don't doubt it. But he's so tied up with all the politicking he's doing these days he barely has time for anything. You'd have thought those few weeks cooped up in the tolbooth would have dampened his enthusiasm for that type o' carrying-on but not a bit o' it. There's even talk of him going over to France to speak to some protesters there.' Betty shook her head at the folly of it all. 'To my mind it wouldn't be a bad idea if he stayed there. He's already been warned by the sheriff here. He'd better be careful, that's a' I can say. He was lucky once, thanks to your good man, Mrs Falconer ma'm, but he might not be so lucky a second time.'

Kate was taken aback at hearing her old friend address her so differently, but she let it pass. Things were no longer the same between them; it was a fact of life. 'Well, I'm sure Davey's wise enough to have worked out for himself exactly how far he can go without getting into any more trouble with the authorities.'

She was about to enquire further into his proposed trip abroad, when she felt that same fuzziness in her head and the accompanying feeling of squeamishness she had experienced so often of late.

'Are you all right, ma'm?'

Kate backed towards the easy chair a yard or two behind her and sat down, pressing her hand to her forehead. 'I'm sorry,' she said faintly, as a film of perspiration covered her brow. 'I don't know what comes over me these days.'

'This happens quite a lot, does it?' Betty queried, pouring a glass of water from a ewer sitting on the washstand and handing it to Kate.

Kate sipped the water gratefully and admitted, 'For the past few weeks. In fact on the morning of my wedding I thought I was actually going to be sick in the carriage on my way to the manse.'

Betty gave a knowing, 'Mmm . . .' as she placed a hand on Kate's forehead; it felt cold and clammy to the touch. 'If it wasn't so soon after the wedding, I'd say there was only one cause of all this.'

'Oh really?' Kate said, sipping on the water. This continual feeling of nausea and lightheadedness was really beginning to worry her. Even Augustus was noticing she wasn't looking herself in the mornings and had asked if there was any sign of blood being brought up with the slight cough she had had during their two days in Montrose. Consumption was the black cloud that hung over all their lives. She looked curiously at Betty who was nodding thoughtfully to herself. 'Only one cause?' she repeated nervously. 'And what might that be?'

'I'd say there was no doubt about it. You're going to have a baby.'

'A baby!' Kate stared at her old friend, relief and shock evident on her face in equal measure as she handed the glass back. Could it be it was not the dreaded consumption, after all? Did all these symptoms simply mean a bairn was on the way?

'You look surprised.'

'Just a bit,' Kate admitted, leaning back on the chair and letting out a sigh.

'Are there any other signs? Are your breasts sore, for example?'

Kate coloured but had to admit they were, and had been for two or three weeks now.

'Mmm . . . How long have you been married?' Betty asked tentatively, knowing she was treading on sensitive ground. From what she could remember it was no time at all.

'Just over a month,' Kate replied truthfully.

Betty frowned and shook her head. 'That's strange,' she said, trying her best to be tactful, 'because if I didn't know better, I'd lay a pound to a penny you're all of six or seven weeks gone.'

Kate stared at her. 'Six or seven weeks gone?'

'Aye, that's about it. If your honeymoon had been at the beginning o' April instead of at the beginning o' May, I'd have said there was no doubt about it.' Then, seeing the shocked look on Kate's face, she added with a smile, 'Come away, you may be my employer and a fine lady now, lass, but we're both grown women. Your guid man may be auld in years, but that doesn't stop him jumping the gun the same as a bridegroom half his age when his bride-to-be is as bonnie a lassie as you. It's not everybody has the patience to wait till the ceremony's out o' the way.'

Kate got up from the chair a trifle unsteadily and walked to the fireplace where she stood frowning down at the empty grate. The phrase 'jumping the gun' kept repeating in her head. But Augustus hadn't jumped any gun. On the contrary, he couldn't even get the damned thing to fire!

'Relax, Kate lass,' she heard Betty's voice saying behind her. 'It might have come as a wee bit of a shock to you, but the father-to-be will be absolutely delighted, you mark my words.'

Kate's face had gone quite white as she turned to face her old friend. The most awful realization had dawned. Surely fate could not be that cruel? 'Absolutely delighted . . .' she repeated in a voice that was more of a croak, as her insides quaked at the thought of Willie sulking down there in Leeds, totally unaware of the news that had just befallen her. 'That I doubt, Betty dear. That I doubt very much.' If there was one thing she was certain of, Willie Falconer would have no more wish to be the father of her child than she would wish to be the mother of his.

* * *

As the weeks wore on and late spring gave way to the fresh verdant days of high summer, so the feelings of nausea and lightheadedness faded and gradually Kate began to feel her old self again. Only the expanding girth of her waistline told her that Betty's prediction looked like it might be coming true. Happily Augustus had not appeared to notice anything, however, merely commenting of late on how well she was looking now that her cough had cleared up. Her hair had never been so glossy, nor her skin so clear. 'And I do believe you're putting on a bit of beef at last, my dear,' he told her approvingly. 'It's good to see that the life of a lady seems to be agreeing with you.'

For her part, Kate viewed the prospect of approaching motherhood with mixed feelings. From what additional information she had gleaned from Betty about the mysteries of conception and birth, she knew that there could be no doubt about it, the child must be Willie's and not his father's. The thought appalled her, but there was absolutely nothing she could do about it. One thing she was sure of, however, neither Willie nor his father must ever know the truth, and her main preoccupation now would be to convince her husband, when the time came, that the baby was his.

At the moment, still only Betty knew of her pregnancy, and the housekeeper naturally assumed that the child was Augustus's. 'You'll have to see the doctor soon,' she told Kate, one bright morning in late June. 'You can't go on keeping it a secret for much longer.'

They were standing in the kitchen of Falcon Ridge and Kate sat down in the rocking chair and began to rock gently back and forth, a pensive look on her face. Augustus was in the neighbouring village of Monifieth today, visiting his old friend Jim Low, the owner of the foundry that made most of the cards and spinning-frames for the Falcon Mills. 'I'll tell Augustus tonight,' she resolved.

'Then you'll have to tell your parents, for the proud father will never keep such news to himself, and they're sure to hear of it before long.'

Kate looked up sharply. She had not seen either of her parents since the wedding, and certainly did not relish the prospect of a visit to the Hawkhill to tell them she was about to father a Falconer child. 'I'll cross that particular bridge in my own good time, thank you, Betty.'

'Oh, I didn't mean to cause offence.' The housekeeper looked mortified, but Kate merely smiled.

'Don't worry, you haven't offended me. God knows, you know my mother as well as I do. She's not the easiest person in the world to get on with, or to break news to that she certainly doesn't want to hear.'

'Your mam's had more than her fair share of grief in this life, and I dare say she'll be none too happy, but you canna live your life to please other folk, that's something I learned a good many years ago when my man walked out on me.'

Kate's brows rose in interest. 'Walked out on you? You mean Davey's father's not dead – you're not a widow?'

Betty Lorimer sat down on the edge of the high-backed settle on the opposite side of the range and stared into the flickering flames of the hearth. 'Jock left when the bairns were only wee. It got too much for him, I suppose. All those mouths to feed and no work coming in. He'd been on the handloom, working for a fella out at Barnhill, but when the war ended and the big mills began opening, well the work just wasn't there any more.'

She sighed, a deep, heartfelt sigh that came from the very depths of her soul. 'I canna say that I blame him for going. He was a clever man, awful keen on the book-learning, and not cut out for the hand-to-mouth life we were forced to live. He always said the Scots were made to fight on the wrong side in the wars with France. The "Auld Alliance" should have held fast. To hell with the English government down in London. They had the right idea over there in Paris, he would say — Liberty, Equality and all that . . . I can see him now, standing in front of our wee bit fire and waving his hands as he railed at the injustice of it all.' Her voice tailed off and a film of mist covered the faded blue of her eyes as she thought of the good-looking young man she had once loved more than life itself.

'Is he . . .? Could he still be alive?'

Betty shrugged her thin shoulders and admitted, 'Och aye. There's no reason why not.' That was what made it all the harder to bear.

'Does Davey know?'

'I've never said a word to him, for he still believes his dad died when he was a bairn. But my Davey tak's after his father all right. And not only in looks.' She shook her head at having to watch history repeat itself in her own family. 'A' that politicking . . . Jock was the very same. He couldna' get his fill.'

'And you think he may still be alive?' Kate pressed the point.

Betty shrugged her thin shoulders. 'Wha kens?' Then she forced a smile to her face, and in an attempt at bravado she declared, 'And, in all honesty, wha cares these days? I tell you this, Kate . . . ma'm . . . Right now I couldna' be happier the way things have worked out . . . Oh, it would have been grand if Jock had been around when the bairns were wee, there's no doubt about that, but had he still been wi' me today he'd never have agreed to me taking this job.' She gave a rueful laugh. 'My God, he would have been worse than Davey in his protests that I should ever consider such a thing!'

Kate gave a wry smile in response. She too had gone through that type of reaction. 'Supping with the devil', her mother had called it. The words still burned in her mind. 'Davey's not been to see you yet? I'm sorry if he's still angry.'

'Oh, there's no need to be sorry, for he's due up tonight. If you come down here at around ten you'll probably find him.' She gave a conspiratorial wink. 'I've told him to say his name's Alec or Joe or something – anything but Davey – if he happens to come upon your good man.'

Later that same afternoon, Augustus sent word that he was staying on in Monifieth for supper with his friend, Jim Low, and, for once, Kate was relieved. She had learned from Betty that Davey was due at around nine-thirty that evening, and resolved to see him before he went downstairs to find his mother.

She thought of taking an evening stroll in the rose garden to the front of the house to catch him as he came up the side drive, but the sky was darkening to an alarming degree, foreshadowing the rain that had been threatening since late afternoon. So instead she positioned herself just to the side of the curtains of the drawing-room window to await his arrival. She could feel her insides churning at the thought of facing him. They had not spoken to one another since her wedding, and she had little doubt he would be feeling both betrayed and sickened by what she had done.

She did not have long to wait, for the longcase clock in the hall outside was striking the half-hour when she saw a stocky, bearded figure come through the pedestrians' gate and begin to make its way up the side drive and round to the servants' entrance.

Her heart pounding, she wasted no time. Her cry of, 'Davey, wait!', as she ran around the side of the house, caught up with him as he was about to descend the stone steps.

He turned and she saw him pause uncertainly for a moment, then begin to walk slowly back towards her through the growing darkness. Her heart was now beating fit to burst. Her whole being sang at the mere sight of him, but there was no reciprocal smile on his face as his footsteps drew nearer.

He stopped several feet from her, and they stood looking at one another beneath the fading blossoms of a magnolia tree that grew against the house wall and scented the bedroom in which she slept with her husband.

The grey, threatening clouds billowing up the Firth hung low over their heads. A stiff breeze was now blowing from the direction of the river, ruffling Davey's hair, and the dampness that had been in the air since afternoon was causing it to curl around the sides of his face. He looked thinner than when Kate last saw him, thinner and older somehow. He had lost the rounded look to his cheeks, and his eyes were grave as they looked into hers. 'I hear you're a married woman now, Kate,' he said, doing nothing to disguise the bitterness in his voice. 'Congratulations should be in order, but you won't mind if I don't offer them.'

Kate looked down at her feet before raising her gaze to meet his. 'I − I can understand how you feel . . .' she began, but got no further.

'Can you?' he interrupted bitterly. 'Can you really, Kate?'

She knew now she shouldn't have come out. It would have been best to let well alone. It was too soon. Far too soon. The wound she had inflicted was still too painful for them to do anything other than hurt each other even more. She half turned from him, unable to bear the accusation in his eyes, but he was determined she was going to face him. Now was no time to take the coward's way out. He grabbed her arm, forcing her round to look at him once more.

Large drops of rain were falling now, splattering off the stone flags of the path, and trickling down their faces. 'Look at me!' he commanded. 'Damn you, Kate, look at me!'

'I can't!'

Then the heavens opened and the deluge that had been threatening for so long came down in torrents. 'Look at me, Kate,' he commanded. 'Look me straight in the face and tell me that you love that old man whose name you've taken and whose ring you so proudly wear!'

161

They stood facing one another on the garden path as the rain poured down. They were both soaked to the skin as he grabbed her left hand and pulled it roughly towards him so he could see the evidence with his own eyes.

'Bought with an old man's gold,' he whispered in disgust. For that's what she had been. 'How could you do it, Kate? You can't love him. You love me.'

'Love him? What is love, Davey?' she cried, as the rain streamed down her face. Was love living your life in a garret like his own mother Betty, and bringing up a clutch of bairns alone while her husband went off to practise his reforming zeal for the benefits of mankind elsewhere?

They were glaring at one another, oblivious to the downpour that plastered their hair to their heads and their clothes to their bodies, as his hand still held hers and his eyes burned into her own.

'You love me,' he repeated huskily. 'You know you love me.'

Then suddenly they were in each other's arms, and he was kissing her like she had never been kissed before, his lips slipping from her mouth over the wet skin of her cheeks, and back again until they were both gasping for air.

'You ask me what is love . . . This is love, Katie . . . This is love . . .' he murmured desperately into the soaking strands of her hair, as his arms moved up and down her back, crushing the breath from her body. 'And you feel it too, I know you do.'

She shook her head in despair, against the wet worsted of his jacket, as she continued to cling to him. Just being with him out here as the heavens opened, touching him, feeling his arms around her, hearing his voice, made every nerve in her body sing out in exaltation.

'How could you do it? How could you marry him?' He prised her from him, his hands on her shoulders, his fingers digging into her skin beneath the wet silk of her

162

dress as he gazed down at her, seeking an explanation for the inexplicable.

She gazed back at him, her tears mingling with the rainwater on her cheeks. She shook her head in despair. How could she tell him that as a small child she had seen her mother kill her own grandchild out of the despair bred of poverty in this city? How could she tell him his own father had walked out on his family for that very reason? How could she tell him she did not want to turn into her mother or his? How could she tell him the truth?

'Leave him,' he implored her, smoothing the soaking strands of hair back from her brow. 'Leave him and come away with me. I'm leaving for France soon. We can go together. We can help change the world, Katie – you and me.'

But Kate could only shake her head once more as she pressed his hand to her lips. 'I can't go with you, Davey lad, for this is my world now. There is no other.'

And inside her, for the very first time, she could feel the new life begin to stir. The tears flowed hot and bitter from her eyes to mingle with the cold rain as she stood looking at the man she loved. If only this child were his. If only it were his.

Chapter Fourteen

After a labour lasting twelve hours, Ewan Robert Augustus Falconer was born in the opening seconds of the first day of January, 1831, in the master bedroom of Falcon Ridge. Outside the wide bay-window a soft snow was falling, drifting down to cover the rooftops of the village with a sparkling white blanket, while four miles to the south the bells of Dundee's Old Kirk steeple were ringing in the new year.

It was ten years to the day since Peggy's child had been born, and heartache mingled with the joy on Kate's face as she was given her first glimpse of her son. Throughout the long hours of her labour she had felt the presence of her dead sister. It was as if dear gentle Peg was here with her now. Despite their mother's anger and bitterness, Kate knew that Peggy would not condemn her for what had happened. She would have understood. And if there really was a heaven, then Peggy was there now, at peace beside her own child whose birth and death she had endured in that small back bedroom on the Hawkhill on that terrible day ten years ago.

Kate had never been one to believe in omens, but somehow she felt it was meant to be that her baby would be born on this particular day: the first day of a new year, a day to remember the past, but also to put it behind her and look to the future.

Outside the snow might be falling, but here in the bedroom the fire crackled in the grate, filling the room with cheering warmth as the elderly doctor stood in front of the hearth, wrapping the irate baby in its waiting shawl.

As Kate watched, a deep peace descended on her as she

held out her hands for her son. 'The Lord works in mysterious ways,' she whispered, touching the red puckered cheek of the infant with her fingertips as he was laid gently in her arms.

The remark, so softly spoken, was lost on Hector Grant, who knew nothing of the significance of the date, but was simply relieved it was all over. As Kate cradled her child, he washed his hands in the basin of water on the washstand by the window, and offered up a silent prayer that things had worked out so well. It had been a difficult birth for a first delivery, due to the size of the child, but the young mother had borne it well. 'You should feel proud of yourself, Kate my dear,' he told her. 'There are not many young women have bairns as big as that first time round.'

Taking the squalling infant back from its mother, he placed it in the basket of a weighing machine on the table by the side of the bed. 'Almost ten pounds, by God!' he declared proudly as the pointer swung resolutely towards the top quarter of the dial. 'A prize-fighter and no mistake, you've got here, lass!'

'Take him to his father,' Kate told him, knowing Augustus had been pacing the house in a state of high anxiety all day. 'Then bring him back immediately, for I want to make sure he's real.'

'Oh, he's real all right,' the doctor assured her, almost shouting to make his voice heard above the crying child as he secured the infant in the crook of his left arm and made for the door. 'I tell you, this young lad will let you know he's around from now on. He's got a pair o' lungs that would do a town crier proud!'

'You've got a son, Augustus man!' he shouted in triumph from the balustrade of the minstrels' gallery into the hall below. 'You've got a braw bonnie laddie here!'

Lying back on her pillow with a wide smile on her face, Kate heard the shout and closed her eyes with a deep sigh. She had done her job, and the relief she felt was not simply because it was all over and she had survived to produce a healthy child; it was as if the personal guilt she had carried with her all these years after witnessing the death of Peggy's child had been washed away. By giving her a child of her own on this most painful of anniversaries, the Lord had shown her his forgiveness. He had told her she had not been responsible for what happened to Peggy or her baby on that terrible day ten years ago, and the infant now on its way downstairs to be presented to its father was the living proof.

Augustus, who had been pacing the floor of the hall for the best part of an hour, looked up and stood stock still as his old friend Hector Grant descended the staircase with the child in his arms. 'How's Kate?' he cried, his first concern for his young wife.

'Kate's grand, just grand. And she's done you proud this day, Augustus. You've got a fine son.'

'A laddie . . .' Augustus breathed in a voice husky with emotion. 'The lass has given me a son.'

Hector Grant passed the screaming bundle to the proud father, who gazed down into the indignant red face of his son.

'There's nothing wrong with his lungs, anyway,' Augustus observed ruefully, touching the soft damp skin of the infant's cheek. 'And, would you believe it, Hec, this little bugger's got black hair.'

Hector Grant gave a laugh. 'Aye, some change from the last time, there's nae doubt about that.' Almost thirty years before he had ministered at the birth of his old friend's first son, and both men had been amazed at the sight of the newborn infant with a crop of carrot-red hair. No one had realized that red hair ran in Emily's family, and there had been much shaking of heads and speculative mirth at their first introduction to Master Willie.

'What does Kate think of him?'

'Why don't you go and ask her?'

'Man, I'll do just that!' Still proudly cradling the child in his arms, Augustus slowly ascended the stairs and knocked tentatively on the bedroom door before pushing it open to see his wife propped up on the pillows.

Kate's face was pale and her hair was plastered to her brow with sweat, but at the sight of her husband and son she broke into a weary smile. 'That was quite an effort,' she said, easing herself up on the pillow and taking a sip from the glass of milk the midwife had provided on the table beside her.

'He's a big lad all right,' Augustus replied, gazing down in admiration at his son before handing him back to his mother. 'And to think I was worried about you going into labour over a month before your time.'

'Aye, with a bairn of that size at eight months, God help me if I'd gone the distance,' Kate said without turning a hair. What he didn't know could not hurt him, and she would make sure he never discovered the truth.

Augustus had never doubted that the child was anything other than several weeks premature, or that he was the father. In fact, the news in the early summer that Kate was pregnant had proved an enormous morale booster for him. He had practically danced across to the drinks cabinet, and his hand had shaken so much that he had spilled a good nip of his favourite malt whisky all over the polished wooden top before raising his glass to toast the unborn child. It was just the tonic he had needed to convince him that he was still the real man he knew his young wife deserved. He might not have quite risen to the occasion on their actual honeymoon, but once back home in Broughty Ferry he had seemed to relax more and had done his duty fairly satisfactorily on at least a couple of occasions. And now he had the living proof; he had confounded the doubters. Kate was pregnant, and it was obviously not necessary to be a young stud to do your duty by a wife less than half your age.

'The old blunderbuss might not fire all that often, but at least it's not firing blanks yet,' he had told his young wife in undisguised delight as they sat together in the rose

167

garden one fine evening in late July and talked of the expected child. 'I can't wait for the great day to come. Kate lass, I'll be the proudest man alive!'

Now he repeated those words as he sat by the side of her bed and together they gazed at the infant safely back in its mother's arms. 'I didn't think it was possible to be so proud of anything at my age,' he told Kate, as a mist of tears blurred his vision. 'This wee lad's birth has given me something else to live for. You've done me proud, lass. You've done us both proud. Maybe the old man is not quite ready for the knacker's yard yet-awhile!'

Kate reached out and squeezed her husband's hand. She knew more than anyone how conscious of the age difference he had been over the past few months, taking every opportunity to assure her she would miss out on nothing and there was plenty of life in the old dog yet. 'Everything worth having improves with age,' she assured him gently. 'Whether it's malt whisky or men, give me vintage any day.'

He raised her hand to his lips and kissed it. It was times like this when she made him feel ten feet tall.

It was almost two weeks before she was allowed on her feet again. 'A bairn that size takes a lot out of you in more ways than one, my dear,' Hector Grant told her sternly when she protested that she felt well able to get up and dressed on the seventh day. 'A quiet half-hour on the day-bed is all that I will countenance.'

The day-bed was consequently moved into the bay of the window where, in the warmth of the fire that blazed constantly in the grate, Kate could look out to her heart's content on the snow-covered rooftops of the village and the turbulent waters of the estuary beyond.

Having to spend her waking hours lying down, she had plenty of time to reflect on the year that had gone, and in a strange way with the birth of young Ewan her life seemed to have come full circle. It was as if she had been bound up with the destiny of the Falconers all her days. In the cot beside her lay a robust young son whom Augustus had named Ewan, after his best friend, a soldier in the Duke of York's army, killed on a battlefield in Flanders in 1793. 'Ewan Falconer . . .' she would whisper against the soft down of her son's cheek. 'My bonnie Ewan . . .'

Yet, sometimes, despite all the pride and adoration, just occasionally a chill would come to her heart, for she knew there were plenty of folk in this great city who still held the Falconer name in scorn. Folk like her own mother who would never forgive the fact that the Falconers were rich and powerful and they were not. Despite all the love she could bestow in the security of their own home, it was a hard world out there. She knew only too well that there were people who wished her son ill. People like Willie, his own father, whom he would never call by that name, and who, from his new home in faraway Leeds, must already wish the child dead.

So the first days and weeks of her son's life passed in a mixture of conflicting emotions for Kate, as her moods swung from elation and pride to fear and trepidation for the future. She also longed for the time when she could get up off her day-bed and carry on as normal. For an energetic young woman, the restrictions being imposed on her life seemed almost unbearable. There seemed to be all sorts of things she could and could not do. Even feeding the baby herself, she learned, was not at all approved of, so, to her great dismay, a wet-nurse was brought up from the village to breastfeed the child. Kate made sure, however, that she had a say in the choosing of the woman for such an important task. She immediately enlisted the help of Betty, Davey's mother, who came up with one of her own nieces through marriage for the job. Susan Lorimer had a month-old baby of her own and a cheerful, pleasant disposition. She was also the proud possessor of a head of nut-brown curls that were heartbreakingly similar to those of her cousin Davey.

'If he can't have Lorimer blood, at least he's having

Lorimer milk to start him off in life,' Kate found herself saying to a puzzled Betty, who looked at her quizzically as the two of them took tea together in the kitchen two days after Kate's confinement period was over.

'Maybe I'm overreaching myself, but you were quite fond of my lad, weren't you, ma'm?'

Kate paused in the sipping of her tea, the cup half-way to her lips. She replaced it in the saucer on her lap and avoided the older woman's enquiring eyes. She had made a stupid slip of the tongue, but there was no use in lying, this was one of her ain folk, after all. This was Davey's mother, and maybe it hadn't been such a slip, if the truth be known. Maybe it was quite a relief to be able to admit it at last: a truth she knew Betty had long guessed at. 'Yes,' she admitted softly. 'Yes, I was.'

Betty Lorimer sighed deeply as she sat back in her chair. It was no more than she expected. From the time they were bairns the two had been inseparable, and she had often wondered what had happened to change things. She had known how upset Davey had been when he'd first learned of Kate taking the post as Augustus's housekeeper. His face had been a picture of misery for days. It was almost as if he had known that would be the beginning of the end between them, and his reaction at hearing of Kate's marriage had left his mother in no doubt. 'Love is a strange thing, and no mistake,' she sighed.

'Have — have you heard from him recently?' Kate asked tentatively.

Betty shook her head. She had not heard from Davey since he'd disappeared to France at the beginning of the summer and, by the sound of things, with the overthrowing of the French king and all those revolutionary goings-on the previous year, God only knew what trouble he had got himself involved in. It was his father all over again. 'No, not since he went to France . . . He may be my own flesh and blood, but you're better off without him.

Love and politics don't mix. They never have and, God help me, I should know.'

Kate said nothing, for there was nothing to say. His mother was right.

The birth of his son seemed to give Augustus a new lease of life. He took the greatest interest in the baby's progress, and the nursery was usually his first stop on returning from the mills in the evening. Kate had had the room done out in shades of blue, with sunshine yellow and blue curtains at the windows, and all manner of baby toys lay waiting in a large wooden kist at the foot of the crib.

'He's a grand little lad and no mistake!' Augustus would declare, dandling the infant in his arms, and even going so far as to ignore his rheumaticky knees, getting down on the floor to play with him once he had taken his first steps.

Mary Jean, the nursemaid who had been engaged to look after him, would give a tolerant smile and wonder at the miracle that could make a man of Augustus Falconer's standing resort to such carryings-on. 'The Master is very fond o' the bairn,' she was for ever telling Kate, who would merely smile and say, 'Yes, Mary Jean, isn't it wonderful?'

Mary Jean was the eldest daughter of Jean Lorimer, one of Betty's sisters-in-law from the village; having so many of Davey's family around somehow gave Kate comfort during his long absence from her life. Not that she spent every day thinking about her old friend. So full was her life during that first year after Ewan's birth that the initial hurt she had felt at his leaving had now faded to a dull ache. Both husband and wife were living life to the full, and so much did their lives and thoughts revolve around the baby that even Augustus no longer fretted over the absence of Willie as he had once done. Young Master Ewan, as the staff called him, had become the pivot around which all their lives revolved.

To Kate it seemed that the only person who seemed impervious to the baby's charm was her mother, Bel, who declared she had no wish ever to see the child. 'Falconer blood is Falconer blood,' she told her daughter on Kate's first visit to the Hawkhill after the infant's birth. 'I'm sorry, Kate, but I would be spitting on Peggy's grave if I recognized one o' them as my own.'

Kate had felt a burning anger at that moment. This was the woman who, more than any other – yes, even more than Willie himself – was responsible for Peggy's death; who had snuffed out her baby's life with her own hands.

The two women faced one another across the kitchen table and the silent accusation hung heavy in the air. Their eyes were locked in an undeclared combat that they knew could destroy them both should the fatal words be spoken.

Kate was the first to break, as she turned abruptly and picked up her basket from the chair beside her. 'I must be going,' she said through clenched teeth. 'I really don't know when I'll be back.'

'Don't judge her too harshly,' her father had said, out of earshot, as Kate slipped him her usual handful of sovereigns at the door. Rob McMahon looked down at the coins in his hand and shook his head at the futility of it all. 'She'd rather die in a ditch, so she would, than take a tainted penny piece, as she calls them, and she'll never accept you bearing a child with Falconer blood. It brings it all back, so it does, and you'll not be changing her now.'

'But she killed Peggy's bairn, Dad! She was the one – '

'No!' Rob McMahon interrupted harshly. 'She did what she had to do to spare that lassie a lifetime o' misery. And she did no more than has been done in almost every other family in this city at some time or other. Sure and you can't condemn what you don't rightly understand, Kathleen. You were just a young thing when it happened, so you were.'

He shook his head in weariness at it all. 'Sure and she did what she had to do – what seemed right at the time.

172

But, by Christ, 'tis a high price she has paid a hundred times over, with poor Peggy dying like that . . . You'll not be blaming her, Katie. You can throw it back in her face and all but, believe me, whatever you want to accuse her of, she has accused herself of it a million times over these past ten years.'

Katie knew he was speaking the truth. She made no reply, but squeezed her father's arm. 'Keep well, Dad,' she said softly. 'Look after yourself.' There was no point in saying more. The best she could do was to visit every so often and see they were still healthy. Her mother might have her pride, but so did Kate and she would not grovel for approval for herself or for her son.

Things were to prove far from easy on the few visits home she made over the following year, for it was not just the baby that remained a touchy subject. Another bitter bone of contention between mother and daughter as the year progressed was the question of Bel's old friend and workmate, Betty Lorimer, taking the job as Kate's house-keeper at Falcon Ridge. After learning about the matter, Bel would not even allow Betty's name to be spoken in her presence, although, by all accounts, she was quick to downcry her old friend at every opportunity outside the house. This attitude upset Kate, for in her eyes Betty had done no wrong, and it was on one of her visits to her parents, just before the Hogmanay of 1831–32, and her son Ewan's first birthday, that she found she could keep quiet about it no longer. As she was leaving, her mother remarked, 'I'd wish you a Happy New Year, but sure and you'll be having that anyway. You and that Lorimer woman will be having no time to think of the likes of us when you're sitting up there in that Falconer mansion, before your roaring fires, drinking old Augustus's whisky and eating his black bun.'

'That's not fair, Mam, and you know it. And at least you have got your family here. You've got Dad and you've got me and your grandchild, if only you'd appreciate us, but poor Betty's got no husband or bairns of her own here to celebrate with.'

'What do you mean poor Betty has nobody?' Bel demanded. 'She's got that no-good son of hers to visit her.'

'Davey's in France, and well you know it.'

''Tis damned that I am if he is! I saw him just the other day. In fact, wouldn't he be after talking in the Community Hall this very night!'

Kate stared blankly at her mother. 'You mean Davey's here in this city?'

'Sure, and he's here in this very road,' her mother said, turning her back to throw another stick on the fire. 'If I'm not mistaken, he'll be after shouting his mouth off as we speak, so he will.'

Davey here in Dundee . . . Here on the Hawkhill . . .

It was with a quaking heart that Kate descended the stone stairs of the tenement a few minutes later and made her way out into the snow-covered street.

'Davey . . .' She found herself whispering his name out loud. 'Davey . . .' She could hardly believe it. But if ever there was a time for a Scotsman to return home it would be now. Tomorrow night would be Hogmanay, the last night of the old year.

In the light from the lamp at the head of the close, Kate peered at the watch hanging from her jacket, inside her cape. It was almost nine o'clock. In order to be at home with his family on what was also his son's first birthday, Augustus had gone to Monifieth tonight instead of tomorrow to have an early New Year dram with his old friend, Jim Low. Kate knew of old that he wouldn't be back till gone midnight once the whisky got flowing.

'The Community Hall . . .' she said, under her breath. Its grey stone bulk stood at the foot of the hill next to the Methodist chapel. She had to pass it to get to the stand of cabs, one of which she would need to take her back to Broughty Ferry.

It took her less than five minutes to get down there, her

breath causing frozen clouds to billow from her lips, her booted feet slipping and sliding on the icy ground as her heart throbbed almost painfully in her breast.

As she neared the hall, she could see that her mother was right, there was obviously something going on. There was a hum of talk in the air, and a crowd was spilling on to the road outside the building. Lamps were still burning within and the doors were wide open. Her steps slowed as she neared the scene and her apprehension grew. The very thought of bumping into him again filled her with a nervousness she could barely contain as her teeth began to chatter.

The air seemed to be filled with excited voices. Leaflets were being distributed. A young lad, no more than waist-high, thrust one into her hand.

She moved into the lighted area of the porch to read:

DUNDEE POLITICAL REFORM LEAGUE
Last meeting of 1831 in the Community Hall, Hawkhill, to herald the Great Reform Bill of 1832.

She could not resist a smile at that piece of presumption, for it was by no means certain that all the agitation of the past year was going to produce the electoral reform being demanded. But the smile faded and she bit her lip as she read on:

Eight p.m. sharp. First speaker the MP for County Clare, Mr Daniel O'Connell, backed by our local representative, Mr David Lorimer, fresh from the political battlefield of France.

Kate read and reread the words on the page that fluttered between her fingers in the yellow glow of the lamp. Another glance at the watch hanging from her bodice told her it was now just after nine. The meeting was obviously over and they were all heading home.

Her heart began to pound once more as the audience continued to drift back out into the street. Most were chatting animatedly to each other, their breath forming white clouds in the freezing night air as they argued over speeches they had just heard. Most were young men, but there was a good smattering of the older generation, with a few serious-faced women amongst them. She recognized several mill-workers from the area, but no one seemed to give her a second glance as she stood uncertainly in the shadow of the door.

As she continued to stand there shivering in the shadows, it took all of ten minutes for the hall to empty, save for a small knot of people left standing by the edge of the stage. She found if she craned her neck she could just make out the stout, bluff figure of the Irishman Daniel O'Connell, who had caused such a stir a couple of years back when he had championed through the Catholic Emancipation Act that enfranchised so many of his countrymen.

The others present were clustered around the MP with their backs to the door, so it was impossible to see their faces.

Kate pulled her cloak more tightly around her shoulders and glanced nervously around her. The crowd had all but dispersed now. Except for the pool of light given off by the lamps at the door, it was dark and freezing cold, and a fine snow was beginning to fall, all but obscuring the road down to the cab-rank.

I'll be better going, she thought despairingly. What good will it do hanging around here any longer? If Davey really was in there he was obviously tied up with the Great Liberator, as his supporters referred to O'Connell.

'Kate!'

The voice made her whirl round in surprise, in the direction of the road.

'Kate? Is that you?'

'D – Davey?' She hardly dared breathe his name.

The owner of the voice came out of the darkness, a huddled figure, unrecognizable in a voluminous tweed cloak and cap.

He hurried across to where she was standing and grasped both her gloved hands in his. 'Kate . . . Kate . . . You came . . .'

'I – I . . .' Reluctant to confess she was there almost by accident, she compromised with, 'I'm sorry I missed your speech . . . Oh, Davey, I had no idea you were home!'

She was trying desperately to see his face in the dim light of the lamp as he stood before her, clasping her hands in his. But just having him near her again was enough. It brought all the old feelings flooding back. No longer was she the responsible wife and mother. She could feel her composure going as she said in a voice shaking with emotion, 'Oh Davey, I've missed you so much.'

'I've missed you too,' he said, gripping her hands even more tightly, then he half turned in a nervous sort of way to glance behind him in the direction from which he had appeared out of the night.

'But what are you doing out here? Shouldn't you still be in the hall with the other speaker and the officials?' She could see from the snow covering his cap and cape that he had obviously been outdoors for a good ten minutes or so. 'What on earth are you doing out here?'

A silence fell between them as Kate waited for the answer to a perfectly reasonable question. There was a strange look on his face that she did not recognize.

He let go her hands and, looking somewhere over her left shoulder, said at last, 'I was seeing my wife to a cab.'

'Your wife?' Kate gasped, taking a step back.

Davey nodded and turned from her, digging his hands into the pockets of his cape as he stared out into the falling snow. 'I'm married, Kate.'

'No!' She reached for his arm, pulling him back round to face her. 'How can you be?' she said, her voice rising. 'How can you be married? You love me.'

'And you love me, but that didn't stop you, did it?'

The words stung her into silence as her eyes searched his face for some explanation. 'But why? Who . . .?'

'She's French,' he said quietly. 'Her name's Marie-Louise. I met her in Paris. Her father's in the movement.'

His simple explanation merely served to increase her pain. The woman he had married, she was one of them – that band of revolutionaries out to change the world. 'I see.'

'Do you? Do you really?'

Kate could feel the bitter sting of tears in her eyes and turned her head so he could not see. 'I – I had a baby last Hogmanay,' she found herself saying proudly in retaliation. 'A fine son. He'll be one year old on New Year's Day.'

He gave a bitter-sweet smile. She always did have to get the last punch in, even as a bairn. 'Congratulations,' he said softly. 'I wish it was mine.'

Chapter Fifteen

Kate's chance meeting with Davey at the end of 1831 and the news of his marriage was the spur she needed to put the past behind her. She had much to be thankful for. Despite what her mother said, Augustus was not a bad man. He was a good husband and a proud father to young Ewan and, with the passing of time, Kate was growing to love the man she married. It could never be the same kind of love she felt for Davey, but she was fond of Augustus and felt a strong bond of loyalty for the affection and respect he had always shown her. Memories of the bitter-sweet love she had known with Davey were no substitute for real life. She knew she owed it to her husband to concentrate on being a good wife to him and a good mother to her son.

For his part, Augustus was more than happy with his lot. Marrying Kate was proving to be the best decision he had made in his life. After thirty joyless years with Emily, he had at last found a companion who not only took an interest in himself but also in his work. There seemed to be no aspect of his life that did not hold a fascination for Kate, and they often spoke long into the night, talking over the future of flax-spinning in Dundee and where the next improvements might be made.

He often wondered how he had borne three decades of marriage to a woman for whom he was little more than a generous provider of the good things in life. Emily had made it more than obvious that as a man he held little appeal. In fact, that whole side of things quite disgusted her. Willie's birth had proved a very convenient way of bringing the physical part of their marriage to an end. Of course he could have forced himself on her, as so many men with similarly minded wives had to do, but he had never been that kind. He might be a hard man at work, he told himself, but as far as home was concerned he would remain the perfect gentleman she had married. There had been no more than perhaps two occasions since Willie's birth and his mother's death thirty years later that Augustus could remember ever having touched his wife in that way, and on both those occasions he had been drunk. But despite her professed constant ill-health, it had never occurred to him that Emily might actually die before him, and he had quite resigned himself to a life of celibacy. Then along came Kate.

Now, after nearly three years of marriage, he still could not believe his good luck. His young wife was not only bright and intelligent, she was beautiful into the bargain, and what was more, she had shown him more affection in these few years than Emily had shown in a lifetime. All right, perhaps their love-life might not be as it could be had he been twenty years younger, but he had fathered Ewan, hadn't he? That proved he was still a man, and any other reassurance he needed she was quick to give. 'Are you sure you never hanker after a lad your own age, Kate lass?' he would often ask as they lay side by side in the big double bed, and she would always shake her head. 'Oh no, Augustus,' she would assure him. 'Why should I when I have everything a woman could possibly want with you and Ewan?'

As she uttered those words, Kate knew her husband would never know the pain behind them, nor the vision of Davey Lorimer that she would continually pray would eventually fade from her mind as she closed her eyes to go to sleep every night. Augustus would never know as he tried so hard to be the man he wanted to be for her that it was Davey's weight on her body that she longed for as she lay there and stroked the grey head that sweated and panted in another vain attempt to defy the passage of time.

In that regard, Kate often found herself wishing she had not been so quick to employ Betty Lorimer as her housekeeper. Seeing and talking to Davey's mother in her own home every day could not help but bring thoughts to the fore that she was trying her best to put to the back of her mind. There were so many little mannerisms that seemed to have passed from mother to son, such as the way they both held their head to one side when they smiled, and a certain way the skin around their eyes crinkled when they laughed, that it was often painful to watch, and she found herself having to make her excuses to walk away.

She had discovered from Maisie, the parlour-maid, that Davey had visited his mother shortly after her fleeting conversation with him outside the Community Hall that winter's night, but when Kate had raised the matter over a cup of hot chocolate in the kitchen one evening, Betty had been cagey about the visit and what had been said between her and her son. It was many months, in fact, before she admitted to Kate that she not only knew Davey was married but that she had actually met the young woman in question.

They had been sitting in the kitchen one evening, after Ewan had been bathed and put to bed for the night, Betty with a pile of household mending on her lap, and Kate sipping her favourite cup of hot chocolate, when the subject was raised in a most unexpected way.

Mary Jean, the nursemaid, entered the room carrying a small package. She looked surprised to see Kate there and hovered by the doorway for a moment, until Betty said, 'What is it, lass? Do you need me for something?'

'Oh no, Auntie Betty,' the girl said quickly. 'I didn't mean to disturb you or the Mistress, but I was asked to give you this. It was handed in for you when you were out at the butcher's this afternoon.'

She laid the package on the table and backed out of the room, nodding her apologies for the interruption to Kate,

181

who smiled and murmured, 'Goodnight, Mary Jean. You will tell me if Ewan wakes, won't you?'

Betty got up wearily from her seat and lifted the package from the table with a frown.

'An admirer's been leaving presents, have they, Betty?'

The housekeeper's tired face creased into a rueful smile. 'Dear me, no . . . "Mony's the day, but noo it's nicht", as the saying goes . . .' She shook her head in bafflement. 'I can't think for the life o' me what this can be.'

'Well, there's only one way of finding out.'

'You're right there.' Betty ripped open the brown paper, then paused, giving an embarrassed, 'Oh . . .' as she gazed down at the contents of the parcel. In her hands she held an oval ebony frame containing the silhouette of what looked like a remarkably pretty young woman.

'May I see?' Kate asked, stretching out her hand.

Betty rather reluctantly gave over the picture.

The young woman was in profile and had fine regular features and a mass of ringlets piled on top of her head. Her shoulders were bare and, by the looks of her, she was from a family of substance. 'She's very pretty,' Kate said, studying the likeness. 'Anyone I know?'

There was a short pause then, avoiding Kate's eyes, Betty said quietly, 'It's Davey's wife, Marie-Louise.' There was a long silence. 'She promised to have one done for me before they went back to France.'

Davey's wife . . . This was Davey's wife . . . Kate gazed down in a mixture of fascination and horror at the silhouette of the young woman now married to the man she loved, and she tried to imagine that black paper profile and those pert, regular features in flesh and blood. She attempted a faint smile but could feel her throat closing as she asked as lightly as possible, 'What colour is her hair?'

'Fair,' Betty said. 'She's as fair as you are dark. And she's a wee bit smaller than you in height, and has the bonniest smile you can imagine. Her English is not so good, mind, but Davey has been learning French, so between them they manage.'

Kate continued to stare at the picture, then when the silence became too oppressive she managed, 'I'm sure she's making him a good wife.'

'Oh yes,' Betty was quick to agree. 'You have nothing to worry about on that score. She worships the very ground he walks on.'

'I'm very happy for them.'

The initial embarrassment over, and sensing Kate had taken it well, Betty went on to explain how they were now spending their time between Paris, London and Dundee, working for the cause of electoral reform and the great people's revolution they knew would come one day.

'Marie-Louise's father is a very prominent man in French revolutionary circles,' Betty informed Kate proudly. 'He produces a regular pamphlet on the reform movement in Europe, and has important folk writing for him from Prussia, Italy and all over the place. Clever folk too – politicians and university professors and the like. The movement's not all students and young folk. She tells me he believes Davey will prove a worthy successor when he himself gets too old to carry on.'

'I'm sure he will,' Kate replied, trying hard to keep her smile intact. Why did it hurt so much to know he was so happy? Why, despite all her good intentions, was she feeling an almost insane jealousy of this young woman, with her bunches of ringlets and her clever father, who adored Davey? 'I'm really very happy for him,' she found herself repeating rather too formally. 'He seems to have found a wife – and father-in-law – perfectly in keeping with his needs. He's obviously perfectly at home in the revolutionary movement.'

'Aye, my Davey's turned out to be his father's son all right,' Betty replied wistfully. 'If only Jock were still here to see the mark the lad's making for himself, it's a proud man he would be. When I think of the chances the likes of your husband's son, Willie, and the other toffs' sons got when they were young: the very best schooling available they had, and where did it get them? Most of them turned into real disappointments, sowing their wild oats all over the town, and then just walking into the family businesses.'

Betty shook her head as she sat back down to finish the mending. 'My Davey had to make do with leaving school at twelve, but he's spent every spare minute since then trying to improve himself. Marie-Louise tells me he regularly has pieces of his writings published in journals here and in France and she even brought one or two to show me.'

She snapped a thread with her teeth and added proudly, 'Naturally, Davey being what he is, he'd never boast about such things himself. But it seems he's really going far in reform circles these days. Making quite a name for himself into the bargain.'

Kate had been standing by the table gazing down at the silhouette as Betty spoke. 'Well, as long as his endeavours don't end up with him back in jail,' she said, sitting back down on the rocking chair and picking up Keiller, the marmalade-coloured cat. She immediately regretted the remark as Betty's face fell.

'Aye, there's always the risk o' that, and don't think I haven't reminded him. But he says he's older now and wiser – like we all are, I suppose.'

Kate gave a wry smile as she stroked the animal on her lap. If only that were true, she thought. But one thing was for certain, there would be even less use mooning over Davey Lorimer from now on. He was not only a married man, but a very happy and successful one by the sound of it.

And so, with her mind concentrated firmly on her husband and growing son, Kate determined to make as great a success as possible of running both the Falconer home, and in finding out as much as she could about the operating of the business. One day, God willing, Ewan would inherit these mills. With Willie gone, Augustus needed someone to turn to and discuss all his plans for the future with. And plans there were: great plans, for this city was going places, and the 'golden fleece', as they called the flax, was the reason for it. The mills could now hardly keep up with the demand, and ships were sailing with every tide, exporting the spun cloth all over the world. They said there was more money being made here than in any other city in the Empire.

There were now well over thirty flax-spinning mills at work in Dundee, and four of those were owned by the Falconer family. Competition was rife, and all the other mill-owning families such as the Gilroys, the Coxes, the Baxters and the like were vying with each other to have the healthiest trade balance at the end of the year.

'They may try but I'm damned if they'll succeed,' Augustus told Kate, and she had little cause to doubt him. Anyway, there was more than enough money being made to go round. The total value of linens exported from the city that year was one and a half million pounds, accounting for fifty million yards of linen, nearly four million yards of sail-cloth, and four million yards of sacking.

'There's no other place in the world can hold a candle to Bonnie Dundee,' Augustus would proudly declare. And it was true, for although Barnsley in England and Belfast in Ireland were the city's two main rivals in the linen trade, the convenience of Dundee's docks for importing raw flax from the Baltic provinces and then exporting the finished products around the world gave it a great advantage over its competitors.

The year of 1832 saw a brand-new dock built to cope with the expansion in trade. It was named the Earl Grey in honour of the prime minister, to mark his success in passing the Great Reform Act. The foundation stone was laid by Lord Kinnaird, and the names of Mr and Mrs

Augustus Falconer were well up on the official guest list for the occasion.

'This new dock will aid our mills more than anything else,' Augustus told his wife as they stood proudly alongside the other dignitaries on the quayside and looked up at the forests of masts that stretched as far as the eye could see. 'Take heed, Kate lass, for the ships that sail to and from here all over the world will bring prosperity to us and our people beyond our wildest dreams.'

Kate did not doubt his words as she stood looking out beyond the mouth of the river to the wide expanse of the German Ocean. She raised a kid-gloved hand to shield her eyes from the rays of the sun that sparkled like sequins on the fast-running waters of the estuary beyond.

She had on the very latest in fashion, with her burgundy velvet outdoor dress sporting the new gigot sleeves, and a fine heather-mixture tweed mantelet on top, to ward off the brisk breeze that always affected this area of the shore. To the world at large she knew she must look every inch the 'perfect picture' that Augustus had claimed her to be before they left the house, but in her heart she knew differently.

The seagulls that soared and swooped above her still produced that same tingle in the blood that she had known as a child, and, despite the fashionable clothes, in her heart she was still that small, ill-clad, barefoot girl who had craned her neck from that bedroom window on the Hawk-hill to catch a glimpse of the great ships that weighed anchor in these waters. The pain of hunger and a fervent longing to escape the poverty had given her the courage to break those invisible prison bars. She had made a calculated decision in marrying for money, but now, surrounded by the trappings of wealth, she felt no shame. She had been determined that no child of hers would ever suffer as she had done.

She smiled quietly to herself as she stood there on the quayside with her husband at her side, for she knew there was little fear of that. Ewan had not only been born in entirely different circumstances, he had been born into a new era. Her own birth had been in the middle of the wars with Old Boney, but now Napoleon, the great French leader, was dead, and the poverty that followed his defeat at Waterloo was a thing of the past. Now you could almost smell the scent of prosperity in the air; change was in the wind that blew in from the sea and played havoc with the feathers of the ladies' bonnets as they stood here witnessing this great event in the city's history. These were exciting times and no mistake. There was a new vigour and energy in the very air they breathed, for changes were taking place at all levels of society. The British Empire itself was expanding, opening up all sorts of possibilities for those willing to take them.

Even proposals once regarded as grave threats by mill-owners such as Augustus were now being seen as opportunities for growth. As he explained to Kate, the impending and much talked about Factory Act – which would undoubtedly lessen the production of yarns due to the shorter hours being worked – was the ideal catalyst for the building of even more factories to make up for the loss of production caused by shorter hours.

He had not always been so positive, however, for earlier that year his reaction to the call for such legislation had been very different. The reason for Davey's return to Dundee during the winter of 1831–32 had been to help organize a petition, later presented to Parliament, which demanded that the hours worked in the country's mills be drastically reduced. The twelve-and-a-half-hour day severely overtaxed the strength of the workers and – so the reformers maintained – the consequent mental and physical deterioration of the younger generation amounted to a national evil that could only be laid at the mill-owners' door.

'A damned liberty!' Augustus had declared on reading the first details in the local newspaper. 'They'll be blaming the bad weather on us next! How dare they make such claims? If it wasn't for the likes of us, most of the population would be out of work. Starving on the street corners they'd be, by the thousand! Mental and physical deterioration indeed! If it wasn't for our mills they'd be starving to death, the lot o' them! Shameless scum that bites the hand that feeds them, that's what they are. And I see that young bugger's name features again as one of the main agitators! There will not be a Lorimer in this village of Broughty Ferry who isn't hanging his head in shame this day!' He grimaced at the thought of all those hardworking God-fearing fisherfolk who had spawned such a discredit to the family name. 'I've no doubt our very housekeeper, good decent Betty herself, would blush with shame at having such a relative if she read this vile rubbish! Here, take a look for yourself!'

With a grunt of disgust, he had handed the paper over to Kate, who could feel herself colouring at the sight of Davey's name amongst those who had drafted and presented the petition to the House of Commons in London.

'I'll not embarrass you by asking you outright, but that's that old pal o' yours, the young devil I helped out of jail, if I'm not mistaken,' Augustus continued in vexation. 'Typical, that is. You give them a hand up when they're down, and what do they do? Bite the bloody thing off, that's what! Stab you in the back once they're on their feet again. He'd better damned well keep out o' my sight, I can tell you, or I'll have him hung from the top o' that new stack o' ours on the Lochee Road when it's finished.'

The new chimney stack, the tallest in the city, was going to be Augustus's pride and joy. Two hundred and eighty feet high and made of one million bricks, it would soar away above its neighbours and would be a symbol of Falconer pride and achievement for all to see. 'It will dominate this city,' he had told his wife. 'There's not a man, woman or child who will be able to ignore it. Far higher than the Old Kirk steeple it will be when it's finished.'

'So you'll be nearer to God than the Kirk and all its Elders, will you?' Kate had teased, and he had had the good grace to blush.

It was later that same year, only a few weeks after attending the opening ceremony of the Earl Grey Dock, that the invitations went out to join in the celebrations at the laying of the last stone of the Falcon Stack, the huge brick edifice that now soared into the heavens over the latest Falcon Mill.

The guest list contained the names of everyone who mattered in both the town and the surrounding county. It was important to Augustus that the laying of each new milestone in the family's business fortunes was witnessed by as many of his friends and competitors as possible. There was a procession of carriages over half a mile long leading up to the Dens Road, where the new factory was sited, and hundreds of townsfolk came by foot to witness the inauguration of what had already become a much talked about city landmark.

Kate cheered as loudly as the rest of the crowd and distinguished guests as the workers threw their bonnets in the air at the climax of the ceremony of 'drinking the riggin' stane'. This ritual had been carried out at the opening of all Augustus's mills, and it involved raising a glass of whisky up on a pulley to be drunk by the mason who had the honour of laying the last brick.

This time, however, things did not go according to plan. It had been raining all morning, only easing up less than an hour before the ceremony was due to begin and, as the young man perched precariously on the very top of the chimney stack reached out to take the glass, his foot slipped on the wet masonry. The scream that left his lips could be heard by everyone in the crowd, and they watched in horror as, arms and legs spreadeagled, he fell through the air, two hundred and eighty feet to his death.

Stunned, Kate could only cling to Augustus's arm as a rush of people ran to help him.

'If he's dead it'll be a bad omen for the mill, all right,' a voice cried out from somewhere in the crowd.

Kate clung even more tightly to her husband. No one could survive a fall like that.

A local doctor pronounced the unfortunate man dead less than five minutes later.

Kate shivered as the news reached her, and a cold feeling welled in the pit of her stomach.

There could be no denying the tragic death of the young man put a considerable dampener on the rest of the proceedings. But it was decided to go ahead with the grand reception hosted by Augustus and Kate at Falcon Ridge for members of the town council, and other eminent friends and business rivals.

'It's not going to help that poor lad any if we go hungry,' Augustus reasoned, and everyone agreed with him. In the carriage home, however, he assured Kate that everything would be done to see that the young mason's wife and family did not suffer more than necessary.

'I'll settle a sum of money on them that'll see them all right,' Augustus told her. 'Now let's see that smile back on your face.'

But, try as she might, Kate could not smile. That shouted comment from someone in the crowd kept ringing in her head. A bad omen, the voice had said. A bad omen for the mill meant a bad omen for her family, and that she could not bear.

Their old friend the Reverend Herbert Mooney was amongst the guests at the reception, and he took Kate aside during the drinks party that followed the splendid buffet. Leading her into the quietness of the conservatory off the main drawing room, he asked if there was anything amiss, apart from her upset over the mason's death.

'Why, Bertie, what a question!'

Herbert Mooney shook his grey head. 'Indeed it's not, Kate my dear,' he said. 'In many ways I look upon you as my own daughter, and I pride myself in being able to tell if something's bothering you.'

Kate gave a helpless shrug. 'It's silly really. Ever since this afternoon, I've had the feeling all this can't last. Our family's good fortune can't go on for ever.'

'Nonsense, my dear. That's silly superstition, that's all that is.'

Kate regarded him thoughtfully over the top of her wine glass. 'Is it? Is it really?' She was far from convinced. Something told her that the poor young man's death this afternoon might well be an omen, and that the future might not be quite as bright as both she and Augustus hoped it would be.

Over the next few months, however, she put such gloomy thoughts to the back of her mind and got on with life. As well as the full social calendar they had to contend with, the growing number of Falcon Mills were now taking up all their free time, which was given over to planning even more expansion. 'We must ride the wave, my dear,' Augustus told his wife. 'Life consists of times of opportunity and times of consolidation. We are now in the former and must not let the chances slip.'

She knew he was right, of course. Since Ewan's birth she had made great strides in her grasp of business affairs. She now prided herself in being able to more than hold her own in talking the language of the other mill-owners whenever the opportunity arose at one of the many social occasions they had to attend.

After she had helped Mary Jean put Ewan to bed, long evenings were spent poring over facts and figures, and she was now well acquainted with both the overall production costs of all their factories, and the price of the raw flax down to the latest bale to be offloaded at the new Earl Grey Dock. More and more Augustus would turn to her and enquire as to the cost of this, that or the other, and she would be able to give it off the top of her head, without referring to any accounts ledger. His own human abacus, he called her, and for the Christmas of 1832, he had presented her with her own personal abacus made up of all manner of precious stones as counting beads. It now sat in pride of place on the white marble mantelpiece in the drawing room, mute testimony to a wife who was as able a partner as any man could wish for.

As Kate's confidence continued to grow, she found herself taking a greater interest in the town as a whole, for Dundee had changed out of all recognition over the past few years. Not only were new buildings drastically altering the skyline of the city, but everywhere one went carriages were getting stuck in ruts, or breaking wheels by falling into potholes, for roads were being dug up all over the place. Gas-pipes were being laid in almost every street, with gas-lighting rapidly taking over from candles and oil-lamps in homes and factories alike. Underground sewers were being laid and pipes were now carrying essential clean water supplies from the main wells in the town to homes and businesses throughout the city, although water was still sold in large quantities on the street corners for those, such as Kate's own parents, who could not afford such luxury.

Determined that his own house should be one of the first private homes to benefit from such improvements, Augustus arranged for both gas and water to be laid on shortly after his latest mill at the foot of the Dens Road was opened in the early summer of 1833.

'But there's no need for you to have to stay here and put up with the mess, my dear,' he told his wife over breakfast one morning in early July. 'I've arranged for you to do a week's shopping in Edinburgh while the worst of the work's going on.'

Kate looked up from her boiled egg and raised her eyebrows. 'Really? Is that so, now?' It was typical of Augustus to just suddenly announce such a thing to her. 'And what makes you think I'd care to go?'

'Because I've booked you into the best hotel on Princes

Street and have drawn twenty guineas from the bank for you to spend on some new summer outfits or whatever takes your fancy. But more than that, I'd like you to do a small favour for me while you're there.'

He paused and gave a quiet smile as Kate looked in curiosity across the breakfast table at him. He had been married to his wife long enough to know that she would not be tempted by a mere shopping trip. She was now an integral part of the business, and keen to become even more involved. 'I'm seriously considering opening a mill in Leith,' Augustus told her. 'There's a site I've heard of that's going cheap down by the docks there. Knox's Wharf, they call it. While you're in Edinburgh, I'd like you to take a cab down there and have a good look at it.' He gave a wheezy chuckle as he dabbed his mouth with the napkin. 'I reckon your judgement's as good as any man's, bar my own of course, on something like that.'

Kate was delighted. She had studied the architects' and surveyors' plans on their last two mills long enough to know exactly what was required of a suitable site. 'Augustus, my dear, I'm truly flattered. If you gave me a million pounds I couldn't be more delighted!'

Augustus beamed and reached over to refill his tea-cup. 'I thought such a proposition might just tickle your fancy. And, with a bit of luck on our side, it might well be worth a small fortune before we're finished with it. If not to us, then certainly to young Ewan.'

All his plans were now made with the child in mind. It had come as a great relief to him to discover that Kate was so interested in the business and, more than that, she was damned good at it. He had to be sensible about these things for, no matter how fit he might feel at the moment, he was not as young as he'd like to be. If he had another ten years in the saddle, he'd be doing well. The young lad would need a steady pair of hands on the reins until he was old enough to take over himself, and his mother would be the ideal person. It certainly didn't look as if Willie had any intentions of coming back and lending a hand.

No matter how much he tried to put it to the back of his mind, Willie's continued absence still rankled with the old man. In some ways he was still angry with his elder son for refusing to accept Kate into the family, and he knew that the birth of Ewan would simply have added fuel to the flames of jealousy he knew were at the bottom of it all. But, for all his faults, Willie was still his son and, deep inside, Augustus hoped that one day the rift could be healed. It would mean a great deal in his old age to know that Kate had someone like Willie to lean on when he himself was no longer capable of giving her all the support she might need.

He reached for his pipe and lit it thoughtfully as he looked fondly at his wife sitting on the other side of the breakfast table. She was a grand lass and no mistake. 'Have I ever told you how proud of you I am, Kathleen?' he asked in a quiet voice. 'If I haven't, then it's high time I did, for, as God's my judge, you're the best thing that's ever happened to me.'

Kate rose from the table and came round to where her husband was sitting. She bent down and kissed the bald crown of his head. 'I love you too, Augustus,' she whispered into the wisps of white hair. 'I really do.'

The old man had tears in his eyes as he reached up and took her hand. This was the first time she had ever actually spoken those words to him.

Chapter Sixteen

Kate arrived in Edinburgh two weeks to the day after Augustus first suggested the trip. To her disappointment, it was decided at the very last moment that Ewan and Mary Jean, the nursemaid, should not accompany her. The toddler had been running a slight temperature and Hector Grant, the Falconers' trusted physician, had suggested it might be better if he stay at home. 'You can't be too careful with bairns of this age,' he told the anxious mother. 'But there's absolutely no reason why you shouldn't go. He'll be as right as rain in a day or so.'

So it was decided, but it was a distinctly subdued Kate who kissed her husband and child goodbye from the gates of Falcon Ridge that bright summer morning. 'You might well see me back here in a day or so,' she warned her husband as she brushed her lips against his whiskery cheek. 'If I find I'm missing you both too much, I'll be on the very next coach available after I've done the business in Leith.'

'Away you go and enjoy yourself,' she was told. 'Have some fun spending that money I gave you, and think yourself lucky you're not having to stay on here and put up wi' floorboards up all over the place for a week or so.'

Kate leant out of the carriage window and waved until Augustus and the baby disappeared entirely from view as the horses rounded the corner of Camphill Road and headed for Dundee and the long ride ahead to Edinburgh, the nation's capital.

It was the first time she had been so far from home, and she was glad of the other occupants of the coach for company as it trundled its way over the twenty miles to

Perth, towards the first change of horses and a half-hour stop for refreshment at the Salutation Inn.

With Perth and the Vale of Strathearn behind them, it was on to the village of Kinross on the shores of Loch Leven. 'That's where that poor soul Mary Queen o' Scots was imprisoned,' an elderly gentleman sitting opposite informed her as they passed the fortified island in the middle of the loch. 'It wasna' right for a lassie to lose her head like that, and Lizzie, the English queen her cousin and a'.'

Kate gazed at the grim-looking remains of the fortress with interest, then sat back in her seat with a shiver. If she remembered rightly, Augustus had a relic of the ill-fated queen displayed in his study at Falcon Ridge, but she was ashamed how little she knew of Scotland's history. She was soon to be enlightened, however, for a lively discussion followed on the merits and demerits of the young queen's claim to the throne. Finally, after an entertaining hour or so of tale-telling, there was another change of horses, a bite to eat, then the dubious excitement of crossing the wide expanse of the River Forth at Queensferry, before heading on for the city of Edinburgh itself.

Accommodation had been booked at the King George Hotel on Princes Street. It proved to be an excellent choice, and Kate was delighted with the air of informal elegance as she entered the marble-pillared foyer, with its huge urns filled with the most magnificent displays of summer flowers.

A young boy, in a gold-braided uniform of the same blue as the Scottish saltire that fluttered from a mast above the main door, took her bags up to her rooms while she completed the formalities at the desk.

Feeling quite the lady, she tipped him on her arrival at the two-roomed suite. Then when he had gone she went to the window to feast her eyes on the breathtaking view of the old Castle on top of its great rock.

Such dusky grandeur clothed the height,
Where the huge castle holds its state,
And all the steep slope down,
Whose ridgy back heaves to the sky,
Piled deep and massy, close and high,
Mine own romantic town!

Long evenings spent lying in bed and feasting on the delights of the Reverend Mooney's library by the light of a guttering candle had paid dividends beyond price as the words that Walter Scott put into the mouth of Lord Marmion as he surveyed this very scene came into her head. To her surprise, she found herself with tears in her eyes.

Yes, Edinburgh was a wonderful city and no mistake. With its historic Old Town and Royal Mile leading from the Castle ramparts to Holyrood Palace, and its impressive New Town of fine Georgian terraces and dignified squares designed by their own Robert Adam, she had no doubt it was a match for any capital in the world. Even the awful expanse of middens and swampland in the deep valley between Princes Street and the Castle Hill was now being turned into flower-filled gardens, with shady walks, for the benefit of the townspeople.

Kate hugged herself in delight and anticipation of the week ahead as she turned from the view and leant back against the windowsill and looked around her. It was a comfortable room, with fine furniture in the Chippendale mode which, as well as the grand four-poster bed with its gold damask drapes, included a writing desk by the window and a large comfortable easy chair to relax in.

'You'll have a rare time raking round the shops here,' the porter on the front desk told her when she set off on an exploratory walk after breakfast the next morning. 'The ladies always tell me they've never found materials o' the like that we've got here in the New Toon.'

A walk down the esplanade of shops that fronted this

Georgian part of the city told her he was quite right, and her first two days were taken up admiring and ordering as much fabric as she knew she could possibly need for at least five years. It was not extravagance, she reasoned, merely prudence, for she was not at all sure when she would get such an opportunity again. She also made two purchases that she knew would delight both Ewan and his father; a wooden monkey that did somersaults between two sticks for the former, and a brand-new German meerschaum pipe for the latter. These, along with several other minor finds, she packed into the spare case she had brought with her and was dismayed to find it was already full with only two days of her trip gone.

The third day she resolved to make the short journey to the port of Leith on the Firth of Forth, just a few miles north of the city.

'Even the weather's smiling on ye,' Jamie, the porter, told her as he hailed her a cab on the morning in question. 'It's no' often we see three days o' sun in a row.'

Kate beamed him a smile and pressed a silver three-penny bit into his hand as the two-seater cabriolet rolled up. 'I have a feeling Edinburgh likes me,' she laughed. 'And I certainly like it!'

The few miles to Leith seemed to be downhill most of the way and on their arrival at the busy seaport the coachman had little trouble finding the proposed site for the next Falconer Mill, for Knox's Wharf was a well-known landmark in the town. It had once contained several large warehouses, but these had recently been destroyed by fire and the site had been cleared for sale.

Kate got out of the cab in the vicinity of the old wharf and instructed the coachman to pick her up from the same spot in two hours' time. 'I think that should give me just about long enough to complete my business.'

The cabbie had tipped his hat and regarded her curiously before driving off. It was not a usual occurrence to transport single ladies on business to this part of the town, but these were changing times indeed.

It took Kate less than ten minutes to find the office building she wanted. It was a large three-storey property by the side of the main road, with several shining brass plaques outside the front door. She saw the one she wanted immediately, and noted the office was on the second floor.

It was with some trepidation that she pushed open the main door and climbed the stairs to call on a certain Mr Walter MacDougal, a surveyor and property investor in the area, but, within minutes of sitting down in his bright office overlooking the docks, she knew she had found a friend she could trust. The elderly man, with the round cherubic face and *pince-nez* spectacles perched on the end of his stubby nose, was delighted to meet her and was a mine of information. He immediately provided her with a refreshing cup of tea and they spent a profitable hour discussing the financial aspects of the proposal before he suggested they take a walk down to the harbour area to see the land itself.

On the way he admitted to her that he had never discussed business with a lady before, but that he was remarkably taken by her grasp of the essentials. 'You'd make a damned fine employer, if you don't mind me saying so, Mistress Falconer, ma'm.'

Kate did not mind at all. She was thoroughly enjoying her new-found responsibility, and enjoyed it all the more once they got to the proposed site. It was a large grassy piece of wasteland, with almost all trace of the former buildings gone. It was just under two acres in area and, most importantly, had direct access to the docks.

'Of course it'll need all the services such as water laid on,' Kate remarked, as they paced the perimeter together. 'But that should not pose too much of a problem. I take it you already have such things provided in your own building, Mr MacDougal?'

The surveyor looked distinctly abashed. There were not even plans laid for such luxuries. 'Not yet, I'm ashamed to say, ma'm. But we're working on it.'

'Mmm . . .' His answer did not surprise Kate as she paused to look around her with a keen eye. 'It seems we're well ahead of you in Dundee in some areas. But very important areas they are. Where would the nearest underground water- and gas-pipes be, may I ask?'

Walter MacDougal looked even more uncomfortable as he scratched his bewhiskered chin and pondered on the question. 'That I can't rightly say at the moment, but I have no doubt I can find out for you.'

'How soon?' She tapped the ground in frustration with the tip of her parasol. 'Time is money in business, as you well know; you don't need me to tell you that the proximity or otherwise of such essentials will directly affect whatever price, if any, we are prepared to offer.'

'Quite so. Quite so.' The elderly surveyor was now distinctly ruffled, but his admiration for the young woman's ability to handle herself in a man's world was increasing by the minute. 'I can have the details over to your hotel by first thing tomorrow morning,' he said in an attempt to regain lost ground. 'Aye, and more information besides that may be of use to you.'

'That's extremely civil of you, sir,' Kate said, extending her hand to bring the meeting to an end.

'Would you care to accompany me back to my office to partake of some more refreshment?'

Kate smiled but shook her head. 'That's very kind of you, I'm sure, but I'd rather like to have a last wee walk around myself to get the feel of the place before I head back for Edinburgh.'

'Very sensible, if I may say so, ma'm.' The surveyor doffed his hat. 'It's been a real pleasure to make your acquaintance. I sincerely hope we'll meet again and might be able to do business on the matter.'

'So do I, sir. So do I.'

It was with a warm, almost smug feeling that Kate took her leave of the old man and turned in the direction of the docks. She knew she had handled the whole thing in a way that would have made Augustus proud of her. And now there was more work to do before the coachman returned. It was important that she acquaint herself with as much of the area as possible so she could give a full report to Augustus. It was also of prime importance to take a proper look at the docks themselves, to compare their facilities with the brand-new ones of her hometown.

After a good twenty minutes walking the length and breadth of the waterfront, it was obvious that Dundee was much better provided for, but the facilities here seemed more than adequate. One thing was for certain, there was plenty of on- and offloading going on this morning, of both goods and passengers alike.

Teams of overworked dray horses stood patiently by on the cobbled quayside, whilst all around them was a frenzy of activity. Barrels of salted fish were being rolled up the gangplank of one ship, while at the next berth bales of what looked remarkably like linen were being hoisted aboard.

Ahead of her she could see what appeared to be a newly berthed ship disembarking a human cargo on to the quayside. A straggle of passengers came wearily down the gangplank. Most seemed to be businessmen, who would no doubt be heading straight on into Edinburgh, and Kate mentally breathed a sigh of relief that she had already booked her cab for the return journey. The row of public carriages that stood waiting at their stance in front of one of the dockside taverns would be full within minutes by the looks of it.

There were one or two families standing disconsolately around at the foot of the gangplank, waiting for their luggage to be offloaded, and Kate's heart immediately went out to them as small children cried and fretted around their mothers' skirts. Each and every one looked tired and dishevelled and more than relieved to be back on dry land.

As she approached the foot of the gangplank, a large travelling chest was being carried down by two hefty seamen and she quickly moved out of the way. The younger of the two called out, "Morning to you, Miss!' and Kate smiled back in return. It was some time since she had been referred to as Miss. She was rarely out without Augustus and the baby these days, and the look of approval in the sailors' eyes made her smile contentedly to herself as she walked briskly back in the direction of Knox's Wharf.

'Hey there!'

At first she did not stop. It seemed like the young man was becoming much too familiar.

'Hey! Wait!'

This time the urgency in the masculine voice made her pause and turn. But to her surprise, the heavy chest had been deposited on the quayside, and the two sailors were nowhere to be seen.

'Kate! Hey, Katie!'

This time the sound of her name being shouted made her look up to the gangplank itself and she let out a gasp. A young bearded man with a jaunty fisherman's cap on his brown curly hair and carrying a knapsack over his left shoulder was running down the wooden boards towards her.

'Kate!' he called out. 'Kate, is that really you?'

She stood gazing in astonishment at the approaching figure.

Then suddenly he was in front of her and they were staring at each other in disbelief.

'Kate, I don't believe it!'

Before she had time to assure him it really was her, he had grabbed her, lifting her at least two feet off the ground, and was whirling her round and round, so that her little feathered hat took flight and she had to put out a hand to catch it as she laughingly begged him to stop.

'Davey! Please! I'm a respectable married woman, remember!'

'And I'm a respectable married man,' he replied, letting her down on to the cobbles with a bump, to stand there grinning at her. 'What does that matter? . . . God, Kate, it's good to see you!'

'It – it's good to see you too,' she found herself assuring him as she took in the tanned face and familiar boyish grin. The blue eyes that smiled down into hers had that same twinkle that made her heart turn over. It really was him. She could scarcely believe it. 'You've just come off that boat, I presume?'

'You presume right,' he said. 'Newly docked she is. Just arrived from London.'

'You – you've come up from London?' It was hard to keep track of him these days.

'Aye. I've a few days' business in Scotland before I head back to Paris. I spend most of my time there these days.'

'My and it's a busy and exciting life you lead, to be sure.' She tried hard to keep her voice light, but it was difficult.

'Yes,' he agreed cheerfully. 'You're right there. But I hear that you're not doing so badly yourself. Old Augustus has been expanding his empire all over Bonnie Dundee, so I hear. Next he'll be setting his sights as far as the banks of the Forth, I'll wager. Are you down here to meet someone?'

'No . . . I – I'm here on business.'

'Well, well . . . You're not really considering hoisting that damned bird over a mill door hereabouts, are you?'

Kate bridled momentarily. 'And what if we are?'

He let out a low whistle and scratched the mop of curly hair beneath the cap. 'Well, I'll be blowed! The Falconer empire is in danger of stretching from the Tay to the Forth.'

He took hold of her arm and asked, 'Are you staying in Leith?'

'No, I'm lodging on Princes Street, up in Edinburgh.' She glanced behind her in the direction she had come from. 'In fact, my cab should be back for me any minute.'

'Will Augustus be in it?'

'No, I'm here on my own for a few days.'

There was silence for several seconds.

'Would it be out of order if I begged a lift?' Davey nodded in the direction of the cab stance. 'By the looks of it, they're all taken already, and it could be ages before a free one turns up.'

'Well, I . . .' Then common sense prevailed. They were old friends, and now two perfectly respectable married people after all. 'No, no, of course not. Why wait around here and then have to pay for transport when I have a spare place in my cab?'

'Why indeed?'

'I'm at the George on Princes Street,' she told him, as they sat side by side in the back of the cab a few minutes later. 'Where are you staying?'

Davey shrugged as he settled back in his seat. 'Oh, I've several folk I can call on to put me up for the time I'm here. Don't you worry about me.'

He turned towards her and his eyes were quizzical in a good-humoured sort of way as they studied her face. 'You're looking well, Kate,' he said quietly. 'Real bonnie these days. Marriage must agree with you.'

'And why shouldn't it?' she retorted, much more indignantly than she intended. 'Augustus is a fine man and treats me well.'

Davey absorbed her words, then surprised her with, 'Do you love him?'

'I'm sure that's no business of yours!'

'Maybe not, but I'd like to know all the same.'

He was looking at her intently as he spoke, and Kate could feel her cheeks begin to burn. 'Love?' she replied, with a forced laugh. 'And just what is this love exactly?'

'Love is when you feel so much a part of the other

person they could almost be your own flesh and blood. It's when your heart beats faster just thinking about them. It's wanting the very best for that person even when they've done you the ultimate hurt by marrying someone else. That's what love is . . . To me anyway.'

His voice was low and intense, and as his lips uttered the last three sentences Kate could feel the words turn a knife in her heart. She averted her face and stared out of the cab window as he continued, 'Can you imagine what that could be like, Kate? Can you imagine the pain of loving someone and hearing they had married someone else? You never even had the decency to tell me. I had to hear it from somebody else – when it was already too late.'

She bit her lip but remained silent as he took hold of her arm. 'Why, Kate, why?'

She turned towards him and there were tears in her eyes. 'I did what I had to do, Davey,' she found herself saying. 'I can't expect you to understand.'

'But you never even told me. I had to hear it from someone else – from my own mother.' He shook his head at the memory. That had been the worst part. They had been far too close for too long for that to happen. 'Why couldn't you have warned me? Why did it have to be like that?'

Kate stared fixedly out of the window. 'Because you might have persuaded me not to,' she answered truthfully. 'And I couldn't have borne that.'

She turned towards him. His face was only inches from hers. His boyish features were now those of a grown man; only the unruly brown curls and the glint in his eye remained in evidence of the Wee Davey she had once known and loved. He was older now, and wiser; they both were, but both knew they were the same people beneath the veneer of adult respectability. 'You should know,' she continued softly. 'You of all people should have understood why I did it. You too knew what it was like to be so poor your whole childhood was one long dream of escape . . . I escaped, Davey. I escaped by marrying Augustus. Can you really blame me for that?'

'"*Être pauvre sans être libre, c'est le pire état où l'homme puisse tomber*,"' he replied softly, in the language of his new land. 'Jean Jacques Rousseau. "To be poor without being free is the deepest pit into which man can fall" . . . You chose to free yourself, whilst I chose to devote my life to freeing others. They are two different choices, but both equally valid.'

'You make me sound very selfish and yourself like some sort of saint.'

He grinned. 'You never did like me to have the last word, did you, Katie girl?'

They sat in silence for the rest of the journey. There was nothing left to say, because both knew there was everything to say; but in saying that everything, the private worlds they had built could be brought tumbling down around them.

As the cab pulled up at the door of the King George Hotel, Davey took hold of her arm. 'May I come in, Kate?' he asked in a quiet voice. 'We can't part like this, perhaps never to see each other again.'

She was trembling inside, but found the strength to shake her head. 'I think not, Davey lad,' she told him. 'We have loved too much and too long for that. It is better that our hellos and goodbyes be said in public.'

She got out of the cab and held out her hand to be shaken. No words were spoken as, instead, he raised it to press her fingers to his lips; then he turned and was gone, a lone figure striding down Princes Street, the sound of his booted feet resounding in her head long after he had turned the first corner into Charlotte Square.

'You had a good morning, I trust, ma'm?' the doorman enquired with his customary smile as she entered the foyer of the hotel.

But Kate neither heard nor saw him as she swept past and rushed on up the wide curve of the staircase to her room.

Once inside, she flung herself on the bed and let out a

long groan like an animal in pain. She rolled on to her back and stared up at the ceiling. She had sent him away, perhaps for ever. She should feel good: the virtuous wife. She could almost hear her old friend Herbert Mooney applauding from the sidelines. But she did not feel good or virtuous. She merely felt a great aching void in her being. He might be gone out of her life, but she knew she would carry him with her always, and the weight on her heart and soul was almost too much to bear.

Chapter Seventeen

Kate ate alone that night in the corner of the dining room on the first floor, with its magnificent view of the Castle and the old narrow stone houses of the Royal Mile. The room itself was furnished with the classic simplicity of the Georgian era, with an enormous gilt mirror above the mantelpiece which reflected the glittering flames of the crystal chandelier hanging from the ceiling in the centre of the room. A large equestrian tapestry of King George, the country's first Hanoverian monarch, hung on the wall opposite the window, whilst the other walls were adorned with large sombre oil paintings of various Edinburgh worthies, such as the philosopher David Hume, and a splendid, newly commissioned portrait of the recently deceased and much-lamented novelist Sir Walter Scott.

There was only a handful of other diners present, mainly respectable married couples considerably older than herself, and one or two city gents obviously in the capital to do business. One particular rather stout, frock-coated gentleman at the next table, who Kate decided had already had perhaps one drink too many with his meal, called for a bottle of the hotel's best vintage malt to be brought and placed at the disposal of all the guests present.

'In honour of our beloved brother – alas no longer with us – dear auld Walter Scott himself!' he declared, rising unsteadily to his feet and lifting his glass high to bow his head in the direction of the bard's portrait.

'Here's a bottle and an honest friend
What wad ye wish for mair, man?

> Wha kens, before his life may end,
> What his share may be o' care, man?

'That's Robbie Burns, but I'm sure Sir Walter wouldna mind,' the generous provider of the Scotch announced to all and sundry as the waiter appeared with the ordered bottle and set it on the table in front of him. 'And in honour of both our illustrious bards, I now take great pleasure in bestowing a glass of the water of life on all my friends gathered here before I retire to my room!'

His eyes fell on Kate who was carefully avoiding his glance by studying the menu. Self-conscious about dining alone and perhaps falling prey to any over-friendly single gentleman, she was already becoming quite adept at making her desire for privacy known in the most polite but firm manner. She had been careful to take a book with her to concentrate on between courses and a leather-bound copy of Sir Walter Scott's *Waverley*, borrowed from the large break-front bookcase in the guests' drawing room lay comfortingly on the table beside her. She had read the novel several times before as part of her self-education whilst with the Reverend Mooney, but found delving into the pages once more was akin to revisiting old friends.

Unable to catch her eye, to her great relief the gentleman with the whisky sat down to enjoy his own main course as hers was being served, and after a tasty dinner of lamb chops and new potatoes, followed by apple Charlotte, she allowed herself the indulgence of a small dram of his specially ordered malt whisky.

> 'Go fetch to me a pint o'
>   wine,
> An' fill it in a silver tassie,
> That I may drink before I go
> A service to my bonnie lassie!'

209

Kate blushed as the gentleman at the next table lifted his glass to touch hers after pouring the drink. 'Burns again, I wit,' she smiled.

'True, dear lady, and very apt, if I may say so! May your stay in "Auld Reekie", our bonnie capital city, be long, and the time between now and your return be short!'

Kate smiled graciously as she took her first sip of the pale amber spirit to please him, and he moved on, bottle aloft, to the next table.

There was a jolly festive air to the dining room now, owing much to the wine and whisky that had been flowing throughout the meal, but she had no wish to remain longer than necessary. Two glasses of wine and now the whisky were making her feel distinctly maudlin and bringing thoughts of Davey back to the forefront of her mind. She had deliberately banished the memory of the afternoon's meeting from her consciousness but now, as she became more tired and thoughtful and the drink began to take effect, it was not so easy to remain in control of her emotions.

By the time she had drained the last drop of spirit from her glass, it was with a distinctly heavy heart that she bade the remaining diners goodnight and took her leave to climb the stairs to her room. She intended writing a long letter to Augustus telling him of the visit to Knox's Wharf. The main event of the day, on which her mind was now well and truly fixed, she would keep strictly to herself.

She had previously ordered a hot hipbath to be prepared, and a bottle of white wine to be sent up shortly afterwards with the girl who came to remove the bathwater. The soak in the warm water was just what she needed to help her relax, and in the space of half an hour she had bathed and changed into her dressing robe and slippers and was seated, sipping the wine, at the small desk by the window as she attempted to turn her mind to composing the letter to her husband.

It was not going to be an easy task, for even thinking of

Augustus and home she found painful after her meeting with Davey. He had stirred up far too many old emotions for her to be happy about concentrating her mind completely on the affairs of the Falconer family once more. Dundee seemed a million miles away. All she was aware of was that she was in Edinburgh and so was the man she loved, but they were not together. They could never be together, for both were now married to other people.

She sighed deeply as she picked up her pen and dipped it in the inkwell. Beside her lay a piece of paper with the dimensions of all the various departments required in the proposed mill. These had to be compared against the space available, plus the cost of the site.

Her eyes scanned the list. 'Warehouse department, hackling department, flax-preparing department, flax-spinning department, tow-preparing department, tow-spinning department, reeling department . . .'

She had got no further when a knock at the door made her turn round in irritation. 'What is it?' she called. She had deliberately told the maid she wanted no further disturbance.

When there was no reply she got up from the chair and threw open the door, ready to complain vehemently at this blatant ignoring of her instructions. Then her hand flew to her mouth before a word could be uttered.

'Hello, Kate.'

He did not wait for an invitation, but strode past her into the room and stood waiting for her to close the door.

'What are you doing here?' she gasped, as the door clicked shut behind her.

They stood looking at one another.

His face appeared even more tanned in the lamplight. 'Why do you think I'm here?' he asked in a quiet voice. 'I couldn't say goodbye, Kate . . . Not like that.'

'Oh, God!'

She walked past him to the window and stood gazing out at the blaze of red sky behind the Castle rock. The sun was going down in all its crimson glory, against the most spectacular backdrop of any city on earth, yet she was unaware of anything but the presence of the man standing behind her. 'You shouldn't have come,' she whispered. 'You know you shouldn't have come.'

'Do you really want me to go?' His voice was low, with a husky intensity to it that made it barely recognizable as he took a step towards her. 'If you really want me to go, I will.'

There was a long silence, filled only with the ticking of the small carriage-clock on the mantelpiece.

Kate's fingers gripped the edges of the windowsill. She was sure he could hear her heart beating.

'I'll turn round and disappear out of your life right now if that's what you want . . . Is that what you want, Kate? Is that what you really want?'

She threw back her head and gave a soft groan from deep in her throat. Why was he torturing her like this? She had not asked him to come and yet now he was here she could not bear him to go. She remained silent, staring out of the window into the darkening sky as burning emotion fought with the cold sanity of reason within her.

He took her silence to be the rejection he was half expecting, and answered for her. 'I'm sorry,' he said, 'it was stupid of me. I shouldn't have come.'

He turned on his heel and, as he made for the door, Kate whirled round, her face distorted with the anguish she felt inside. 'No, don't! . . .Wait!' She made a despairing gesture with her hands. 'Oh God, Davey, help me!'

He stood with his hand on the doorknob. 'I can't help you, Kate, for I can't help myself,' he answered wearily. 'God only knows why I came up here like this tonight.' Then he gave a sheepish half-smile at such a charade. 'I'm also a liar, for you know as well as I do why I came. I came because, God help us, we love each other, and that's the truth of it.' He could not lie. Not to her. Not at a time like this.

'But you're a married man yourself now,' she reminded him, her voice breaking. 'Do you love her — that girl, Marie-Louise?' She could barely bring herself to speak the name.

He thought for a moment, then shrugged his shoulders in a helpless motion indicative of the confusion he himself felt about the situation. 'Aye, you could say I love her. But not the way I love you — never that.'

He took a step towards her, then paused, unsure of what he should either do or say next. She herself was making it no easier, for she had made no move and was still standing with her back pressed hard against the windowsill.

'I'm going back to France soon, Kate. Perhaps for ever. My wife's father, he's not a well man. If he dies then I'll have to take over his work. I may never be back in Scotland. I may never see you again.'

His words, so quietly spoken, appalled her. 'No,' she whispered. 'No, I couldn't bear that.'

Their eyes held. 'That's why I came,' he said huskily. 'For I couldn't bear it either.'

Then she was in his arms and was clinging to him, as if to assure herself that, for now at least, for this one precious moment in time, he was really here, they were together at last. 'I'm glad you came,' she told him, her face pressed against the soft wool cloth of his jacket. 'Oh Davey, I'm so glad you came.'

'Kate . . . My Kate . . .'

She did not object as his lips found hers. She was not kissing a stranger. His body, his taste, his smell were as familiar to her as her own. As their kisses became stronger and more urgent she found herself crying, whether from happiness or despair she could not be sure. And as he carried her to the bed, she buried her head in his shoulder and whispered his name over and over as if to convince herself it was really him.

No more questions or answers were needed as they made love long into the night, until, finally exhausted, they fell asleep in each other's arms. When they awoke, the first fingers of dawn were piercing the night sky above the Castle.

Kate opened her eyes to find him looking down at her. She reached up and gently touched his lips. 'I love you, Wee Davey,' she whispered.

'And I love you.'

As they made love once more, silently and tenderly on the crumpled sheet of the bed, there was an almost quiet desperation about it. Neither wanted it to end, but end it must, and soon, and both knew it.

When it was over, and Kate lay resting with her head in the hollow of his shoulder, Davey uttered the words she was dreading to hear.

'If you don't want me to go back, I'll stay,' he told her. 'I'll bide here in Scotland with you, if you say you want me to.'

The words whirled in her head. What was he telling her? What exactly was he saying?

'But if I bide, then you must be with me, Katie. You must promise me that. You must leave him and come to me.'

Her heart stopped. He was asking her to leave Augustus and live with him. He would not return to his wife in Paris if she would live with him. 'But – but your work,' she whispered back. 'What about your work?'

'There's plenty of the same here in Scotland,' he told her. 'Freedom for the working man will be hard won, whether here or in France. I'll not be short of things to do.'

She moved on to her side to face him, her eyes taking in every feature of the face she loved so well. How many times had she lain in bed beside her husband and wished with all her heart for a moment such as this? Sometimes the ache in her had been so hard to bear she had even groaned out loud and had to make some excuse to Augustus for the great sadness welling within her. But now, as she lay there next to the man she loved, she was shaking her head. 'I have a child, Davey,' she heard herself telling him. 'I have a son who needs me and needs his father too.'

'I should have been that bairn's father, Kate.' The words were spoken harshly, through gritted teeth, for her second great betrayal of him had been in having a Falconer child. 'Your son should have been mine.'

'Please, Davey . . .' She could not bear him to spoil the moment with recriminations. They were both too aware of the hurt that had occurred. 'Let's just accept the past,' she implored him. 'What's done is done. I'm not proud of it, but there's nothing we can do to change it.'

'But we can change the future. If you come away with me, Kate, we can change that.'

She shook her head in despair. If only life were so simple. 'I can't do that, Davey,' she told him. 'I could never leave my son, and I could never take Ewan from his birthright. To deny him that would be to go against all that I have fought for in this life.'

'And what of love, Kate? Would you never fight for love, only for money?'

'That's cruel, Davey . . . That's so cruel.' Life was always black and white with him. But it wasn't like that at all; it was all different shades of grey. She saw things differently now. She had grown up, and hoped that he had too. This was not the time to torture each other with recriminations about the past. 'This is no time to be glib, to hurt each other with clever jibes. Life is not so simple. You must see that.'

'But you won't come,' he insisted. 'You say you love me but you won't leave him.'

There were tears in Kate's eyes now as she nodded weakly. 'You're right. I love you but I won't come. I won't leave him because I can't, Davey. Don't you understand? I can't, for my child's sake.'

They could both see the pain in each other's gaze. Slowly he sat up on the bed and looked down at her. She was lovelier than he had ever remembered. During all those nights with Marie-Louise, it was Kate's face he had seen when he closed his eyes. It would always be Kate's face.

He reached out his hand and touched her hair, letting it slip through his fingers before his hand moved down her arm to reach her hand, which he held up before him. His gaze rested on the slim gold band on her third finger. 'It might as well be an iron shackle,' he said bitterly. 'For he has bound you to him with invisible bars of gold that I can never match. I am but a poor man, Kate, and I can offer you nothing but a life of pain and hardship. Maybe you are right to refuse me.'

She wanted to shout out, *'No!'* It would never be right to refuse him. He was the man she loved, the man she had always loved, and would always love. But instead, she clasped his hand to her breast, then kissed it one last time before letting go and turning from him. 'Please go, Davey,' she pleaded. 'Go now, before I beg you to stay.'

She buried her face in the pillow and he stood looking down at her. Neither was making it easy for the other. He could beg her, plead with her once more to change her mind, but his pride would not allow yet one more rejection.

He dressed mechanically, his mind numbed with the thought of never seeing her again. For a moment he almost regretted having come to her last night, but only for a moment, for in his heart he knew this one night of love would last a lifetime in his mind. No matter what life did to him now, he would have this to remember.

He threw one last glance over his shoulder before he left the room, but she had not moved. She was still lying with her back to him, her face buried in the soft white linen of the pillowcase. Only from the gentle heaving of her shoulders could he tell that she was weeping.

His face was set as he opened the door, and the closing click of the lock was like the sound of the prison gates in his mind. The stark finality of it almost had him turning round to fling the door open once more and run to take her in his arms. But it could not be. It would only serve to torture both of them again.

Instead he continued down the stair and raised his hat to the janitor who sat dozing in the large armchair behind the desk in the foyer. He was walking out of this hotel and out of her life. Outside on the road, a stout, well-dressed gentleman, a guest of the hotel, with a whisky bottle in his hand, reeled towards him.

'A very guid nicht to you, sir!' the man declared.

Davey looked right through him. It was far from that. It was the worst night of his life.

Chapter Eighteen

It was four days after Davey's departure that Kate returned home to Broughty Ferry. Her first inclination was to leave Edinburgh immediately and hurry back to the security of her home and family where she could put the whole episode behind her as quickly as possible. But that, she told herself, would be running away from herself. Her love for Davey Lorimer was something she would simply have to learn to live with. She had done so in the past and must do so again in the future.

Had it not been for their chance meeting and what followed, she would have regarded her visit to Edinburgh as a great success. Three days after her first trip to Leith she had held a second meeting with Mr MacDougal and his associates over the proposed purchase of the Knox's Wharf site and, as a consequence, she was now armed with a whole host of facts and figures to present to Augustus when she returned home.

She had also taken the time to acquaint herself with most of the historic buildings in the city, and even summoned up enough energy to tackle the steep walk up the extinct volcano, Arthur's Seat, from where she had the pleasure of witnessing one of the finest panoramas her country had to offer. From the glittering snake of the River Forth, with the green hills of Fife to the north, to the whole of the Old and New Towns of Edinburgh itself, nestling in the bosom of the Pentland Hills, never could a nation be so favoured by a capital city.

As she had stood there with the summer breeze blowing the sorrow of Davey's departure from her mind, she thought once more of that small child craning her neck from that tiny window high on Dundee's Hawkhill and dreaming of a moment such as this. She had come a long way since then, and knew in her heart that, however painful it might be, she had made the right decision. To have contemplated giving it all up to follow Davey would have been folly in the extreme. There were many different types of love in this life, and who was to say which was the greater? What she felt for her husband and son was every bit as real as the feelings she had for Davey Lorimer, and she knew she must now concentrate on what was real in her life, and no longer hanker after what might have been.

The journey back to Dundee seemed long and tedious compared to the outward journey, for it lacked the excitement of the unknown. Her companions in the coach were pleasant, however, and between the towns of Kinross and Perth, things became decidedly more lively on the arrival of a young solicitor's articled clerk with a fine tenor voice. On mentioning his gift, he was persuaded by the others present to entertain them to a sing-song to help alleviate the tedium of the journey. This he consented to and, before departing the coach at Perth, he asked each of his fellow travellers for a request, which he then serenaded them with as the carriage wheels trundled the last few miles through the fertile Vale of Strathearn.

Kate paused for a moment in making her choice, then asked tentatively, 'You wouldn't know Burns's "Ae Fond Kiss" by any chance?'

'Indeed I would, ma'm,' the young man replied. 'And, if I may be so bold, I would venture that never was a finer song written to the cause of lost love.' And as she sat there, oblivious to the other passengers, his voice filled her senses and memories of that last night with Davey filled her soul.

> 'Ae fond kiss, and then we sever!
> Ae farewell, and then for ever!
> Deep in heart-wrung tears I'll pledge thee,
> Warring sighs and groans I'll wage thee . . .

Had we never loved sae kindly,
Had we never loved sae blindly,
Never met – or never parted,
We had ne'er been broken-hearted.

Fare-thee-weel, thou first and fairest!
Fare-thee-weel, thou best and dearest!
Thine be ilka joy and treasure,
Peace, Enjoyment, Love and Pleasure!

Ae fond kiss, and then we sever!
Ae farewell, alas, for ever!
Deep in heart-wrung tears I'll pledge thee,
Warring sighs and groans I'll wage thee.'

As the last note died on the young man's lips, Kate had tears brimming in her eyes, and to her amazement she was not alone. There was hardly a dry eye amongst her companions.

Instead of the customary cheer and polite clapping, the end of the song was greeted with a decided hush as each of the listeners remained caught up in their own particular memories of the past.

'I seem to have put rather a blight on the company with that one, unless I hit the wrong note once too often,' the young man said apologetically as he looked around him in some concern.

'Nah, nah, lad,' an old man on the opposite side of the coach to him sighed. 'It's nae reflection on your singing. I wis, yon sang says mair aboot things guid folk would like to forget than ony other . . . Love's a funny thing, there's nae pain quite like it, even in auld age.' He blew his nose noisily in a large white handkerchief and glanced across at Kate in the window-seat opposite. 'But I hae my doubts if a bonnie young lassie like you would ken about that yet.'

Kate managed a weak smile as she blinked back the tears. It was just as well the old man was not a mind-reader as well as a philosopher.

It was a good three hours after the young songster disembarked at Perth's Salutation Inn before the replacement coach and fresh horses pulled up outside Falcon Ridge on Broughty Ferry's Camphill Road.

'Do you want a hand with those bags, ma'm?' the driver asked, as Kate stood outside the wrought-iron gates and searched inside her purse for a shilling to tip him with.

'No, thanks, I can manage,' she assured him, glancing up at the red sandstone castellated mansion that was home, before pressing two silver sixpences into his waiting palm.

It was just after eleven at night, and she could see lamps lit in several of the windows, but thought it strange that Augustus had had no one positioned at the gates awaiting her arrival. She had sent word the previous day advising him about which coach she would be arriving on, and it was not like him to be forgetful. It looks like it must have been a bad day at the mill, she told herself as the coach pulled out on the next stage of its journey.

She rang the lodgekeeper's bell. Joe Patton, the retired mill warehouse clerk, who lived in the ornamental two-roomed lodge at the gates, opened the door almost immediately and stared in some consternation at Kate. 'Why, Mrs Falconer, ma'm, I wasna expecting you the nicht!'

'But I sent word to my husband that I was coming,' Kate assured him in some irritation. 'Didn't he inform you?'

'Well, now . . .' This was much worse than he expected, and Joe Patton's normally pallid face paled even more in the lamplight. 'Did – didn't they tell you?' he stammered.

'Tell me what?'

He scratched his whiskered chin and looked truly perplexed. 'I could swear the housekeeper said they had sent word to Edinburgh.'

'Sent word about what?' Kate demanded, her irritability now tinged with concern. 'What's been happening, Joe? It's not Ewan, is it? He's not got any worse?' The toddler had never been far from her mind since she'd been away, but she had comforted herself with the knowledge that the slight temperature he had been suffering from before her departure must have come to nothing, for Augustus would have informed her immediately should there have been any real cause for concern.

'I think you'd better step inside here,' the old man said, taking her arm and attempting to escort her inside. 'My Martha will make you a cup o' tea while I go up to the big hoose and get help.'

Kate shook her arm free from his grasp. 'Forget the tea!' she declared. 'I'm going nowhere but home, to find out exactly what's been going on since I've been gone!'

Leaving her bags sitting on the ground at the gate-keeper's feet, she pushed open the great iron gates of the big house. They creaked loudly on their hinges and she called after her for Joe to close them and see about some oil, before picking up her skirts and setting off at a run up the gravel drive.

She had barely gone more than a few yards when she tripped over a displaced edging stone and had to steady herself against a workman's barrow parked at the side of the front lawn. 'This really is the limit!' she exclaimed. 'Someone could be killed falling down one of these holes!'

The mess ahead of her was indescribable, for the pipelayers had dug up all of one side of the drive, displacing most of the stones that edged the wide sweep of front lawns and leaving piles of earth several feet high on the other. By the time she reached the main door of the house, her boots and the bottom of her skirts were covered in dirt.

She took hold of the brass knob and turned it, murmuring, 'Thank God for that!' on finding the door unlocked. On closing it behind her, she stood for a moment looking around her in the great hall. An eerie hush seemed to hang over the place, and only half the candles and lamps were lit. There was a gloomy, neglected air that she could not quite comprehend, for Augustus was always most particular about things like lighting.

'Augustus!' she called. 'Augustus, I'm back!'

When there was no reply, she ran to his study on the far side of the ground floor, but to her consternation it was empty. No fire burned in the grate, and no papers were strewn on the leather top of the desk. It looked as if it had not been used for days. What on earth was going on?

More anxious than ever now, she made for the stairs and ran up them, losing her hat in the process, so great was her concern to get to the top and find out exactly what was happening.

When she was only a few steps from the first-floor landing, she was met by the startled face of Mary Jean, Ewan's nurse, looking over the balustrade. 'Mistress Falconer, ma'm, I wasn't expecting you back tonight!'

Kate stopped in her tracks, panting for breath. 'Maybe not, Mary Jean, but by the looks of things it's just as well I've come. What in heaven's name's going on? Where is my husband?'

At that another voice intervened. 'Your man's in here, Kate,' Hector Grant said, coming from the direction of the master bedroom. 'But there's no reason to upset yourself.'

Kate was standing on the landing now, looking from one to the other in growing anxiety, her chest still heaving from the exertion of the stairs. 'And Ewan? What of the bairn?'

'Ewan will be fine,' the doctor assured her. 'With the right medicine and plenty of rest, they'll both be fine. There's no need to go upsetting yourself.'

Kate could feel herself begin to panic in earnest now. Something was wrong, very wrong, with both her husband and her son. She looked frantically from one to the other. Whom should she go to first? 'Take me to Ewan!' she commanded a nervous-looking Mary Jean. 'Quick, girl! And you come too, Hector, please!'

Despite her lack of breath and shaking legs, Kate beat them both to the door of the nursery and threw it open to rush inside.

The toddler was lying in his cot on the far side of the

room, the sheets pushed down from his perspiring body by his chubby little legs, which lay on top of the embroidered coverlet. His eyes were closed and he was breathing noisily. His face was the colour of parchment, his dark curls plastered against a damp brow. Kate gasped at the sight of him.

'Don't touch him,' Hector Grant ordered, as she made to pick him up. 'It's better for him and yourself if you don't.'

'But what's wrong? For pity's sake, Hector, what's wrong? He had no more than a wee stomach upset when I left.'

Mary Jean drew in her breath and glanced nervously at the doctor, who looked distinctly uncomfortable. The last thing he wanted was to worry her unduly but, on the other hand, he knew Kate was no fool and certainly wouldn't thank him for being less than frank. 'That stomach upset,' he began. 'We've had a bit of a job in clearing it up. The wee lad has lost a lot of fluid.'

Despite Mary Jean's valiant attempts to keep the nursery spotless, Kate could smell the stench of sickness in the air, and there was something more. 'He's had diarrhoea as well, hasn't he?' she cried, looking around her for more tell-tale signs. Sickness, diarrhoea, a high temperature . . . The symptoms rang dreaded bells in her brain. She looked from one to the other, aghast. 'It's not . . . ? It can't be . . . !'

'There's no real evidence it's the cholera,' the physician hastened to assure her. 'But we're doing everything we can. With something like that you can't be too careful.'

'And Augustus? He's not . . . ?' Surely it couldn't have attacked him as well?

'The Master was concerned about the bairn ever since Ewan took really ill after you left,' Mary Jean informed her. 'He even stayed away from the mill to tend to him. He couldna bear him greetin' his heart out for you, you see, ma'm. He said if his mama couldn't be with the wee lad, then his daddy should be.'

224

'Oh God!' Kate groaned, looking at Hector Grant who could only nod in agreement.

'There's no doubt about it, Augustus did himself no favour by tending the bairn himself.'

Kate clenched her fists and shook her head in frustration and disbelief. She hadn't been gone that long, for heaven's sake. How could things have got so bad in so short a time? 'How long have they been like this?' she demanded.

'The best part of a week as far as Augustus is concerned, and Ewan a good bit longer,' the doctor replied. 'But by my reckoning the bairn has turned the corner. His crisis has passed.'

'Thank God for that!' Kate's heart missed a beat as she glanced down at the sleeping face of her son. 'And his father?'

'There's still some way to go before we can be sure.'

'I see.' Kate felt herself go weak at the knees, and Hector Grant took hold of her arm to support her.

'We're doing all we can, lass,' he told her. 'For both of them. And, God knows, there are plenty of others in this city right now who know what you're going through.'

'You mean there's an epidemic?' She looked up at him, aghast at the thought as he sat her down gently on a nursing chair by the side of the cot. 'What's caused it, for God's sake?'

The elderly man shrugged his shoulders. 'We can only make a calculated guess, and they're blaming the water. All this upheaval in the town with the new water system being laid at the same time as the gas; they reckon it's contaminated the main water supply. It's only a guess, of course. With cholera you can't be sure of anything and, as we all know, there have been such epidemics long before they thought of laying water-pipes.'

Kate's face was drained of colour as she leant her head against the tall back of the nursing chair. Cholera. Here in Dundee. In her own home. On the Hawkhill, yes, she could believe that. But here in Falcon Ridge itself. It

225

seemed like only yesterday that Augustus was assuring her that the new water-pipes that he was having laid on would totally eliminate all forms of water-based contamination. 'There'll be no more bouts o' gut-rot or the runs in this house, Kate lass,' he had assured her. 'Nothing but good clean water will come out of those lead pipes.'

And the awful thing was that she had believed him.

'I must go to him,' she said, rising from the chair. 'I must go to my husband!'

Neither the doctor nor Mary Jean attempted to follow her as she rose unsteadily to her feet and half walked, half ran the twenty yards or so to the master bedroom.

Only one single lamp was burning, giving the room a sombre, shadowy appearance as she pushed open the door.

Augustus was lying in the middle of their double bed, his whiskered face grey against the white pillowslip. His eyes were closed and his breath was coming in short, whistling gasps. The few strands of white hair that he possessed were plastered with sweat to the crown of his head, and beads of perspiration stood out on his brow.

Gently, Kate took a handkerchief from her pocket and dabbed the damp skin. 'I'm here, my love,' she whispered. 'I'm back. You're going to be fine now.'

It was all of two hours before his eyes opened; she had not moved from his bedside. On the table beside her stood a half-drunk cup of tea that Mary Jean had kindly brought, and Hector Grant had looked in once or twice before excusing himself to return to his own home for the night. He would have a hard day ahead of him on the morrow, for news was reaching him that many other cases had been reported both in the village and in the city itself.

'I'll pray for you both,' he told a pale-faced Kate as he called into the bedroom for the last time. 'There's a good chance the crisis will be tonight. If so, you know where to reach me.'

She had nodded silently and kept hold of her husband's

hand, as if the act of physical contact could somehow invest him with enough of her own vitality to see him through the night ahead.

Just after the doctor left, Betty Lorimer came to the door of the bedroom in her nightclothes, her face beneath the linen nightcap a picture of concern. 'Mary Jean woke me and told me you were back,' she whispered. 'Is there anything I can do?'

Kate shook her head. 'There's nothing any of us can do right now, Betty dear,' she replied wearily. 'You go back to bed and get some sleep, for I'm sure to need you in the morning.'

It was about ten minutes after that that Augustus's eyelids flickered for the first time.

Kate's grip on his hand tightened as she leant forward over the bed. She was now so exhausted it was almost impossible to keep her own eyes open, but she was determined he should know she was here. 'Augustus . . . Augustus, my love . . . It's me, Kate . . . I'm back . . .'

His lips opened a fraction and a faint sound was emitted. Her heart leapt. He had heard her.

She stood up, leaning over the bed as she smoothed the damp strands of white hair back from his brow. It was the face of an old, old man beneath her. He had lost so much weight since she last saw him that the translucent grey skin was pulled tight across the bones of his cheeks, and his pale eyes were sunken in the deep, dark sockets. 'Can you hear me, my darling? Do you know I'm here?'

'Kate . . .' Her name came as a faint whisper from between the parched lips as his lids flickered open long enough to catch sight of her face.

She bent down and kissed the damp skin of his brow. 'You're going to be fine, just fine, my love,' she whispered. 'I'm back to look after you.'

His eyes were red-veined and brimming as they found hers. She had come back. She had come back to him at last. 'Kate, my dearest Kate . . .' he whispered, then his voice faded.

She took a damp sponge and ran it over his flaking lips, then across his brow.

His hand fluttered up towards her face. He wanted to touch her, to prove she was really here beside him. 'Kate . . .'

'Hush, my love, don't try to speak.'

But he wanted to speak. He wanted to tell her how much her being here meant to him. How in all his three-score years he had never loved anyone as he had loved her. But try as he might, the words would not come. All day the strength had been ebbing from him and his body felt like a great weight, far too heavy for him to cope with any more.

She could see him struggling, and her heart went out to him. Somehow she knew what he was trying to say, for the faded gaze that met her own was filled with so much love she thought her heart would break.

'I love you too, beloved,' she whispered, her lips pressed to his hand which was clasped tightly in both of hers. 'I love you so very, very much.'

His eyelids flickered in response, and she could swear she felt his fingers move in hers as she continued, 'We have had the best of marriages. These past few years with you have been the happiest of my life.' She wanted him to know that. It was so very important that he know it. 'I will always be here, my love,' she told him. 'I will take care of everything, and one day our wee laddie will be the finest son a father could wish for. Ewan's going to be just grand, Augustus, and he'll grow up to do us both proud.'

It was what he wanted to hear. All his life he had craved for love and had never known it. But now he had it in plenty. It was surrounding him in a cloud of happiness as his wife's face swam in and out of his consciousness. He was slipping from her, and from their braw wee

228

laddie, but he felt no fear, no sorrow, for her love was bearing him along.

A solitary tear trickled slowly down the ashen skin of his cheek as a deep sigh shuddered through his body. It seemed to breathe her name . . . Kate . . .

'No, God . . . *No!*' In desperation, Kate threw herself across his lifeless body. She clung to him, willing the life force that pulsated through her to fuse with his, but the heart beneath her was no longer beating.

'Don't leave me,' she begged, as her tears caused a damp patch to form on the shoulder of his nightgown. 'Don't leave me, my love!'

She sobbed herself to sleep at his side, one arm thrown protectively across his chest. He had been more than a husband to her, he had been a father and a friend. He had given her the world, but that world was now no more, for he was dead; Augustus, her beloved husband, was dead, and it would be a far colder world without him.

Chapter Nineteen

In memory of my beloved husband Augustus:

> The bridegroom may forget the bride
> Was made his wedded wife yestreen;
> The monarch may forget the crown
> That on his head an hour has been;
>
> The mother may forget the child
> That smiles sae sweetly on her knee;
> But I'll remember thee, my love,
> And a' that thou hast done for me!

'I hope Robbie Burns will forgive me for taking a small liberty with his "Lament", for never was a sentiment more apt,' Kate murmured as she signed her name beneath the two lovingly transcribed verses on the black-bordered card.

The Reverend Herbert Mooney, who was standing pensively by the drawing-room fireplace, nodded his agreement. 'Aye, you've lost one o' life's finest in Augustus's passing,' he agreed. 'And I've lost my best friend.'

Kate got up from her seat at the writing desk, a sombre, dignified figure dressed entirely in black. She handed the card to the minister. 'Place this on the roses for me,' she said quietly. There were to be only her flowers: a bunch of one dozen red roses in the centre of the brass and finest walnut coffin that money could buy. It would be borne by four black-plumed horses that very afternoon to its final resting-place in the Falconer family vault in the local cemetery.

'You're looking tired, lass. Can I be of any more help?'

'I feel redundant, Bertie,' Kate said with feeling, as Herbert Mooney slipped the card safely in his coat pocket. 'I wish women were allowed to attend funerals. I shouldn't be left sitting here in the house this afternoon. I ought to be there with him at the very end.'

'You *were* there at the very end,' her friend reminded her. 'You were with him when it mattered. It is not Augustus we are burying this day, Kate my dear, it is a mere empty vessel, the shell of the man that was. His soul has long departed this life and is, no doubt, watching over us now as we mourn his passing.'

At that, Kate gave a wry smile. 'If that be true, I know exactly what he would be saying. Why are you not offering my good friend a wee dram? Is that not right, Bertie?'

The minister gave a half-laugh, half-cough. 'Aye, you could be right there, my dear. You ken your man all right. And if that's an offer from the dear departed himself, I'll better no' refuse. We can't go offending Augustus on his big day now, can we?'

They both laughed. The tension was lifting. It really was as if Augustus was here now, telling them to cheer up and not be so long-faced on his behalf.

It was arranged that the minister would return to conduct the service in the house at three that afternoon, then the mourners would follow the cortège to the cemetery. Kate would remain behind, as was the Scottish custom, and pay her last respects at the graveside later. It was not what she wished, but now was no time to go offending public convention.

Between the time the Reverend Mooney left and the funeral service got underway, she seemed to acquire a new strength as she put the finishing touches to the arrangement of white flowers in the hall, and checked with Betty that the catering arrangements for the mourners after the funeral were well in hand. It was estimated that several hundred friends and business acquaintances would be attending, and nothing could be left to chance. She knew she owed it to Augustus, who had been so generous with his hospitality in life, to make sure his friends were well catered-for after his death.

'You've done me proud, Betty,' Kate told her housekeeper, as she stood in the kitchen and surveyed the mountains of cut cake and freshly baked bannocks, with a selection of cold meats and cheeses to accompany them. Everything was ready to be taken upstairs and laid out on tables in the dining room. On the floor beside the food stood several cases of Augustus's favourite malt whisky. Nothing was to be too good for his friends on this day.

For her part, Betty Lorimer was filled with admiration for her young employer. Although obviously grief-stricken, Kate had knuckled down to supervising the arrangements for the funeral, overlooking nothing in her determination that Augustus should be given a send-off worthy of his status in the community.

'Will you be involving the bairn at all?' the housekeeper asked, knowing there was very little the child was excluded from at Falcon Ridge.

'Of course,' Kate replied. 'Ewan will remember this day, young though he is. I'm determined of that.'

At one o'clock precisely, before any of the mourners had begun to arrive, Kate went up to the nursery and collected her son. She thanked God who had made it possible for her to perform that task, for there could very easily be two coffins waiting downstairs to be buried this day.

Happily, Hector Grant had been right, and young Ewan really had already been on the mend when she returned from Edinburgh; in the four days since Augustus's death there had been a remarkable improvement in the child. The fever had quite gone, as had the sickness and other symptoms that had had them all so worried. To counteract what little dehydration might still be lingering, he had been drinking boiled sugar water by the gallon over the past few days, and now even his appetite was almost back to normal. Only in the fact that he had lost several pounds in weight and no longer had that much-admired chubby look was there any indication of the illness that had threatened his young life such a short time ago.

Under Kate's orders, dispensing with his usual toddler's white lace gown, Mary Jean had dressed the child in a miniature sailor suit, with a black band around his middle. All agreed he looked a proper picture, with his head of dark McMahon curls and thick-lashed Irish eyes.

'You really don't know what this is all about, do you, son?' Kate sighed as she picked up the boy and carried him to the window to look down on the rooftops of the village below.

Outside the sun was shining through the clouds that billowed over the estuary of the river. It glinted off the sails of the boats that plied their way through the sequined water towards the open sea, and she could hear the emotive cry of the gulls that followed in their wake.

A playful breeze was blowing, and she could see the washing of the fisher families flapping on clotheslines along the shore. Old men would be sitting there contentedly smoking their clay-pipes as they baited their lines and talked of the days of 'auld lang syne' when things were not so rushed and folk had time to stop for a bit of a crack.

In the garden of Falcon Ridge itself, work had stopped for the day and what workmen could still be seen were all wearing black armbands out of respect for the deceased. Despite the mess created by the pipe-laying, the roses alongside the dug-up driveway were in their full glory, splashes of blood-red, gold and white against the green of the well-cut lawns. All in all, it was a perfect summer's day. It seemed grotesque that such a tragedy had befallen their small family and yet the sun went on shining and the world carried on revolving.

An elderly man in a black frock-coat similar to one Augustus used to wear appeared on the road beneath them, and Ewan's small face brightened. 'Dada!' he shouted, waving a stubby hand and reaching towards the glass. 'Dada!'

The child wriggled in her arms, eager to make contact with the father he had not seen for so long, as Kate turned from the window and looked in despair at Mary Jean. 'I really don't know what to do for the best,' she said. He was still far too young to take in the fact his father was dead, yet she felt she should do something to let him know Augustus would not be here in their midst ever again. His father's body was about to leave their family home; this was a special day for both of them, and somehow Ewan should be made aware of it.

'Have ye thought o' taking him down to see his dad?' the nursemaid asked in a hesitant voice. Mary Jean was a quiet, retiring girl, and not one for making suggestions to her Mistress. But she had not been much older than wee Ewan when her own father had drowned in an accident just outside the harbour, and her first memory was of being taken by her mother to see him lying in his coffin, laid out on the table in the front room.

'Do you think that's wise?' It was a thought Kate herself had been toying with all day.

Mary Jean's freckled face was pensive. In her mind's eye she could still see her own father's face in that wooden box. She had felt no fear, for he had looked at peace with the world. She had been allowed to reach over and touch the mop of curly hair on his brow that was the mark of all the Lorimer men. It was a memory she cherished. 'It could just be that he'll thank you for it some day, when he's grown.'

So, carrying her small son in her arms, Kate descended the wide sweep of the staircase to enter Augustus's study, the room she had chosen for his last resting-place at home. It was a place Ewan already knew and loved, for it was in here before the child's bedtime every night that Augustus would bring his son for a few precious minutes to play with the many curios that lay enticingly on the shelves of the mahogany bookcases and in the several display cabinets that stood around the walls.

It had been a family joke that Ewan knew the room even better than she did and, as Kate closed the door and stood looking around her, she felt no chill at the sight of the open coffin. On the contrary, there was an almost sacred feel to the room; if Augustus's spirit was anywhere in the house, it was here in this his most beloved of places.

The heavy velvet curtains were half drawn across the wide bay-windows and she could still smell the pungent aroma of his tobacco in the air. She had deliberately requested the ashtrays not be cleaned to cling on to as much of him as she could for as long as possible. This was the room she knew he would want to spend his last moments at home in, the room he had loved above all others, the room which housed all those treasures collected over a lifetime which meant so much. Each and every one had had a special place in his heart for, despite what some might have thought, the owner of the Falcon Mills had been the most sentimental of men.

With Ewan still in her arms, before going near the coffin, Kate walked slowly round the room letting her gaze and fingers rest momentarily on many of her husband's treasured possessions: his ancient meerschaum pipe that she had been going to replace with the new one bought in Edinburgh, a signed copy of *The Lord of the Isles* by Sir Walter Scott, a framed fragment of tapestry said to be done by Mary Queen of Scots during her internment in Loch Leven Castle and, most recent and touching of all, a small curl of Ewan's baby hair which he had had placed in a tiny gold and glass orb that had hung proudly from his best watch-chain.

Her eyes moved to the wall above the mantelpiece; here there was a large patch of wallpaper where the burgundy-striped pattern was much darker than in the rest of the room. For three decades Emily's portrait had hung there, but on his marriage to Kate Augustus had removed it, promising his young wife that her own would be the only one to grace that spot from now on. Kate gave a wan smile as she glanced at the still-vacant space, for he had been nagging her for years to sit for her portrait, but she had always put it off with a nonchalant, 'Och, Augustus, there will be time aplenty for that later on!'

But there was not to be time aplenty, for Augustus had gone, and now she bitterly regretted not giving him the pleasure of that picture.

'We're going to see Dada now,' she whispered into her son's ear as she turned from the fireplace and walked slowly towards the open coffin in the centre of the room.

As if aware this was a special moment, the child had stopped squirming in her arms as they approached the body of the man who had meant so much to both of them. The small arms clung even more tightly around Kate's neck as they both looked on the beloved face. To her surprise, Augustus looked younger than she could ever remember. It was as if death had wiped away all the lines of sorrow that had accumulated over his three-score years. The undertaker had done his job well, for there was little evidence of the illness that had taken him. His white hair was brushed and bushy around his side-whiskers, and beneath the bristling moustaches he even seemed to be smiling as they stood there looking down at him.

'It's Dada, Ewan son,' Kate said softly, seeing the perplexed look on the child's face. 'But he's no longer ours. He is asleep now with Jesus. He will never wake up. God has taken him home.'

'Dada!' The child reached out and Kate leant over to allow her son to touch the whiskery cheek of the man who had loved him so much. 'Dada!'

Then, setting the child on the floor, she herself bent over and placed a kiss on the old man's brow. 'Goodbye, my husband,' she whispered. 'May God keep you and love you as we have done.'

The official service that followed passed in a haze of

biblical platitudes and an endless round of handshakes and condolences from friends and acquaintances. It seemed that the whole ground floor of the house was a sea of black coats and hats as the city of Dundee came to pay its last respects to one of its most successful sons.

The closed coffin was moved to a catafalque in the centre of the main hall for the service, and Kate greeted the mourners herself from a straightbacked chair to the right of it, by the side of the marble fireplace, which contained a display of white lilies. On the coffin lid lay her single bouquet of red roses and card. She appeared to all to be a solitary, dignified figure and, even amongst those who had shaken their heads at hearing of the match several years earlier, there was nothing but admiration for the way the young widow was deporting herself at so painful a time.

The funeral procession itself stretched all of half a mile, and Kate watched, with Ewan in her arms, from the window of the master bedroom, as the black-plumed horses pulled the carriage containing the remains of her husband towards his final resting-place.

She stood watching until the last mourner was out of sight, then turned, aware of someone standing at the door.

'I've made you a cup of tea, ma'm,' Betty Lorimer said, her normally cheerful face showing all the signs of the tension of the day. 'Will I bring it up here to the bedroom for you?'

Kate looked at her and was about to say she would have it in the kitchen, but something stopped her. Something inside her told her that those days were now gone. No longer was she the uncertain young wife still clinging to the familiarity of the past by spending hours in the kitchen drinking tea and hot chocolate with Betty. Now, until Ewan came of age, she *was* the Falcon empire. 'I'll have it in the drawing room, thank you, Betty,' she replied in a tired voice.

Betty continued to hover in the doorway.

'Was there anything else?'

'I – it's just . . .' The housekeeper fumbled for the right words. 'Well, I thought you might like to know that I heard from Davey last night. He's been down in Edinburgh most of last week and is here in town for a couple of days before going back to France. He heard of Augustus's death and felt really bad about it for you . . . He – he was to be attending the funeral today – the cemetery bit, I mean. He asked me to see if you'd care to meet him before he leaves – so he can offer his condolences.'

Kate's heart had stopped at the first mention of the name. Davey was here in town. Not only that, he was attending her husband's funeral. As she stood looking at her housekeeper, she could feel her eyes begin to fill. Exactly who she was crying for she could not be sure. Was it Augustus, Davey, wee Ewan, or herself? Perhaps it was a combination of all four.

Slowly she began to shake her head. To see him at a time like this would be to compound the sin she had committed as her husband lay on his deathbed. Nothing she could ever do could atone for that in her mind. Her heart felt like an open wound, for the pain she had felt at rejecting Davey had been surpassed fourfold by what she had found on returning home. To even set eyes on him right now would be to repeat the betrayal. There came a time in everyone's life when the head must rule the heart. 'Thank him, but tell him no, Betty, please. I don't feel like seeing anyone right now.'

Betty looked surprised and a trifle uncertain. It was not the reply she had been expecting. Davey had been so insistent she speak to Kate, to tell her he was here. She could not remember him so on edge before. It was all she could do to stop him going on up the stairs himself to offer his sympathy. 'He – he says he might not be back to Scotland,' she said hesitantly. 'It might be your last chance to see him, your last chance to say goodbye.'

Her last chance to say goodbye. Kate managed a wan smile. 'I fear the goodbye I have said to my husband today is more than enough to cope with,' she said in a resigned voice. 'Tell Davey I regret I have no wish to see him, but I wish him well in his life to come.'

Betty Lorimer reached for the doorknob and paused, half turning towards her employer. 'You have changed, Kate,' she said in a quiet voice. 'You are no' the lassie I knew.'

'No,' Kate agreed, clutching her small son to her breast. 'You are right. I have grown up.'

Chapter Twenty

The sun was just beginning to sink behind Dundee's Law Hill when, taking Ewan by the hand, Kate walked through the cemetery gates and on up the winding path towards the marble vault that had been newly closed over the body of her husband.

The plot was on the south side of the graveyard, in the shadow of a high stone wall and sheltered by a tall chestnut tree. Augustus used to call it his tree, for it had supplied him with many a contest-winning conker on Sunday visits to his dead grandparents as a young child. Kate knew he could have been no more than Ewan's age when he made his first pilgrimage to this quiet spot, and she felt a strange sense of timelessness as she stood in front of the black marble and grey granite edifice with her son and read the names of those of the Falconer family who had gone before.

Augustus's grandfather, William Augustus Falconer, Willie-Gus to all but his wife, had walked into this city as a barefoot boy from the green fields of the Carse of Gowrie over a century ago, and had begun work apprenticed to a handloom weaver in the Cowgate for the princely sum of sixpence a week. When he died he left sixty thousand pounds, a sum that was doubled by his own son, and now trebled by the grandson at whose grave Kate and her son now stood. The men who were buried here had been of pious, hardworking stock in the best Scottish Presbyterian tradition, and it was quite a legacy for young Ewan to live up to.

Kate clutched her son's hand that bit tighter as she contemplated the future ahead of them. It was funny how true the old saying was that you never really appreciated what you had until it was taken from you. Only now she had lost him did she fully realize the tower of strength that Augustus had been. He had stood head and shoulders above all other men, a giant amongst his contemporaries, just as his beloved chimney stack had towered above his rivals' in the town. In a hostile world he had been her shelter against the storm, and she wished with all her heart she had not made that fateful trip to Edinburgh, but had been here at his side during that last week when he really needed her.

'Forgive me, Augustus,' she whispered. 'Forgive me.' If there really was a God, then her husband would be with him now and would understand the pain she was going through.

She was not sure how long they had been standing there when the shadow appeared. It came silently up the path behind them to pause only a few feet behind. It was Ewan who saw him first, turning round, pointing his stubby finger and shouting, 'Mannie, Mama! Mannie!'

Startled, Kate turned to find herself looking into a face that at first she did not recognize, for the familiar features were half obscured in a thick auburn beard. But the eyes, there was no mistaking those glittering hazel eyes.

'Willie!' she gasped. 'What brings you here?'

'What do you think?' came the deadpan reply. 'My father's dead after all.'

'But . . . but . . .'

'But it would have been too much to inform me of his death and invite me to the funeral, would it? I'm only his first-born son, after all.'

'I – I couldn't,' Kate flustered. 'I – I swear I didn't even know where you were – or how to contact you.'

'Liar!'

'It's no lie,' she protested. Willie had been a taboo subject in their home ever since his departure and, although she had often thought of him after Augustus's death, she had been too caught up in her own grief to even contemplate ways of tracking him down. 'How could I know where you were?' she said defensively. 'You never informed either of us of your whereabouts after you left Dundee.'

'Balderdash. You knew I was in Leeds.'

'Well, yes . . .' That much was true, but the Yorkshire mill town had only been mentioned in the passing. 'Leeds is a big place.'

'Not that big.'

He looked older and more mature as he stood there glaring at her. His lanky figure had filled out, and gone were the dandified clothes. In fact, he seemed every inch the prosperous city gent in his well-cut funereal black frock-coat and grey leg-hugging pants. Even his hair, now slicked back and well-groomed beneath the high hat, seemed not quite the fiery red of memory.

'Mannie, Mama!' With a child's natural curiosity, Ewan began to toddle towards him, and Kate was quick to snatch at his hand.

'No, pet, bide here!' She bent and picked up the child, who grizzled and held out his arms towards the tall stranger.

'So this is your brat,' Willie said, eyeing the boy coldly. 'This is the new heir to the Falcon empire.'

'This is Ewan,' Kate confirmed, her heart pumping inside her, for she knew she was looking at her child's father. She searched his face for any sign that he might suspect, but there was none, only an icy coldness in the eyes that told her he had not come back to this town to mend bridges. Quite the contrary.

From the branches of the chestnut tree in whose shadow they stood came the sound of birdsong, and there was that sweet scented hush to the air in which the notes floated that could only be felt at this time of the year. It seemed so sad that they should be facing one another in anger over Augustus's grave.

Willie began to tap his malacca cane against the side of his thigh, a nervous mannerism that Kate remembered of old. 'Just why have you come here?' she asked in a tired voice. 'Your father's dead, Willie, coming here can't bring him back, and I can't imagine that you've come to pay your respects to us.'

'Come to pay my respects to you!' Willie gave a bitter laugh. 'I doubt if there's a need for that, for it'll be more a case of the merry widow than the grieving one from now on, I'll be bound.'

'That's a cheap jibe, even for the likes of you.' She put up a hand to stop Ewan pulling too hard at her veil, and pressed Willie harder on the point. 'Just why are you here? If it's not to make up, then it's obviously to cause trouble.'

Willie allowed himself an enigmatic smile at that. It amused him to keep her guessing. Little did she know he had already been here in Dundee on business when he'd learned of his father's death, having arrived by boat from Hull several days previously. It had been his second trip to the city in as many months. Having made more money than he had thought possible in England over the past few years, he now had the financial backing required to set himself up in the flax trade.

There was never any question in his mind that Dundee was the place he would settle. There was nothing he wanted more than to beat the Falcon Mills at their own game, and he knew with his intimate knowledge of both English and Scottish spinning practices that there was no one in a better position to do it. He was well aware that, apart from his own father, no one knew more about the running of a flax-spinning mill and its financial affairs and markets than he did. He was in the perfect position to undercut his rivals at every turn.

'No, I certainly haven't come to pay any respects, Kate,' he informed her coldly. 'But cause trouble . . . ?' He smiled that enigmatic smile again. 'Well, you could say that, for I have certainly come to put you and that little brat of yours out of business.'

'I – I don't understand.' There was a venom and bitterness in his face and voice that quite took her breath away. This was not the Willie she knew; this was an older, harder version of the young man who had left here in such high dudgeon at the time of her marriage to his father. 'You mean you're coming back to Dundee?'

'Indeed, that I am – and what's more I'll be bringing with me the very latest in machinery and working practices. I aim to be the biggest manufacturer of spun yarn in the world before this decade is out.'

She laughed out loud at that.

'You can laugh now but you won't be laughing later on, I can vouch for that . . . As a matter of interest, how many spindles a day per horsepower are the Falcon Mills managing to produce at the moment?' Not for one minute did he expect her to know the answer.

'Upwards of thirty,' Kate replied, quick as a flash.

Willie's brows rose a good half-inch. She was better informed than he imagined. 'Is that so? Well, my mill will be producing half as much again, with each spindle producing an average of sixteen cuts of yarn, both of lint and tow, per working day.'

'I don't believe you!'

He merely smiled once more. She could doubt all she wanted, but he would show her. 'I expect you'll be putting my father's mills on the market now he's gone,' he said. He was twirling the cane in his right hand now, deliberately avoiding her eyes. 'After all, the brat is far too young to run the show.'

'Ewan won't have to,' Kate retorted. 'I will manage the mills myself until he comes of age.'

'You!' Willie laughed aloud, his teeth glinting white behind the auburn beard. 'But you're a woman!'

'Aye, that I am, but I have a brain in my head the same as you and I fully intend to use it.'

'You've taken leave of your senses, woman!'

'No, on the contrary, I've only just come to them.' Kate's eyes narrowed as she looked up at him. 'This is not quite what you expected, is it, Willie Falconer? You actually thought I'd have to sell wee Ewan's birthright because, as a woman, I wouldn't be capable of running the business. Then, lo and behold, you would step in and buy back the mills from me. You really are even dafter than I took you for if that's what you thought!'

'You're mad,' Willie retorted. 'Quite mad. There's not a female alive who could run those mills. You'll come begging to me before long to take them off you. And you know what I'll do, Kate McMahon? I'll spit in your face, that's what! I'll spit in your avaricious little Irish face for cheating me of what's rightly mine. The Falcon Mills were *my* birthright, not that young brat's, and you have denied me that. You have stolen from me what three generations of my family sweated to build!'

He flicked his cane in the direction of the marble vault. 'My father, grandfather and great-grandfather lie in there,' he reminded her bitterly. 'Three fine men who spent their lives building a future to pass down from father to son. And you, Kate McMahon, have spat on their graves, for you have denied them what they spent their lives working for. You have broken the line.'

His eyes fell on the face of the child in her arms. 'As long as there is a breath left in my body, that usurper will never profit from my inheritance – *never*, for it will never be rightly his.'

Kate's heart was cold as she looked at the man who was the father of her child. 'You are so wrong, Willie Falconer,' she said in a voice as cold and hard as the marble tomb which now held his father. 'You are so very wrong.' Just how wrong he would never know.

It was three months later almost to the day when she heard the rumour that the newly opened Dundee branch of the Bank of Scotland, along with Marshall's Mills of Leeds, were lending Willie the money to build Dundee's biggest mill yet at the top of the Hawkhill. Just why the news it would be on that particular site should have hurt Kate so much, she was not quite sure, but hurt it did. The whole city was a-buzz with rumours. They even said, so determined was Willie to get his own back on Kate, that the chimney stack he was building would look down on old Augustus's highest stack by a good twenty feet.

The last piece of information was given to her by her old friend Hector Grant, who had recently treated Willie in his surgery in Union Street for a septic index finger – got, he claimed, by too much bookwork, working out the facts and figures necessary to complete his plans by the end of the coming year. 'It seems he's hell-bent on surpassing his father in just about everything,' the elderly physician told Kate as he rose from his chair by the window of her drawing room. 'But he'll never be half the man Augustus was. I'm just heart-sorry my old friend will not be here next spring to celebrate, for he would be the proudest man alive.'

'You mean at the opening of Willie's mill?' Kate asked, surprised at his tactlessness.

'Good God, no, lass. At the birth of your baby, I mean.'

Kate stared at him in incomprehension. 'My – my baby?'

'You mean you really didn't suspect when you asked me here today?'

Kate shook her head, quite speechless. She had been feeling quite exhausted and run-down of late, and had even been sick for a week or two just after the funeral, a fact she had put down to picking up a touch of the cholera-type infection that had made Ewan so ill and carried off his father. The sickness had abated now, but the tiredness had continued, so she had at last taken Betty's advice and asked Hector to call.

'Well, suspect it or no', you're pregnant all right, my

dear. By my calculations you are all of three months gone.'
He gave a rueful smile. 'I reckon this must have been old
Augustus's last present to you before he took sick.'

Kate stared at him, shocked into silence. She had not
slept with her husband in that way for over six months.

'Aye, its father would be a proud man all right, and it's a
crying shame he will never know.'

Kate listened to his words and felt the room sway
around her. Automatically her hand went to her stomach,
where already a new life was forming, a new life that
would bear the Falconer name but possess not one drop of
Falconer blood.

'Maybe it would not be out of order to have a wee dram
to celebrate this happy event, if I may be so bold?' Hector
was saying, eyeing the array of bottles on the table by the
window.

Still speechless, Kate gave a wan smile and nodded to
him to help himself.

He poured himself a whisky and then half filled a wine
glass with claret, which he handed to her with a fatherly
pat on the shoulder. 'You're a wee bit taken aback at the
news, my dear, and I can understand that, but look on it as
a bonus. You will now have another living reminder of the
bairn's father around the place – something you could
never have expected. Is that not right?'

'A living reminder of the bairn's father,' Kate repeated
after him in an incredulous voice. 'You're right, Hector, I
never expected that.'

Hector beamed down at her as he raised his glass. 'Here's
to the new bairn!' he said with feeling. 'Whether it be a
laddie or a lassie, may it turn out to be someone who will
do their father proud!'

It was just over six months later that Laura Elizabeth was
born, on a morning that saw the village of Broughty Ferry
and the city of Dundee washed by a flurry of April
showers.

Hector Grant was there to deliver the child, who was pronounced as bonnie a bairn as he had seen in many a long day.

So quick was the labour that the midwife was not even called, and Betty Lorimer stood in to do all that was necessary to see to the comfort of the new mother and baby.

'My but she's a bonnie wee thing,' the housekeeper declared as she cradled the infant in her arms. 'And just look at those eyes. They will break many a heart in their day, you mark my words!'

She handed the child back to its mother, and Kate gazed down in awe at the dark blue orbs that looked straight back into her own. One day soon they would turn that peculiar shade of slate-greyish-blue, and that fine down of dark hair would fall out, to be replaced by a head of nut-brown curls. Somehow she had absolutely no doubt of that.

As she sat there cradling her daughter in her arms, Ewan clambered on to the bed and snuggled down beside her.

Lying across the foot of the eiderdown was a copy of that morning's *Advertiser*, its front page carrying a notice of yet more vacancies at the new Golden Eagle Mill on the Hawkhill. Willie had got his way and his new mill had opened two weeks previously, with a chimney stack that soared into the Dundee sky a good twenty feet higher than any of his father's.

At the opening, he was quoted in the paper as saying that he had chosen the name 'Golden Eagle' as Scotland's national bird signified the finest of its species. 'And so our mill will prove to be the finest this country has yet seen,' the proud owner had declared as he pulled the Scottish saltire from the carved granite replica of the great bird that stood guarding the main entrance.

Kate had felt no envy that day, only a great sadness. For all his faults, Willie was still Augustus's son and her own son's father. She had no wish to spend the rest of her life in competition with such a man. She had even sent him a

248

note of congratulations by special messenger, but it had come back torn in two.

And now as she lay in bed with her son and newly born daughter in her arms, she wondered on the strange fate that had brought three such very different men into her life, yet left her a woman alone to cope as best she could in a man's world.

'Is there anything else you need?' Betty enquired, picking up a soiled towel and making for the bedroom door.

Kate looked up and shook her head. 'No, Betty, thanks all the same. I have all I could possibly want.'

And only she knew the pain and the irony behind those words.

BOOK TWO

A Land of Dreams

Ah, love, let us be true
To one another! for the world, which seems
To lie before us like a land of dreams,
So various, so beautiful, so new,
Hath really neither joy, nor love, nor light,
Nor certitude, nor peace, nor help for pain;
And we are here as on a darkling plain
Swept with confused alarms of struggle and flight,
Where ignorant armies clash by night.

MATTHEW ARNOLD: *Dover Beach*

Chapter Twenty-one

Dundee, Scotland.
24 January, 1855

Kate's eyes glowed with pride and the faint hint of a tear added to their sparkle as she gently wafted a lace fan in front of her face and watched her daughter's slim figure whirl past in the arms of the man whose wife she had just become.

'Did you ever see such a bonnie couple?' the Reverend Mooney declared as the bride and her kilted groom swept past them, their faces glowing in the exertion of a Scottish reel.

'Never!' Kate agreed. With his fair colouring and tall, broad-shouldered figure, the groom had always been known as 'a strapping lad' in his younger days, and his new bride was every bit a match for him as they whirled around the dance-floor in each other's arms.

Laura was taller than her mother, and had a slim athletic figure, born out of a childhood where competing with her older brother Ewan at games had been her main joy in life. And as Kate sat beside her old friend Herbert Mooney and watched her daughter float past in her wedding dress, now the most feminine and ethereal of visions, she could not help but wipe away a wistful tear as she recalled the tomboy of yesteryear. There could not be many brides whose knees still carried the scars of so many tumbles, or who could still climb a tree as well as any monkey, given a little encouragement.

In many ways Laura reminded her of her own mother. There was that same streak of stubbornness in her that was so typical of her grandmother and a certain way she sometimes held her head that never failed to bring a pang to Kate's heart. Bel and Lang Rob McMahon were now long dead, but their memory lived on in the heart of their daughter as she watched her own child sweep past in the arms of her new husband. And, for a moment as she sat there, Kate felt quite alone, with neither parents nor husband to share her joy on this special day.

But perhaps more than parents or husband, there was another person on her mind as she sat tapping her foot to the music and, today of all days, Kate's heart ached for what might have been.

But it was no good living in the past. Both she and Davey had married other people, for better or worse. And for her own part, her marriage to Augustus had been good while it had lasted, but it was God's will that he had been taken from her so soon, no matter how often she had railed against the cruelty of fate that had left her alone with such a wilful child to bring up. Yes, Laura had been quite a handful for a widowed mother to handle on her own, and many times over the years Kate had wished she had still had Augustus to turn to. There were times when a woman needed a man around the place; someone to lean on at the end of a tiring day, or when there were decisions to be made. For almost a quarter of a century now she had had to make those decisions alone and, despite her wistfulness, she felt a deep sense of pride that it seemed a job well done. Augustus would have been proud of her this day.

She found herself sighing deeply behind her fan. It was a bitter-sweet thought that her responsibility for her daughter's welfare was now at an end. Today, for good or ill, Laura had become Mrs Blair Baxter, and Kate could only pray the marriage would turn out to be as great a success as her own had been. They had both married older men, and that at least might prove a good omen.

Remembering her own low-key affair, Kate had been determined that the wedding would be the most memorable possible. Nothing was to be too good for her only daughter. It was what Augustus would have wanted. She had set about transforming the family home for the event with great gusto. Flags in the personal tartans of all the guests hung from poles suspended around the hall, and tartan bunting fluttered between the coloured lanterns from the main gates right up the drive of the big house. Almost the entire male guest list was in national dress, either in the kilt or tartan trews, with their womenfolk resplendent in white dresses with tartan sashes. They made a splendid sight as they filled the dance-floor, often singing along as the band on the minstrels' gallery played all the well-loved national airs. For a young couple about to embark on a life abroad, Kate was determined it would be a wonderful memory of home to cling to in the years ahead.

Only the bride herself was without a tartan sash, and everyone agreed that Laura had never looked lovelier in an off-the-shoulder dress of white organdie, with her nut-brown curls transformed into a halo of long ringlets that cascaded down her back, intertwined with streamers of Macmillan tartan ribbon, in honour of her new husband, the Baxters being a sect of that great clan.

'I can't believe my wee girl is actually married,' Kate murmured as much to herself as to her companion, as she sipped a glass of wine and, from her seat by the side of the great fireplace, watched the dancers form up for a schottische.

'Aye, it was a surprise to us all,' Herbert Mooney agreed. You could have knocked him down with a feather when Kate told him just before Christmas that Major Baxter had proposed to Laura and had been accepted.

Laura had first met Blair Baxter two years previously, when the thirty-six-year-old officer of the Black Watch had been home on leave in Dundee. They had been introduced during a Hogmanay party at the home of a near relative of his, Mr David Baxter, of Baxter Brothers, one of the Falcon Mills' biggest rivals in the flax- and jute-spinning trade. Kate had thought little of it when the major had made two formal house calls at Falcon Ridge during the following fortnight, before returning to his post as British military attaché to the King of Oudh, a northern province of India.

Whether Laura herself had given the dashing army officer much thought during the two years he was away, Kate could not be sure, but it was certainly a surprise when just before Christmas a letter arrived informing them he would be home on leave over the New Year period and was looking forward to calling on them once again.

To everyone's surprise, not least Laura's, he had proposed during his third visit, after asking Kate's permission in front of the fire in the main hall as the object of his affections waited innocently in the drawing room.

'He certainly makes good use of the time available, I'll say that for him!' Ewan had declared over supper that evening, not a little put out that, in the absence of their late father, the major had not seen fit to consult him first.

The news of the sudden engagement had thrown the whole household into confusion, and whilst Laura herself seemed quite sure she had made the right decision, both Ewan and her mother were by no means certain.

While there was no doubt in Kate's mind that Blair Baxter was an officer and a gentleman in every way, she felt the two had barely had time to get to know one another properly. There was also the small matter of age. The major was now thirty-eight to Laura's twenty-one, and seventeen years was quite a difference in anyone's book. It was only when her daughter gently pointed out that there had been forty years between herself and Augustus that for once Kate had been left speechless and had been forced to give up that particular battle as well and truly lost.

'You'll miss her, there's no doubt about that,' Herbert Mooney sighed, stating the obvious, as he sipped his whisky at Kate's elbow and his gaitered shoe tapped in time to the music. 'But it could be worse. At least you'll still have Ewan.'

'Aye, I'll still have Ewan.' Kate glanced towards the other side of the hall where her handsome kilted son stood talking and laughing with a group of his friends.

While she loved her daughter dearly, there was no denying that Ewan was the light of her life. Now in his middle twenties, the young owner of the Falcon Mills was in the prime of his manhood. He stood a good six feet tall, with a head of dark brownish-auburn hair and a full beard that seemed to have become more red with the passing of time. But if that aspect of his appearance reminded his mother uncomfortably of her son's natural father, in every other way he was a McMahon, right down to the sparkling green of his eyes. He was also the most good-natured young man one could wish to meet, a trait she was happy to lay at the door of her late father, for he had all of Lang Rob's easy-going ways, without too many of his weaknesses.

As to her son's real father, she had seen little of Willie Falconer over the past two decades, although she had heard plenty in the business capacity. Willie had returned to Dundee shortly after his father's death to set himself up in business, and one of his first creditable transactions appeared to have been his decision to marry a local girl. 'Far too good for the young rascal,' the Reverend Mooney had informed Kate at the time, for once allowing his Christian charity to take a back seat to the truth.

Helen Munro was the daughter of one of St Andrews University's most distinguished professors. A talented local amateur soprano, her beautiful voice and delicate blonde good looks had captivated many a heart before Willie came back on the scene and, despite all the shaking of heads and ominous mutterings at the surprising match, by all accounts the marriage had turned out to be a great success. Two children had been born: a daughter, reported to be the spit of her mother, whom they had named Emily after

257

Willie's own beloved parent; and four years later a son they had called Ian. From what Kate had heard, it seemed Willie had become even more devoted to the youngsters than ever after his wife's untimely death some years ago. 'Keeps them wrapped up in cotton wool, he does,' Herbert Mooney had told her. 'He'll pay for it one of these days. You can only shield youngsters from the real world for so long. They have to be allowed to make their own mistakes. We can't live their lives for them.'

Those words now echoed in Kate's head as she sat beside her old friend and watched her daughter on the dance-floor. Laura was going out into the real world all right. To the other ends of the earth her husband was taking her, and Kate prayed with all her heart that she was not making a mistake. She was still so young, so very young.

The dance was ending and the young woman in the bridal gown turned her head in her mother's direction. 'Won't you take the floor, you two?' she called out as the participants of the schottische began to drift back to their seats. 'Ask her up, Mr Mooney. It would do you both good!'

'What? Me and my gammy leg?' the minister retorted with a shocked look. 'Have a heart, Laura lass!'

The exchange was heard by a stockily-built, bearded man in middle age, who had entered the hall as the dance was ending. Although smartly dressed, unlike the other male guests he was not wearing Highland dress, and his serious expression was at odds with the merrymaking going on around him. For a moment, he wavered uncertainly at the side of the floor, then, taking his courage in both hands, he walked resolutely up to Kate's chair and executed a perfect bow.

'May I have the pleasure of the next dance, ma'm?'

Kate looked uncertainly at the stranger for a second or two, then her eyes widened and she let out a gasp. It was as if a bolt of lightning had hit her. Those eyes . . . That hair . . . 'Davey!'

She put down her fan and almost toppled from her chair, so surprised was she to see her old friend. Never for one moment had she expected him to accept the invitation to attend the reception of her daughter's wedding. The gilt-edged card sent out in the name of Mr and Mrs David Lorimer had been an impulsive gesture on her part, and one that she had had second thoughts about ever since.

She had tried so hard to push him to the back of her mind. As Laura had grown to adulthood, it had become increasingly obvious to her mother how like her real father she was. Not only did she resemble the Lorimers in looks, with her head of nut-brown curls and eyes as grey as the German Ocean on a winter's day, but she also had Davey's spunk, that same stubborn streak to her character and inborn sense of justice and feeling for the underdog. Although Kate knew her old friend had no inkling he was Laura's father, she had wrestled with her conscience about whether or not to give him the chance to see Laura on her wedding day. Not for one moment, however, did she expect him to come, and now she stared with a mixture of apprehension and delight at the figure in front of her. How was it possible her heart could still beat as fast at the sight of him after so many years? She fought desperately to compose herself. 'Davey! I — I do declare this is a surprise indeed!'

'A pleasant one, I hope?' her old friend said, offering his arm as Kate rose a trifle unsteadily from the chair to accompany him on to the dance-floor.

'How are you, Kate? You're looking as bonnie as ever, if I may say so.' His voice had a strange intensity about it as his eyes gazed down into hers. Apart from a single silver streak in the dark hair above her brow and a few fine lines around the eyes, there was little sign of the years that had passed since they had last met.

Kate flushed. 'You may indeed say so!' she laughed. 'Compliments are richly prized at my age.'

'How did you know we were back in Dundee?' He was curious. The wedding invitation had arrived less than a week after his and Marie-Louise's return from France, and it had come as a real surprise, awakening old memories he had fought so hard over the years to bury.

Kate inwardly tensed at the 'we', but was lighthearted in her reply. 'Oh, I don't have the second sight, if that's what you're thinking! Your cousin Mary Jean informed me. She still does occasional part-time work for me, and has been helping out with the preparations for the wedding. She told me you were due home a few days before the wedding and would be staying in your mother's old house on Shore Terrace.'

Due to a combination of old age and ill-health, Betty Lorimer had retired from her post as housekeeper at Falcon Ridge over two years previously. Kate had bought her a small two-roomed cottage on the foreshore that had become vacant, and the old lady had valiantly tried to cope on her own for several months, but after a prolonged spell of illness had had to give up her independence and had gone to live with her married daughter in Perth. Since then the cottage had stood empty, and Mary Jean's news that Davey was to return to Dundee over the New Year and would be staying there had filled Kate with an excitement she had not known in years. Over twenty years of running the mills had given her little time to dwell on too many sentimental feelings that might have remained from her youth, but all of a sudden, just when she least expected it, they were back. The combination of Laura's impending marriage and Davey's imminent arrival had left her in a tangible state of tension by the time the wedding day actually arrived, due in no small part to the presence of Mary Jean around the place and her incessant chatter about the goings-on within the Lorimer clan.

'Isn't your wife with you tonight?' Kate glanced enquiringly over Davey's shoulder. She had met her old friend only once since he went to live permanently in Paris over twenty years previously, but she had never been introduced to his wife.

'Marie-Louise's health's not so good,' Davey informed her, rather more curtly than he intended. 'She doesn't socialize much these days. She prefers to have friends to call.'

'I'm sorry to hear that.'

He made no reply as his arms encircled her and they took the floor. Memories came flooding back. Memories of an evening when the heavens opened and they had stood out there in the rose garden, clinging to each other as the rain mingled with the tears from their eyes. Kate could feel herself tremble in his arms and wondered if he remembered too. They had met only once since Laura's birth. Just over a decade ago, but there had been too many people around to say anything other than a few pleasantries. He had grown a beard since then; it was now quite grey and his curly hair was streaked silver at the temples. 'It's been a long time, Kate,' he told her. 'How many years would it be?'

'Almost ten and a half.' She had not meant to answer so quickly or to be so precise, and her cheeks flushed with more than the exercise as he grinned, 'You wouldn't happen to know the exact days and hours too, would you?'

She was conscious of them being the object of several speculative glances as they danced past knots of old friends and acquaintances, many of whom she knew were scratching their heads to place the bearded stranger who had suddenly appeared in their midst.

'You don't mind the looks we're getting, do you? It seems I may not have aged as well as you, and they'll all be wondering to themselves just who this auld grey-haired rogue is who is commandeering the bride's mother.'

'Heavens no! They can stare as much as they like. If gossip had bothered me I'd have been a nervous wreck years ago. I . . . I really appreciate your coming, Davey.

This day means a lot to me, as you can imagine – and even more now.'

He smiled at that. 'You've every right to feel proud,' he told her. 'Your daughter's as bonnie a lassie as I've seen in many a long day. In fact, I'd go as far as to say I've not seen a bonnier one since her own mother was that age!'

Kate laughed as his arm tightened around her waist and they whirled past the minister sitting by the fireplace. 'Wee Davey, you can't soft-soap me like that!' she chided him. 'I know you too well.' But a warm glow remained. That old feeling between them was still there. She could feel it, and knew that he could too. 'I'm only sorry you won't get the chance to get to know Laura better. They sail for India at the end of the week.'

'India, is it?' He whistled softly. 'That's a mighty long way . . .' Then his face took on a pensive look. 'So one of Katie McMahon's offspring is off to serve the Empire? Well, I dare say it'll be all the better for it. But you'll miss her, I have no doubt.'

'Aye, I will that.'

'But you'll still have your son.'

'Oh yes,' she agreed. 'I'll still have Ewan. A woman needs a good man around these days.'

For a fleeting second their eyes met, and she could swear she could feel the pressure of his fingers on hers increase at the words. 'You've never married again, Kate,' he said quietly.

'No, I never have.'

'I can't believe it's been for want of offers. Have you never met a man to tempt you?'

'Oh aye, I have that,' she assured him. 'But he was already married.'

She could feel his fingers stiffen over hers, and he made a strained attempt at a smile. He had asked for that, and had the good grace to blush beneath his beard as the dance came to an end and he guided her off the dance-floor back in the direction of her seat.

To her great regret he stayed for only the one dance, telling her he had not come to join in the festivities, but had merely intended offering his good wishes to herself and the bride and groom. He and his wife would be returning to Paris shortly, he said, but they might be spending a great deal more time in Scotland in the future. 'Those mills of yours still have a long way to go before they're fit for human beings to work in,' he reminded her. 'And it's up to the likes of me to put that right.'

'If you'd played your cards right you could have been on the board of directors by now,' Kate replied with a smile that could not disguise the truth behind the words. 'Then you could have had mills here to rival those of Robert Owen himself.'

'Alas, Bonnie Dundee will never be New Lanark,' he sighed, for the great industrial reformer's custom-built mill village was the showpiece of the Capitalist world. 'But where men like him lead, others must follow. I'll take you there some day, Kate. We'll go down there and I'll show you how workers really should be treated.'

'Enough about workers,' she said, determined to lighten the mood. 'Today of all days let's just concentrate on wedding guests and their needs. You'll have a drink before you go?'

To her disappointment he shook his head. 'Thank you, but no. A wee dram on an occasion like this could turn into one too many. The last thing I want is to end up embarrassing you or that bonnie lassie o' yours on her wedding day.'

'You'd never do that.'

Standing there at the side of the floor, they were both aware of the curiosity they were arousing. Davey glanced around him and with a wry smile said quietly, 'It seems I've hogged your time long enough. I'd better let you return to your mother-of-the-bride duties, but it's been grand seeing you again, and I just wanted you to know how much I appreciated the invitation . . . *Au revoir*, dear Kate . . .'

He took her hand and pressed her fingers in his until she could feel her heart beginning to race and a film of nervous perspiration breaking out beneath the blue shot-silk of her dress.

'Goodbye, Davey . . . I hope it won't be another decade before we meet again.'

He gave a quiet smile but made no reply. None was really needed. Then he turned on his heel and strode off in the direction of the door, where Laura and her new husband were chatting to a few old friends.

'He said he's an old friend of yours, is that right, Mother?' Laura asked, coming over after shaking hands with the bearded stranger and accepting his best wishes for her future.

Kate gave a wistful smile as she turned to the enquiring face of her daughter, uncanny in its resemblance to the man who had just gone. 'A very old friend, Laura dear.'

'Was he a friend of Father's too?'

The question took Kate aback, but only for a moment. 'Well, your father once helped get him out of prison.'

'Prison? Goodness me! What company you keep! Is he a thief?'

Kate laughed. 'Something much worse – a Communist!'

'Really?' Laura had little idea what exactly the term meant, only that they were meant to be very unsavoury characters indeed. 'How exciting! You must tell me about him some time.' Then she was off again, this time accompanying the groomsman in another reel and leaving her bridegroom still standing by the door, after chatting amicably for a few minutes longer to the rather intense, bearded local man who had just left.

'That's quite a daughter you've produced, if I may say so, ma'm,' Blair Baxter told his new mother-in-law as he strode across the floor to where she was sitting. They watched Laura dance by in a swirl of white organdie and merry laughter. 'I feel honoured to have made her my wife.'

'And so you should, young man,' Kate agreed. 'My daughter is quite a character. She may look like she's made of porcelain, but her backbone's forged from finest Sheffield steel. In fact, she's the most stubborn person I've ever met, bar one.' And that one had just left, but she knew her new son-in-law had not an inkling as to the true relationship to his wife of the man whose hand he had just shaken on his way out.

Blair Baxter's bluff face took on a more serious look as he nodded thoughtfully. 'A strong character, eh? Well that will certainly come in useful out East. India is no place for shrinking violets.'

Kate knew very little about that faraway land, other than that it was the producer of the jute fibre that was now taking over from flax as their main raw material in the spinning mills. They already had several members of their firm based in Calcutta, and over the past ten years had opened three mills on the Hooghly River, with Dundonians supervising production. By all accounts it was in Indian jute that the future of the Falcon Mills now lay, and it was strange indeed that her own daughter should be heading for that land as the wife of an officer of the Empire. 'You will look after her, won't you, Blair?' she said, as the major helped himself to another whisky from a passing tray. 'You'll take care of her and make sure she has the best of everything.'

'The best of everything and more,' Blair Baxter assured her. 'Laura will not only be my adored wife, she will be the toast of the station – the best loved *memsahib* in the whole of Lucknow!'

And it was those words of comfort that echoed in Kate's head one week later as the newly married couple said goodbye to herself and Ewan on the quayside of Dundee's Earl Grey Dock.

Laura's fair skin was streaked with tears as she hugged her mother for the last time. 'Look after yourself, Mam,' she said for the third time in as many minutes. 'Write me often and let me have all the news from home. Every last tiny bit of it. I swear I shall die if I don't hear from you regularly.'

'Of course I will. I'll try and write a wee bit every day so you'll know all that's going on,' her mother assured her. 'And you see you do the same, for I won't rest until I have all the details of your new life.'

'Down to every last creepy-crawly whose acquaintance you make!' Ewan put in mischievously, knowing his sister's abhorrence of everything in the insect kingdom. 'They say they've got women-eating spiders as big as my fist over there.'

His sister aimed a playful punch in her brother's direction. 'I've got my husband to protect me, don't forget,' she reminded him. 'I've no doubt he's well-trained in killing pests of all descriptions, so you'd better watch out!'

Kate glanced at Blair who was standing a foot or two away, conscious this was a special moment for the three of them. 'You're sure you'll have everything you need out there?' she queried him anxiously. 'If not, just let me know and I'll see it's sent out straight away.'

'I'm quite positive,' he assured her. 'I'll be much more concerned that you two are faring well back here, without Laura to boss you both around any more.'

'Don't you go worrying your head one whit about Ewan and me, we'll be just fine. Won't we, son?'

Ewan nodded in agreement as he put a comforting arm around his mother's shoulders. 'You just concentrate on making that man of yours a good wife, Lala,' he told his sister, reverting to a childhood nickname that had not touched his tongue in years. 'Ma and me, we'll be just grand. We've got the mills to keep us out of mischief, while you'll have nothing to do all day but lie around being waited on hand and foot by servants.'

'That's absolutely true,' Blair Baxter broke in with a smile. 'It's a hard life and no mistake as a colonial wife, with punkah-wallahs waving fans over you all day long as you lounge about on your couch!'

Laura made a face. 'Well hard or soft as the life may be, and punkah-whatevers or not, I can assure you all, here and now, I'll be the best colonial wife in the business,' she declared confidently as she reached for her husband's arm. 'But pray for me, both of you. Pray for both of us.'

'Always one to hedge her bets, my sis!' Ewan grinned as, gripping tightly to Blair's arm, Laura turned and they headed for the waiting ship that would take her to her new life half-way across the world.

Mother and son stood on the quayside and waved until their arms ached and the vessel was a mere speck in the distance, as it sailed out of the Tay estuary and headed on into the open sea.

'Good luck!' Kate called into the icy wind that gusted in from the north-east. 'Good luck!'

'They've gone,' Ewan said in a choked voice, but in a funny way relieved it was all over. 'They'll be fine, Ma, don't you worry.'

'Will they?' Kate's glance lingered for the last time on the dot on the horizon. 'Will they really?'

As she turned and slipped her hand into the crook of her son's arm, something deep inside told her that, despite the brave words, her daughter was going to need every ounce of that luck once she reached her destination.

Chapter Twenty-two

Lucknow, India.
September, 1855

'Don't whine so much, woman! You've only been out here four months. How can you possibly be bored? Think of the other ranks' wives. They would give their right arms to be in your position!' Major Blair Baxter threw the words over his shoulder as he picked up his files and made for the door of their bungalow. Why did she always choose breakfast to start moaning about life out here? She was far better off than the vast majority of women, and the quicker she came to realize it the better for both of them. 'I haven't time to listen to a catalogue of complaints about the servants or anything else this morning. I'm already late and the finance officer is expecting me at nine.'

Laura's expression was thunderous as she stifled the retort she was about to throw back at him, then, as the door slammed, she picked up a cushion from a nearby chair and threw it with all her force after him. 'Go to hell, Blair Baxter!' As far as she was concerned, she was already there. Then, mortified, she watched as Ali, the cook-cum-housekeeper, appeared as if out of nowhere to pick up the cushion and put it back in its proper place.

'Thank you, Ali,' she heard herself saying automatically. What on earth could the servants think of them? She could just imagine what her mother would say if she had witnessed this scene. But sadly it was far from unusual. There had been too many such exchanges of late, too many days when her husband had gone off to work at the palace in high dudgeon, leaving her to vent her frustration on the nearest object, then wander disconsolately around their quarters wondering if every married couple out here went through a bad patch such as this. It was a far cry from what she had imagined married life would be like when she entered into it such a short time ago.

'God give me strength!' she pleaded as she pushed a hand through her tousled hair and made her way through to the bedroom.

Beneath the green mosquito netting of the bed, the linen sheet was crumpled, but not from lovemaking, that had not taken place for almost a month now. How quickly dreams could die . . .

Sitting down at the washstand that served as a dressing-table, she propped up Blair's shaving mirror against the ewer and began to put up her hair. Like everything else around here, it felt dank to the touch as she pulled a brush through it a few times before twisting it into a figure of eight behind her head and sticking the pins in.

The more she thought about it, the harder it was to put her finger on exactly when things had begun to go wrong in their marriage. During her first few weeks in Lucknow she had been too busy adapting to her new life to pay too much attention to how their personal relationship was faring.

The town itself was a beautiful, dirty, noisy kaleidoscope of a place, the novelty of which had been all the more intense after being cooped up on board ship for almost four months.

They had arrived in India at the end of May, just over a fortnight before the rains came. The weather had been much hotter and more sultry than she had expected, and she had blamed this for her constant headaches and feeling of lethargy on her arrival. 'You'll get used to it in the end – we all do,' the other wives had told her, but that was of little comfort as she lay on her bed for hours on end with cold flannels across her brow.

She had tried to alleviate her tension by taking walks around the palace compound, or occasionally venturing out into the countryside beyond, where the cracked and dusty earth, baked brown like the people, seemed to be crying out for the rains that hovered just over the horizon. When they finally unleashed their torrents, the spectacular tropical storm that broke in the morning skies over their bungalow had had her rushing for her pen to describe the experience to her family back home.

Before she arrived here she had barely known what to expect. Blair himself had been infuriatingly enigmatic about the place, telling her only that Lucknow was the capital of Oudh province and India's third largest city, with around half a million inhabitants. And he had added disconcertingly, 'The King of Oudh may seem like an odd cove to you, but he likes me and this is by far the best posting I've ever had. I don't expect you to say or do anything that might jeopardize my position there.'

'Ye-e-s, *sir!*' But her mock salute had brought no smile to his face. His job here was not to be joked about.

Her husband had originally enlisted in Dundee's own regiment, the 73rd Highland, better known as the Black Watch, but had been seconded to the post in Lucknow as a senior British military attaché at the suggestion of Lord Dalhousie, an old friend of his family, when the Scottish earl was appointed Governor-General of India in 1847.

Despite her husband's philosophic toleration of the hereditary nabob, Laura considered the King quite repulsive. She soon found she was not alone in this, for neither the British government nor the East India Company had any time for the young debauched monarch. King Wajid Ali Khan, who was nominally in charge of the strategically important northern province of Oudh, was considered not only sexually depraved but corrupt and unbearably conceited into the bargain. Their solution was to place spies in his camp, as Laura put it, or – as Blair preferred – to place trustworthy British personnel in key positions to constantly monitor the situation and report back.

Like Dalhousie, his overlord, Wajid Ali Khan had come to power in 1847 and, despite Blair's more tolerant attitude,

Laura was appalled at the King's lifestyle, which was a constant source of amusement and gossip amongst the other British residents. It took her very little time to realize just how sheltered an upbringing she had had in Scotland. 'But can't something be done to curb his excesses?' she had asked Blair shortly after her arrival. But her question had been met with much mirth, for just before his last trip home, Blair had been asked by the British authorities to suggest very diplomatically to the King that he at least cut down on the number of concubines in his Farhat Bahhsh – the aptly named Delight-Giving Palace. 'And you know what the young devil did?' Blair asked his wife. 'He showed us what he really thought of us and our suggestion by immediately ordering ninety more young virgins for his harem that very same day!'

Laura listened and learned. The private quarters of the palace where her husband went to work each day were full of sex slaves with sycophantic eunuchs to guard them and, to a sexually ignorant young bride from Scotland, it was an introduction into a new world she could never have imagined in her wildest dreams.

For his part, Blair merely laughed whenever she appeared shocked by any of the excesses he delighted in recounting to her over supper at night. 'Far be it from me to sit in judgement on anyone. There's nothing wrong with the man having a healthy sexual appetite,' he told her. 'In my opinion there is hardly a British man-jack over here who wouldn't give their eye-teeth to be in the King's position.'

'And I suppose that includes you?' she had hit back.

He had merely smiled and got on with his meal.

At first she had tried to tell herself that she was the one who was out of step. She simply did not understand how it was over here. Her husband was an old India hand and was bound to view things differently. He had been in North India for over nine years now, and had been a senior military attaché in Oudh province for seven. During that time his old regiment, the Black Watch, had been on active service in South Africa, with several of his closest friends killed, so, as he pointed out to Laura, he had more than one good reason to be satisfied with his own lot. As one of the King's favourites, he was also in a position of some influence, and this could only bode well for his future career. 'You must realize, my dear, that whilst your life here is very different to that you had been living in Dundee, it is, nevertheless, one of great privilege and standing.'

She could almost have believed that when she had her first sight of the strange complex of buildings and sumptuous gardens in which her new home was situated. The royal compound lay to the north of the city, on a hill that sloped gently down to the River Gumti. It consisted of the palace itself where the King and his entourage lived, and where much of the administration was carried out, plus the church and other staff houses, and all the other offices and outbuildings so essential in maintaining such a lavish lifestyle.

Her first surprise had come as their carriage drove past the well-tended lawns that surrounded the palace. There the King's pet tigers, leopards and cheetahs prowled aimlessly on the ends of long gold chains, while peacocks strutted proudly, displaying their fantastic tails and giving their spine-curdling cries.

'More impressive than the Scottie dogs and marmalade cats we go in for back home, wouldn't you agree?' Blair had remarked, and there was no arguing with that.

The palace was built on classical lines, and around the outside of the building were wide verandas, where they had sat to sip their tea and chat to the other members of staff and their wives who had been waiting to welcome them.

With tiffin over, Blair had asked permission to take his wife up on to the roof for a bird's-eye view of her new home, and there Laura had gazed out through the shimmering heat on to a panorama of gracious public buildings and picture-book palaces set amid the lush greenery of public and private parks. Below them the grey-green snake of the Gumti river divided them from a city that appeared to be shot through with nuggets of glittering gold. The sight rendered her almost speechless, as she feasted her eyes on the shining cupolas, golden domes and slender minarets that sparkled against the azure blue of the sky. It was quite unlike anything she had ever seen, and both excitement and fear tingled through her, for this was indeed a strange land; a land whose ways and whose gods were not her own; but a land which, for better or worse, was now home.

From their position on the rooftop, Blair pointed out their own new home. 'I think it's about time we went down to see it, don't you?'

All the simple cantonment bungalows were built on the same lines: a rectangular block of rooms, with concrete floors and whitewashed walls, each one leading on to the next, and all opening on to a wooden veranda which ran along the front and back of the house.

'They're plain but practical,' he had observed as half an hour later they opened the door of the one that was now theirs.

After the splendour of the palace, Laura's first impression as she crossed the threshold was of a bare empty shell of a place, with battered rattan furniture her mother would not have given house-room. Most peculiarly, the legs of the furniture were sitting in bowls of water. 'To ward off the white ants,' Blair told her. 'They're house guests we can't get rid of, I'm afraid.'

She tried hard not to let her feelings show as she hurried through to the next room. After the comfort she had been used to at home, it was spartan in the extreme. It contained no furniture but a basic wooden bed, almost completely hidden by the drapes of thick green mosquito netting which surrounded it, a washstand, and two rattan chairs.

Above the bed hung a contraption called a punkah. This long wooden frame had wet towels draped over it, which were meant to keep one cool by creating a damp breeze as it swayed and creaked above the bed. There was one in every room, and they worked by a system of pulleys and ropes that led out to the back veranda where two punkah-wallahs were stationed, their duty being to sit there all day and pull on the cords which were attached to their big toes. Only a thin curtain flapping in the faint breeze divided the room from the veranda and its occupants.

Through the open weave of the curtain, Laura could quite easily make out the hunched shapes of the servants on the other ends of the rope. They were obviously well within earshot of everything that was said or done within the room. 'Will they be here all the time?' she had asked in growing dismay, already fearful of the answer.

'Night and day,' her husband assured her. 'And you'll be very glad of them, I can tell you. A punkah-wallah is as essential to life out here as the air you breathe. In fact,' he added with a laugh, 'you wouldn't have any air without them!'

She had looked up with a sinking heart at the monstrous thing above her head. The relentless swaying and creaking she was sure would drive her completely mad within days, quite apart from the omnipresence of its operators. 'But — but we shall have no privacy!' she had protested as she turned helplessly to her husband.

But Blair had merely laughed. 'This is India, my dear. One learns to leave one's British sensibilities on the boat. It's the only way to survive.'

She had bitten her tongue at that and tried desperately not to let her dismay show. She was determined to make a real success of life out here, but this was far, far worse than she had anticipated. This was positively primitive.

But even that shock had been as nothing when she passed through into the bathroom and caught sight of two fat lizards snoozing on the concrete floor. 'Get those creatures out of here!' she gasped, rushing back into the bedroom, to be followed by a grinning Blair.

'Don't be silly, darling! Regard them as household pets. They'll do you no harm and are essential here if we're to keep the mosquitoes and other insects at bay.'

She still squirmed at the thought. Even after several months she had not come to terms with those lizards, whom she had irreverently nicknamed Victoria and Albert, but as they were deemed essential to life and limb, she had eventually reached a sort of wary truce with the unwelcome guests, just as she had had to do with the punkah-wallahs and so much else that was strange in this most foreign of places.

Perhaps the worst aspect of life here, she decided, was the fact that they were never really alone. Night and day there were servants within earshot: dark, hovering presences whose inscrutable faces betrayed no emotion, but who she knew missed nothing. She was sure that was part of the reason for her increased bickering with her husband. Trapped inside because of the rains, she had had little means of escape, and these silent, white-robed spectres seemed to be everywhere, flitting like ghosts on the edges of her life. 'They haunt my every waking moment,' she complained. 'It's those bare feet, I can't even hear them as they creep up on me!'

'Tosh, my dear!' had been the retort. 'You're well used to having servants around the place. Falcon Ridge was full of them.'

She had made no response to that, for she had grown up with the parlour-maids and grooms and such like back in Broughty Ferry; they were her own people, they spoke her language, she could laugh and joke with them. Here it was so different. This whole colonial ethos made the Indian people inferior beings in their own land. And she knew she would never get used to all the bowing and scraping that went on.

As well as Ali, the cook, and the ever-present

punkah-wallahs, there was the dhobi-wallah who arrived twice a week to do the laundry, and a special servant known as a *bhisti*, whose job it was to keep the tatties wet. These screens of dried grasses placed in front of open doors and windows were kept constantly soaked, so that they tempered the blistering Indian winds to a damp breeze more reminiscent of the British seaside. But Laura could find no resemblance at all between the fetid air that came through the tatties and the refreshing zephyrs she had known down by the harbour in her home village.

It hurt her to think of Scotland now, and she was almost embarrassed to remember the high hopes with which she had set sail for India that cold winter's morning. The voyage out had not been the best start to any marriage. As well as her sadness at leaving home, she had been seasick for the first few weeks. Blair, however, seemed to enjoy every moment of it. Drinking until late in the evening with the captain or other members of the crew, he had spent little time in their cabin sympathizing with his young wife's predicament.

Laura had had no inkling beforehand of his partiality to the whisky, other than the odd drink he had accepted socially. On board ship, however, each new day would see another bottle opened, to be discarded empty before night-fall.

When she had commented on this, he had been quite acid in his response. 'Look to your own behaviour before you seek to chastise me,' he had told her bitingly. 'Lying around a cabin all day complaining about your health does not exactly make for good companionship!' The remark had cut deep, for it had been the first suggestion that he was tiring of her company and was, perhaps, not quite the besotted husband he had originally made himself out to be.

After that she had forced herself to socialize and go on deck more often. There had been several older women on board who had already spent several years in India, and

276

they had confided in her that her husband's behaviour and partiality to the bottle was far from unusual. 'It's spending all those years abroad without a decent British wife to keep them in hand, you see, my dear,' a chaplain's wife bound for Cawnpore had told her. 'Believe me, we have seen it all. If it's not the drink, it's the women that do for them.'

'The women?'

Laura had sat on the edge of her deckchair as her companion put down her needlepoint and nodded emphatically. 'Oh, my goodness, yes. There's many a good white man succumbed either to ill-health – or worse, brought on by associating with the scores of fallen women out there; or – God forgive them – taken on a . . . a . . .' and her small eyes had darted furtively in the direction of their nearest neighbours, lest they be overheard, 'a native companion, shall we say?'

'A native companion?'

'Oh yes . . . And some have several children by these women. Poor pathetic little creatures they are too, recognized by neither side.' And she had shaken her head in recollection of the numerous dusky offspring of white fathers she had herself encountered in her years of outpost living.

Laura was both shocked and curious. 'But – but this consorting with natives, it can't be commonplace, surely?'

The chaplain's wife had nodded sadly. 'I'm afraid it is, my dear. It's all too common. But I wouldn't worry yourself on that score. Most of the men who have "consorted", shall we say, choose to remain bachelors. I'm sure your handsome young husband has never had any need to stoop so low. Why, he must have had all the eligible young ladies in Oudh province living in hope for some time now! You'll have broken quite a few hearts in marrying him, I'll be bound!'

Now when Laura recalled those words, it was with a wry smile. She had not the faintest doubt that her husband had his admirers amongst not only the unattached sector of the white female population of Lucknow, but amongst the married ones as well. She was not so innocent that she had not picked up some of the many innuendoes that had passed between Blair and several of the wives at the numerous social functions they had attended since their arrival. Were it not for the fact that she herself was the object of so much male attention, she knew she would have felt a great deal more jealous than she had done.

But despite the compliments, in some ways she hardly recognized the person who was now Mrs Blair Baxter. She did not have to look in the mirror to know that the handsome major's wife was now rapidly becoming a mere pale, listless shadow of the energetic young woman who used to be known as Laura Falconer. As she lay on a couch all day, beneath the swaying, creaking punkahs, she often wondered if she would ever be her old self again, and if her energy and enthusiasm for life would one day return.

One day, she hoped, she would get used to this type of existence and learn to put up with the heat and the insects and all the other inconveniences of day-to-day living. Maybe she would come to actually enjoy the constant round of socializing, where she would sit and exchange polite small-talk with the other wives whilst their husbands drank at the bar and laughed heartily at the male banter she knew would be much more entertaining than the inane pleasantries that passed between the women. Maybe . . . Maybe . . .

Laura sighed deeply as she walked from the drawing-room window to the rickety rattan table in the middle of the floor. She knew that Blair would have totally forgotten their morning tiff by now as he threw himself into another day in Wajid Ali's employ, but the bitter words exchanged at breakfast seemed to lie heavily on her heart as the hours ticked past.

Her face was pale and tiny beads of perspiration stood out like pearls on the smooth skin of her brow as she sat down and opened up her writing case. A clean sheet of white paper lay in front of her and slowly she dipped her pen in the inkwell and began to write:

Lucknow,
15 September, 1855

Dearest Mother and Ewan,

It is now over a week since I put pen to paper, but I hasten to assure you that there has been no cause for concern. Our life here is so hectic but unbelievably happy that a week seems to flash past in the blink of an eye . . .

Chapter Twenty-three

Falcon Ridge
February, 1856

Ewan's brow furrowed as he sipped his tea and read the letter on the table in front of him:

> *Dearest Mother and Ewan,*
>
> *It is now over a week since I put pen to paper, but I hasten to assure you that there has been no cause for concern. Our life here is so hectic but unbelievably happy that a week seems to flash past in the blink of an eye. My days are full of all manner of interesting occupations that one could not begin to comprehend back home in Scotland.*
>
> *I do hope this finds you both in the best of health and spirits. I expect you will have been out in the garden this weekend dead-heading the roses. Autumn in Scotland was my favourite season and oh how I would long to see the trees begin to change into all their golden glory as the days grow short and the wind from the Tay grows snell and keen . . .*

'Would you say Laura sounds a wee bit homesick in this one?' Ewan queried as he finished reading and handed the letter to his mother who was sitting on the other side of the breakfast table. 'It strikes me she was just beginning to miss the old place as she sat down to write this.'

Kate glanced at the date at the top of the page. 'Last September . . . Aye, well she'll have been out there almost four months at the time.' The latest batch of letters had arrived that morning. The mail from India took all of five months to get to Scotland and this was only the fourth bundle they had received since Laura and Blair set out for their new home. 'It's to be expected, I suppose, that she feels a wee bit homesick now and again. It takes time to get used to marriage itself, let alone in a strange country. The first few months are always hard, no matter where you are.'

Ewan listened as he spread a piece of toast with marmalade. 'Did you find it strange – when you were first married to my father?'

'No, I can't say that I did, but then Augustus was a very special man.'

'I wish I could remember him.' Ewan's normally cheerful face took on a pensive look as he thought of the man who had died when he was no more than a toddler. He had inherited his father's study and all his possessions, so loyally kept by his mother, just as they had been when the old man died. He had grown up knowing the meerschaum pipes, the leather-bound books, and all the cherished curios as well as he knew his own toys, but that was not the same as knowing the man. 'It grieves me to think that I can only remember him in his coffin, but I suppose I should be grateful even for that memory.'

Kate gave a sympathetic smile as she stirred her tea. Somehow she had always known that memory would remain. Augustus's funeral had been over twenty years ago now, but it was still as clear in her mind as if it were yesterday. 'Do you remember anything else about that day?' she asked tentatively, for she had never before talked in depth with her son about that terrible time. Ewan looked thoughtful as he munched on the toast and sat back in his chair, scratching the auburn hair of his beard. 'Well, I can remember going with you to the cemetery, if that was the same day.'

Kate paused with her cup half-way to her lips. The cemetery – that was the most painful part of all. 'Anything else? Do you remember meeting anyone there?'

Ewan shook his head and looked surprised. 'Meeting

281

anyone there? No, I can't say that I do. As far as I remember it was just the two of us, with me holding on tight to your hand as we walked between all those tombstones that looked so huge to me at the time.'

His eyes narrowed as he cast his mind back to that summer's evening so long ago. It was funny how certain scenes remained imprinted on the memory, while others disappeared like morning mist over the estuary. Those few minutes in front of his father's grave would never leave him. 'I remember we stood in front of the family vault and it seemed awful strange to me as a wee lad that we should go all that way just to stand in front of a big stone square thing.' He gave a wry laugh. 'It seemed even stranger when you told me Dad had gone to join his father and mother and his grandparents in there!' Then his brow furrowed as he looked across at his mother. 'Why do you ask if I remember anyone else there? I've only ever remembered the two of us. There wasn't anyone with us, was there?'

'No,' Kate lied. 'There was only us.' Never in her wildest dreams could she admit to her son that it was not his father in that marble tomb but his grandfather, and that his real father had stood beside him in the graveyard that day, just as unaware of the fact that he was looking at his own son for the first time. She knew Ewan would be horrified to learn that Willie Falconer was his natural father. As far as he was concerned, Augustus's eldest son was no more than his own distant relation and now the Falcon Mills' greatest rival.

Unlikely though it had seemed at the time, Willie's prophecy over his father's grave was just about to come to fruition. Since the arrival of jute on the mill scene a decade ago, it had almost totally taken the place of flax as the city's biggest money-spinner, and Willie's own Eagle Jute Mills were on the verge of taking over from the Falcon Mills as Dundee's main employer.

The outbreak of the Crimean War three years previously had seen the Falcon Mills lose thousands of pounds that had been tied up in flax awaiting dispatch at the Russian seaport of Archangel. Once the government had declared war against Russia, there could be no question of continuing to trade with the enemy, so to Kate's dismay their firm had lost not only a major supplier of raw materials, but a vast amount of money already paid for the expected orders which never arrived. Willie, who by then had diversified almost totally into Indian jute, bore no such loss, and had made no secret of the pleasure he was taking in his rival's misfortunes.

That major financial loss had dealt a severe blow to the Falcon Mills. For several years previously the firm had been struggling to replace machinery far older than that employed in Willie's brand-new factories, so the thousands lost in the Baltic trade was a burden they could scarcely afford to bear.

The rise of the Eagle Mills to rival their own in output had rankled both Kate and her son more than the success of any of their other competitors, for Willie made no attempt to disguise the fact that his main aim in life was to outdo his father's old firm at every turn. His bitterness at what had happened had not abated over the past two decades. On the contrary, it had hardened into an abiding hatred of both Kate and her son.

As far as Kate was concerned, his determination to better them in every way was beginning to verge on the obsessional. Only the previous month he had taken out a writ to prevent them building a new mill in Lochee, one of the city's western suburbs that now housed a surfeit of Irish immigrant labour. He was claiming the land in question was legally his as it had belonged to his mother's family, although it had been listed as part of the Falcon Mills property when Kate inherited the business. Kate's lawyer, Henry Graham, maintained Willie was bluffing, as he had only stepped forward to claim the land when it was announced that the Falcon Mills were planning to build a major jute mill on the site to rival his own mills on the Dens Road.

As if reading her mind, Ewan suddenly said, 'Tell me, Mother, did Willie Falconer attend the funeral?'

Kate's heart turned over. 'What makes you ask that?'

'Oh, I was just thinking back to what I remember of that day. I know you said it was the biggest turn-out for any funeral the city had seen in years, and that all Father's friends and associates attended, but I can't recall you ever telling me that he came to pay his respects . . . Not that I'd expect him to. That man doesn't have a decent bone in his body.'

Kate toyed with the handle of her tea-cup. She hated having to lie to her own son. 'No,' she said quietly. 'Willie never turned up, and I can't say that I'm sorry. He was a bitter man then and has remained one to this day.'

'Do you think he'll be in court himself for the hearing tomorrow?'

'I really have no idea. But I shall certainly be there.' She had always been a great believer in facing down the opposition, and she certainly wasn't afraid of Willie Falconer, no matter how big a man he might now be. She gave a wry half-smile as she took another sip of her tea. 'I do believe that it might be quite a novelty for the town to have a woman take on such a case.' Her management of the business had caused quite a bit of controversy in the town before Ewan came of age, but over twenty years on she was justly proud of the job she had made of it. She had asked no quarter and none had been granted. And that had made her initial success all the sweeter.

'If you're determined to go, then I shall go with you.'

'I think not, Ewan lad,' Kate said, rising from the table. 'This is one battle I'd rather fight on my own. I just hope I'm right in thinking Willie is bluffing on this one and he doesn't have any real proof that the land in question is his.'

She was still unsure of that one vital fact as her carriage rolled up to the steps of the Sheriff Court in West Bell Street just before two o'clock the following afternoon.

She was sombrely dressed in a fine worsted dress of Black Watch tartan plaid, beneath a long jade-green cape lined with the same material. 'Blair would be flattered,' Ewan had commented as she came downstairs ready to leave, and Kate had merely smiled, knowing that not only her son-in-law but Sheriff Muir, the presiding judge's own father and brother had been officers in the illustrious Highland regiment. She had been around long enough now to know to use every wile in the book. The more she could do to give Lady Luck a helping hand the better, for she had no doubt that Willie would not miss a trick.

'Don't bother to wait, Charlie,' she told the driver of her carriage as he came to a stop outside the Palladian columns of the fine Georgian building that was the Court House. 'I really have no idea how long this is going to take, and I can easily get one of the public cabs home.'

To her surprise there was quite a turn-out of the general public to hear the case, as well as a couple of journalists from the local papers. 'You'd think this was some sort of romantic scandal they've all come to hear,' Kate commented wryly to Henry Graham, her defending solicitor, as they stood at the top of the steps and looked down on the milling crowd.

'Aye, well, the feud between you and Willie has certainly kept the tongues wagging over the years,' the lawyer reminded her as they entered the building and he made way for her through the crowd jostling in the aisle of the court. 'I'd say the town's split about fifty-fifty on the outcome of this case.'

'Those odds will suit me just fine,' Kate assured him as they took their seats. 'It's always a mistake to be the public's favourite, in my view. I'm sure when every Tom, Dick and Harry are all clamouring for a certain outcome, the judge gets wind of it and often brings in a contrary verdict to spite them all.'

'Aye, well, I'll better not comment on that,' the lawyer

said. 'But Sheriff Muir's as fair as they come in my experience.'

'We'll see about that,' Kate said, reserving her judgement for the outcome, and craning her neck in the direction of the door as Willie and his legal entourage entered.

A buzz went round the court.

Having now reached his half-century, Willie Falconer was a fine figure of a man who in size and stature bore a disconcerting resemblance to his late father. His red hair was now steel grey and receding at the temples, and his waistline was almost double what it had been in his twenties, but he had a commanding presence about him that had been the mark of all the Falconer men. In the main hall at Falcon Ridge hung portraits of three generations of the male line of the family, and there was no mistaking the lineage from which he had sprung as Willie made his way confidently down the centre of the aisle. At the sight of him, Kate could not help but wonder if she was looking at her own son in thirty years' time.

Willie was surrounded by an entourage of two lawyers plus several friends as the opposing party took their places on the benches opposite. He exuded an air of total confidence, and did not so much as cast a glance in Kate's direction. Suddenly she felt very isolated sitting there alone, apart from Henry. All her carefully cultivated bravado of a few minutes ago seemed to be vanishing by the second, and she could feel herself becoming more and more tense as they waited for the sheriff to enter. Every so often her eyes would dart in Willie's direction. He was looking so sure of himself, sitting there sharing a joke with his lawyers, she was now certain he must have something up his sleeve.

She did not have long to wait to find out. It took less than an hour for the evidence to be presented and disputed, and whilst it very quickly became clear that the land had indeed been owned by Willie's mother's side of the family, and she had willed all her Dundee estates to him, that particular site had previously been marked out in Falcon Mills' plans for expansion as far back as five years before Emily's death. Henry Graham, Kate's solicitor, argued persuasively that the late Mrs Falconer must have accepted that particular piece of land to be part of the Falcon Mills estates and it would be quite unethical for Willie to attempt to claim it back now.

In the end the sheriff found the case against the Falcon Mills unproven; the land would remain as part of their estates, but that 'as an act of goodwill, Mistress Kathleen Falconer and Mr Ewan Falconer must pay Mr William Falconer the current market price for the land as a compromise of their being allowed to build on it.' Costs would be shared.

Kate was far from happy with the verdict. 'I really don't see why we should have to pay for what is already ours,' she told Henry Graham in some irritation as they rose to leave the court. 'There obviously wasn't a case to answer on the evidence. That Sheriff Muir was frightened of Willie, that's all.'

Henry Graham's face was grave as he gathered up his briefs. 'Aye, well, there may be some truth in that. Whether we like it or not, Kate, Willie Falconer is a powerful man in this city. There are not many would care to cross him – and that goes for the high and mighty as well as the lowly.'

The lawyer's admission quite took her by surprise. 'Are you really admitting you agree with me that Willie may even have the judiciary in his pocket?'

'I'm not telling you anything,' her lawyer replied, stepping aside to allow her to leave the building first. 'You're a bright woman, Kate, you're perfectly capable of working these things out for yourself.'

Kate gave a bitter smile as she walked ahead of him down the aisle of the court. It was just as she expected all right. There was no more to be said.

Willie himself was standing outside at the foot of the stone steps when they walked out into the grey drizzle of the February afternoon. There was a lot of laughter, back-slapping and handshaking going on within the group that surrounded him. It included his counsel and his teenage son, Ian. Although she had seen Willie himself several times over the years, Kate had never actually met the boy before. It was interesting to note that now he was at that awkward stage between adolescence and manhood, he had become the spitting image of his mother Helen.

As Kate paused uncertainly on top of the steps, Henry Graham noticed the two local journalists standing at the foot making notes. 'I think it might be a good idea if the warring parties shook hands, don't you?' he whispered into Kate's ear as they started down the steps. 'It would certainly read well in the papers tomorrow.'

'A very good idea, Henry,' Kate agreed, pulling herself together. After all, she had always prided herself on being unafraid of her stepson.

Lifting her head that bit higher than usual, she began to walk purposefully down the steps, heading straight for the opposing group.

She knew Willie saw her with her hand outstretched before he deliberately turned on his heel to head off in the direction of his carriage. She could feel her cheeks begin to flame in embarrassment at the obvious snub when the slim, sandy-haired young man who had been standing beside him came striding across.

'We haven't met before, but my name is Ian Falconer, ma'm. I'd just like to say there are no hard feelings on our part.'

Although taken aback, as they shook hands, Kate found herself smiling back into the serious young face. 'You do your grandfather credit, young man,' she told him. 'He died before you were born, but Augustus would have been proud of you this day.'

'Well, thank you, ma'm.' The youth's beardless cheeks became even pinker in tone as he absorbed the observation, both embarrassed and flattered by the unexpected compliment. 'I appreciate that. I'm sorry I never had the chance to meet my grandfather . . .' He glanced round nervously at his father, and Kate sensed he would like to say more, but this was neither the time nor the place. Instead he raised a slim hand to his brow in a farewell salute. 'A very good day to you, ma'm.'

Kate watched as Ian Falconer hurried down to rejoin his father. She was aware of a peculiar knotted feeling in the pit of her stomach. She had just shaken hands with her own son's half-brother, but neither would ever know it. Suddenly it felt as if she was bearing all the secrets of the world on her shoulders. Families were a funny institution all right.

'There goes the younger generation,' she told her lawyer, standing by her side. 'It seems the old can learn a thing or two from the young now and then, wouldn't you agree, Henry?'

'Indeed I would, Kate. Indeed I would.'

Chapter Twenty-four

Although her mother's court case took place in Dundee in February, Laura did not read about the outcome until the latest bundle of letters arrived in Lucknow in the middle of July. The accumulated correspondence always covered several weeks, and she had got into the habit of only reading one letter a day so as to spin out the pleasure for as long as possible.

She broke the seal of the latest one at five o'clock in the morning, standing on the veranda of her bungalow in the cool darkness of the early dawn. Scotland seemed a million miles away as she leant back against the wooden rail and tried to visualize her mother shaking hands with Willie Falconer's son. From what she could gather, young Ian Falconer appeared to be anything but a chip off the old block. Her mother had seemed quite touched by the lad's gesture after the verdict, writing with some feeling, *'It's a pity the father is not as adult as the son, for young Master Ian could teach Weary Willie a thing or two when it comes to good manners and sound common sense . . .'*

Most of the two pages were taken up with the story of the trial, which was obviously a major concern to all back home. *'I admit to losing quite a bit of sleep over the whole affair,'* her mother had gone on to say, and Laura could well imagine the atmosphere in the house during the few days before the case came to court.

It was funny how awful people like Willie Falconer meant almost nothing to her out here. Even Blair, whose own family were big in the jute business, barely gave Dundee and its problems a second thought. It was as if they had stepped on to another planet coming to India.

Life, particularly over the past few months, had seemed full of their own special Indian intrigues. Things were changing and changing fast out here. Rumour had it that Wajid Ali, the King, was about to be sent into exile in Calcutta by the British, and his kingdom of Oudh annexed and a resident commissioner installed to run the province. Of course His Majesty was up in arms over this, and his English personal surgeon, a Dr Bell, was having a terrible job calming him down. He had even called in Blair to help convince him that it was just wild speculation. What was said between themselves, however, was a different matter entirely. There was not a single high-ranking Briton out here who did not believe the rumours to be true, and Blair had even been briefed to this effect by his old friend, Lord Dalhousie, just before His Lordship handed over the Governor-Generalship of the country to Lord Canning earlier in the year.

Laura had mixed feelings about the imminent overthrow of the King. On the one hand she was quite appalled by the decadence of his lifestyle, but she also knew his departure would cause great offence amongst his people. He was a strange spoilt baby of a man who had oozed charm on the few occasions they had met. Rumour had it he had even asked Blair to name his price for her, and that her gallant husband had replied that all the gold in his kingdom could not buy a single hair from her head. It was Dr Bell who had recounted this exchange to her in their own home after rather too much wine one evening. While she had almost choked on a mouthful of mutton chop, Blair had thrown back his head and roared with laughter. 'Aye,' he had agreed, 'but I added I'd consider letting him have first refusal as soon as I got fed up with her!'

Laura now smiled wryly at the memory as she leant against the balustrade of the veranda and mused on the incident. Good old Blair, the reply certainly ran true to form.

From her vantage point on the crest of the hill, she could see the compound and city below begin to stir as the sky began to lighten in the east. If there really were dramatic changes in the offing, she knew they would not be noticeable to most of the inhabitants who went about their daily tasks with the same dull listlessness that seemed to characterize so much of life out here. Even the very air one breathed seemed to stultify the senses, making one so lethargic that even the thought of now walking back into the house and getting into bed again seemed like a major exercise.

The rains had come early this year. It had been the morning after Blair's birthday, on the first of June, when she had awoken just after dawn feeling oddly chilly. The room had taken on a ghostly silver-grey appearance, and everything had been clammy to the touch as she got out of bed to walk to the veranda to be greeted with a swirling grey mist rolling in over the compound from behind the palace, to the north-west. And the thunder and lightning that followed was so spine-chilling and awe-inspiring that even today the memory of it was enough to bring her skin out in gooseflesh.

Old hands said that the monsoon was mild this year, but this was hard to believe. The drenching stair-rods of water that fell incessantly on to the flat roof of the bungalow and turned the dry earth to mud, causing rivers to run down what were once the well-kept pathways, were more confining than any prison bars. It was akin to living under a waterfall, waiting patiently for chinks in the deluge when one could rush out and do all the things taken for granted at other times of year.

The humidity made proper sleep impossible. An hour or so of tossing and turning on the damp sheet, inside the confines of the mosquito netting, was as much as she knew she could expect at this time of year. Instead of lying and suffering, she had got into the habit of slipping out on to the veranda to breathe deeply of what would undoubtedly be the freshest air of the coming day.

There was a special magic about the dawn, when into the sky from the east would come a faint red glow that gradually turned to flame and, as the silver moon faded from sight, the other buildings of the compound became tinged a dull bronze colour. It was like looking at an old painting that would disappear before one's eyes as the purple-grey clouds began to roll in from the hills to the north-west and the deluge began again.

Laura sighed as she slipped the precious letter from home into the pocket of her robe and took one last look up at the sky where the purple rain clouds were already gathering. High overhead, a flock of birds were passing, a black blur silhouetted against the silver-grey heavens. As she watched they disappeared over the far horizon to follow the meandering river on through the fertile plain of Oudh. Out there countless peasants would now be rising to begin another day's toil in the fields. There were times when she even envied them the simple ordered lives they led. And, as she stood there in the silent dawn, she wondered at the strangeness of fate that had brought her here to the other side of the world, and had visited this vapid, aimless lifestyle upon her. Unlike her husband, she had no office to go to, no piles of documents awaiting her perusal, no orders to give, other than the same ones she gave day after day to the same servants, who could quite easily run the household without her.

A few yards from where she stood, the two punkah-wallahs lay sleeping beneath a makeshift shelter, their thin worn faces the colour of well-tanned leather and their toothless mouths beneath droopy grey moustaches letting out rhythmic whistling sounds as they slept. What did they dream about as they lay there, she wondered? They owned nothing but the garments they slept in. Did they envy her her lifestyle and so-called riches and think her stupid and selfish for complaining of boredom? She would probably never know, for their thoughts were as inscrutable as their faces as they sat out here day after day pulling on the worn cords of the punkahs in a vain attempt to keep her cool.

Restless now, she left the veranda to wander back into the house, padding through to the drawing room on bare feet. She had tried her best to make this shell of a house into a home. The basic rattan furniture had been brightened up with rose-pink and purple Bokhara silk cushions she had made herself from a selection of materials offered by a box-wallah who had turned up with his case of glowing silks and embroidery threads shortly after her arrival. She had also bought a hand-printed Sind cotton chadar in a green leaf pattern to be used as a bedspread for the cooler weather, plus a roll of silvery-blue Benares silk that she had put aside as a present for her mother, for never had she seen such exquisite materials back home.

Home . . . How sweet was that word! And how far away was all that she held so dear. As she looked around her in the half-light of the new dawn she knew that, try as she might, this could never take the place of that beloved house where she had grown to womanhood; these rainwashed streets could never be her own.

She placed her precious letter with the others in a carved teak box she had bought, before slipping back into the bedroom where her husband lay asleep beneath the thick green folds of the mosquito netting.

She paused at the foot of the bed to look at him. He was snoring gently, his naked body sprawled across the crumpled sheet. Even through the net she could see the faint sheen of perspiration covering his skin. On the small rattan table by the bed stood a half-empty bottle of whisky and an overturned glass. In all the time she had been married to him, she had never known him go to bed without a drink – without several drinks. But he was not alone in that. There were few husbands out here who did not regard the bottle as their best friend. Maybe that's what makes him sleep so well, she thought wryly. Maybe she ought to try it.

She slipped off her robe and parted the net to slide back in beside him. He gave a half-conscious groan as she laid her head on the pillow next to his, and one of his arms flailed out and flopped heavily across her breast. She could still smell the whisky on his breath. There was no other smell quite like it, and somehow it always reminded her of this time of day. Perhaps that was why she had always managed to resist the temptation to indulge. Whisky would always be associated in her mind with a naked, sweating body and slow rhythmic breathing that stank of the excesses of the night before. But, despite the temptation of oblivion in a bottle, something told her that to join him in the nightly ritual would be the beginning of the end. She knew many wives who had teetered uncertainly at the top of that particular slippery slope, only to slide headlong into an abyss out of which it was almost impossible to climb.

Breakfast was a simple affair of tea, boiled eggs and bread and butter, eaten by lamplight. By the time Blair set off for work the streets were already awash, and Laura watched him go, picking his way across the torrents of red water that rushed anew down the road outside.

Once he had gone, she bathed in the zinc tub in the bathroom, pouring pan after pan of the cool water over her perspiring body, knowing full well that within five minutes of getting dressed she would be as sticky as ever.

She was just finishing her ablutions when there was a noise outside the window. The sweeper woman had come to clean out the earth-closet. One of the Untouchables – the outcasts of Indian society – she appeared, a thin frail figure, basket in hand, dressed in the dark, earth-coloured cloth of her class. She gasped aloud, her skeletal brown face contorting in embarrassment at the unexpected sight of a naked Laura finishing her toilet. The poor creature flattened herself against the wall, as if wishing to disappear into the masonry as Laura reached for her robe. The incident had a peculiarly depressing effect on her as she returned to the bedroom to attend to her hair.

Blair returned home as usual for *chota hazri* – little breakfast – at around eight. Another highly confidential dispatch had arrived from the Governor-General's office concerning the imminent take-over by the British. Laura knew that the whole situation was making everyone edgy, and Blair seemed preoccupied with his own thoughts as he sipped his tea and scanned his papers. But although uncommunicative, he was not as irritable with her as he had been of late, even going so far as to bend down to kiss the top of her head before leaving for work again an hour later.

'I may be late back this evening, my dear,' he told her. 'I have a special meeting with Cargill. He's due at my office at six. There's some problem arisen about his replacement when he retires, and I want to get the thing sorted out.'

How many times had she heard such an excuse? If it wasn't confidential dispatches from the Governor-General it was something else. It seemed that she ate alone more often than not these days. 'Don't worry,' she told him, with just a trace of irony. 'I'm sure I'll find plenty to keep me occupied.' But as she said the words all her nerve-ends were screaming. The supreme effort she had been making of late not to row with him in the morning was beginning to take its toll. Sometimes she felt she would explode with the frustration she felt at the thought of being cooped up here for yet one more day. She could run the household blindfold, with one hand tied behind her back.

In the months she had been out here she had wrought several changes for the better. Ali, the cook, now no longer stirred the eggs for the custard with his fingers, and in general the hygiene of the place was much more to her liking.

Bracing herself for the monotony that lay ahead, she set about her first task of the day, to see that the *bhisti* had refilled the water pots and that the sweeper had not forgotten to clean out the previous day's ashes from the stove.

She was still supervising the cleaning of the stove when she heard a cry from the next room. Rushing through, she saw that the maid, who had been spreading the damp sheets over wicker cages set out on the bedroom floor, had dropped one of the charcoal *sigris* that had been lit to place inside the cages to dry the bedding. The burning ashes were strewn all over the floor, and Laura was aghast to see that one had landed on the roll of Benares silk she had bought specially for her mother.

'You stupid, clumsy woman!' Laura looked askance at the cinder burning its way through the precious fabric, and dashed across the floor to snatch up the roll. It was obvious that several yards of the silk were now ruined.

'Look what you've done!' Suddenly all the frustration within her boiled over and she flung the singed material at the crouching figure of the maid who was desperately trying to pick up the burning charcoal with her fingers and replace it in the *sigri*. The roll caught her on the side of the head and she toppled over on to the remainder of the burning ashes.

'Oh God, I'm sorry!' Appalled at what she had done, Laura rushed across and helped the poor woman to her feet. Her right arm where she had landed still had burning pieces of charcoal clinging to the skin, and the poor creature was too cowed to attempt to remove them.

Pulling her into the bathroom, it took several minutes to clean the maid's arm with cold water from the newly filled ewer and then bandage it. Throughout the procedure the woman did not flinch or make the slightest sound as Laura dabbed at the scorched flesh. When at last she had finished, the woman pressed her hands together and bowed in gratitude, whispering softly, 'I am so sorry, *memsahib*.'

The simple words and gesture were too much for Laura, who shook her head vehemently. 'It's me who should be apologizing to you,' she said, impulsively putting her arm around the woman's narrow shoulders. 'It was unforgivable of me to lose my temper like that.'

On the washstand in the bedroom next door lay her favourite brooch, an opal set in pearls. She picked it up and thrust it into the woman's hand. 'Please,' she told her. 'Keep it. And don't think too ill of me.'

The startled woman gazed down at the gift and fear came into her eyes. To own such a thing could be dangerous indeed as one could easily be accused of stealing it. It took Laura several minutes to persuade her to accept the gift, and somehow the woman's reluctance only added to her own feelings of guilt.

Exhausted before the day had barely begun, she lay down on the bare mattress as the maid resumed her duty drying out the bedding. It was a stupid, thankless task at the best of times, for no matter how much energy went into drying things out, they still smelt fusty at the end of it all. Whatever they did, mould and mildew still seemed to cling to their clothes and possessions no matter how many ingenious methods were tried to prevent it.

It was about an hour after that, and less than an hour after Blair had left, that on rising and going through to the drawing room, Laura discovered he had forgotten the small leather case containing his essential files for the day. With so much secrecy over the planned annexation, she knew his papers were of a highly confidential nature, and not something she could trust to a servant. She had no choice but to deliver them to his office herself.

Rainwater gushed from the overloaded gutters and poured down over the ends of the veranda as, cowering beneath her umbrella, she left the house. It was a ten-minute walk to the palace building, and part of the way she attempted to keep to the scant shelter of the dripping branches of the trees.

Her leather boots were soaking wet, her stockings inside them uncomfortably damp, and the hem of her linen dress was spattered with red mud when she eventually reached the outer room of the suite of offices where Blair worked. Normally she enjoyed visiting his headquarters, for the large, high-ceilinged rooms seemed so much cooler and more fit to live in than those of her own little bungalow.

A handsome portrait of Queen Victoria hung on the wall opposite the door, with an enormous mahogany desk beneath it.

Samit Chaudri, the honey-skinned young man who was employed as a clerical assistant, got up quickly from behind the desk and bowed, pressing his hands together in the traditional greeting as Laura entered the room. The sight of his boss's wife in such a bedraggled state had him hurrying round to the front of the desk. 'Mrs Baxter, *memsahib*. How very nice to see you . . . Allow me . . .'

Laura pushed a soaking strand of hair from her eyes and gasped, 'Thanks, Sam!' as he took her umbrella and placed it to dry in the far corner of the room. She bent to dab ineffectually at the dirty hem of her dress with a handkerchief as she exclaimed, 'This awful rain!' then enquired, 'Is my husband around?'

The young man opened his mouth, then closed it again. To her surprise, he looked distinctly uncomfortable at the question. 'I'm sorry, *memsahib*, he is not.' His dark eyes swivelled towards the door behind him as he shook his head.

'Well, when will he be back?' Laura asked in some irritation, thinking her husband must just have slipped out of the office for a minute or so.

Samit lifted a chair to offer his unexpected guest a seat as he told her, 'I am very sorry, Mrs Baxter *memsahib*, but the major – he won't be back here today.'

'What do you mean, he won't be back today?' Laura demanded, smoothing her damp hair and tucking a stray strand back into its net at the nape of her neck. Blair had left her in no doubt he had a hard day in the office ahead of him. 'He told me himself he has a particularly busy day today and he has an important meeting with Mr Cargill in his office at six.'

'Oh no, not today, *memsahib*, I'm afraid.'

'Look here, Sam,' Laura said, refusing the offered chair. 'You can be afraid all you like, but my husband told me quite distinctly he was in for a hard day at the office and afterwards had a meeting scheduled with Mr Cargill at six. Now either my husband was lying or you have been misinformed.'

The young man made no reply, but avoided her eyes as he replaced the chair he had brought out for her, then resumed his stance behind the desk.

'Where is Mr Cargill?' Laura asked, her patience running out. 'I'll speak to him myself. You are obviously going to be of no help at all.'

'Mr Cargill — he is off today, *memsahib*,' Samit replied, his discomfort increasing. 'He has been confined to bed with Delhi-belly for two days now.'

Laura stared at him in confusion. 'Confined to bed? Did my husband know this?'

The clerk made a helpless gesture with his hands. He had no doubt at all that Major Baxter knew of his colleague's illness, but now was not the time to be adding fuel to the fire. 'I — I am not sure of that, *memsahib*.'

This was too much. Laura strode round the side of the desk and pushed open the door to the suite of two inner offices occupied by Blair and his staff. A young English army lieutenant and an Indian office-wallah both looked up from their respective desks in astonishment as Laura marched in. They sprang to their feet immediately and the soldier saluted. 'Mrs Baxter, ma'm. How nice to see you.'

'I've come to see my husband,' Laura announced in an I-want-no-more-of-this-nonsense voice. 'Will you tell me where I can find him, please?'

The two men exchanged nervous glances, then the lieutenant cleared his throat. 'The major was called away on business, ma'm.'

'Am I allowed to know where to?'

There was an uneasy silence as both avoided her eyes.

'Is he still in the compound then?' She had to find out; he would be requiring his files.

'I – I'm afraid I'm not at liberty to say, ma'm.'

'Oh tosh, Lieutenant!' Laura declared impatiently. 'I'm his wife and I demand to know where I can get hold of my husband.'

The young Englishman took a deep breath as he came forward and took her by the elbow. 'If you care to wait in the other room, ma'm, I'll see what I can find out for you.'

Laura allowed herself to be propelled back into the outer office and into the chair Samit Chaudri had offered her a few minutes earlier. The latter glanced across at her in some embarrassment as she sat there glowering out of the window at the rain as the officer took his leave and disappeared through the door.

'Does my husband often get called away like this?' she asked the distinctly nervous-looking young man behind the desk.

The clerk shrugged his shoulders. 'Now and again,' he answered hesitantly as his slim fingers toyed with a stick of sealing wax.

Laura made no reply, but sat looking at him as he lowered his head and began to scribble into a large ledger in front of him. He was a good-looking young man, in his mid-twenties, perhaps. Slightly above average height, his features were fine-boned and he had a sensitivity about him that told her he was far from comfortable with the situation. She had got to know Sam quite well in the year she had been out here, and had always found him the most helpful and honest of men.

At one point, quite soon after her arrival, she had even found herself making excuses to come up to the office to see him. For, discovering he was as keen a reader as she was, they had taken to exchanging books until Blair found out and put a stop to it. 'For God's sake know your place, woman,' he had told her. 'One doesn't consort with the lower orders on any basis other than business!'

At no time had Laura considered herself 'consorting' with the well-mannered young clerk, but she had been married long enough to know when to adhere to the word 'obey' in her marriage vows, and no more was ever said on the subject. She still missed her chats with Samit, though, and as she sat there she longed to ask him if he had read a copy of Tennyson's latest poem, *Maud*. She herself had been sent one from home and longed to share her enthusiasm for it with someone who would understand. Poetry had never been her husband's strong point.

When there was no sign of the officer returning after ten minutes, to fend off boredom she opened the leather-bound file on her lap. She had been loath to hand it over, even to the likes of Sam or the lieutenant, for Blair always made quite an issue about it being highly confidential and for his eyes only.

Feeling more than a little guilty, she glanced across to see if Samit was watching, but the clerk's dark head was bent over the ledger in front of him. Tentatively, she opened the file. Most of the papers inside were covered in her husband's own spidery handwriting, but as she flicked through them one stood out as it did not bear the usual British government heading or royal crest and it was scrawled in a totally unfamiliar hand. Her brow furrowed as she read on. It was a receipt for the renting of a property in the name of Major Blair Baxter at 21 Wellington Road, Lucknow. The sum paid was twelve pounds and six shillings. It was stamped and dated only four weeks previously.

'Does the King own any property in the Wellington Road area of town?' she asked Samit, totally puzzled now, for she had been here long enough to know that that particular part of the city was far from salubrious, and she couldn't imagine why either the British authorities or the royal family should consider renting property there.

Samit looked up and, to her astonishment, began to colour beneath the light tan of his complexion. 'Not that I am aware of, *memsahib*,' he answered hesitantly. 'But I couldn't swear to it, of course.'

Laura sat in silence for a moment. Thoughts were forming in her head that had no right to be there. It was as if the rain that was pouring down beyond the window just behind her had turned to ice-water and was now trickling down her spine. Her mouth had gone quite dry as she looked across at the young man in front of her and said in a quiet voice, 'That soldier who just left – he's not going to come back, is he? He's going to wait until I get bored and leave before he returns, then he won't have to tell me where I can find my husband.'

Samit twiddled his pen nervously between slim fingers and his brown eyes were troubled as they looked at her from behind the desk. 'I – I really can't say, *memsahib*.'

Laura got to her feet, shoving the leather case with the files beneath her arm. Her face was set as she walked across and picked up her wet umbrella.

Samit immediately got to his feet. 'Where are you going?'

'I'm going to find out where my husband is,' Laura replied in a voice that made clear her resolve. 'If you won't help me, then I'll have to find out for myself.'

'I – I wouldn't do that if I were you, Mrs Baxter, *memsahib*.'

'And why not, may I ask?'

The young man gave a helpless shrug of his shoulders and his lips made no response, but his eyes, dark and distinctly troubled, were already saying much more than she wanted to hear.

Chapter Twenty-five

Twenty-one Wellington Road turned out to be a side street off one of the city's main thoroughfares. It was an area Laura had never visited before. As her palanquin left the palatial villas and well-kept gardens behind and headed for the sprawling hinterland of inferior buildings and shanties, she began to experience a growing sense of unease. Here there were no longer any white faces, and there were few well-dressed people to be seen. Emaciated dogs scavenged for scraps in the open sewers, and ill-clad children with stick-insect limbs watched wide-eyed as her palanquin-wallahs splashed their way to their destination.

It came as some relief to find that the house in question was in a street that still looked relatively prosperous compared to most of its neighbours. There was even the odd tamarind tree to be seen and a few shops, plus a large, shakily written sign stating 'Doctor and Dentist' propped up outside an open doorway as the palanquin slowed and Laura craned her neck for a better look.

'Here, *memsahib!*' the cry went up from the front bearer as they stopped outside an archway that seemed to open on to a covered courtyard leading into the houses beyond. The number '21' was scrawled on the wall next to what she took to be the equivalent in Hindustani.

'Wait here,' she told the two native bearers as, still clutching the leather case with the file, she climbed out of the shaky contraption that had borne her the two miles through the rainwashed streets. 'I shouldn't be too long.'

A thin, sad-looking cow, with dark mournful eyes, a deep hanging dewlap and a hump between its bony shoulders stood watching by the side of the road as she looked up at the shuttered windows of the surrounding buildings.

The two bearers who had carried the palanquin were now squatting inside a nearby doorway, watching her in growing curiosity as they popped fresh betel-nuts into their mouths. She threw an anxious glance their way and they grinned back at her, their few remaining teeth stained blood-red from the juice. In all their years of ferrying palace personnel to and from the city, they had never been asked to convey a single white woman into this part of town before.

Sheltering beneath her umbrella, Laura began to panic, wondering what was the next best course of action. This was the house referred to on the receipt in her husband's file all right, but what did she do now? Should she enter the courtyard and bang on the door demanding to see Blair? Suddenly coming here in person did not seem such a good idea after all. Her mother had always told her she was far too impetuous. 'Act first and think afterwards, that's you, Laura,' she used to say. And now, as she stood there beneath her umbrella, gazing at the strange doorway, Laura knew that to be true.

'Oh God!' she groaned aloud. Her impulsiveness had got her into some scrapes in the past, but this had to be the worst yet. Maybe she had come here on a wild-goose chase . . . But no, something inside her told her that was not the case. White men did not rent houses in this part of town without a good reason. Why hadn't Blair told her about it if it was so innocent? And why wasn't he at the office today? She had no doubt his clerks knew far more than they were letting on.

She gazed through the open archway into the courtyard beyond. She was sure he must be in there. Perhaps she should scout around a little first and find someone to ask if a *sahib* had just moved in?

The downpour began to subside a little, allowing a watery shaft of sunlight to break through the clouds, and she glanced up at the sky wondering what to do for the best when a small girl appeared at the gate of the court-yard.

'Well, hello there . . . Aren't you pretty!' Laura found herself staring down at the child, for she was truly beauti-ful. Two curtains of dark hair framed a perfect oval face, with skin the colour of golden honey, and beneath a thick black fringe, a pair of luminous brown eyes observed her with a shy curiosity. She could be no more than five or six years old and, although she was barefoot, she wore a pretty European-style dress and carried a doll with real hair, a rare luxury indeed for an Indian child, let alone one from this area.

Her back pressed up against the mellowed stone of the arch, the child was watching her with an unblinking stare that was quite unnerving, but as she began to back away into the courtyard Laura immediately attempted to move closer.

'Don't be afraid,' Laura told her in a reassuring voice. 'I won't hurt you. I have come to see your mama. Can you take me to your mama?'

To her surprise the child seemed to understand and, after thinking for a moment, nodded, gingerly holding out a hand towards her.

Both flattered and taken aback by the reaction, Laura smiled down at the tiny figure, then followed, with a rapidly beating heart, as her young guide turned and led her into the courtyard.

The rain was now no more than intermittent large spots, and in the watery sunlight a few scrawny hens pecked aimlessly in the mud in front of them. She could smell the pungent aroma of spices cooking through one of the windows. Almost all had their shutters half closed, making it impossible to see inside any of the dwellings, although the sound of distant female voices could be heard, and somewhere there was a baby crying.

Laura could feel beads of perspiration trickling down her

back as the child wended her way around the flooded patches of ground and up to the door of one of the houses. Letting go her hand, the small girl pushed open the door and disappeared inside, leaving Laura standing uncertainly on the step.

She was sure she was being watched as she glanced round at the windows; they were like blinkered eyes, staring at her from all angles. This had been a really stupid idea, she decided. Her mother had been right; her impetuousness was bound to get her into real trouble sooner or later.

She was on the point of turning to leave when the door opened a fraction, and a tall, slim, dark shape appeared in the semi-darkness behind it. As Laura adjusted her eyes to the gloom of the house's interior, she could make out the figure of a young woman in a red and gold sari. She had long, waist-length dark hair, and her face was half covered but, even so, from her bearing and demeanour, it was obvious she was very beautiful. She had that dignified serenity about her that only Indian women seemed to possess.

'I've come to find someone,' Laura found herself saying in far too loud a voice, to cover her embarrassment. 'A Major Baxter. I understand he has bought this house. You wouldn't know him, by any chance?' In her eagerness to appear completely in control of the situation, she knew she was verging on making a complete fool of herself as she stared through the gap in the door, praying that the woman spoke English and understood.

'Not here.'

The words, so softly spoken, took Laura aback. 'What do you mean, not here? You know him then?'

'Not here,' the woman repeated, louder this time, as she attempted to close the door in Laura's face.

'Please don't!' Laura leapt forward and found herself pushing on the door as the woman tried to close it. 'Please don't go. I – I must find him. It's important!'

307

'Not here!' the woman repeated, her voice much louder this time as she pushed on the other side, the sari falling from her hair as she tried desperately to keep the stranger out. 'You go, please! Major Blair not here!'

'A-*ha!*' Her husband's first name hit Laura like a bolt, and she pushed even harder now. The woman actually knew his name.

Then suddenly, with all her weight behind it, the door was thrust open and she found herself stumbling into the darkened room and face to face with the young woman, whose hand flew to her face as if she had been physically struck.

As the Indian woman reached down to comfort the small child who was now cowering behind the narrow skirts of the sari, Laura could see that both the woman's slim wrists and upper arms were covered in gold bangles, as were her ankles above the bare feet. She had an exotic, compelling presence about her that was quite unlike the other native servant women she had been used to meeting in the confines of the palace compound. For the most part, they were submissive, cowed creatures like her maid, a breed apart from the tall, dignified figure whose dark eyes were full of anger as she now pointed to the door and said, 'You bad woman. You go. Husband not here.'

Exactly which husband she was referring to, Laura could not be totally sure as she glared back at the woman in mounting anxiety. A shaft of sunlight found its way through the open doorway, enabling Laura to see more clearly the features of her reluctant hostess. A jewel sparkled on the woman's forehead, between a pair of dark eyebrows that flared delicately above the black lustrous eyes; the nose was small and aquiline, the mouth full and sensuous. It was a face quite startling in its dusky beauty, a fact that did little to put Laura's mind at rest.

Nervously she glanced around her. 'I'm not going until I get some answers,' she said in an agitated voice. 'This house is in my husband's name, and if he owns a house here I want to know the reason why. I'm not leaving until I get to the bottom of it.'

She pushed past the woman, looking for anything that might answer the questions that were eating at her insides.

It seemed a typical Indian house, with little to betray any European occupation. A black beetle scuttled across the floor at their feet, and the whole atmosphere had an uncomfortable, dank feel to it. There was a neglected air about the place, due mainly to the lack of furniture. The walls were whitewashed and a picture of Queen Victoria's wedding hung on the far wall, next to a picture of the god, Shiva. Beneath it stood a long couch similar to those issued by the British government to its employees abroad; most *dak* bungalows had one. Laura glanced at it, then her gaze returned and she stared hard for several seconds. Then a cry of recognition escaped her lips. There, lying on the worn upholstery, was a jacket similar to one worn by her husband.

'That's Blair's!' she shouted triumphantly, rushing across to snatch it up. Then immediately she leapt back as if stung when, to her astonishment, a startled, wailing cry was emitted from beneath the garment.

She gazed down in consternation as she clutched the jacket to her. There, on the faded fabric of the couch, lay a small boy of no more than two years old. He was curled into a ball and was naked save for a striped cotton shirt. He had obviously been fast asleep until so rudely awoken. He sat up on the couch rubbing his eyes and, after fixing Laura with the gaze of a frightened rabbit, he began wailing even more loudly at the sight of the strange young woman staring down at him. Both his hair and skin were much lighter in colour than his sister's – far too light for him to be a true Indian.

'Don't cry,' Laura implored him as the wails reached screaming pitch. 'Please don't cry. I haven't come here to hurt you.'

At that, the young Indian woman came forward and picked the boy up, glaring at Laura as she did so. The child wrapped his thin arms and legs around his mother as she murmured soothing words in his ear in an attempt to pacify him. Despite her cool demeanour, Laura could sense the woman was nervous, for her upper lip was covered in beads of sweat which she wiped away with the stiff, embroidered corner of her sari as she turned to face her unwelcome visitor. 'You go now,' she said, in a voice full of accusation at this upsetting of her children. 'You not good here. You go, please.'

'Soon,' Laura assured her. 'Soon.' She wanted proper answers and wasn't getting any. All she was doing was upsetting innocent children. Her despair became tangible as she gazed down at the jacket in her hands. But she must not jump to conclusions, she told herself. Many men on the station had similar jackets, so she couldn't be entirely sure this one belonged to Blair. Then something made her look inside. The label said: '*MacDuff and MacDuff, Gents' Outfitters, George Street, Edinburgh.*' Her stomach turned over. 'Oh God . . . No . . .' It was Blair's favourite tailor.

Indignation flooded through her; indignation, hurt pride, and most of all a deep anger that she could have been such a fool as never to suspect. She could feel the blood coursing through her veins, and two red patches stung her cheeks as she threw the jacket back down on the couch and turned to the woman. 'Where is he?' she demanded in an icy voice. 'Where is my husband?'

'Not here,' the woman repeated, clutching the child more tightly to her and backing nervously away towards a door that led into another room. 'Husband not here!'

'Bitch!' Laura yelled back, her reserve crumbling. 'Can't you say anything other than that? If you can't tell me then I'll have to find out for myself!'

Pushing the woman out of the way, she ran through to the next room, looking around her wildly for any other sign of her husband. To her frustration, she could see nothing that spoke specifically of Blair, although several items of male apparel lay on the double bed and a few European masculine toilet articles stood on the dressing chest alongside it.

The woman and her children watched her in silence from the open doorway as she continued to search the room for evidence.

Laura could feel tears of anger and frustration welling in her eyes. She felt demeaned by what was happening. Then the small boy began to cry once more and the sound made her stop her wild search. She had not come here to frighten children. Whatever was going on was none of their doing. She took a deep breath and raised her eyes to the ceiling. 'You do understand English?' she said to the woman in as measured a tone as possible.

The woman nodded uncertainly.

'Good. Then I want to tell you that I am Major Blair's wife . . . He is my husband.' She wanted absolutely no mistake made about that and pointed to the gold ring on the third finger of her left hand. 'My wedding ring. I am married to Major Blair. Do you understand me?'

The woman nodded.

'Good. Does he sometimes live here with you?' She spoke the words loudly and clearly as one would address someone with a hearing problem.

The woman's expression was totally impassive as she shook her head. 'No. No,' she insisted. 'Major Blair. He not live here. He good man. He help me.'

'Yes,' Laura said patiently. 'I understand that. And I know he lives at the palace with me, but does he some-times live here with you?' She pointed in the direction of the bed but could not bring herself to actually look at it. 'Does he sometimes sleep there – with you?'

At that the woman turned abruptly on her heel and walked back into the outer room.

Laura looked down at the bed and felt sick in the pit of her stomach.

She followed the woman and children out of the room. 'I would be very grateful if you would not tell him I have been here,' she said in a cold voice. 'If he finds out it wouldn't do either of us any good. Do you understand that?'

The woman made no response.

'Good,' Laura replied briskly as she fought back the tears. 'I'll be going then. I think I've found what I came for.'

Then, without as much as a backward glance, she walked out of the room and on out of the house.

The rain had stopped completely now, and a shaft of midday sun almost blinded her as she stepped back into the courtyard. Fighting back the tears, she leant back against the wall of the house and closed her eyes as she tried to calm herself. She was living out her worst nightmare. She had been a fool to come here.

Despite her attempt to stop them, tears streamed down her cheeks as she made her way back to the waiting palanquin.

She was totally unaware of the dark eyes watching her from the shadow of a doorway across the street.

Samit Chaudri watched her stumble blindly back into the conveyance and he shook his head in silent despair. He knew as soon as she entered the building with that case under her arm that she would find out about the house. The whole office knew the receipt was in there, but the major had become far too blasé about the whole thing. For seven years his relationship with the woman had been an open secret to his staff and, although he had been more discreet at the time of his marriage, he had been becoming careless again of late. It happened so often out here. He had seen it so many times over the years. And the wives coped with it in different ways.

As the bearers picked up the shafts of the palanquin and started off back down the street with Laura inside, Samit wondered how she would live with the knowledge. She was not like most of the others. She was not one of those females content to spend their days lying idly beneath the swaying punkahs or drinking tea on the palace veranda. She was far too lively and independent for that. He had enjoyed their chats on the few occasions she had come in to see her husband and had had to wait in the outer office until the major found time to see her. They had discussed literature together and music, and she had asked him all sorts of questions about the country and its people. But those conversations had come to a sudden end and, although it was never mentioned, he was sure the major had been the cause. Samit knew that as a non-white he was deemed fit to work for the British government, but not to consort socially with its subjects. The fact that so many white men, like the major himself, had secret Indian wives did not seem to come into the reckoning.

The young man's face was pensive as he came out of the shadows of the doorway and watched the spindly brown legs of the dhoti-clad palanquin bearers disappear into the distance. Laura Baxter had lost a husband in this shabby little street today. She would need a friend.

Chapter Twenty-six

Laura arrived back at the bungalow in a state of desperation. If Blair really did have a native 'wife' and family, then
who was she to turn to for support? Who out here would
understand? From the bits of gossip she had overheard,
her husband's behaviour was far from unusual. On the
contrary, it seemed almost the done thing, and most British wives simply cultivated a stiff upper lip and put up with
it. Maybe it was innocence, or maybe just plain stupidity,
but never for one moment had she believed it could
happen to her. This type of behaviour seemed so far removed from the view of love and marriage she had experienced at home. It was as if she had entered an entirely new
world where people played the game by rules she could
not begin to understand. While she could just about comprehend what would make an unmarried man resort to
liaisons with native women, to carry on such behaviour
after marriage was truly despicable. Perhaps he had never
really cared for her. Perhaps all those words of love he had
uttered on the sofa in her mother's drawing room were
simply that – mere words, with no real emotion behind
them. It was a chilling thought.

Once home, she found she could not rest. She wanted to
run – run as far away from here as possible. The bungalow
seemed an alien place as she paced the concrete floors and
fought with her emotions, which swung between a burning jealousy and an ice-cold hatred for the man who was
causing her such pain.

Did she still love Blair? Had she ever really loved him? It
was true she had been both intrigued and flattered by the
attentions of so mature and attractive a man when he had

314

first come to call at her family home. Compared to the young men paying court to some of her friends, the dashing major had appeared so much more worldly-wise and interesting. And there was no denying she had been attracted by his fine figure and craggy good looks, even if his fair hair was growing a bit thin on top and his blue eyes were already pouched by rather too many late nights. Those physical signs of maturity had merely added to his attraction, as had his tales of life abroad, which had made India seem such an exotic and appealing place. But did all that add up to love? She had convinced her mother and brother that it did and, in truth, had also convinced herself. But what now? The one thing that was for certain was that she had left Scotland a girl, with a head full of romantic notions, and a year and a half later she was now a woman with few illusions left.

Watching her husband drink himself into a stupor almost every night had not exactly enhanced her romantic picture of him, but this had to be the ultimate insult. It would have been a big enough shock to learn he had been consorting with a native woman before they met, but to discover he actually had a family by one and was still supporting her . . .

She shuddered at the very thought. Had this been Scotland she would simply have left him – gone back to her family in disgust; but this was India, and there was no family round the corner to run to, no one to give her any advice on how to handle such a situation.

How she wished Ewan were here. She knew her brother would understand even better than her mother. From earliest childhood he had been there, her rival and her protector rolled into one. He had even taken the blame for several of her misdemeanours over the years, both of them knowing that the maternal wrath would be that bit less severe if Ewan owned up to being the guilty party. She had always accepted that, although her mother loved her dearly, he was the real favourite. Her happy-go-lucky, loving brother could do no wrong in anyone's eyes at home. Oh how she longed for him now!

Laura could feel her eyes begin to mist at the thoughts of home as she paced from room to room, wringing her hands, under the curious eyes of the watching servants. She knew they could sense something terrible was wrong as they threw wary glances in her direction and silently went about their business.

Finally, at around six o'clock, when Blair had still not returned, she knew she could stand it no longer and, lifting her umbrella from the stand by the front door, she decided to go back to the palace. What she was going to say to Blair if she found him there, she had no idea; all she knew was that she could not remain at home alone one minute longer.

'If the major returns home, tell him I've gone to the palace,' she told Ali, the cook. 'I don't know when I'll be back. And you can forget about supper.' The very thought of food made her feel quite ill.

She ignored the two punkah-wallahs squatting on the veranda as she closed the bungalow door behind her.

'Good-day, Mrs Baxter, ma'm!' Dandi, the tiny Bengali schoolmaster who assisted in the teaching of the English children on the compound was passing the foot of their steps as she came out. Sheltering beneath his oversize umbrella, in his tight-fitting black coat, white dhoti and fawn sock suspenders over his bare legs, he was a comical sight, but she had a soft spot for him; he could recite Burns better than any man she knew, and had a fair knowledge of Byron into the bargain.

'Good-day to you, Mr Dandi. I trust you are keeping well these days and the mixture was of some help?' She knew he had been suffering with his lungs and had loaned him a very good chest mixture she had brought with her from Scotland.

'Indeed I am, *memsahib*. I am much better. The mixture was quite excellent.' He bowed low as she descended the bungalow steps. 'You are indeed a gracious lady.'

'It was my pleasure.'

'God bless you, *memsahib*,' he called after her as, umbrella held high, she picked her way over the wet ground. 'And may he keep you dry!'

Laura gave a wan smile in response. If there really was a God she would need a bigger favour than that if she was to get through today without going out of her head.

The rain was lighter now, and the nearer she got to the palace itself, the more solid the path became beneath her feet. Here the ground was covered in stone flags and much less prone to turning itself into a muddy quagmire in the rainy season, or into a dust bowl in the early summer heat.

Around her, sheltering beneath the ubiquitous umbrellas, she could see people going about their business totally unaware that her world was falling apart. It seemed incredible that she could smile, murmur greetings, and chat to Mr Dandi about his chest complaint at a time like this.

She was approaching the hospital block when she recognized another familiar figure coming towards her. She could tell from the tall, lithe-limbed gait that it was Samit, her husband's clerk.

She managed a strained smile as they neared one another and their steps slowed down. They paused awkwardly a few feet apart on the path.

Sensing the young man's innate shyness, Laura forced herself to speak first. 'The major – he isn't back yet, is he, Samit? Has he been in the office at all today?' Then, to her embarrassment, she heard her voice break as she added, 'I've been looking for him.'

The young man looked at her in consternation. 'Mrs Baxter . . .' He made a move forwards, his hand out towards her, then checked himself. His arm was left in mid-air. It was not done for him to touch her. He was of a much lower social standing; the rules were immutable and must be observed. 'Come to the office,' he found himself saying. 'Come back with me and I will make you a cup of tea.'

Grateful for his concern, Laura followed his hurrying figure towards the palace. She walked several steps behind him so it would not appear they were together, and she kept her umbrella low over her face as they passed other clerical workers leaving for home. She felt angry at herself for almost breaking down like this. It made her look weak and silly, when she had every reason to be furious, for she had never been so humiliated, or felt so betrayed.

To her great relief, the other staff had already gone home, and there was no one in the outer or inner offices of Blair's suite when they arrived.

Laura and the young man looked at one another as she closed the door behind her. There was an awkward silence. She felt a strange sense of guilt, as if they were naughty children doing something they shouldn't, and she knew he could feel it too.

'Please . . . take a seat. Make yourself at home.' Samit broke the silence as he motioned for her to take the most comfortable chair in the room. 'I will be back in a moment.'

He disappeared down the passage outside in the direction of the small kitchen shared by those on that floor.

Laura sat motionless until he returned. A slight buzzing was the only sound to be heard. On the windowsill beside her was a glass jar with vinegar and honey in the bottom, put out to catch flies, and she watched listlessly as the trapped occupants flew round and round in a frantic search for freedom. She had a sudden urge to tip the jar up and release the demented prisoners, but at that moment Samit returned.

'I have taken the liberty of adding the milk,' he told her as he handed her the cup and saucer he had brought. 'Please drink it. It will do you good.' He stood and watched until she took the first sip, then he sat down on a chair opposite.

Laura was thankful he had not disappeared behind the desk. Somehow that would have put more than a physical distance between them. There was something comforting about his presence. He had a calm, gentle nature, quite unlike most of the British officers she knew, and quite unlike her own husband. No one could ever accuse Blair of being either of those things. The major was a typical, down-to-earth – sometimes dour – Scot, who could be either devastatingly charming or cuttingly sarcastic at the drop of a hat.

The tea was strong and piping hot and she nodded her appreciation. 'Thank you, Sam. This is very thoughtful of you.'

He smiled. It was a wide, rather bashful smile that revealed a row of perfect white teeth beneath the thick black moustache. 'It is nothing.' Then his eyes were serious once more. 'You must not worry, Mrs Baxter,' he told her. 'These things – they are not important. They sort themselves out. I swear to you they do.'

And as she looked at him, and saw the concern in his eyes, Laura had no doubt that he knew. His sympathy was genuine, for he knew exactly what was upsetting her. It was both a humiliating thought and at the same time an enormous relief. 'You – you've known my husband a long time, haven't you, Sam? Far longer than I have.'

'Almost five years.'

'And you've known about that Indian woman and the children.'

There was a long pause as he looked down at his hands.

'Please,' Laura begged him. 'You must be honest with me. There is no one else I can talk to about this. No one. You are my only real friend.' No matter what the British authorities thought, in her eyes at least they had been friends. Since the early days of her arrival here he had been the most helpful of all her husband's personnel. None of the other wives she had met were in the least bit interested in discussing anything other than local gossip or bemoaning their lot, but with him she could talk about things that really interested her. They had read the same books, thought the same thoughts. 'You've got to tell me the truth. Please. I shall go mad otherwise.'

He looked at her and sighed as he shook his head. 'I can't. It is not my place to say anything –' he began, but Laura burst in.

'– Place! I'm tired of hearing about place out here. The whole country seems to be run by keeping people in their places. And the Indians are no better than the British. In fact, if anything they are even worse with their ridiculous caste system!'

He was silent after her outburst, his dark eyes inscrutable as she continued wearily, 'I'm sorry . . . Please forgive me. I'm a stranger to India. I can neither fully understand nor accept certain things that happen here – on both sides of the social divide. Things that other Europeans take for granted seem terrible to me. It's a whole new world I have found myself in and I need a friend. I need a friend more than anything. Someone to help me understand. Will you be that friend?'

'I would be honoured,' he said quietly. 'But I cannot.'

'Why not? Because you work for my husband?'

'Not only that. I am only half-British. My mother was Indian. It would not be considered suitable for me to be your friend.'

Laura stiffened in her seat. She had had no idea he was a half-caste. In many ways they were thought even less socially acceptable than the pure Indians by the Europeans who considered them neither fish nor fowl. Accepted by neither side, they inhabited a curious no man's land in between both cultures. 'I didn't know that. I really had no idea.' Although he was much lighter skinned and better educated than most of the local clerical staff, it had never occurred to her that he was half-British, and the knowledge both intrigued and appalled her. She had come to him for a solution to her dilemma to find that he was part of the problem – her problem. He was a product of the very situation she was now finding it so impossible to cope with. 'You come from one of these –' she searched for the right word – 'these *liaisons?*'

He nodded, his face impassive, but he said nothing.

She was examining his features in detail now, and felt foolish that the thought had never occurred to her. It was a handsome face, but more angular, more square-jawed than the usual fine bone structure of the Indian race. It was an Anglo-Saxon face with a pleasing pale, coffee-coloured skin, dark glossy hair and an Indian sensitivity about it that combined to make an intriguing mixture. 'Your father – he was a British soldier?'

Samit nodded, and when he spoke there was a noticeable note of pride in his voice. 'He was a colonel in the Engineers.'

'And he had a British wife as well as an Indian one – your mother?'

'Yes, he had a British wife. In fact, his English wife was a very fine lady. He always spoke most highly of her to us.'

Laura drew in her breath and threw up her hands in a gesture of incredulity. What kind of society was this? 'You mean – the colonel's wife – she knew about your mother – about you?'

Samit nodded, his expression softening as he confirmed, 'Oh yes, she even gave us presents before she left to return to England.' His voice was wistful as he remembered the tall, fair-skinned woman with the gentle eyes who had given him a red cloth-bound set of Shakespeare, and his younger sister Sushila a beautiful doll dressed as the unfortunate French Queen, Marie Antoinette. 'She went back to the English south coast, Hampshire I think it was, because of her health. My father retired and returned to England two years later. He wrote to us regularly until he died four years after that. That was ten years ago.'

Laura inhaled deeply and let out a deep sigh. This was indeed another world entirely. She had come here expecting tea and sympathy, and instead was listening to another version of the story that had just shattered her own life, and from the lips of someone intimately concerned.

For once she was lost for words. 'I – I really don't know what to say.'

He was looking at her intently, as if summing up the effect of his story upon her. She got up from the chair and walked to the window and looked out at the rain that was now falling again, sending fresh rivulets down the sides of the path and causing small lakes to form in the overflowing flower-beds. Somehow, although she knew it was not his fault, she could not bring herself to look at him. He seemed to represent the very cause of her own life falling apart.

Samit got up from his chair and walked up behind her. Tentatively he placed a comforting hand on her arm. 'Don't be angry with me,' he said in a quiet voice. 'We cannot choose our parents, neither can we be held responsible for their actions before we were born.'

Laura listened but made no reply. He was right of course, but that did not help. All her dreams had crumbled in that shabby side street this afternoon. How could she ever allow Blair to touch her again? How could she remain married to a man who had betrayed her like this? How could she bring children into the world who would have a half-brother and -sister they would never know; a half-brother and -sister who would live their lives in poverty in this alien place? Her mind flew back to that strange, beautiful creature in those shabby surroundings. 'Do you know her?' she asked in a terse voice. 'Have you ever met my husband's native wife?'

'I know of her,' Samit replied truthfully. 'And I have seen her, but we have never met.'

Laura turned to face him. 'What do you know of her?' The question was almost accusatory.

'It is not a pretty story.'

'I don't expect it to be.'

'And you really want to know?'

322

'Yes. I really want to know.'

'Her name is Jaya,' he began slowly, as if pondering the best way to describe the woman his employer had been supporting for about seven years. 'I think he met her on a visit to Madras before he came here . . .'

'And?' Laura sat back on the edge of her chair, her voice betraying her impatience. 'Where exactly did she come from? How did they meet?'

Samit was silent for a moment. He had been told Jaya's story by Nirad, the old man who had preceded him as the major's personal clerk. It was a story that was not unfamiliar to Indian ears, but might not transfer too well in the telling to a European. 'I cannot expect you to understand,' he told her. 'All I can say is that certain customs have existed here for hundreds of years, and some can have a terrible effect on people's lives.'

'Go on,' Laura urged him, sitting forward on her seat.

'In certain parts of the country, such as Madras,' he began, 'there is a custom among Hindu parents where, in order to persuade the gods to grant them a particular favour, they promise their next-born girl child as a sacred gift to them. Or if they have a particularly beautiful daughter they exchange her for a special favour.'

'But that's terrible!' Laura had heard that girls were not as highly valued as boys out here, but to simply give them away . . .

'No,' he said in a calm voice. 'It is not so terrible. Not in their eyes.'

'But what becomes of her – this sacrificial offering?'

'As an offering to the gods, she is presented to the temple as an infant to be trained in singing and dancing.'

Samit paused, his face reddening beneath the cool coffee colour of his skin. He sat down on his chair with a sigh. Despite his attempt to make it acceptable to European ears, it was not a pretty story at all and he was loath to go on.

'Please continue,' Laura implored him. 'I must know all if I am to even attempt to understand.'

He took a deep breath and avoided her eyes. 'By the age of five – when she is considered to be at her most sexually desirable – she becomes the priests' own personal plaything.'

'Plaything?'

'Prostitute.' There, he had said it!

Laura gasped and sat up in her chair. 'At the age of *five!* You can't possibly be serious!'

'Unfortunately I am.'

They looked at one another and he looked away, unable to bear the recrimination in her eyes.

'That is quite the most hideous thing I have ever heard. That – that could kill the poor creatures!' The horror in Laura's voice and face was all too obvious.

'Yes,' he agreed. 'You are right. And very often it does. And perhaps they are the lucky ones.'

'And those that survive? What of them?'

'If the child survives into adolescence she serves as a dancer before the shrine in the daily temple of worship . . .' He moved uncomfortably in his seat, reluctant to continue.

'And?'

'And there she must at all times be prepared to be used not only by the priests but by all the male visitors to the temple. She is there for one purpose – to fulfil their every sexual desire. It is what she has been trained to do.'

Laura looked at him in increasing horror. 'And – and what eventually becomes of her?' she whispered. Surely no one could survive that sort of life for long?

Samit shrugged. 'Once she is used up and her charms have faded, she is turned out on to the street with the acknowledged right to beg for a living.'

Laura shook her head in incredulity. 'But her parents . . . ?'

'Oh, it is no shame on them. They may be people of excellent caste and lose no face at this disposal of her. What they did is perfectly acceptable. The girl is no longer one of them. On her arrival at the temple she entered a quite separate caste peculiar to her kind. They call them *"devadassis"* or "prostitutes to the gods". They have existed from time immemorial. The temples could not survive without them.'

Laura was stunned into silence.

'I think perhaps I should not have told you of this.'

She shook her head. 'No – no, I had to know . . . But – but that's totally inhuman,' she said at last. 'Those poor girls.'

Samit gave a philosophic shrug. 'Most do not survive long enough to be sent out on to the street. And occasionally one has the courage to escape while she is still young and beautiful . . . Like Jaya.'

The name resounded in Laura's head. Jaya . . . Jaya . . . 'You think my husband met her after she ran away from the temple in Madras?'

'I know nothing for certain, but that is the story I was told.' Jaya herself had told the story of her past to Nirad, when the old man had been sent on an errand by the major to her first rented room in Lucknow. From then on Nirad had visited her many times, and they had become firm friends before the old clerk died.

Laura sat in silence letting the knowledge sink in. Then, as if reading her thoughts, Samit added, 'Former temple dancers, especially beautiful ones, are often very sought-after as second wives for they have been so well trained in all the *devadassis'*s skills . . . These things matter a great deal to some men.'

Laura shuddered as the image of her husband and that woman on the bed in that shabby little room flashed into her mind. She felt physically sick at the thought. How could she, as a decent wife, ever share a bed with him again? 'Does my husband know that you know all this?' she asked quietly.

'All about her past, no. But about Jaya herself and the children, yes. Although he has never spoken to us of his exact relationship to them . . . I understand Rajiv, the mail clerk in the inner office, has been on several errands to the lady. It is not uncommon for British officers to use their staff as go-betweens.'

Laura felt as if she had had all the wind knocked out of her. 'As usual the wives are the last to know.'

Samit shrugged and gave an understanding smile. 'There are many such stories, not only here in the palace but everywhere in our country where the white men rule. Life is hard here for the Indian in his own land – man or woman.'

Laura made no reply. Her mind was still on that slim, dusky figure in the red and gold sari. By the looks of her she was not much older than herself, and yet she had two children. At what age had she run away, she wondered? Fourteen or fifteen perhaps? A look of horror crossed her face at the thought of her husband consorting with a mere child.

'You are shocked,' Samit said. 'I should not have told you.'

'Oh, no! I'm very glad you did.'

'Are you? Are you really?'

Laura attempted a smile. 'I don't know. I really don't know.' Sometimes the truth was even worse than the imagination. 'It – it's knowing what to do about it, that's all . . . Where to go from here.' She made an imploring gesture with her hands. 'Tell me, Samit. What do most wives do when they find out something like this? Because it does happen, doesn't it? I am not the only one.'

'Oh no,' he assured her. 'You are not the only one. It happens to many wives. Many . . .'

'And what do they do? Do they go home? Do they simply pack up and go back to Britain?'

He looked shocked at the very suggestion. 'Good gracious, no! That would bring great shame to their husbands.'

Laura let out a half-laugh. 'Shame to their husbands!' Nothing was too absurd to believe any more.

'They carry on,' he told her. 'They seem to regard it as

326

one more problem to put up with, along with the rains, the heat and the insects.'

'Do you think they are right to do that?'

'It is a matter of honour.'

'A matter of honour,' Laura repeated, as the door opened. Both heads swivelled round at the noise.

'Major Baxter!' Samit jumped to his feet, his face and whole demeanour betraying his embarrassment.

Blair ignored his clerk and looked in surprise at his wife. 'Laura! What brings you here?'

Laura was aware of Samit's eyes on her as she rose a trifle unsteadily to her feet. Incredibly, her husband looked completely normal. So grotesque had he become in her mind over the past few hours, she would not have been surprised had he grown a pair of horns and a tail. But here he was, as large as life and looking at her in some astonishment as he placed his umbrella in the stand and repeated, 'What on earth are you doing in my office?'

'I could ask you the same thing,' she answered in a voice that quavered only slightly. Surprisingly she felt a curious detachment now as she looked at him. The initial insane jealousy and then the bitter hatred had abated and she felt a strange sense of superiority. She was possessed of knowledge that he was not aware of and it was up to her to decide what to do with it.

'I told you I had an appointment with Cargill at six.'

'You did indeed,' she replied, feeling on much safer ground. 'And I must admit to being slightly puzzled, for I understand the gentleman in question is laid low with a rather nasty attack of Delhi-belly and has been for a couple of days now.'

'I was indeed, Mrs Baxter, but thank God I'm well on my way to recovery now,' a male voice declared from the passage beyond.

Laura and Samit exchanged surprised glances as Blair stood aside to allow the older man to enter. Angus Cargill's double chins quivered as he nodded courteously in their direction and beamed them both a smile. 'It must have been the Bombay duck – the dried fish I ate for supper the other night. I told my dear wife it did not taste quite as it should.'

'I'm relieved the worst is now over,' Laura said, forcing a smile to her lips as she pulled on her gloves. 'Do give my regards to Mrs Cargill.'

'I will indeed, my dear.'

'By the way, tell Ali I won't be home for supper,' Blair said to his wife as he ushered his older colleague towards the door to the inner office. 'I rather think Mr Cargill and I will fancy a game or two of cards after we've done with the business of the day . . . You're welcome to join us, of course, my dear.'

'I think not,' Laura replied coldly, reaching for her umbrella.

'My wife doesn't play cards on principle,' Blair explained to his colleague with a smile. 'It's the Calvinistic Presbyterian in her. Isn't that right, my dear? Pleasure is a thing to be resisted at all costs.'

Laura raised her brows a good half-inch, then smiled sweetly as she made her way to the door. 'I rather think you were born a Presbyterian too, dear heart,' she reminded him. 'And even you must have had principles at one time.'

Despite the smile, there was no ignoring the cutting edge to her remark, and Blair looked distinctly nonplussed. 'Aye, well, we're a long way from John Knox out here,' he reminded her. 'And India is not Scotland. We do things differently under the Indian sun.' He gave a bit of a cough and a wry smile as he glanced at his young clerk. 'Is that not right, Samit?'

'Indeed it is, *sahib*.'

Laura turned and caught Samit's eye.

'Very differently indeed,' the young man added with feeling.

Chapter Twenty-seven

The day Laura visited 21 Wellington Road, Lucknow, was a happy one indeed for Kate and Ewan. After the court verdict on the Lochee building site in February, they had paid Willie's firm the current price for the land and commenced building on it straight away. The mill, spinning both flax and the more profitable jute, was now in operation and was, in every respect, the biggest and best in the city. Congratulations were pouring in from far and wide, and Kate and Ewan spent the whole of the first day in production going round speaking to the workers and shaking hands with all the well-wishers.

Many of the new hands had been with the Falcon Mills for over thirty years, and had been brought from factories in other parts of the city to instruct the new labour force. To accommodate them, a brand-new tenement had been built adjacent to the mill, and from the beneficiaries of this modern miracle the good wishes were particularly warm. The clean, airy rooms were a far cry indeed from the rat-infested hovels many of them had previously inhabited.

Although Kate spent a great deal of her time in the administrative offices of the individual mills, it was very seldom she had ventured on to the factory floor, with its all-pervading smell of oil and dust-laden atmosphere. She could not be sure what kept her from seeking personal contact with the hands; perhaps it was a basic insecurity bred from her past on the Hawkhill. Many of the families whose wages she now paid had been her neighbours in the past. All the Moran family worked for her, except Mamie who had married a locksmith from St Andrews and now lived in that ancient town on the other side of the Tay. It took quite a bit of persuasion from Ewan to break with tradition and go with him round the mill floors on the first day, but her trepidation soon vanished as the warmth of the welcome extended to them both completely overwhelmed her.

'Maybe you should do this more often, Mother,' Ewan commented, noticing how shining her eyes were, as they neared the end of their walkabout. He himself was no stranger to the various departments, and seemed to be on intimate terms with most of the original workforce as well as many of the new arrivals.

As they passed the rows of frames, greetings were called out to them in both Gaelic and the Scots tongue, and the mixture of different languages and accents came as a delightful surprise to Kate, particularly the lilting brogues of her parents' blighted land. The last decade had seen thousands of Irish immigrants flood into Dundee, refugees from the desperate famine conditions that had killed so many in the late Forties. Part of the village of Lochee itself was now being referred to as Tipperary, and Kate was quite surprised to see how popular her son seemed to be with the dozens of smiling, dark-haired Irish girls who called out to him from their places at the gleaming new machines. Their nimble fingers seemed to shift the bobbins in the blink of an eye. Three hundred and twenty-eight empty bobbins to take off per hour and as many to replace, with 500 knots to tie, 208 hanks to knot with twine and four times to strip the full reel and take off and twist the hanks. This was no job for a slacker, but the females whose fingers flew so deftly between the bobbins still had time to laugh and share a joke as their employer passed.

'You'll have to watch your head doesn't turn with all this attention,' she told her son, as one particularly forward young miss executed a coy smile and winked in his direction as her hands flew as if of their own accord.

But Ewan merely laughed. 'If I had a mind to it, Mother, I could take my pick of any one of them any time, but

I'll confess I've rather outgrown that sort of carrying-on.'

'Oh really?'

Kate's amazed look resulted in a laugh and shrug of her son's broad shoulders. 'Come, come now. It's not a monk you've raised. I'd have to be some kind of saint not to have taken advantage of what's been offered to me on a plate for so long!'

Kate was dumbfounded. With the pick of Dundee society to choose from, it had never occurred to her that her own son could have been trifling with mill girls over the years. The knowledge was like a physical stab of pain to the heart.

Seeing the stricken look on her face, Ewan put a consoling arm around his mother's shoulders. 'Ma — for heaven's sake! You wouldn't want me to be taken for a jessie now, would you? There's nothing wrong with sowing wild oats while you're young. It's when you do it after you're married that's the terrible thing.'

They were standing at the end of the spinning floor, and the clanking of the frames resonated in Kate's head as she looked up at her son and said quietly, 'The trouble with sowing wild oats, Ewan lad, is that some of them take seed. And what happens then?'

Ewan's fair skin began to colour beneath his beard and he avoided her eyes as he shuffled his feet. 'Aye, well, there are ways and means o' dealing with that . . . We're not exactly a poor family, Mother. If anything happens then I see that nobody suffers . . . I don't think I have to say any more.'

Kate took a deep breath. 'No, lad, you don't have to say any more.'

But that conversation was to remain with her throughout the rest of the day. Had this been years ago, she would have said he was his father's son all right. But she was older now and not so quick to judge. With all those pretty girls to choose from, what young, red-blooded bachelor in his position could easily turn down such offers? And it

331

must have been the same in Willie's day. Suddenly her sister Peggy's death took on a quite different hue. But try as she might she could not compare dear, gentle Peg with any of these black-haired, brazen young misses who smiled and winked their blue eyes in Ewan's direction every time he passed by. Maybe she was simply getting old, but young women these days seemed so much more forward than they used to be; at least the ones who worked in the mills certainly were.

'I hope you take your time in choosing a wife,' Kate told her son as they sat side by side in the Victoria on their way back to Broughty Ferry that evening.

Ewan looked surprised. 'Really? Whatever brought that up?'

'Oh, I suppose it was seeing all those good-looking young women in the new mill today and seeing the way they were making eyes at you. I can quite understand how a young man could be led astray . . . I just hope you take your time, that's all, and look in the right places. That's very important.'

He smiled and patted her hand. 'You mean marry within my own class?'

Kate flushed. She was extra sensitive on that point, and he knew it. It was odd how she automatically regarded anyone of her own class who cast an eye in her son's direction as a gold-digger, when the very same could have been said about herself in the past, and no doubt was. 'I just think you ought to mix more with some of your own type, that's all. You don't want to wait until the best are all snapped up now, do you? There's an invitation to that garden party at Carbet Castle this Saturday. Why don't you go to that?'

Ewan sighed. He saw plenty of his own type on numerous social occasions, but attending garden parties was not exactly his favourite occupation. And his mother was a fine one to speak. When was the last time she had been to one? He had noticed the invitation stuck behind the clock on the morning-room mantelpiece for over a week now, but had expected it to be politely declined like all the rest. 'I'll go if you go,' he said, reckoning he at least had a fifty-fifty chance of escaping the ordeal.

That seemed eminently fair. 'Right! We'll shake on it!' Kate proffered her hand and, very reluctantly, Ewan took it.

'You're a hard woman,' he told her. 'But a fair one. I'll grant you that.' He knew she hated such meaningless socializing but was obviously doing this for his sake. She actually seemed to think he was lacking female company. The thought quite amused him, for nothing could be further from the truth. But now was not the time for any more confessions. 'I'll even make you a promise,' he told her. 'When we get to the Grimonds', I'll make a beeline for the bonniest lassie in the place, and if she's lucky enough I might even ask her out.'

They stopped off at the cemetery on the way home and laid a bunch of red and white roses on the family vault. It seemed right somehow to involve Augustus in this special day in the Falcon Mills' fortunes. 'Your father would have been a proud man,' Kate told her son as they stood before the marble and granite tomb. 'And if there's a heaven above, I know he'll be watching us now.'

Ewan put his arm around his mother's shoulders. He had been thrust into the position of being the man of the house at far too early an age, but they had worked well together over the years, the two of them. 'We're not a bad partnership,' he said, giving her a comforting squeeze. 'I reckon Dad would have been pretty proud of the pair of us.'

Before heading back to the waiting carriage, they paid a visit to the grave of Kate's parents. After her mother's and father's deaths, she had erected a stone Celtic cross in their memory, not far from where Augustus was buried. She had also added her sister Peggy's name to the stone, feeling

333

it was the least she could do, for poor Peg was still lying in some unmarked grave, after that pauper's funeral all those years ago.

For many years she had kept the existence of the stone to herself, and the first time she had taken a fourteen-year-old Ewan to see it, he had been naturally curious to know about the additional name. She had been guarded in her reply, merely telling him that she had had an older sister who had died long before he was born. It seemed to satisfy him.

In many ways she was relieved that Ewan was the sort of person who seemed to have very little curiosity about the past. Happy-go-lucky by nature, and unquestionably accepting about his good fortune in being born into one of Dundee's wealthiest families, he had never displayed the slightest interest in either her own background or that of his father's side of the family. And although he would never know that Willie Falconer was his real father, Kate was not even sure that he realized Willie was, in fact, Augustus's son. Unable to tell him of the bitterness there had been over her marriage into the Falconer family, as far as she knew, Ewan had grown to adulthood believing that Willie was simply a cousin of his father's who had come back from England determined to put them out of business.

Their carriage passed Willie's home in West Ferry about ten minutes after leaving the cemetery. The Eyrie stood on a grassy bank half-way between Dundee and Broughty Ferry, and had been built on Willie's return to Dundee shortly after his father's death, just before his marriage to Helen Munro. Kate had watched it go up in some amusement, for it was almost an exact replica of Falcon Ridge, but on an even grander scale. Rumour had it, it was now to be extended, with the front rebuilt to resemble Balmoral Castle, the Gothic fantasy Prince Albert had recently designed for himself and the Queen on Deeside.

'I see Willie's got the scaffolding up again,' Kate commented wryly to Ewan as they passed the magnificent red sandstone gates, with the same eagles on top as graced all Willie's mills. 'It looks like the Queen had better watch out, for Balmoral won't be able to hold a candle to that place before he's finished.'

Ewan grinned. 'I wonder what he thought of all the stuff in the papers this week about our new mill. It can't have gone down too well, just when he was getting used to being cock of the heap in the town.'

Kate gave a weary smile as she sat back in her seat. 'To tell the truth, son, I'm really sick and tired of it all. This silly rivalry is getting out of hand. I'd as soon have built a smaller mill if I thought it would put a stop to this stupid nonsense once and for all. I sometimes think that some men never grow up. Willie will go to his grave trying to better the Falcon Mills, and precious little good it'll have done him. Thank God you're not out of the same mould.'

'Och, I don't feel the need to prove anything to anyone,' Ewan agreed, then he grinned. 'But then, I *know* we're better than anybody else, maybe that's why.'

If he had imagined that his mother might forget their agreement to attend the garden party in the grounds of Carbet Castle, the home of the Grimonds, their rivals in jute and their near neighbours on Camphill Road, he was wrong. The Saturday in question dawned bright and sunny with just the hint of a breeze to flutter the washing hanging on the lines in front of the fishermen's cottages down by the harbour. The sky was that comforting shade of duck-egg blue, with a trace of white feathery clouds high above the seagulls who emitted their raucous cries as they followed in the wake of the fishing boats heading back into harbour. Kate had been standing at the morning-room window watching the scene with a quiet sense of well-being, and the first thing she said on her son's arrival at the breakfast table was, 'The Grimonds will be relieved it's not raining.'

'Aye,' Ewan agreed. 'I expect they will.' He took his seat at the table and looked across at his mother. 'You're looking well pleased with yourself this morning, Ma.' So often these days she seemed to be tired and preoccupied with business worries, but not today. The tense look had gone from her face, and her eyes had that clear look to them again that seemed to say all was well with the world.

'I think we have every right to be well pleased, don't you?' Kate said, taking her seat at the opposite end of the table.

'Aye, it's been a grand week all round.' And so it had, for as well as there having been almost no rain, which always raised the spirits, the new mill had exceeded their greatest expectations, with the workers breaking all records for production in the city and the local newspapers now stating that the Falcon Mills had resumed their rightful place at the head of Dundee business.

It was difficult to concentrate on anything other than the good news from the mill for the rest of the day and it was still on both their minds as they walked arm in arm the few hundred yards from their own home to the garden party that evening.

'Those figures the papers published certainly won't please Weary Willie,' Ewan commented. 'But I don't think we can afford to rest on our laurels just yet. Knowing him, I imagine he's still got a trick or two up his sleeve. I just hope he's here this evening, for I'd love to see the look on his face when we walk in.'

The road outside the Grimonds' residence was already blocked by carriages, and they could hear the noise of laughter and conversation long before they rounded the castle walls and entered the back gardens. A large marquee had been erected, beneath which white damask-clothed tables were spread with all manner of delicacies, and black-coated waiters were flitting between the knots of guests, carrying silver trays laden with glasses of finest French wine.

'It seems all Dundee's here and half the county into the bargain,' Kate remarked as she accepted a drink. At a first glance she could see representatives from most of the mill-owning families: the Baxters, the Coxes, the Gilroys, the Cairds, the Ogilvies, the Sharps, the Walkers; they were all there, dressed to the nines and quaffing the Grimonds' wine with relish.

'Aye and they'll all be talking about us, so hold your head high, Ma,' Ewan whispered in her ear as he glanced around him. Then he added, 'It's funny, but the only person I can't see is Willie.'

'Oh, have no fear, he'll turn up like the proverbial bad penny,' Kate told him. She had little doubt about that.

They had no sooner emerged into the throng when they were surrounded by a host of friends and acquaintances offering their congratulations at the opening of the mill. 'You're pioneering a new era,' one of the local councillors told them. 'It can bring nothing but good to the city, and where there's full employment, there are full stomachs. Folk don't make revolutions on full stomachs.'

There were murmurs of agreement from the group surrounding them. The city had been getting quite a reputation of late for revolutionary rhetoric. During the period of Chartist unrest in the previous decade, the marches on the city centre demanding a political voice for the common people and the riots that followed had had the city fathers sweating on several occasions.

A conversation then ensued about the lot of the working man, with complaints about the number of skilled mill-hands being enticed away to the likes of Glasgow to earn higher wages in the shipbuilding trade. An elderly uncle of Mr Grimond had family contacts in shipbuilding; he was informing Kate of the average weekly wage now expected on the Clyde, when she became aware of someone watching her. It was one of those eerie moments when she simply knew she was the object of someone's attention. Anxious in case it was Willie looking daggers at her from the crowd, her eyes scanned the gathered guests, taking in Ewan chatting to a very pretty girl with reddish-blonde hair. Then her heart stopped. She saw him. He was staring at her from about a hundred feet away. It was not Willie at all.

He was in a small knot of people standing by the garden steps. Next to him was the tall, angular figure of Father Risi, the local Catholic priest, and, although Davey's mouth appeared to be taking part in the conversation, he was looking straight at her across the crowded lawn.

Kate went hot and cold as old Mr Grimond's voice droned on in her ear.

She could make out the greying curly hair and beard. It was him all right. She had not seen him since Laura's wedding eighteen months ago, and he was the last person she would have expected to see at such a gathering as this.

She deliberately pretended not to notice him, turning her attention back to her elderly companion, when, to her dismay, the old man asked to be excused.

'I'm afraid I must slip away for a few minutes, Mrs Falconer. Do forgive me. It has been very interesting talking to you.'

As the elderly gentleman made for the outside earth-closet that had been put at the disposal of the guests, Kate felt hopelessly exposed. She glanced about her looking for a likely group to join, when Ewan came over, striding across the lawn in his kilt, the pretty, strawberry-blonde girl on his arm.

'Mother, I'd like you to meet Emma. She tells me she has just arrived back in Dundee after being "finished" in Switzerland for the past two years.'

The young, blue-eyed woman bobbed a curtsey, balancing one hand prettily on her white lace parasol as she smiled her greeting. 'How do you do, Mrs Falconer? It's a pleasure to meet you.'

Kate shook hands and murmured a platitude back. Happy though she was to see her son with such an attractive partner, this was not the moment to get into a conversation about the merits of being 'finished' in Switzerland or anywhere else for that matter.

She forced herself to stand and chat for a few minutes until she could bear it no longer. He was still watching her, and she felt as awkward as a young girl in the first flush of romance. And to make matters worse she had spotted Willie holding court inside the conservatory. All she wanted to do was to get out of here. Staying could bring nothing but complications. 'I – I think I'll be getting back home now, Ewan. There are some letters I must write . . .'

She took her leave of the young pair and could feel her heart beating furiously as she realized that she must pass within a few feet of where Davey was standing to get out of the garden.

Replacing her glass on a nearby table, she began to make her way towards the gate.

To her surprise, and then consternation, as she neared the group, she saw that her old friend was not alone. A petite blonde woman was clinging to his arm. Marie-Louise . . .

Kate's heart sank. She had never actually met Davey's wife before and realized she had no wish to. A momentary panic enveloped her. Should she turn and go back the way she had come? Should she simply ignore them?

Her dilemma was solved for her as Davey leant over and said something into the woman's ear, and they immediately took their leave of the group to walk in her direction.

Kate could feel herself come out in a cold sweat as she stood rooted to the spot.

'Hello there, Kate . . . I didn't expect to see you here!' Even his very voice still had the ability to bring her skin out in gooseflesh.

He held out his hand and she took it, murmuring, 'Hello,

Davey, I could say the same about you.' Then her eyes met those of the woman by his side.

'I don't believe you've met my wife . . . Marie-Louise, this is Mrs Kate Falconer, a very old friend of mine.'

Kate noted that Marie-Louise was a good head shorter than herself and had small bones and delicate, bird-like features. Although she must now be in her forties, her hair was still fair in colour and fashionably arranged in a cascade of ringleted curls behind her head. She wore a becoming pale blue watered-silk crinoline, trimmed with white lace, and held out a lace-gloved hand in greeting. 'How lovely to meet an old friend of Davey's,' she said in a sing-song voice with a distinct French accent. 'Do you live here in Broughty Ferry?'

'Kate lives in Falcon Ridge,' Davey informed her, and his wife's fair brows rose in interest.

'Falcon Ridge? That is the big house with the birds on the gates at the top of the hill, no?'

'Yes,' Kate confirmed. 'That's it.'

Marie-Louise smiled sweetly. 'You must be very rich to live in such a house. You must be a Tory, yes?'

Kate opened her mouth but no words would come. She glanced at Davey who she was sure was stifling a smile. 'I – I really don't know what I am,' she flustered. 'I've never pinned any kind of label on myself.'

Marie-Louise nodded gravely. 'We must not be ashamed to admit to being what we are,' she observed solemnly. 'You are a Capitalist – and why not, if that is what you believe in?'

'I beg your pardon?'

Marie-Louise's bright blue eyes crinkled prettily at the corners as she smiled. 'It is simple. That is what you are. You are a Capitalist, *non?*'

Davey gave a sheepish grin. 'In our circles we always pin labels on folk, as you may already know, Kate. But it's not as bad as it sounds. Some Capitalists are very nice people.' His smile widened that bit more. 'Misguided maybe, that's all.'

340

'You will never change, will you, Davey? You will never grow up. You are still as idealistic as ever. The dreams of youth will still be with you in old age!'

'"*Jeune, on est riche de tout l'avenir qu'on rêve; vieux, on est pauvre de tout le passé qu'on regrette!*"' Marie-Louise told her.

'"Youth is made rich by its dreams of the future; old age is made poor by its regrets for the past,"' Davey interpreted before Kate's embarrassment showed.

Marie-Louise nodded emphatically. 'We are the lucky ones. We are rich in a better way than the Capitalists. We 'ave reached middle-age and still 'ave our dreams,' she declared. 'We will 'ave no regrets in old age. We can be proud of that, *non?*' She slipped her hand into Davey's arm and gave it a squeeze.

It was a proprietorial gesture, so intimate in its familiarity that it brought a pang to Kate's heart. No one else had the right to be that close to him. No one, not even his wife. It was a crazy jealousy she was feeling, and totally absurd after all these years. 'I can see that you have like minds,' she told her old friend. 'Unlike some of us who have grown a wee bit cynical in our old age, you have both obviously retained the ideals of youth. You are fortunate indeed in your choice of partner.'

'Fate was with us the day we met,' Marie-Louise agreed, smiling up at her husband.

Davey smiled back with his mouth, but not with his eyes as he gave a half-laugh. 'Well, it was certainly a fateful day all right.'

'And when might that have been?' Kate hated herself, but could not contain her curiosity.

'Och, it was during the weavers' uprising in Lyons, in '31. I was there with some union friends from Scottish mills giving them a wee bit of moral support, and Marie-Louise was with her father who was reporting the riots for his journal in Paris . . .'

'And you both ended up in jail in the same cell until Papa gave the chief of police all the money we 'ad with us to set you free!' Marie-Louise interrupted, laughing merrily at the memory of a day that had been far from funny.

Kate's brows rose in feigned amusement. 'It seems you make quite a habit of getting arrested,' she told her old friend.

Davey ignored the remark but added, 'We've certainly come a long way in the movement since then.' That weavers' uprising in Lyons, France's major textile centre, in 1831, had led to another riot three years later, in which Davey had also taken part, afterwards passing on his knowledge to political activists back here in Britain who were preparing for the struggle ahead. Unknown to Kate he had made several trips back to Dundee during that decade, advising leaders amongst her own workers on how to organize and agitate for reform. He had felt no shame at doing so, for he believed totally in the righteousness of his cause. Conditions in Dundee's mills were as deplorable as anywhere in the world, and while there was breath in his body he would fight to change things.

'Are you back here for long?'

'As long as it takes,' he answered enigmatically. Then added, 'Aye, we'll be spending a fair bit of time here from now on.' Then, changing the subject, for his wife was not totally reconciled to leaving Paris for good, he said, 'I take it the family are all well? I can see Ewan seems to be enjoying himself this evening, but Laura? Is she happy in India?'

Looking into the grey-blue of his eyes was like gazing into her daughter's own as Kate nodded in confirmation. 'Oh yes, Laura seems to be really enjoying life out there. I suppose I should worry more than I do, but it put my mind at rest, her marrying someone mature like Blair Baxter and not some silly young army lieutenant still wet behind the ears.'

'Mmm . . . No sign of a family yet?'

'Good God, no! And maybe it's just as well, for I don't see myself as a grandmother yet-a-while!'

'We would 'ave liked children,' Marie-Louise broke in with a sigh. 'But it never 'appened.' Then she shrugged her narrow shoulders and laughed. 'But, 'oo knows, God might still bless us. We still live in 'ope and keep on trying.'

Kate's cheeks flared and at that moment she felt real hatred for the middle-aged woman, with her faded doll prettiness, who clung on so tightly to Davey's arm. 'I – I must be going,' she said much too abruptly. 'It's nice to have met you.'

'You must come to visit us,' Marie-Louise said politely, holding out her hand. 'We do not 'ave many Capitalists come to our 'ouse.' Then her face lit up. 'We can per'aps introduce you to M'sieur Proudhon, then you would become a Socialist *tout de suite!'*

'M'sieur Proudhon?'

'Old Pierre Joseph,' Davey explained with a wry grin. 'If committed Socialists' children had godfathers, then he'd be Marie-Louise's. He's a writer friend of her late father's and has been like a second father to her . . . But she means introduce you to his writing, not him. He'd never leave Paris and come this far north, even for the sake of the revolution.'

Marie-Louise pulled on his sleeve. 'Remember your talk, *mon cher*. Maybe your friend would like to attend?'

Davey looked a bit abashed. 'Och aye, the talk . . . I'd quite forgotten about that. I'm giving a talk on his book *What is Property?* at the Town Hall in Dundee next Wednesday . . . but you'd not be interested.' His right eyebrow quirked quizzically as he looked at Kate.

Kate knew that nothing would give her more pleasure than to go and hear her old friend speak. But knowing it was Marie-Louise's suggestion, and the sight of her clinging on to his arm, would not allow it. She had her pride after all. 'No, you're right, I don't think I would be very interested,' she told him as she held out her hand. 'We old Capitalists are too busy making money to think about changing the world . . . Goodbye, Davey . . . Mrs Lorimer . . . It's been very interesting meeting you.'

It was five days later that she learned that Marie-Louise was dead and that Davey was being held for her murder.

Chapter Twenty-eight

‘Kate . . . You shouldn't have come.’ Davey's complexion was grey, his eyes bloodshot; two nights without sleep had taken their toll as he gripped the iron bars of his cell and gazed out at the woman standing in the passage beyond. They had arrested him within an hour of his finding Marie-Louise's body and calling the police. He had still not recovered from the shock. ‘You should have stayed well clear of this. You mustn't get involved.’

Despite the fact it was high summer, Kate shivered as she stood in the vaulted passage of the jail and looked at the man she loved. ‘How could I stay away? I had to come,’ she told him. ‘I came as soon as I heard. Oh, Davey, what happened? For God's sake tell me.’

But Davey could only shake his head. ‘I wish I knew. I wish to God I knew!’ The memory of that moment when he had opened the front door and found her lying there seemed like a nightmare from which he had yet to awaken.

‘Tell me what happened. All you can remember.’

He ran a hand through his greying curls and let out a low groan. ‘Christ, Kate, I can't . . .’ He had already gone through it so many times in his head that his brain was bursting.

‘Talk me through it,’ she insisted. ‘Where were you on Wednesday evening? What happened when you got home?’

‘I was here in town giving that talk on Proudhon's book I told you about on Saturday.’

‘And?’

‘And there was quite a lively audience, with a fair bit of

argy-bargy after it. There were a couple of Tory fellas sitting at the front who began to give me stick, so we got into a debate and . . . Well, I never was one to sidestep an argument, so I went off with them to the pub for a dram or two. I never looked at my watch to see what time I left, but I got home a bit later than usual, I know that. About half-eleven it must have been . . .'

He paused and closed his eyes, as if to visualize the scene that confronted him on returning home. Then he sighed deeply and shuddered. 'The front door was half open, and that surprised me for a start. Marie-Louise always closed it and made sure it was locked before she went to bed. We'd had some trouble lately wi' drunks from the Fisherman's Tavern on their way home at night just barging in . . . Anyway, our door opens straight into the front room, and as soon as I stepped in I saw her. She – she was just lying there on that rug my mother made, in front of the fireplace. I – I couldn't quite take it in. I thought she was asleep at first, but when I couldna rouse her, I noticed the marks around her throat . . .' His voice tailed off and there were tears in his eyes as he looked at Kate. 'I swear to God I didn't kill her. I loved her, Kate. And in her own way I know she loved me.'

'In her own way?'

Davey sighed from the heart, his grief deeply etched on his face as he slumped against the barred door. How much of the truth was it necessary to tell? How could he explain, to Kate of all people, that he and his wife had seldom been physical lovers for all of ten years now? They had gone through so much together, all the troubles in Paris several years back when the people overthrew the old king, Louis Philippe. The two of them had been there that day in late February, 1848, outside the Tuileries, when inside the mob had overturned the royal throne. It had been history in the making and they had been a part of it.

She had even travelled with him to London later in the year for the great marches on Parliament demanding a People's Charter. And it had been in London, the previous year, when they had sat with British Chartists, and members of the League of the Just, and other kindred revolutionary spirits from all over Europe and founded the Communist League ... *WORKERS OF THE WORLD UNITE, YOU HAVE NOTHING TO LOSE BUT YOUR CHAINS* ... *Tous les hommes sont frères* ... *Alle Menschen sind Brüder* ... Brave, noble words for the new world of justice and international brotherhood they were helping bring about ... So much they had gone through together. So many dreams they had shared.

But despite it all, that vital spark that had been there between them in the beginning had simply gone out, with recriminations on neither side. No longer in love, they had still remained the best of friends. He had had his work to immerse himself in. He required little more, but he knew it had been different for her of late. Although she often pretended otherwise, since her father's death her interest in the political causes that dominated their lives had waned, and since moving to Scotland she had found little to occupy her time. The mill women from the city who were active in the workers' cause were a different breed. They knew nothing of the Paris salons of Marie-Louise's youth where the great political thinkers of their day would gather to put the world to rights. And who was left? Middle-class women, who cared little for politics, bored her, with their constant talk of children and household matters. Was it little wonder that she had preferred the company of men? She had grown up as her father's disciple and constant companion, and now he was gone that need to be adored still remained. She was an attractive woman and there had been other lovers over the years, several of them, but she had been discreet. She had been a lady to the end and had never embarrassed him. How could he embarrass her now in death by telling the truth about the other men, even if he knew their names?

Kate saw the haunted look on his face and felt his pain.

'Was she seeing someone else?' she pressed, sensing his reluctance to talk about his wife.

'I – I wouldn't know about that.'

'But you suspect so.'

He made no reply.

'Please, Davey, be sensible!' she implored him. 'This is no time to be chivalrous. It's your life that's at stake. Have you any idea who it was she was seeing?'

He gave a hopeless shrug of his shoulders, then admitted, 'I have my suspicions, and I suppose I could find out for sure.'

'How?'

'Villages are small places, Kate, and Broughty Ferry is no exception. Auld man Campbell who bides next door is a nosy auld bugger. There's not a lot he misses. If anybody's been round there when I've been away, then he's bound to have spotted them.'

'But surely he would have told the police by now?'

'I doubt it.'

'Why ever not?'

'Folk don't want to get involved, that's why. Especially where the law's concerned.'

'Dear God!'

'It's a hard world out there, Kate. Good Samaritans are hard to come by.'

'Would he speak to me?'

'He might. You can be a very persuasive woman.'

Kate made a poor attempt at a smile. It looked as if she had work to do and there was no time to be lost. The murder had made headlines in the local paper that morning and Davey's arrest would be the talk of the town by now. 'REVOLUTIONARY'S WIFE FOUND MURDERED' had been the heading at the top of the page, followed by a column making much of how his political meeting had been a great success and how his Reform League was gaining support in the city.

The newspaper had gone to press before his arrest had

been made public, and Kate knew that as soon as the news leaked out there were many in this town would be only too pleased to see him either hanged or put behind bars and kept there. Her own kind most of all. 'I'll have to go now, but I'll be back, Davey,' she said, squeezing her fingers through the iron grille to touch his. 'You must believe in me and mustn't give up hope.' They were brave words, much braver than she actually felt, for this time she had no idea where to turn for help, even if she got the evidence she was looking for.

She turned to leave, and he called her back. 'It's funny,' he said quietly, 'how life repeats itself, isn't it?' As they looked into each other's eyes, it seemed only yesterday she had visited him in just such a prison cell all those years ago.

'Aye,' she replied in a tired voice. 'That it is. But, sadly, this time I've not got Augustus to turn to for help.'

She relayed the conversation to Ewan over a glass of port in the drawing room of Falcon Ridge that same evening. He listened in silence, a deepening frown on his face. When she had done he said firmly, 'Ma, you're to keep well out of this.'

'I can't,' Kate protested. 'He was my best friend, Ewan. I can't have him hanged for a murder he didn't commit.'

'You only have his word for that.'

'That's quite enough for me,' she snapped.

Ewan looked at her quizzically from across the room. He had hardly even heard the man's name spoken in their home until this had happened. Up till now he had simply been a political agitator whose mother had once been housekeeper here. Now all of a sudden he was his mother's best friend. 'This Davey Lorimer – he was the one with the beard who looked in for a few minutes at Laura's wedding, wasn't he?'

'That's right. I'm sorry I never got a chance to introduce you.'

Ewan grunted. 'I'm not. I've seen him before speaking at

various meetings around the town. From what I can gather he's all hot air. He and his cronies are all for bringing about a second French Revolution right here in Scotland and, from what I can gather, if they succeed, then the first to be guillotined would be the likes of us . . . A fine type that is for a friend! I can't for the life of me imagine why you should get yourself involved with somebody like that.'

Kate gave a wry smile. 'One day you will understand,' she told him quietly. 'One day.' But not now. Now was not the time to tell him how much Davey Lorimer had meant to her; how much he still meant, despite the years in between. Now was simply a time for action.

She called on old Jock Campbell in his cottage on the foreshore the following morning. The retired fisherman was standing enjoying the sunshine, leaning against the window of his two-roomed but-and-ben that adjoined the one in which Davey and Marie-Louise had lived since their return from France.

The old man took his pipe out of his mouth and raised it in greeting as Kate approached. In years gone by he had enjoyed the occasional crack with her when she was down this way visiting Davey's mother. For one of the nobs from the top of the hill, she was far more sociable than most, and had even handed him in the odd bag of apples from her garden on occasions. 'Well now, Mrs Falconer, it's a braw day, is it no'?'

His thin whiskery face was the colour of old leather, tanned by over seventy years at sea, and his blue eyes were faded to a dove grey, but they had lost none of their sharpness as he watched her cross the road towards him.

This time she had brought with her two ounces of Indian tea and a jar of her own tomato chutney, which she warned him would make his moustaches curl, for it was laced with a generous dash of fine English mustard.

A few minutes later the gifts stood proudly on the small oak table in front of the fireless grate as they sat down opposite each other and the old man scratched his head as he listened politely to her request for information. 'Well now, it's a terrible business and no mistake, but I doubt very much if I can help you.'

'But you can, Jock,' Kate insisted. 'You must have seen who has come and gone next door, especially when Davey himself has been away.'

'You wouldna be accusing me o' spying on my neighbours by any chance?' His pale eyes narrowed beneath the shaggy brows. He would have none of that, for he prided himself on minding his own business. There were quite enough busy-bodies in this place without him joining in.

'Good grief, no!' Kate exclaimed. 'I'd never do that. I'm simply asking you to try and remember any particular male friends Mrs Lorimer might have had visiting her in the past, especially on the night she died.' She bent forwards, her hands clasped in her lap as she implored him. 'She did have men friends, didn't she?'

The old man rubbed the rough stubble of his chin. 'Well now, she was a fine-looking woman and there may have been one or two, I'll grant you that,' he admitted. 'I'd have to be deaf and blind not to notice. But on that particular night – no, I canna say any o' the regulars visited.'

Kate's heart sank. 'You're quite sure about that?'

'Aye, I'm quite sure.'

Kate watched him suck quietly on his pipe. Had he any idea how important this was? She was not even sure that he and Davey had got on as neighbours. Her old friend's politics did not go down too well with everybody in the village, there was no doubt about that. For all she knew he could be quite happy to see him behind bars. 'These men friends Marie-Louise had,' she continued. 'Would I know any of them?'

The white smoke curled its way lazily to the black rafters as Auld Jock thought for a bit, then slowly nodded his head. 'Faith, I dare say you would.'

'They're local then?'

'Aye, that they are.'

She shifted anxiously in her chair, terrified to ask their names outright in case she got a refusal. 'Are — are they neighbours — fishermen, maybe?'

Jock Campbell let out a wheezy chuckle. 'I doubt you didna ken the French lassie very well,' he told her. 'She had expensive tastes that one, in men as well as clothes.' His eyes twinkled at her from behind the smoke. 'They werena fishermen, I can assure you o' that, but I'll no' give you any names for that could land me in trouble. I'll just say one o' her best friends, you could say, was an old relation o' your ain.'

'An old relation of mine?' Kate repeated in confusion. But she had no living relatives in this country! Then realization dawned. 'You don't mean Willie?' The horror was evident on her face.

'I'll no' deny he has been known to cry in next door from time to time when her guid man was awa'.'

'Dear God!'

'Mind you, I've not seen him doon here for a good six-month.'

'Really?' That came as almost a relief. 'And the others?'

The old man waved an impatient hand behind the smoke of his pipe. 'Since they're no kith or kin of either o' us, I see no reason to blacken any other man's name.'

Kate swallowed her disappointment with difficulty. But it seemed quite clear that despite Marie-Louise's many visitors, Jock had not seen anyone call that night.

She stood up to go, finding it hard to conceal her disappointment. 'You've been more than kind, Jock,' she told him, holding out her hand. 'I'm sorry to have bothered you.'

'It's no bother,' the old man assured her, rising stiffly from his chair to make his way to the door. 'And if you don't mind me asking, why would somebody like yourself be bothering like this anyway?' As far as he knew, although Kate had once employed Davey Lorimer's mother in her big house at the top of the hill, she was no great friend of her son. 'You've no' become one o' they holy wifies who go round prisons fighting for prisoners' rights, have you?'

'Dear me, no. I'm no Mrs Fry,' Kate assured him. 'I'm simply helping an old friend, that's all.'

The old man nodded. 'I just wondered . . . It'll be for his late mother's sake, no doubt. She was as decent a woman as they come, and it's as well she didn't live to see this day.'

They shook hands again on the step, and as Kate was on the point of turning to go, she paused. 'If you can by any chance remember anyone that might have called on Mrs Lorimer that night, you will let me know, won't you?'

'Na, na, lass,' the old man said. 'I've already told ye, there was nobody next door that night, the priest can vouch for that.'

'The priest?'

'Aye, the Papist fella.'

'I don't understand.'

'Yon Mrs Lorimer – Marie-Louise – she was French like, and they're a' Catholics o'er there. The priest, Father Risi, he was a good friend o' hers and a regular visitor. Usually when her man was oot o' the hoose. I reckon Davey didn't care too much for Papists,' he added with a chuckle.

Kate's heart was beating much too fast. 'But you said none of her men friends visited her the night she died.'

'Aye, that's right enough.'

'But now you're telling me he visited her – Father Risi was there the night she was killed?'

'That's right. But he was surely no' one o' her friends, if you ken what I mean. I might no' ken much about the Catholic religion, but I ken enough to know the Pope doesna agree wi' that sort o' thing.'

Kate nodded impatiently. He quite obviously made a distinction between the priest and ordinary mortal men. Auld Jock was a God-fearing man and that dog-collar counted for a lot.

'He was a man o' the cloth, even though he was a Catholic. He told me they did regular Bible readings together and I have no reason to doubt it.'

'What time was he here?' Kate could scarcely disguise her impatience.

'Around eight o'clock I think it was. About his usual time at any rate. I'd just made myself a cup o' tea and a bit bannock for supper when I saw him pass the window and heard the latch closing next door.'

'And did you hear him leave?'

Jock Campbell shook his head. 'No, I canna say that I did. I must have dozed off after supper, for the next I knew o' it was when the bobbies started to arrive about half-eleven or a wee bit later. A right stushy there was, I can tell you. It didna surprise me when they told me next day that her man had been arrested.'

'What makes you say that?'

The old man sucked on his pipe and shook his head at the memory of the broken nights he had had over the past few years. 'She was a bonnie wee thing, yon Marie-Louise, but she had a temper on her, a' richt. Many's the nicht I've had plates crashing against yon wall.' He indicated with his pipe to the dividing wall between the two houses. 'God knows what they got to row about. Everything under the sun by the sound o' it. And many's the scratch I've seen on Davey's cheeks.' He chuckled once more. 'If he hadna had that beard to protect him, I doubt if he'd have had an inch of skin left after some o' their battles. No wonder he was out such a lot. It was safer than biding at hame!'

'But you never saw him hit her, did you?'

'Dear me, no. Though I've no doubt she asked for it often enough . . . That's why it didn't surprise me when they found her dead like that. A man can only take so much.'

Kate gave a wry smile and patted the old man on the shoulder. 'Thanks for all your help,' she said. 'And by the way, regarding Father Risi – you won't mind repeating what you've told me about his visit later on if you're asked to, will you?'

The old man looked surprised. 'Well, we'll have to see about that. But I dare say, there's no harm in telling the truth.'

Kate's heart was thumping as she bade her goodbye. The knowledge that the local Catholic priest had visited Marie-Louise the night she died lay like a stone on her heart. She had met Father Paolo Risi on several occasions over the years, mainly at the Reverend Mooney's house, and she had been quite drawn to the handsome Italian. He had been in the village for over ten years now and had quite a following amongst the female population. She had even joked with her old friend Bertie Mooney about him losing his own Church of Scotland parishioners to the charming cleric. It came as little surprise to learn that Father Risi and Marie-Louise had become close friends. But exactly how close, that was the question?

'Bertie!' Kate uttered her friend's name aloud as she hurried away from Jock Campbell's cottage. Who better to turn to for advice?

It was early afternoon when she rang the bell of the manse in Grey Street and was ushered into the familiar parlour that had once provided her with such a happy home. The minister was seated in his favourite chair and enjoying his first whisky of the day. He asked her to join him but Kate politely refused and made do with tea as she told him the story of her friend's predicament.

Herbert Mooney listened intently as he sipped his drink. When she had finished he put down his glass and said in a resolute voice, 'It seems to me there is only one course open to us, Kate my dear. We must pay Father Risi a visit without delay.'

Kate drew in her breath. 'Do you really think that's wise?' She had not expected quite so positive a reaction.

'Most certainly I do.' There was very little passed him by in the way of gossip in the village, and it was not the first time he had heard of the handsome cleric making special friends of certain attractive young wives whose husbands happened to be away from home a great deal. Personally he liked Paolo Risi; he was an amiable fellow and good company on a social occasion, which was more than could be said for many of his own Presbyterian colleagues, but he had had his suspicions about his private life all right, even if he had not aired them in public.

He rose from his chair and set down his empty glass. 'If he has nothing to hide then he might well be of some help in other ways, such as letting us know if the good lady was expecting any other visitor that night.'

The priest lived a few hundred yards away, in a small grey stone house on the corner of King Street and, twenty minutes later, Kate's heart was in her mouth as she stood outside the front door and watched Herbert Mooney knock firmly on the varnished wood.

When there was no reply to the third knock, he tried the handle. It would not budge. Kate's heart sank, but the minister was undaunted. 'There's a back door,' he informed her. 'We'll try that.'

They entered the garden by a side gate, and made their way past a hedge of sweet-scented climbing roses, round to the rear of the house. A washing line with certain items of gentlemen's undergarments flapped listlessly in the breeze, and Kate averted her eyes as Herbert gave three sharp taps on the peeling paint of the door before trying the handle. It opened at once.

The hinges creaked loudly, advertising their arrival as they entered the small kitchen. It was sparsely furnished but immaculately tidy, save for a half-full jug of water which stood on the well-scrubbed table next to a small blue glass medicine bottle.

'No sign of any meal being made yet,' Herbert commented as he looked around him. 'Let's take a look next door.'

Kate followed close behind him and yelped in pain as,

on opening the parlour door, her old friend took an immediate step back on to her toes.

'Good Lord!' Herbert Mooney quickly closed the door and turned to face her, shielding the handle. 'I think you'd better stay where you are for the moment, Kate.'

There was something about his face that told Kate not to argue, and she stood nervously aside as Herbert entered the room, closing the door behind him.

The priest was lying on the sofa, with one hand trailing over the side. On the polished wooden floor beside him lay an upturned glass.

For a few seconds Herbert Mooney stood quite still, staring at the sight. From the look of him, he was quite sure he was dead and had been for some time.

Steeling himself, he bent down to pick up the glass. He held it to his nose and sniffed. 'Laudanum,' he murmured. It was the easiest way in the world to leave this life, and no one would ever know if it was an accident or otherwise. There was not a man, woman or child did not take it at some time to relieve pain.

He sighed as he looked down at the lifeless body of the priest who had also been a friend. Pain came in many forms, as did our ability to deal with it.

He placed the glass on the table beside the body and was about to return to Kate when he noticed the note. It was lying on the floor where it had obviously fallen from Paolo's hand.

Herbert stooped to pick it up. He took his spectacles from his pocket and put them on. It was written in Italian in the priest's own hand: '*Al male estremo, rimedio violento,*' he read. Remembering just enough Latin, he mentally translated, 'Desperate ills require desperate remedies.'

He turned to gaze upon the upturned face of the young man. Paolo Risi's dark eyes were still open, looking heavenwards as if in search of his God.

Whatever sin he had committed he had now paid the ultimate price.

Herbert Mooney's face was grave when he returned to Kate, who was still standing anxiously behind the door. 'There has been a tragic accident,' he told her, for the Catholic Church did not forgive suicides. They buried them in unconsecrated ground. The knowledge lay heavy on his heart. No one deserved that fate. 'It seems Father Risi took rather too much painkiller for that headache he complained of to me this afternoon,' he told her.

She frowned, uncomprehending, as he put his hand on her arm. He would explain everything later. Now his heart was too full for a fellow servant of God fallen from grace. 'Even the worst sinners amongst us deserve to be buried with Christ's blessing,' he told her as they made for the door.

She did not have to ask. She knew he was dead. 'May God forgive him,' she said softly, for he obviously could not forgive himself.

Chapter Twenty-nine

'You've completely taken leave of your senses, Ma! I just don't know what's got into you!' Ewan paced the drawing-room carpet and glared at his mother. He had never questioned her judgement before, but this was different. Couldn't she see she was making an utter fool of herself by championing that Lorimer fellow? The man was not only accused of murdering his wife, he was a known political agitator – the very last type of person he would have expected his mother to claim as a friend. 'The man calls himself a Communist. To my mind, he's a common criminal, and they're one and the same anyway. They all want to put us out of business. And if they force us to close our doors with their ludicrous demands, they send half of Dundee to the Poor House into the bargain. Why, all of a sudden, does he become your best friend – someone you'll risk your good name to help – when we've barely heard of him for the past twenty years?'

Kate had been waiting for just such an outburst, so it came as no surprise, but it still hurt. 'I really don't have to explain myself to you or anyone else,' she replied, stabbing the needle into her *petit-point* with more vigour than usual. 'Davey's a very old friend who is in grave trouble. He has lived abroad for most of the past two decades, that's why you've not heard of him. Trying my best to help him now he's in trouble is the very least I can do.'

'The very least you can do – spending our good money on lawyers to try to get him off the charge he's probably guilty of in the first place!'

'I'll have no more of that type of talk in this house!' Kate flared. 'Davey's no more guilty of his wife's murder than I am. As for spending money on his defence, you need have little fear on that score, for I don't think it will even go to court.'

'I know – I know. You're his guardian angel, beavering away behind the scenes making a complete fool of yourself trying to get him off.'

'Not just trying – succeeding,' Kate informed him icily. She had been present in the ante-room of the sheriff's chambers that very afternoon when both Herbert Mooney and Jock Campbell had given their statements. From what Henry Graham, her lawyer, told her, it was now just a matter of days before Davey was released. Bertie's and Auld Jock's evidence had been backed up by the police surgeon who had put the time of Marie-Louise's death at mid-evening, at which point Davey had been talking to a crowd of almost five hundred in the Town Hall.

Ewan paused in his pacing, leaned with one elbow on the mantelpiece and glared into the empty fireplace. Could his mother not see that her getting personally involved in this type of thing was doing the family name no good at all? Even if the man *was* innocent, tongues would wag. Good-for-nothings like that Lorimer fellow were spending their lives making things difficult for mill-owners such as themselves. Chartists, Socialists, Communists – whatever they now liked to call themselves – they were all the same, all tarred with the same brush, they were all their enemies. His mother must be mad. And what she had told him about finding Father Risi's body had made the whole episode even more sordid. He had met the fellow on several occasions and, even though he was a Catholic, Ewan had liked him enormously. He could take a drink with the best of them. There was nothing po-faced or puritanical about him, not like some of the Presbyterian clerics he knew. He was good-looking into the bargain, with those dark Italian eyes of his; no wonder the ladies of the parish all took to him so much. He could charm the birds from the trees, that one. 'It may have come as a relief to you when they found the priest's body, so you could put two and two together and make five, but I think it's monstrous they should be trying to pin the blame on that poor man when he's no longer here to defend himself.'

'Have you never asked yourself why he's no longer here to defend himself? Wearing a dog-collar doesn't suddenly turn you into a saint, you know. Paolo Risi was a man as well as a priest. I'm not blaming him for Marie-Louise's death, I simply wouldn't be surprised, that's all.'

Ewan grunted. 'There's no real evidence that he was guilty of the murder, or that he committed suicide. From what I can make out, it was a simple accidental overdose.'

Kate laid her needle in her lap with a sigh. 'Look, Ewan, I really don't want to get into any more arguments with you over this. Whatever I say, it looks like you've already made your mind up. What has happened is regrettable, and very sad for all concerned. I am merely doing what little I can to see that another tragedy is averted. My relationship with Davey Lorimer is entirely my own affair. I don't interfere with your friendships . . . Suffice to say, I feel a lot happier today than I did yesterday. Things are looking much better for Davey now and I hope very much to have him back here before long, a free man.'

'What do you mean – back here? He's not coming into this house!' Ewan's hackles rose at the very thought. 'I'll not have him over that doorstep!'

Kate sat up straight on her chair. 'Oh, is that a fact now? And when was it your house to keep him out of? The mills may officially belong to you now you're of age, young man, but this is still my home.'

Ewan clenched his fists, his mouth pursing beneath the auburn of his beard as he struggled to control his tongue. It never failed to upset him when his mother brought up the fact that the Falcon Mills now belonged to him. Since his father's death she had made them what they now were. He owed everything to her, and he knew that was why he became so ridiculously protective whenever he felt she might be being used by anyone. Maybe he was being irrational. She had certainly accused him of that over the past twenty-four hours, but he was deeply suspicious and resentful of this Lorimer character. The trouble was he didn't seem to be able to put his point across to her without them falling out about it. That upset him more than anything, for they had always had the best of relationships in the past. They could talk about anything and everyone. It was only since this damned Communist had come back into her life that things had begun to change. 'I'd better get ready,' he said abruptly. 'I'm going out tonight . . . It's the meeting to finish the arrangements for the Trades Ball next week, remember?'

'Goodness, yes. I'd quite forgotten.' Kate thawed immediately at this welcome return to normality. 'How time flies! Have you a bonnie partner picked out for it?'

'You'll find out soon enough.'

She smiled to herself as she bent her head to resume her sewing. When he wasn't telling her how to run her life, her son was quite the young man-about-town these days. Before she knew it, there might be wedding bells in the air for the second time in as many years.

As Ewan left the room he could sense the irritation he had felt over the Lorimer affair begin to lift as he made his way upstairs to prepare for the evening ahead. He was really looking forward to tonight, for the pretty strawberry-blonde he had first met at the Grimonds' garden party had promised to be there, and she was really something special. Definitely a cut above the normal homegrown produce these events usually came up with. Maybe the Swiss finishing school had had something to do with it, but, whatever it was, he was looking forward to getting to know her better.

He left for the meeting at a little after eight and, alone in the house, apart from the servants, Kate found she could not rest. She decided to take a walk down to the shore. It was a lovely evening, mild and clear, with just enough of a breeze to ruffle the petals of the roses that scented the driveway as she walked past on her way down the hill. Whisky, one of the kitchen cats, accompanied her as far as the gate, then leapt on to the stone wall to watch her continue the walk down the steep brae that led to the shore.

The old village that lay at the foot was a world apart from the great houses of Camphill Road and West Ferry. The whitewashed cottages were mainly of the single-storey, two-roomed, but-and-ben type, and the families who lived there and earned their living from the sea had done so for generations. Davey's own family, the Lorimers, had fished out of these waters for centuries, and Kate smiled wistfully to herself as she wondered what his fisher grandfather would have made of the international political agitator his grandson had become. One thing was certain, he would be horrified at the predicament Davey now found himself in, for scandal was anathema to the God-fearing folk of the foreshore who attended the 'Wee Free' every Sunday.

As she reached the road that skirted the water, she passed the time of day with several of the fisher wives who sat at their doors baiting lines from buckets overflowing with juicy-looking mussels. They were healthy-looking, jovial women who worked every bit as hard as their men-folk, many of whom were now back from the day's fishing and were sitting mending their nets in preparation for the next day's catch. Several of the smaller boats were pulled up on to the grassy beach, and barefoot children clambered over them, their carefree laughter carrying on the breeze as Kate strolled past.

Against the growing pink of the evening sky, a flight of wild swans headed northwards. She stopped to watch them, shading her eyes with her hand from the bright glow of the setting sun. Where were they headed, she wondered? The mudflats of Montrose basin, perhaps, where she had first walked with Augustus on their honeymoon all those years ago?

'Wild geese, wild geese gangin' tae the sea,
Good weather it will be.
Wild geese, wild geese gangin' tae the hill,
The weather it will spill.'

The speaker of the lines was a rosy-cheeked young woman standing at the door of her cottage as Kate craned her neck skywards.

'Since they're swans and not geese, and are headed for neither the sea nor the hill, it seems we may have a surprise ahead of us,' Kate remarked with a smile.

'You're helping Davey, aren't you?' the young woman said, abruptly changing the subject.

Kate looked surprised. 'Well, I'm doing what I can.'

'My man's a cousin on his mother's side – Jock Guthrie.'

'Ah . . .' Kate recognized the name. Hurricane Jock. She had occasionally heard Betty, Davey's mother, remark on the young man who would be loath to leave harbour if there was as much as a breath of wind stirring.

'I'd just like you to know we appreciate it,' the young woman continued. 'Davey's a grand man, but yon Marie-Louise . . .' She cast her eyes down to her bare feet which shifted uncomfortably on the stone step. 'Well, far be it for me to speak ill o' the dead, but he had his hands full wi' that one and no mistake.'

'Yes, well, I'll certainly do what I can to help him,' Kate assured her. She had no wish to get into a conversation on the merits or demerits of Davey's late wife with Marie-Louise still warm in her grave.

She could see Auld Jock Campbell standing at his favourite spot in front of his cottage window further along the street, and she used the sight of him to excuse herself. 'If you'll forgive me, I'd better go and have a word with Jock . . .'

The old man looked pleased enough to see her, and when she began to thank him for speaking up for Davey to the sheriff, he raised a gnarled hand in protest. 'There's nae need to thank me,' he told her, taking his clay pipe from his mouth. 'I told the truth, that's a'. Naebody can do mair.'

'And I'm sure Davey's more than grateful,' Kate assured him, bending to pat Bess, the collie dog, now sniffing around her skirts. 'It's at times like this you need your friends.'

'I ken that fine, for he told me so himself not an hour syne.'

'Pardon?'

The old man jerked his head in the direction of the Fisherman's Tavern. 'He's in yon pub having a dram or twa and nae doubt thankin' the good Lord for his freedom. You can see for yourself.'

Kate turned open-mouthed in the direction indicated.

'There's nae use staring. Why not go and hae a look?'

'But I – I've never been into a pub before,' she confessed, her stomach churning at the thought.

'Dearie me,' the old man chuckled. 'They're only human beings in there like you and me. Faith and they'll no' eat you.'

She made a brave attempt at a smile. 'I'll take your word for that.'

The noise that greeted her from the interior of the public house almost had her turning back before opening the door. Someone was playing an accordion and, as well as the shouts and laughter, there was the sound of the raucous singing of 'Loch Lomond' as it was never meant to be sung. But there was no time for second thoughts, for the door was opened for her by a tall youth in the traditional dark blue fisherman's jersey and stuff trousers who came lurching out. 'Begging your pardon, Missus!' he mumbled, stumbling into her and sending her half through the open doorway, where she stood looking about her in confusion.

A shout went up at her arrival, for well-dressed middle-aged ladies were not a common sight in the bar.

'What can we do for you, lass?' an older man, sitting at a side-table, asked.

'I – I'm looking for a friend of mine. Davey Lorimer's his name.' The music and singing came to a discordant halt as she looked around her at the sea of laughing, talking faces. It was impossible to make out anyone in the crowd.

'Davey!' a shout went up. 'Hey, Davey! You're wanted!'

Kate stood awkwardly in the doorway while Davey's name was bandied through the crowd. Then a rough-looking young man came from somewhere in the back of the room to take hold of her arm. 'Come wi' me,' he told her. 'He says for you to come through.'

Kate shook her arm free from his grasp, but did as she was told as the young man pushed a passage clear for her to follow him into a crowded snug in the back of the bar.

Davey was sitting on a high wooden chair at the far side of the room, surrounded by a crowd that contained one or two rather tough-looking women. The room was thick with a fug of smoke, for most had pipes in their hands, but he saw her immediately and raised his glass in delighted recognition. 'Kate! I don't believe it!'

Grinning broadly, he rose to his feet and beckoned her towards him. 'Well, I'll be damned! Come away in!'

Kate stood uncertainly in the doorway and shook her head. For some reason she felt like bursting into tears as she looked at him. He had obviously been drinking but was not quite drunk. And these people that surrounded him – what claim did they have on his attentions at such a time?

'Ellen, shove up and let the lady take a seat!' he commanded a youngish woman nearest to the door. 'Sit yourself down, Kate, there's a good lass!'

But Kate had no intentions of sitting down, here or anywhere else. She felt betrayed that he should be sitting here, carousing with these folk, when she had not even known he had been released. How could he be so thoughtless after all she had done for him? Without a word, she turned on her heel and stalked out of the pub.

She had got less than twenty yards when she heard feet behind her. Then she felt the tug on her arm.

'Kate! Kate! Wait!'

She turned to face him. 'You could have told me,' she said angrily. 'You could have let me know you were out.'

He shoved a hand through his hair. 'I – I would have told you,' he sighed. 'But I only got out an hour or so ago. I was waylaid as soon as I appeared in the Ferry. They insisted on buying me a dram.'

'And you insisted on drinking it by the looks of it,' she added, looking ruefully at the state of him. 'Just take a look at you. You look as if you've slept in those clothes!'

'I have,' he reminded her, his face suddenly serious. 'I've just come out of prison, remember?'

'I'm sorry. Forgive me . . .'

Davey glanced around him. Jock Campbell was watching them curiously from the front step of his cottage, and a raggle-taggle group of children was beginning to gather. 'Look, we can't talk here,' he said, taking her by the arm. 'And I certainly don't feel like going back home just yet.' The very idea of entering that house where Marie-Louise's dead body had lain so recently made him feel quite ill. 'Do you fancy a walk along the shore? We could take a wander along by the Castle.'

'We'll go up to Falcon Ridge,' she told him. 'There's no need for you to go back to the cottage. You can stay there until you feel better.'

To her surprise, he did not demur, and she took his arm as they walked together up the hill that led to her home.

Ignoring the curious look they got from Maisie, the parlour-maid, Kate ordered tea and some food to be brought to the drawing room and they went in and sat down together on the two-seater sofa that stood in the bay-window on the west side of the room.

It was the first time Davey had been in this particular room, and she could see his eyes scan the tasteful heavy brocade curtains that framed the two magnificent bay-windows, and take in the rich red Honduras mahogany furniture. She had had it almost totally refurnished since Augustus's day, keeping only the very best pieces and adding more of her own. He nodded thoughtfully, a quiet smile on his face, as if to say he approved, she had done all right for herself.

A warm feeling came over her as Kate adjusted her skirts on the firm brocade cushions of the sofa, and Davey made himself comfortable alongside her. The last rays of the evening sun were shining through the glass of the bay-window and highlighted the silver in his hair as she reached out and touched his hand. 'You've had a narrow squeak, my lad,' she told him. 'You can relax now, and I don't know about you, but I swear I don't know how much more of this I can take.'

He gave a wry smile in response as he took her hand in both of his. 'Katie lass, you have been my saviour,' he told her. 'But it should never have come to this. No man likes a woman to come to his rescue, and you've come to mine twice now – albeit with a quarter of a century in between.'

'They say things come in threes,' she warned him with a laugh. 'But you'd better not try it a third time!'

He leant back on the buttoned cushions and sighed as he shook his head. 'I've had enough of the insides of prisons to last a lifetime,' he told her. 'It's a quiet life for me from now on.'

'Will you be staying on in Scotland?' She held her breath, hardly daring to listen to the answer.

His face was pensive. 'I've thought about that quite a lot over the past few days.'

'And?'

'And I can't really see any good reason to return to Paris now that Marie-Louise has gone ... Anyway, there's plenty of work to do here. I was seriously considering

368

staying on anyway. Charity begins at home and all that.' He grinned at her. 'How do you fancy having such a troublemaker on your doorstep?'

'Oh, I think I could put up with it.'

'Maybe. Maybe not. But I'd advise you to steer well clear of me,' he warned her. 'For if not, then I'll convince you of the error of your ways. We'll have the Falcon Mills turned into another New Lanark before you can say Robert Owen!'

They were both laughing at the thought when the maid came in with the tea-tray. She put it down on a low table in front of them and Kate told her to leave the tea, she would pour it herself.

As she set about filling the two cups, Davey got up and walked slowly around the room, his eyes dwelling on all the cherished artefacts she had collected over the years. Every so often he would reach out and run his hand over the smooth wood of a writing box or finger the silk tassel of a chairback. As her gaze followed him, that same warm glow returned. How many times over the years had she sat here and envisaged such a scene? How many times had she wondered how he would look amid the cherished possessions of her own home? Never had she believed it would ever come about; but now he was here, only a few feet away.

He paused in front of the fireplace to gaze up at the wall to his left. On it, to the side of the marble mantelpiece, hung a large watercolour portrait in a slim gilt frame. It was a picture of Laura that Kate had had done before her daughter left for India. She was wearing her favourite dress, a crinoline of cream wild silk, and with her head of nut-brown curls and large blue-grey eyes, the resemblance to her father, and the whole Lorimer clan, was quite striking. There was absolutely no resemblance to Augustus or any of the Falconers with their red hair and distinctive freckled features.

Davey stood before it without speaking for some time,

then he turned to Kate. 'She's a bonnie lassie, all right,' he said quietly. 'But she looks nothing like you.'

Kate nodded in agreement; only one of her children had inherited her dark Celtic looks. 'You're right there. There's nothing of the Irish in my daughter.'

'She looks nothing like her father either.' He was looking straight at her, and his grey brows quirked in a silent query as he awaited her reply.

Kate held her breath, then let it out slowly as she shook her head. It was an innocuous comment and she could take it either way, but could tell from his look that only the truth would do. 'On the contrary,' she said softly. 'She looks exactly like her father.'

Their eyes met and held for what seemed like an eternity, and that look said more than a thousand words.

When he sat down next to her, the years between had melted away. Even the heartbreak of the past week seemed little more than a faded memory. They said little as they sipped their tea and Davey helped himself to the fresh bread and butter and cold cuts of meat from the supper tray.

Despite his attempts to hide it, she could see he was all in, for his eyes were red-rimmed and bloodshot through lack of sleep and the skin of his face was grey and drawn over the fine bones. After supper he fell asleep on the sofa and, leaving him to his rest, Kate lit the lamps then went to see about preparing the old housekeeper's annexe for him to move into. It had been empty since Davey's mother had moved out, with the current housekeeper preferring to sleep in her own house in the village.

When she got back to the drawing room at a little after ten, he was just beginning to wake up. He sat up shame-faced on the sofa as she stood looking down at him, her arms full of clean, aired bedding.

'God, I'm sorry, Kate. I must have dozed off. It was unforgivably rude of me.'

'Rude perhaps, but understandable,' she told him, feeling

a glow inside that he should have felt comfortable enough in her home to do such a thing. 'After a day like today, I expect you could sleep for a week. And you'll get the chance, for I've prepared the wee place your mother used to have. Nobody will disturb you there. I'll see to that.'

To her surprise, Davey made no response, but sat quite still, looking over her shoulder, a concerned look on his face.

She turned in the direction of his gaze to see Ewan standing in the doorway. Her heart sank but she could not let it show. 'Ewan! I didn't expect you back so soon!'

'Obviously.' There was ice in his look and voice.

Kate pretended not to notice as she turned to Davey. 'This is my old friend Da –'

'You don't have to introduce us. I know fine who he is,' Ewan cut in. 'What's he doing here?'

Kate stiffened. She had never known him be so rude before. 'Mr Lorimer is spending the night here,' she began with as much authority as she could muster.

'No, he's not!'

'Ewan!' Kate was aghast. How could he shame her like this?

Davey got up from the sofa. 'It's all right, Kate,' he said quickly. 'I – I never intended putting you to any bother. I'll be heading off down the road to my own place.'

He walked over to where Ewan was standing. 'It's all right, son,' he said wearily. 'If she was my mother I'd be just as protective. The last thing I'd want would be for her to be consorting with an old jailbird like me.'

He turned to Kate. 'You've got a fine laddie here, Kate,' he told her. 'Be proud of him. I certainly would be if he were mine.'

He put out his hand and Ewan found himself shaking it.

Kate and her son watched in silence as Davey left the room. Then, almost beside herself with rage, Kate hurried to the window to watch Davey walk down the long drive leading out on to Camphill Road and the village below.

Ewan came and stood behind her, his hand resting on her shoulder. 'I'm sorry I was so rude, Ma,' he said quietly. 'I didn't want you to be taken advantage of, that's all. He may be charming and plausible face to face, but men like him, they're out to destroy the likes of us . . .'

She shook her head vehemently at his words, without turning round, for she could not trust herself to speak.

'It's true,' he insisted. 'And I know it'll be hard for you but I don't want you to see him again, and certainly not under my father's roof.'

Kate could stand it no longer. She whirled round. 'I'm sorry, Ewan, but you've gone too far. It's not up to you to choose my friends for me, or to tell me who can and can't enter my home. And if I don't see Davey here then I'll see him in his own place in the village.'

'Then you'll bring shame on this house,' Ewan told her angrily. How could she do this to them? The man was notorious before and would be even more so now. The whole town was talking about the affair. The best thing he could do would be to take himself back off to France or wherever it was that he came from and leave decent people to get on with their lives. His mother had taken leave of her senses. 'Consort with him and you'll blacken the Falconer name with a vengeance! Is that what you want?' he asked her.

'The Falconer name!' Kate laughed bitterly at the phrase that sounded so fine on the tongue. 'What, for pity's sake, is the Falconer name anyway?'

'It's the name my father bequeathed to me and I'm proud of it!'

'Your father!' Kate scoffed, seeing not Ewan's but Willie's leering face before her. 'Your father is the biggest scoundrel this city has known in a generation! Davey Lorimer is twice the man he could ever be!' Then, seeing the look of incomprehension on her son's face, she realized what she had said and quickly made amends. 'I'm sorry, Ewan son,' she said, sitting down heavily on the nearest chair. 'I'm tired, that's all. I don't know what I'm saying.'

Ewan stood looking down at her in silence as a cold hand took hold of his heart. He had the strangest, most terrible feeling that she knew exactly what she was saying. In her concern to defend Davey Lorimer, she had let her tongue run away with her. He had never enquired into his mother's past before, but something told him old ghosts were stirring. Never for one single second had it entered his head that he was not his father's son. But if his father was not Augustus, then who was he? The very question was almost too painful to contemplate.

His mother was looking imploringly at him. Her face had a strained, haunted look to it, and there were tears in her eyes. He wanted to reach out to her, to tell her that he was sorry. They were both sorry. But something held him back. The past was standing between them. A past he had never bothered to enquire into before. He had just confronted one of the ghosts of that past, but how many more were there yet to be discovered? He felt a chill run through him and he wished with all his heart that he had more guts. For that was what it took to ask those sorts of questions. All around him everything was as familiar as ever, but it had all changed. Suddenly he was a stranger in his own home. He had never cried in living memory, but tears spiked his eyes as, without another word, he turned and left the room.

Kate watched him go. 'God forgive me,' she pleaded. 'Dear God forgive me.'

But exactly for what, she was not quite sure.

Chapter Thirty

Davey spent the night at his cousin Mary Jean's in the village. He had no wish to return to his cottage until the shock of Marie-Louise's death had subsided, so he was grateful for the box-bed in the kitchen that they made up for him.

He was dog-tired but found he could not sleep. The confrontation with Ewan had upset him more than he had realized but, more than that, finding out the truth about Laura had shaken him to the core.

It had never dawned on him that she could be his child until the day he attended her wedding. It was the first time he had seen her face to face, and the shock of instant recognition had been severe. It had been like looking at a feminine version of himself twenty-odd years ago. And now to have that suspicion confirmed ... The very thought brought him out in a sweat. She seemed a bright, lively, intelligent young woman, but had she any idea, he wondered? How could she? He had been no more than a passing stranger on her wedding day, and the knowledge turned a knife in his heart.

But as Davey lay tossing and turning in the confines of the box-bed in that small Broughty Ferry kitchen, his daughter, thousands of miles away in India, had little thought of the man who had sired her. In fact, she had little thought for anyone or anything other than her disintegrating marriage. Since discovering the truth about Blair's native wife and family, she had been living in a dark tunnel with no light at the end of it.

Her first reaction had been one of total shock combined with a deep sense of betrayal. She had wanted to confront

Blair with it at the first opportunity, but Samit had convinced her otherwise, telling her of several wives who had done just that and lived to regret it. So that evening when her husband had returned home, and every evening after that, she had simply pretended that things were just as before, with one exception. In a voice that was as cold as her heart had become, she had informed him she would no longer be sleeping in the same room as him. From now on he would be required to sleep on the couch in the drawing room.

When he had asked why she had said only one sentence. 'I will not be used as a common *devadassi*.'

The sound of that word had brought the colour flaring to his cheeks. He had simply sat quite still for several seconds, staring at her across the table, then got up and left the room. In his silence she had learned all she needed to know.

Their bungalow in the confines of the palace walls had become a virtual prison since then. Her discovery seemed to have completely sapped her confidence, so that venturing into the city itself became a real ordeal. Apart from their obligatory social evenings at the palace, or at the nearby homes of local dignitaries, the only daily exercise she got was in walking up to the administration offices for the occasional chat with Samit. She was no longer afraid of incurring her husband's wrath in that regard. She knew he would no longer have the gall to attempt to choose her friends for her.

The alternative to the occasional welcome chat about books and poetry was to take tiffin on the terrace with other young wives, surrounded by their attendant *ayahs* and pasty-faced infants who had been unfortunate enough to be born out here.

Most of her day was spent on the veranda of the bungalow writing letters home, where she would occasionally be afforded a moment's amusement watching the Reverend Hudson, one of the Residency chaplains, riding his horse at 'Sindhi pace' down the path past their house. He had taught the poor animal to run with the legs on either side working in unison, rather than using its natural gait. This peculiar method of riding had become very fashionable, with several others on the compound trying it, so that some evenings as many as four or five of the poor horses would pass by the window, more resembling half-demented, speeded-up camels than the noble creatures they were.

Such light moments were rare, however, and about a week after the discovery of her husband's secret life, the gloom she was feeling was deepened by the murder of the wife of one of the junior clerks who was found dead in bed, with a regimental dagger through her heart.

'This truly is a depressing place,' Laura told Samit when they ran into one another outside the palace the day following the murder. 'That poor woman! Her husband must be distraught.'

But he had merely given a sad smile and shaken his head. 'I think not. *Zam, zar, zal,*' he had murmured. 'Land, gold and women . . . He has lived here long enough to know that those are the three most common causes of such a deed.'

'I don't doubt it,' Laura had countered. 'But what difference does that make? Of course he must be distraught!'

'He is better off without her.'

'Why do you say that?'

Samit shrugged. 'They say she has been unfaithful.'

'Oh? So it is perfectly all right for husbands to be unfaithful, but not wives. If they stray, they deserve to be murdered, is that it?'

Samit had looked quite shocked. 'Oh no, that is a terrible thing to say!'

Infinitely weary of it all, she had let the subject drop and returned home to write a letter to her mother and Ewan, telling them of how happy she was, and how wonderful life was out here, despite the monsoon rain that fell incessantly, and the insects that made meals of her skin as she sat there, pen in hand, and dreamt of home.

'*Have you a special lady friend yet?*' her pen enquired of Ewan, and she smiled to herself at the thought of her handsome older brother taking his first steps down the path towards matrimony. It would be easier for him, much easier, when his time came. He would not have to journey half-way across the world with a new partner. He could remain in their beloved Scotland.

> Scotland! the land of all I love,
> The land of all that love me;
> Land whose green sod my youth has trod,
> Whose sod shall lie above me.
> Hail! country of the brave and good!
> Hail! land of song and story!
> Land of the uncorrupted heart,
> Of ancient faith and glory!

The favourite poem learned at her mother's knee repeated itself in her head, and Laura laid down her pen and sighed. Would she ever see home again? Dundee, her own city on the banks of the silvery Tay, had never seemed so far away. How she wished with all her heart she was Ewan. He had inherited the mills and would one day own Falcon Ridge itself. And, sitting there thousands of miles away, she knew she envied him those two things more than anything on earth.

But Ewan's own mind that day was far from dwelling on the mills or on his family home. It was the night of the Trades Ball and he was looking forward to it more than he had looked forward to a dance for many a long day. After all, *she* might be there . . . He had never quite got her out of his head – that strawberry-blonde he had first met at the Grimonds' garden party. With her slim figure dressed in the latest Paris fashion and her bright laughter, she was quite unlike any female he had ever met.

He resolved to make a special effort to outshine any would-be competitors for her attention. It was not usual for him to wear full Highland dress to local dances, but having had a new kilt and jacket specially made for Laura's wedding eighteen months previously, there was no use letting them simply hang in a cupboard gathering dust.

'How do I look?' he asked his mother as he presented himself for her inspection before leaving for the dance. The pleats in his kilt hung perfectly above the well-muscled legs in their knee-length woollen hose, with the horn hilt of the *skean-dhu* just visible above the top of his left sock. His dark brownish-auburn hair was perfectly combed, his beard was neatly trimmed, and in the left lapel of his jacket he wore a sprig of white heather.

'You'll pass,' Kate told him, adhering to the old maxim of praise the child, spoil the child. She patted his jacket pockets.

'No wee bottle of the craetur hidden away,' he assured her, but omitted to add that he had already had a good dram or two from the whisky bottle in the drawing room before he got dressed.

'Well, enjoy yourself, son,' she told him. 'God knows you work hard enough these days.'

She watched him go from the steps of the house. He had borrowed her new carriage, telling the driver to return for him at midnight.

As she stood there waving goodbye, Kate was surprised to find how much she envied him. She had never been in a position to attend any dances when she was young, nor known the thrill of expecting the unexpected. After she married Augustus it had not been quite the same. He had been well past the age of kicking up his heels, and she had had no burning desire to partner any of his ageing business associates around the floor.

She breathed deeply of the evening air as Ewan's carriage disappeared out the gates. The spell of fine, dry weather was lasting, and she had no wish to return indoors immediately, so she spent the evening pottering in the rose garden, dead-heading the bushes, and thinking how quickly the summer would be gone and the cold winds of autumn would come whistling up the Tay. Already they were well past the longest day and the evenings were drawing in.

No more mention had been made of Davey taking over his mother's old quarters in the house. She had seen him only once in the week or so since his release from prison, when she went down to visit him two days after his confrontation with Ewan. He was not at home, and Auld Jock had directed her to Mary Jean's. He had been pleased to see her but was still concerned about Ewan's reaction. 'We'll play it canny for the time being, Kate lass,' he told her. 'The last thing I want is to cause trouble between you and your son.'

It was with a heavy heart that Kate now remembered that conversation as she walked with her basket filled with dead flower-heads towards the compost heap and emptied it on to the mound of grass-cuttings before returning to the house. How she would have loved his company at a time like this, just pottering around the garden. Summer evenings were not meant to be spent alone.

She was already in bed and reading by the light of her lamp when she heard the wheels of the Victoria crunch to a halt on the gravel outside the front door, followed by the faint sound of voices. She smiled quietly to herself as she got on with reading her book. No doubt she would hear all about the dance in the morning: who had got drunk and had been slung out of the hall, and who had stolen whose partner. Such were the events that Trades Balls were made of, for they belonged much more to the young than to the old, who had merely made the money that allowed their offspring to enjoy themselves in such a fashion.

'Ma? Are you awake, Ma?'

The light knock at the door and the whispered question had Kate putting down her book in curiosity. 'The door's open. Come in!'

She sat up in the bed, modestly pulling the quilt up to cover the lace bodice of her nightdress as Ewan pushed open the door and entered. His face was flushed with the excitement of the evening and he was smiling.

'I didn't mean to disturb you,' he said, pushing a hand through his tousled hair. 'I hoped you would still be awake. There's someone I'd like you to meet.'

'Oh?' Kate clutched at the edges of the quilt as she shifted uneasily in the bed. 'Really, Ewan . . . At this time of night?'

'You must,' he told her, his eyes shining. 'She's leaving for Belfast tomorrow and won't be back for almost a month.'

'Belfast?'

'Her father's got business interests there. She'll be staying with family friends.'

'She?'

'Emma.' He spoke the name with reverence. 'She's waiting downstairs. I wanted you to meet her before I take her home.'

'Tell her I'll be right down,' Kate said, casting her book aside. 'Take her into the drawing room and pour the lass a wee drink and I'll be with you in a tick.'

'Thanks, Ma!'

After a buoyant Ewan had disappeared out through the door, Kate got out of bed and pulled on her best quilted dressing gown before going to the mirror to tidy her hair. It was hanging down her back in a single long braid and, so she wouldn't look quite so *déshabillé*, she pinned it into a quick knot behind her head before making for the bedroom door. This young lass must be someone quite special, she told herself, for Ewan had never invited anyone home before, especially not at this time of night.

The two of them were standing chatting and laughing by

the fireplace when she entered the drawing room, and they came forward immediately to greet her.

'Ma, I'd like you to meet Emma,' Ewan said, leading the young lady by the hand. 'You've met momentarily before – at the Grimonds' garden party – but not quite as officially, one might say . . . Em, this is my mother, Mrs Kate Falconer.'

The young woman dropped a curtsey as she shook Kate's hand. 'How do you do, Mrs Falconer?' she said. 'I'm very pleased to meet you again.' She had quite the prettiest and most disarming smile one could wish to see.

'The pleasure is entirely mine,' Kate told the young woman, who she certainly wouldn't have recognized again. 'I'm trying to place your accent. It certainly isn't local.'

The young woman laughed. 'Oh dear! I've been away to finishing school on the Continent, so that might have something to do with it.'

Such establishments were a mystery to Kate, who smiled politely. 'And you're originally from?'

'Oh, right here in the Ferry . . . Well, West Ferry actually, if one must make a distinction.'

'Really?'

'Emma's a distant relative of our family, Ma,' Ewan broke in. 'She lives in The Eyrie.'

There was a stunned silence. Kate felt she had been delivered a physical blow as she looked from the young woman to her son and back again. 'You mean you're Willie's lass?'

'Yes,' Emma replied, rather startled by the reaction. 'My father is Will Falconer . . . Ewan and I were just saying, we think we must be third cousins or something away back.'

Kate took an uncertain step backwards and made for the nearest chair. This was her worst nightmare come true. Ever since he was old enough to understand, she had wrestled with her conscience over how much to tell Ewan about the man who was his real father. Several times over the years she had even found herself forming the words in her head that she might say if the right moment came around. But somehow it never did, and Ewan never asked. Somehow he had got it into his head that Augustus and Willie's fathers were brothers, and to deliberately feed him the lie that Willie was in fact his own half-brother, when he was in fact his father, was more than she could bring herself to do. The longer time went on the harder it had become. To lie by omission, she now told herself, was every bit as bad as to actually mouth the untruth. In taking the easy way out and simply saying nothing she had stored up more trouble than she had ever realized.

'Are you all right, Ma?' Ewan looked genuinely concerned. He had not expected this sort of reaction, although he had been almost as surprised himself when his partner told him the name of her father. But he didn't really see that it should make that much difference. After all, it was Willie who was their business rival, not his daughter, and whatever ill feeling there might have been between Emma's father and his own was surely water under the bridge long ago. 'Can I get you a drink or something?'

'A wee drop of Madeira will do fine.'

Kate could barely recall drinking the wine, or the short and decidedly strained conversation that followed between herself and Ewan and the young woman. All she knew was that she was still sitting there in stunned silence when her son eventually arrived back from taking Emma home about forty minutes later.

The concerned expression on his face was mixed with disappointment as he entered the drawing room and confronted his mother. 'You could have been a bit more understanding when you discovered who her father is,' he told her. 'Old family feuds belong in the past. Anybody would think you had something against the poor lass herself.'

'I do, son . . . She's Willie's daughter.'

'So?' Ewan demanded. 'What of it? That doesn't make her an Untouchable, does it?' He had been reading up on India and their strange caste system since Laura's departure, but had never expected to encounter a version of it on his own doorstep.

'Yes, yes, I'm afraid it does.'

'But that's stupid! Why should Emma and I be stopped from seeing one another just because her father's a business rival?'

Kate sighed, her fingers nervously smoothing imaginary creases from the skirt of her dress. 'It's not just because Willie's a business rival.'

'Well, because our fathers were related or whatever and fell out years ago. It happens in all families, and it's not as if they were brothers or anything like that.'

Kate sat quite still, her mind numb. Never in her wildest dreams had she imagined this would happen.

'You might have known we would meet,' Ewan was saying to her. 'Dundee's not that big a place, and it's not exactly a huge social circle we move in. If you had something intrinsically against me taking an interest in anyone with the Falconer name, you could have said so before now. You could have warned me.'

'It – it was just one of those things . . . I – I suppose I just hoped it would never happen.'

'Well, it has happened, and there's nothing you can do about it. It's not that long since you told me not to interfere with your choice of friends, Ma, so now the boot is on the other foot. I'm a grown man. I'm not your wee laddie any more. Don't you try to tell me who I can or can't see. I like Emma and she likes me and there's absolutely nothing either you or Willie Falconer can do about it!'

And with that he was gone, leaving his mother staring at a closed door as it rattled on its hinges.

There was nothing either she or Willie Falconer could do about it . . . 'God help us!' Kate groaned aloud. And God help her son, most of all, when Willie got to hear of it.

Chapter Thirty-one

The morning after Kate's argument with Ewan over his friendship with Emma, instead of taking her carriage into one of the mills as usual after breakfast, she walked down to the village to have a word with Davey. The verbal spat with her son had given her a sleepless night, and she had got out of bed distinctly on edge. The last thing she wanted was to carry the bad feeling between them into the business. She needed time and space – they both did.

To her relief she found that Davey had now moved back into his own cottage and was sitting writing at the kitchen table when she peered in at the window.

'Kate!' He rose immediately, his face lighting up as her shadow obscured the sunlight that filtered in through the tiny panes. 'The door's open!' He pushed back his chair with such haste that it tipped over, clattering to the floor as he rushed to the door. 'How are you, lass?'

'I should be asking you that,' she said, taking off her bonnet and following him into the small room that served as both kitchen and parlour. 'I've been so worried about how you've been coping.'

The room was dark and cool compared to the bright sunlight outside. They stood looking at one another, just glad to be in each other's company once more. Then Davey picked up his own chair from the stone floor before pulling one forward for Kate.

'Take a seat, lass. I'll make a cup of tea.'

'No, don't bother for me. I've just risen from one,' Kate said as she looked around her.

It was the first time she had been in the house since his mother's death, and she was surprised to see it had changed so much. Gone was that cheerful, cosy atmosphere Betty had created, with everything polished to within an inch of its life, shining as brightly as a new pin. The room now had a bleak, soulless look to it; the grate was choked with old ashes and everything was covered with a thick layer of dust that must have predated Marie-Louise's death by several weeks. But, despite the neglect, it was obvious the last woman of the house had once come from circumstances far removed from this humble cottage. Instead of the array of Betty's cherished wooden Riga bowls on the shelves of the dresser, there stood a collection of fine Sèvres china figurines and part of a gilt-edged dinner service, exquisitely painted with fruit and flowers. Above the wooden mantelpiece was a signed etching of the storming of the Bastille, and a collection of silhouettes in oval black ebony frames hung on either side of the fire. In the middle of them hung the one of Marie-Louise herself that Kate had first seen in the kitchen of her own home so long ago. She felt that same pang looking at it.

Davey noticed her interest in them. 'You're admiring the silhouettes. They're of Marie-Louise's family. And the rest of the stuff was hers too, needless to say.'

'I gathered that.' Kate gave a wry smile. 'They would all have been a bit beyond your mam's reach . . . Not that she wouldn't have appreciated that lovely china, mind!' Betty always had a taste for quality, even though she could never afford it.

Davey resumed his seat at the table, moving his chair round to face her as she sat down on the far side of the hearth. She found herself nervously fingering the long ribbons of the straw bonnet on her lap as she tried to picture his life here with the French woman. They had come from such very different worlds. She could not imagine Marie-Louise ever getting down on her knees to clean out that grate, or do anything around the house that meant dirtying those pretty little hands of hers. She must have been the very opposite of his mother, who could not bear to see a speck of dust anywhere without wiping it. 'Did they get on well – your mam and your wife?'

'Aye, I suppose they did. They certainly never had cross words, if that's what you mean. I don't think Mam quite understood Marie-Louise, mind. To her, being a wife meant you spent your life looking after bairns and doing housework. But Marie-Louise was never brought up to be like that. Her mother died young and she was her father's right-hand disciple from the age of nine until his death. Politics was her life-blood, although to be honest with you, after her old man passed away she seemed to lose a lot of her enthusiasm for putting the world to rights.'

'Do you miss her?' It was both a stupid and insensitive question but she could not help herself.

Davey reached for his pipe and took a long while lighting it. 'In some ways I do,' he said eventually, puffing the reluctant flame into life. 'But I'm not stupid. I knew what was going on.'

Kate raised her eyebrows but said nothing.

'Aye,' he continued. 'I might not have admitted it at the time – in fact I'm damned sure I wouldn't have – but I knew she had visitors, all right – men friends who called when I was away speaking somewhere or just out at meetings.'

He puffed thoughtfully on the pipe and paused, then his voice took on an infinitely weary tone, as if what he was about to say he had gone over in his own head a thousand times. 'I ken fine there are some who would call me less of a man for turning a blind eye to what was happening behind my back, but I knew my wife. I knew Marie-Louise better than anyone apart from her father, and he was dead. And I knew better than to ask what she was doing or who she was seeing when I wasn't here. She was like a caged bird after we returned here. A beautiful, wilful caged bird, flapping her wings against the bars of a cage not of her own making – a cage I had put her in by returning to

Scotland. But with her father dead and no real family to speak of left in France, she would have had nowhere to go had she escaped.'

'So you opened the cage door occasionally,' Kate said softly.

He took the pipe from his mouth and examined the smouldering bowl in his hands as his voice dropped. 'Sometimes it doesn't do to go probing too deeply into things,' he told her. 'It's like taking the wings from a butterfly to try to understand its beauty, or catching a snowflake in the palm of your hand to examine its make-up. The magic of what so entranced you is gone in an instant . . . Suffice to say, we had grown apart over the past few years and she took her pleasure where she could find it. I could see nothing wrong in that. God knows she had little enough joy in her life of late. I just wish to hell she had stuck to the laity, that's all. When you start combining sex with religion you end up with a mighty potent mixture.' He gave a disparaging half-laugh. 'And to think that I always breathed easier knowing it was Father Risi who had been round when I was out!'

Kate looked at him, her heart full. This was the man she had loved for a lifetime. The man she would always love. The man with whom she had laughed and cried from the time they had taken their first tottering steps together up there amid the grey stone tenements of the Hawkhill. There were deep lines etched on the skin above the blue-grey eyes and dark circles beneath. The skin that had remained so smooth and boyish for so long was taut and drawn over the cheekbones, and the curly hair of his beard was grey and grizzled. He had lost weight, and his neck appeared scrawny inside a collar now too big for him; his dark blue stuff jacket hung loosely on what had once been a stocky frame. 'You need rest,' she told him. 'A period of quiet rest and recovery to get your strength back.'

'Fat chance of that!' Davey gave a short laugh as he stuck the pipe back in his mouth. 'I've a series o' political meetings lined up for September — Edinburgh, Glasgow, Manchester . . .'

'I don't approve! Not one little bit! You need looking after, not spending your time traipsing round the country fighting the good fight, as you like to put it.'

'Then come with me. Make sure yourself that I don't overdo things.'

She was taken aback and showed it. 'But . . .'

'But nothing. You're your own boss, aren't you? And there's still Ewan to see that the whole business doesn't fall apart if you're away for a wee while.'

At the mention of her son's name, the mounting excitement she had felt at the suggestion subsided and her expression changed. 'I'm afraid Ewan and I are not exactly the best of friends at the moment.'

'Oh? What's wrong? Or am I not allowed to know?'

'Oh, you can know, all right,' Kate sighed. 'We had an almighty row last night, that's all . . . It's my worst nightmare, I suppose. He brought Willie Falconer's lass, Emma, to meet me. They've taken a fancy to one another.'

'Good God!' David took the pipe from his mouth and stared at her. 'But Willie's his half-brother.'

Willie's his *father!* she wanted to scream, but couldn't. Never to a living soul could she admit such a thing. Not even to Davey. Especially not to Davey. It would be tantamount to admitting to having slept with the devil. Instead she nodded bleakly in response to his statement.

'Does he know? Have you told the lad?'

Kate picked nervously at imaginary specks of fluff on her skirts. 'We've never discussed the exact relationship,' she confessed. 'It may sound stupid, but it has just never arisen. Ewan has always been one of those happy-go-lucky young lads who never had any interest in the past. He knew Willie was a relative as well as a rival, that was all. His exact family relationship to Augustus was never gone into.'

Davey let out a low whistle and shook his head. 'We pay

dearly for our silences in this life,' he told her. 'What are you going to do about it?'

'I don't know. I really don't. Have it out with him, I suppose. But the thought terrifies me.'

'Then don't.'

'What?'

'Say nothing,' he told her. 'Let it die a natural death. Most first romances do.'

'It's a dangerous game,' she said hesitantly.

'No more dangerous than spoiling your relationship by having an almighty row, with you laying down the law about who he can or can't see, and then discovering there was nothing much in it anyway. Forbidden fruit is always the most attractive to the young. I'd wait, if I were you, and chances are you will never need to lay down the law. Just carry on as normal until such time as circumstances force you to act.'

'You mean if they come one day and tell me they're getting married?' She gave an uneasy smile at the appalling thought.

'Exactly. But, of course, there's always the possibility of Willie finding out himself long before then, and your problem would be solved, for he would not stand the idea of his darling daughter consorting with his half-brother for a single second.'

'That's certainly true!'

Davey got up from the table and walked to the dresser, bending stiffly to take a bottle of whisky out of the bottom cupboard. As Kate watched, he poured two drams into a pair of glasses. 'Here,' he said to her, handing one across. 'Let's drink to happier times – like when you join me on one of my speaking tours!'

They touched glasses and she smiled back at him. Maybe it might not be such a bad idea after all.

When she got home, Ewan had already left for Dundee. It was his day in the Lochee jute mill. Quite against the trend for the trade as a whole this year, their showpiece factory was producing even better results than they thought possible, and there was now talk of perhaps opening another mill over by Invergowrie.

For their main rivals, however, who were still basing most of their production on flax, the latest figures were disappointing. Rumours of peace in the Crimea were now having a lulling influence on production. The demand for coarse linen for the war effort over the past two years had been great, creating maximum profits for the mill-owners, but with talk of peace around the corner, the flax trade had now almost ground to a halt. More and more were now considering turning their production over to jute, and looked with envy on the Falcon Mills who had been concentrating most of their production on that fibre ever since the outbreak of the war, when they had lost tens of thousands of pounds' worth of raw flax which had been unable to leave the Russian port of Archangel.

Knowing that Ewan would be coping more than well enough with the work in hand, Kate decided to give the mills a miss for one day. Sometimes, she told herself, it did one good just to forget work for a while and try to wind down.

The sun was now streaming down out of a cloudless sky, and it certainly was not a day for staying indoors. Her favourite straw gardening bonnet was hanging enticingly just inside the conservatory door and, after a light lunch of mackerel salad and fresh mint tea, she happily donned it along with her old cotton gardening gloves, and went out to tend to her roses.

She was still pottering in the garden when she saw Ewan's carriage drawing up at the front door just after five-thirty.

Laying down her hand-trowel, she took off her gardening gloves and bonnet and followed him up the steps and through the front door.

She found him in the drawing room, helping himself to a dram of whisky.

'Would you care to join me?' he asked as, wiping the perspiration from her brow, she appeared at the door.

'I might just do that.'

He poured two generous tots and took one across to her. 'I'm sorry about the row, Ma,' he said. 'Let's forget about it, all right?'

'That's fine by me,' Kate replied with relief as she lifted her glass in salute.

Ewan gave a quiet smile as he walked to the window and looked out over the sparkling waters of the Tay in the distance. After that ill-fated introduction to his mother he and Emma had made a pact that they would keep both parents in the dark about their relationship for as long as possible. What they felt for one another was a purely private affair. Neither of them had experienced anything like it before, and for it to remain a secret for the foreseeable future only added to the excitement.

'I got the latest accounts on the Leith mill in today,' he said, turning from the window to his mother. 'They're ripe for expansion down there.'

'Oh really?' The Leith mill had remained dear to Kate's heart, even though it had been built in the terrible period after Augustus's death. At one point she had considered not going ahead with the scheme, but that had seemed the easy way out. To grit her teeth and go ahead and build it during the first year of her widowhood had been a challenge she knew she could not refuse. It would be the touchstone for all other thoughts of expansion she might have in the future. And it would show the good citizens of Dundee that women in business could take big decisions too.

'The manager's wondering if one of us could take a look down there shortly.'

'I don't mind going,' Kate told him. 'I'll drop him a line tomorrow and arrange a date. Some time around the beginning of September would suit me fine.' She knew someone else who would be in the Edinburgh area then, and the thought brought a tingle of excitement as she sipped the amber spirit.

'There's another matter I thought we'd better have a word about,' Ewan said, studying the liquid in his glass. 'I'm thinking of branching into shipbuilding.'

'Shipbuilding!' Kate could barely contain her surprise. 'But we've never even considered that before!'

'All the more reason to think about it now,' he told her. It was something Emma had mentioned about her father contemplating just such a move that had set him thinking. 'It seems a sensible way forward, with the jute trade between here and India requiring ever more ships, and the whaling industry and the like still flourishing in the city. Why should others make money from the shipyards here while we stand on the sidelines and watch?'

'But it's so different,' Kate began. Buying into Dundee's booming shipyards was something that had never crossed her mind. 'We don't know the first thing about building ships. Spinning and weaving are our trades.'

'That's the very same attitude the handloom weavers had when the first machines were introduced here,' Ewan told her with some impatience. 'It's Luddite thinking. Money makes money in this life, Ma. I thought you would know that by now.'

Kate looked at her son. His eyes were shining at the thought of a new enterprise that could out-perform the mills themselves in profit-making. But shipbuilding . . . She shook her head. Suddenly she felt very old. Too old for new ventures such as this. 'I – I don't know, Ewan lad,' she told him. 'I'll leave such decisions to you to work out.' To tell him she felt he was overreaching himself would not go down at all well; he had to win his spurs, after all. She could not remain with her own hand fixed firmly to the tiller for ever. He was now the major partner in the business and was obviously keen to prove himself.

'You're not agin it, though?'

Kate shook her head. 'No, I'm not agin it.'

'That's grand!' He strode over to pour himself another whisky in celebration. He would outstrip Willie Falconer as the most successful businessman in this city if it was the last thing he did. Emma would be proud of him, just wait and see.

Chapter Thirty-two

While, back in Scotland, her mother came to terms with having her old friend Davey Lorimer around once more, the weeks and months following Laura's discovery of her husband's unfaithfulness were ones of dramatic change at the palace of Lucknow in faraway India. The rumours had proved correct, and the British were now in control of the whole province of Oudh, with the King and royal family, plus all their entourage, in reluctant exile in Calcutta.

The annexation of the territory had not gone down at all well in Indian quarters where it was thought the British had gone much too far in getting rid of the King and commandeering his palace, but no one was brave enough to say so in public.

The whole operation had been carried out with a military precision that had taken everyone by surprise. Not a single shot had been fired in defence of the King, and his departure seemed to cause little more upheaval than if he were going on holiday.

Diplomatic noises about his being allowed to return when the time was right were made, but Laura and everyone else with access to the palace knew they were just words. Within days of the royal family leaving, the palace had been reorganized as a British Residency, with the existing staff being told they would be allowed to remain in post should they choose to do so.

During the whole procedure, Blair was cock-a-hoop. As an intimate of the retiring Governor-General, Lord Dalhousie, he was assured an even more privileged position once the new resident commissioner was safely installed in the new year; until then he would simply carry on as usual without the added burden of having to kow-tow to 'that bloated barrel of debauchery' as he now referred to the King.

For Laura, however, trapped at home in her small bungalow, life was not half so exciting. Her husband's unfaithfulness lay on her heart like a stone, and she could see no way out of her misery. Never had she felt so alone or missed her family so much. It was true she had learned more of how to cope with the many physical inconven-iences of life in Lucknow, such as how to cure the infuri-ating creaking of the punkahs, or how to get rid of white ants, and how to best deal with the prickly heat rashes that constantly covered her skin, but physical problems were the least of her worries. Since her emotional detachment from Blair, she felt alienated from the world around her. Life went on as usual, but now she found she viewed it at a distance. It was as if the Residency was a grand theatre and her life was some strange foreign play being enacted before her eyes, and in which she had no part.

Her daily routine rarely varied. She would rise around six o'clock, bathe, then have *chota hazri* – her little break-fast – of tea, buttered toast, a newly boiled egg and fresh fruit brought to her on the veranda, where she would watch the daily round begin. From her canvas chair she could sip her tea and watch as, in the distance, the sad-eyed, emaciated bullocks began to plod their weary way down to the river to carry water back for the residents' cultivated patches of ground, while others would begin their monotonous toing and froing in the gardens of those fortunate enough to have their own private wells. Small boys, with brown, toothpick-thin limbs, would be paid a pittance to whack the animals every so often with a cane, and she would wonder which of them had the more wretched lives, the boys or the bullocks.

The quiet of that hour after daybreak would not last for long as to the rear of the house she would hear the ser-vants begin their early morning squabbling. The bungalow had verandas back and front, with the one at the back constantly crowded with servants of varying degrees of social standing, from the punkah-wallahs who lay there activating the punkahs with their big toes, to the dhobi-wallah, a wrinkled little prune of a man, with only one eye, who seemed to be for ever squinting at the world as he bent over his zinc tub. The larger and more soiled items of their household laundry he would take down to the river, and occasionally she would see him there, squatting in the shallows as he flogged and battered the wretched items against the rocks.

They were all so busy, each with their allotted task to perform. Their lives were ordered and straightforward and in their own way they had peace of mind, and Laura knew she envied them that, for her main function in life had been taken from her that day in the house on Wellington Road. All the dreams she had dreamt on the boat coming over here, all the plans she had had for the future of the children she would have, and of the pride and joy she would feel in taking them back to meet her mother and brother, they had all died that day in that squalid little room in downtown Lucknow. She might still wear a gold ring on her finger, but she was no longer a wife except in name.

After breakfast, she would take her time dressing and then take a walk around the compound. She usually ended up at Blair's offices in what was now referred to as the Residency building, and as the morning was the time he spent giving his orders for the day, he was rarely in his own quarters. His absence gave her a chance to stay and chat to Samit before wandering round to the veranda to drink tea or take tiffin with some of the other wives. There the talk would usually be of the latest box-wallah to have visited the compound, and of their respective purchases. These travelling salesmen were one of the few distractions in the lives of the women, with their samples of gloriously coloured carpets, rolls of different silks and gleaming brass artefacts. The *Koi-Hais* – the old Indian hands who had been here for years – would impress upon Laura the benefits of bargaining, but that was something she still could not bring herself to do. Somehow it seemed innately immoral to be trying to prise a few extra rupees from someone who so clearly needed the money more than she did.

After tiffin, it was usually back to the bungalow to check that the servants were attending to their duties properly, perhaps potter around the garden for a little while, then lie down on the bed and read or write letters before Blair returned about six o'clock and they either ate a silent dinner together or prepared for yet another social evening out.

Uneasy in each other's company, they both preferred going out as the lesser of two evils, but they were very much occasions for the benefit of the men. How she would envy them at the end of the evening when the *hookah* was passed around. If the dinner was an official one taking place in the palace itself, it was quite a ceremony, with the *hookah* being borne into the centre of the room on a solid silver tray, its silver chains and mouthpieces gleaming in the lamplight. The familiar gurgling sound that followed was the signal for the most irascible gentlemen amongst them to mellow as each pungent mouthful was gratefully inhaled; even Blair seemed rather less likely to over-indulge with the whisky bottle if he had had a fair go with this communal pipe of peace.

Evenings that ended with the *hookah* she found she could cope with, as they usually went home straight after-wards, with Blair in a much more amenable mood, but about twice a week, after dinner at a friend's house, Blair would get involved in a card game; unwilling to sit there for hours on end watching, Laura would return home alone, often taking the long way around the perimeter of the compound. That often turned out to be the best part of the day. There was a special magic about the place at night.

There was a balminess in the air that made her want to prolong the return home to the stifling confines of her small house, with its interminable creaking punkahs and inscrutable servants round every corner.

She took just such a walk on the first Saturday evening of the new year. To her relief, the Christmas celebrations of 1856 were over and, being the first without the King in residence, they were now being spoken of as the best in a decade, although she had found little enjoyment in the usual round of functions with the same faces evening after evening.

What had really spoilt everything for her was that Blair had disappeared for almost five hours during Christmas Day itself, taking with him a large box he had had secreted for two weeks at the bottom of one of his travelling trunks. Laura had had little doubt that it contained toys for the two children she had met that day six months previously, but her pride would not allow her to comment as he carried it from the house, inadequately hidden beneath the folds of his cape. Instead she had fought with herself to remain cool but friendly when he returned five hours later to prepare for the grand ball in the palace that evening. Convention required her to smile happily as they skipped merrily through countless cotillions together, though it had been almost too much to bear. They were playing an elaborate game of charades with each other that seemed to have no end in sight, and that was the really awful part of it.

As usual that evening he had been the centre of attraction with the other ladies present, and even more so the following week when the annual Hogmanay dance was held to celebrate the Scottish residents' special festival. In keeping with tradition, several of the Scots personnel present had sung their favourite national songs, and Blair had had no need to volunteer. 'We'll have Major Baxter first!' the cry had gone up, and Laura had watched from her seat at the side of the room as, kilt swaying, her husband strode into the middle of the floor as if taking the stage at Dundee's Albert Hall itself.

'In honour of my dear wife, I will sing one of our favourite songs, "Bonnie Dundee"!' he had declared, with a sweeping bow and another swing of the kilt. And she could still hear the resounding cheer that had followed the line, *'And it's up wi' the bonnets o' Bonnie Dundee!'* Paper hats and dress caps of all descriptions had been hurled in the air as he was cheered to the echo.

How on earth had she managed to sit there smiling in the middle of it all, she wondered? After all those glasses of fine wine, how in heaven's name had she succeeded in remaining silent about the secret that was tearing her apart? But who could she have told? Who could she ever tell? Blair had been here for so many years and was so well liked by all that, even if she was believed, they would see nothing wrong in what he had done. Had not a thousand others done it before him? And would not another thousand do it after him? This was India, after all . . .

She found her thoughts returning again to that night, and the lilting tunes of her hometown's favourite song echoed once more in her head as, a week to the day later, she left Blair seated around the card table in the home of a Major Anderson of the Engineers and she set off for home alone.

It was a particularly beautiful starlit night, and she was not in the least bit sleepy as she left behind the lighted windows of the Anderson bungalow and the clinking of glasses and conversation still going on behind them. The meal she had just eaten lay heavy on her stomach. A *'troisième service'*, Blair jokingly called the three courses of stodgily cooked food usually served up on such occasions. 'Very bad third-class French restaurant food . . . You get used to it, Laura old girl. You even come to enjoy it, after a fashion.'

But, try as she might, Laura knew she would never come to enjoy the continual servings of tepid mutton cooked in grey dishwater gravy, or the caramel custards made with watery skimmed goats' milk that smelt of old socks. The drink was the only bearable part of the endless round of dinners they had to endure, and it was little wonder so many out here became addicted to the fruit of the grape or the bottles of Scotch that arrived in endless supply from her homeland.

She had just rounded the corner of the Baillie Guard Gate, a continuation of the hospital that had once been the ceremonial entrance to the royal palace, when she saw what appeared to be a light on in her husband's front office. Summoning up her courage, she decided to investigate. Petty thieving was not unknown on the compound, and she had no wish to see Blair carpeted for carelessness in locking up.

She could make out nothing from outside the window, for the shutters were closed so, tentatively, she pushed on the outer door. To her surprise it gave way under her hand, and it was with some trepidation that she then pushed at the inner one immediately behind it.

'Mrs Baxter, *memsahib!*' A startled Samit jumped up from behind his desk, scattering a sheaf of papers all over the polished surface. 'I didn't expect to see you!'

'Nor I you,' Laura replied in relief, closing the door behind her. She glanced at the clock on the wall. It was just after ten-thirty. 'Do you usually work this late?'

'Only when there is something pressing to deal with.' Just before five o'clock they had received reports of disturbances in Dum-Dum, the military station and headquarters of the Bengal Artillery just outside Calcutta. The Governor was returning to the Residency the following day and would require a full report on his desk first thing in the morning. The dispatch concerned disquiet in the ranks of the sepoys – the Indian soldiers – and the information was taking much longer to collate than he had anticipated. Rising stiffly from having been crouched over his desk far too long, he came out from behind his untidy pile of papers and was his usual polite self as he ushered his unexpected visitor to a chair. 'May I take your wrap?'

'No, thanks, I'm fine.' Laura sat down in the wicker armchair. It was difficult enough sitting with such a wide crinoline at the best of times, but it was especially difficult in such a chair. As she battled with the hoop, she let the cloak slip from her shoulders, revealing an expanse of pale creamy skin and a distinct swell of cleavage never seen in daytime or in such a situation before. She felt a flush of pleasure as she glanced across and caught Samit's eyes on her and saw the colour suffuse his face.

Embarrassed beyond measure, he quickly averted his eyes and went back behind his desk. He immediately set about retrieving his scattered papers with much more gusto than was necessary. 'I see you have been out for the evening,' he said politely, keeping his eyes on the task in hand. 'I trust you had a pleasant time.'

'I don't know if pleasant is exactly the right word,' Laura mused. 'But yes, I have been out for the evening.'

His head was still bent over his desk, but she knew his mind was not on what he was doing as papers flew in all directions. For the first time she felt a certain tension between them, an excitement almost that was making her own heart beat faster. There was something about the intensity of his concentration – or lack of it – on the task he had set himself that told her he was every bit as aware of it as she was.

She found herself looking at him quite differently as she sat and watched him tidy up. A stray lock of black hair was loose over his brow as his hands busied themselves with the papers on the desk and, studying him, she realized for the first time how good-looking he was. It was something that had never really struck her before. So grateful had she been in the past for his friendship that she had never really looked at him as a young man of her own age. Now, as she followed every movement, and saw the pink flush that still lingered beneath the tawny skin of his cheeks, she realized how much she was attracted to this sensitive, bashful young man, with his lustrous black hair, dark, soulful eyes and soft, sing-song accent. 'Do you never get invited to any of these social evenings, Sam?' she asked him.

He shook his head. 'No, *memsahib*.'

'Please don't call me that. My name is Laura.'

He looked up and met her gaze. 'I cannot call you that.'

'Yes, you can. At least when we're alone . . . Say it, Laauurraa . . . Go on, it's not difficult.'

He smiled back at her. 'Laura.'

She clapped her hands in delight. 'There, I told you it wasn't difficult!'

Their eyes held until the smiles died on their lips, then Laura shook her head in frustration. 'I can't make any sense of all this British class and Indian caste nonsense,' she said. 'You can't join in our socials because you're not the right class, or you're half-Indian or whatever, and amongst the Indians themselves – even amongst my servants, for heaven's sake! – there are so many different castes and taboos that I get quite dizzy trying to remember them all. Don't you get tired of it, always having to remember your place when there are officers such as my husband around, or just plain ordinary white people that you're expected to bow and scrape to?'

His lean fingers shuffled the papers in his hands for the umpteenth time. 'Why get angry about what we can't change?' he said. 'That does nothing but make one dissatisfied with one's lot.'

'But you have every right to be dissatisfied,' Laura told him, feeling angry for his sake. 'I would hate it, having to sit here every day tugging the forelock to people often not fit to clean my shoes. Deceitful, lying people with white faces and black hearts. People like my husband, for instance.'

'You are still very hurt over that.'

'Hurt?' Laura gave a strained laugh as she thought about the word, then she shook her head. 'No, I'm not hurt. Angry maybe. And frustrated, deeply frustrated that I can't do a thing about it. I must just sit here and endure all the humiliation like a good Raj wife . . . It's not as if I am some old crone who is long past caring if my husband loves me or not. I'm still young and I still have feelings. Surely I'm not so ugly that he still has to look elsewhere for his pleasure?' She looked across at him imploringly. 'You don't think I'm ugly, do you, Sam? You wouldn't need to visit that – that whore in Wellington Road if you were married to me?'

She could see the blood rush to his cheeks once more as he shook his head quite vehemently. 'Oh no . . . Never. Never that. And you are not ugly . . . You – you are beautiful.'

Laura beamed as a warm feeling surged through her. At least someone thought she was beautiful. And it pleased her even more that that person was Sam. She got up from her chair, letting her cloak slip to the ground.

Before she could stoop to retrieve it, Samit came round the desk to pick it up.

'Allow me.'

As he placed it around her shoulders she could feel the touch of his fingertips on her bare skin. A tremor ran through her.

She turned to face him. His eyes were only inches from hers. 'Tell me I'm beautiful again,' she begged. 'Please, Sam, tell me I'm beautiful. Please . . .'

For a moment there was the hint of fear in his eyes, then, as her lips silently formed the word 'Please' once more, his right hand reached up tentatively to touch her cheek and she shivered as his fingertips lightly brushed the pale skin. 'You are beautiful, Laura,' he told her. 'You are so very beautiful.'

He was barely half a head taller than her, and their lips were only inches apart as she gazed up at him. With all her heart she wanted him to kiss her but she knew he never would. It would be going against all that was ingrained in him, all that was sacred in his life. She could feel the softness of his breath against her skin and, as they stood there so close that the tension between them was tangible, she could feel every part of her body tauten as all the loneliness and misery of the past six months welled up within her. Her eyes began to fill as her body ached for him to reach out to her again, to touch her just once more and ease the pain of this living widowhood.

There was tenderness in his eyes such as she had never seen in a man's before. Real tenderness that told her he could feel her pain. It made her heart ache so much that a faint sigh that was half a groan welled in her throat. Then, slowly, a single tear began to trickle down her cheek. For a second or two he watched it, his dark eyes luminous in the lamplight. Then, very gently, as it met her mouth he reached out and wiped it away with his forefinger, before pressing the moist fingertip to his own lips.

He could taste the salt as he looked down into her brimming eyes. 'Don't cry, Laura,' he said softly. 'Don't cry. He is not worth it . . . It is the beginning of a new year. Things will get better, I promise you.'

'You promise me?' she whispered back. She had already had enough broken promises to last a lifetime. 'It's not promises I need, Sam, it is love . . . And who can give me that?'

His eyes were devouring her and she could feel herself trembling as she reached out to touch him.

'It is forbidden,' he told her huskily, but he made no move to back away.

'Then let us go to hell together,' she implored him, as her fingertips gently stroked the tawny skin of his cheek. 'If this is a sin then I will happily pay for it, for hell cannot be any worse than what I have been going through.'

He reached out and touched her hair. She was so beautiful he thought his heart would break. But what she was now offering him was against all that he had ever held dear. He would put his whole soul in jeopardy if he moved one step closer. Heaven or hell, what was it to be? She was offering him both on a plate.

'Could you love me, Sam?' she whispered. 'Could you love me as I could love you?'

Then, without another word being spoken, she was in his arms and his mouth was on hers as their bodies melded into one. He knew he would be damned for all eternity, but at that moment he did not care. For so long this woman had invaded his dreams, had tortured his soul. And now she was in his arms, begging him to love her.

'Tell me you love me, Sam,' she implored him, as his lips moved hungrily down the soft curve of her throat. 'Tell me you love me.' She craved love as a blind man craved the light. All her life she had longed for someone to love her. She thought she had found that person in Blair, but he had cheated and deceived her. Her whole being was crying out for someone to give her the love that she needed as much as the air she breathed. She could no longer live without it. 'Say it, Samit,' she begged him. 'Tell me you love me.'

'I love you, Laura,' he told her. 'God help me, I love you.'

His whole body and soul was on fire with desire for her. Since he first set eyes on her, she was all he had ever dreamt of in a woman. But she was white and she was married. She was both heaven and hell. 'God help me,' he groaned as his lips moved down to the enticing swell of her breasts. 'Dear God, help me . . .'

But in his heart he knew that neither God nor anyone else could help him now.

Chapter Thirty-three

The weeks that followed Davey's release from prison were some of the happiest as well as some of the saddest of Kate's life. She felt elated to have him back in her life again, but at home she was increasingly uneasy about her relationship with Ewan. He had taken to going out on his own a great deal more, and in contrast to his usual open character he had become cagey as to where he had been and whom he had been seeing. She also discovered he had been taking time off work without telling her, which worried her a great deal. It was an easy thing to do. For years now the two of them had been in the habit of spending the best part of the day in different mills, only meeting up in the late afternoon to discuss whatever business problems had arisen. At first she suspected he might still be seeing Willie's daughter, Emma, but as she had no proof of that she kept her fears to herself and prayed they would prove unfounded.

In September she went ahead with her plan to pay a visit to their mill in Leith, and she was careful to see that this coincided with Davey's talk in Edinburgh. He was delighted she had found the courage to join him, and he made sure she had a seat in the middle of the front row of the audience, 'So I can keep an eye on you and make sure you don't fall asleep.'

In the event, there was never any question of falling asleep, for his rousing words had had the Edinburgh audience on its feet on several occasions during his forty-minute oration, and no one cheered louder than she did at the end. There were moments during it when she thought her heart would burst with pride as he stood there centre-stage and raised his voice to the rafters in the cause of the common man. When he railed against the factory- and mill-owners who exploited the youth of the country – 'our land's finest resource' – she found herself clapping harder than anyone and joining in the cries of 'Hear! Hear!' until she was sure she would lose her voice. And afterwards she had the good grace to blush when he up-braided her for clapping and cheering the proposed demise of her own class.

'Did you not realize it was the likes o' you and your kind I was protesting against, Kate lass?' he said with a rueful smile as he took her arm and they made their way out into the chill of the autumn evening after the crowds had gone home. 'If rabble-rousers like me have our wicked way, then there will be no such thing as Capitalist mill-owners like you making money out of the sweat of other men's brows.'

'Oh Davey, Davey,' she sighed, squeezing his arm. 'I hear what you say, and fine sense it makes, that's for sure. But where would those same folk be if it wasn't for the likes o' my mills, tell me that? They'd be starving on the street corners in even greater numbers than they are now, that's where they'd be.' And she squeezed his arm that bit more as they continued their way along George Street to the small guest-house where they were booked into single rooms.

There had been no question of signing in as Mr and Mrs Smith, or anything like that. He had never suggested it, and anyway it was too soon, she told herself, as she signed the register under her own name. Then, as she watched him bend his greying head over the book and write David G. Lorimer, with a flourish across the page, a chill hand took hold of her heart. Maybe it wasn't too early at all. Maybe it was already too late . . .

When she got back home she did not tell Ewan she had met up with Davey in Edinburgh, for that part of her life was as great a secret from her son as his own private life had become from her. It was not a situation she was happy with, but for the time being she could see no other choice.

'The lad will grow to accept I'm not the devil incarnate he takes me for,' Davey told her. 'Just give it time.'

But waiting had never been Kate's strong point. She looked at herself and the man she loved and saw them both getting older, and she cursed the fate that had put them on opposing sides of the social fence. Already Davey's name was anathema amongst all the other mill-owners and businessmen in the city, who saw him only as a political thorn in their flesh. Although never alluded to openly in her presence, it was an open secret that she had helped him get off the charge of murder that had hung over him after his wife's death, and there were even those who whispered that 'the poor fool of a Catholic priest had been made to pay'. Exactly how that state of affairs could be arrived at she had no idea, but it was indicative of the hatred there was in the city over the growing workers' movement of which Davey was the acknowledged leader. 'You're playing a dangerous game keeping me as a friend, Kate lass,' he would often say to her, usually at the end of a long day when he was both tired and almost defeated by the task he had set himself.

But at such moments she would merely smile quietly to herself and say, 'We'll have less o' that talk, Wee Davey. You've been my friend longer than most o' these fine mills have been standing, and nothing can change that fact, nor would I want it to.'

Yes, she thought to herself, they made an odd couple right enough: the mill-owner and the revolutionary who would destroy all that she had spent a lifetime building; but she would have it no other way. She loved Davey for what he was: the most honest, finest man she had ever known, and if Ewan could not recognize that fact then it was his loss.

And so Davey's tour of the big industrial cities came and went, and as autumn gradually gave way to winter, and the trees grew bare and the waters of the Tay turned to silver-grey under the darkening skies, so Kate found herself living two separate lives. During the day she was still the conscientious businesswoman who put the fear of God into her office staff by turning up to go over the books with a fine-tooth comb, but come evening she was the regular attender at most of the political rallies in the town. Sitting in her usual place she would watch and listen to all that took place, then, after the speeches were all over, she would quietly slip away with Davey to go back to his cottage on the foreshore for a cup of tea, or occasionally something stronger, and they would talk about the issues raised.

The more they talked, the more Kate found herself being convinced by the arguments. And as he talked to her of Robert Owen and the other great mill-owning reformers, she found herself agreeing that such measures should indeed be brought into effect right here in Dundee, and as quickly as possible. If a man like Owen could do it in New Lanark, then surely the Falcon Mills could do it here in Dundee? The only thing stopping her at the moment was Ewan.

'He'll be a terrible hurdle to overcome,' she told Davey as they sat together in front of his fire one cold winter's evening just before Christmas. 'I often think he'd see me hanging from a gibbet on the Law Hill rather than turning myself into a "bloody Communist" as he calls them.'

But Davey merely smiled as he sipped his whisky. 'Even a headstrong lad like your Ewan can't stop progress,' he told her. 'One day "the meek shall inherit the earth" as the good book tells us, and I only pray to God that I'm still here to see it.'

She had smiled at that, for Davey had not believed in either God or the Bible since he was ten years old, but she would never have dreamt of reminding him of that fact.

'Are you going to the Hogmanay Ball this year?' he asked her at the door as she prepared to take her leave.

She paused and thought for a minute, then shook her head. Normally she had put in an appearance for the sake of the business, but this year she had no inclination to obey the proprieties of society. 'Somehow I think I've outgrown all that,' she told him, pecking his cheek in farewell. 'I'll leave that type of thing to the likes o' Ewan and his crowd from now on.'

The answer seemed to please him for, quite out of character, he took hold of her by the shoulders and planted a kiss firmly on her lips. 'Sleep well, bonnie lass,' he told her. 'Sleep tight and don't let the fleas bite.'

'You're so romantic,' she chided, as she prised herself from his grasp. 'A typical Scotsman and no mistake!'

The morning of the Hogmanay Ball, the last day of the old year, dawned with a glowering white sky that meant only one thing. 'It looks like we're in for snow before the day's out, Ma,' Ewan commented as they sat at opposite ends of the breakfast-room table, drinking the last of the tea in the pot. 'We'd better not get snowed up here in the Ferry, for I'm not missing the dance tonight, that's for sure.'

Kate got up and went to the window where big soft flakes were beginning to drift down. 'You can always take your evening clothes with you and book into the Royal Hotel,' she suggested. 'That way you'd be sure of attending. It's being held there this year, isn't it?'

'Aye, it is. And that's not such a daft idea,' Ewan said, rising from the table. 'Has my kilt been pressed yet?'

'You'd better cry in downstairs and check for yourself. You're not a wee laddie any more, you know. You don't need me to see to that sort of thing any longer.'

'Who told you that nonsense?' he grinned. 'I'll always need my mammy!'

'Only till you get a wife.'

Their eyes met and the smiles died on both their lips.

'Aye, well, that's some time off yet,' he said, picking up the daily paper as he made for the door. 'But it looks like

I'll not see you till the wee small hours if I'm taking my stuff with me.'

'Happy New Year then, in advance, Ewan lad,' she told him. 'I'll raise a glass to you when we hear the Auld Kirk bells.'

She was watching him load the carriage with his dress kilt and jacket some ten minutes later when the maid came to take the breakfast things away. 'You'll not miss going to dance yourself tonight, Mrs Falconer?'.

'Lord no,' Kate said, shaking her head.

'Will you be staying here at Falcon Ridge to see the new year in?'

Kate's brow furrowed as she pondered on the question. 'I might just take a walk down the village to see a couple of old friends,' she told her. Yes, that wasn't such a bad idea. Old Bertie Mooney would be glad of her company, and it would come as quite a surprise to Davey to see her appear at his door.

It was a day to be spent in front of the blazing fire in the drawing room, and Kate made the most of it by catching up on her letter writing and poring over the latest batch of reports from their managers in India.

She waited until eleven-thirty that evening before donning her warmest fur-collared cape, bonnet and muff and, carrying two new bottles of finest malt Scotch whisky in a bag over her arm, she set off down the hill in the snow. A good six inches had fallen during the day, and the temperature had plummeted even further with the advent of darkness, so that a crisp coating of frost sparkled like a crust of hard icing sugar on the surface as she carefully picked her way down the steep brae by the light of her lamp.

On reaching the Church of Scotland manse in Grey Street, she was concerned to find that her friend Herbert Mooney had been confined to bed with bronchitis for the past two days.

'No more than to be expected at my time of life, Kate,'

he told her, sipping a hot toddy made with whisky, honey and hot water, as he sat up in bed in his best nightcap and grey flannel nightshirt. 'You can forget all that nonsense about old age bringing wisdom and serenity – it's a lot of baloney. Old age is a damned inconvenience and brings all sorts of things we can best do without, such as this dicky chest of mine. But it comes to us all whether we like it or not, and there's no use complaining about it.' Then he peered at her quizzically in the dim light of the oil-lamp. 'I haven't seen much of you over the past couple of months. Have you been keeping well?'

'As well as can be expected. Why? Did you hear otherwise?'

He blew his nose noisily into a large red handkerchief, then took another sip of the toddy and made a dismissive gesture with his hand, as if to brush aside her question. 'Och, I hear perhaps more than I should in my particular walk of life. Little birds whisper things often better left unsaid.'

The fire in the grate had died down giving the room a chill feel to it, so Kate went over and took a log from the wicker basket by the side of the hearth and placed it in the centre of the grate before raking at the ashes beneath with the brass poker. 'And what might these little birds have been telling you?' she asked, rubbing a hand in the small of her back as she stood up and looked at him questioningly.

'Oh, just that you might not have been quite as prudent as you could have been over the past few months.'

'And what might that mean?' She tried not to bridle too much as she perched herself on the edge of the mattress at the foot of the bed.

'They say you've been seen a bit too much in the company of yon Lorimer fellow since he got out of prison. You've even gone as far as attending some of those rabble-rousing meetings of his.' He looked at her searchingly over the rim of his glass, before dabbing at his nose. 'It doesn't do to offend society too much, you know, my dear. Not in your position.'

'My position?' Kate gave a derisory laugh. 'Bertie, old friend, those little birds you speak of are no better than a pack of vultures getting ready to pick to pieces anybody who happens to offend their own narrow sense of morality. They can say what they like about me. Davey Lorimer is my oldest friend, and I will continue to see him whenever and wherever I think fit. In fact, I'm off to see him right now.' She took the other bottle from her bag on the floor and held it up for him to see. 'In fact, I shall be his first foot!'

The minister gave an approving chuckle. 'I knew you'd say that,' he said, placing his empty toddy glass on the pot cupboard by the bed. 'And I'd have thought the less of you had you felt otherwise.'

Kate came round the bed and placed an affectionate peck on his brow. 'Goodnight, you old devil,' she said softly. 'And a Happy New Year to you and many more.'

It was snowing again when she closed the manse door behind her and began to make her way towards the fore-shore and Davey's cottage. The flakes were drifting down covering everything that stood still in a thick white blanket, and she could feel them clinging to her eyelashes as she picked her way carefully across the road. Already there were small bands of revellers on the street, some distinctly the worse for drink as they staggered across the rutted ice to hail acquaintances on the opposite side who had just emerged from a pub two doors down from the manse.

Thankfully it was no more than a few minutes' walk between the two houses and, as she got within sight of Davey's cottage, she could already hear the sound of music and singing from within. Although this was Hogmanay and she should not have been surprised by it, she could feel her heart drop. Tonight of all nights she did not want to share him with anyone.

413

A glance through the open curtains of the window told her that the small kitchen was packed with people already well advanced in their celebrations.

She groaned inwardly at the sight. Somehow she had imagined it would just be the two of them, and an irrational resentment welled within her towards all these strangers keeping her from the man she loved.

She was on the point of turning to leave when the door was thrown open and a bearded middle-aged man stood there, a trifle unsteadily, bottle in hand. She recognized him from the many political meetings she had attended over the past five months but could not put a name to him.

'Good God, if it's no' Lady Muck herself!' He was quite clearly drunk, and his attempt at an elaborate bow had him staggering forward to almost collide with Kate, who stepped deftly sideways so he collapsed in the snow at her feet.

'Pay no heed to Jim, he's shit-marak and has been all evening,' a shawl-covered woman told her as she came out the door to haul at the man lying in the snow. 'I take it it's Davey you've come to see?'

Kate knew that to have denied it would have been ridiculous as she stood there at the door with the bottle of whisky in her hand, but nothing on earth would get her over that threshold. 'I – I think I'll come back later,' she began, but got no further as the woman released her grip on the drunk at their feet.

'Dinna be daft! Come away in wi' me,' the woman told her, grabbing her by the arm and hauling her towards the door. 'Davey will be fine pleased to see you.'

Her feet sliding on the hard-packed snow, Kate found herself being bundled through the open doorway into the midst of the party going on within.

An old man with an accordion, and a younger one wielding a fiddle were playing just inside the door, and Davey himself was sitting by the fire, surrounded by a swaying, singing group of friends. On his lap sat a good-looking woman in early middle-age; her arm was around his neck and in her free hand she raised a glass at the sight of Kate. 'Well, if it's not the fine lady herself!'

'Kate!' Davey waved a welcoming hand that was clutching a glass in her direction. 'Come away in! Welcome to the party!' His words were slurred and he had difficulty focusing.

'You're drunk!' she told him in disgust, her words almost drowned out by the din going on around them.

'I'm pissed out of my head,' he confirmed proudly, as the woman on his knee whispered something in his ear and they both laughed.

Then his attention turned back to Kate. 'I'm bloody sozzled and I make no bones about that because so is every good Scotsman worth his salt this guid nicht! It's a time for celebration, for partaking of the water of life, for forgetting one's sorrows!

> 'So here's a hand my trusty friend
> And gie's a hand o' thine,
> And we'll tak' a right guid willy waught
> For auld lang syne!'

His tuneless singing of the last verse of Burns's Hogmanay anthem was accompanied by a beseeching hand held out in Kate's direction. His eyes were imploring her to come to him, to take his hand, and there were the beginnings of a sob in his voice as he told her, 'You are my auldest friend, Kate . . . My auldest and best. Have a drink wi' us for auld lang syne!'

But Kate could only see the woman on his lap and her laughing face as she continued to whisper something intimately in his ear. As she stood there, Kate was convinced it must be something about her, and when, grinning back, Davey fondly slapped the woman's backside before taking another drink from the glass in his hand, it was the last straw.

Kate had had enough. Gathering up her skirts she turned and fled the room, rushing across the open threshold and banging the door closed behind her to stand panting in the frosty air.

She could hear a commotion within; fearing Davey was trying to follow her she immediately turned on her heel to flee. As she did so her booted feet skidded on the frozen ground. The bottle in her hand took flight and landed a few feet ahead of her with a dull thud, its contents forming a yellow stain on the snow amid the shattered glass.

As she stood there looking down at it, through the night air there floated the sweet sound of the Auld Kirk bells bringing in the new year.

She turned back towards the cottage where the sound of revelry had been interrupted by a raucous rendition of 'Auld Lang Syne'.

'Happy New Year, Davey,' she called to the closed door. 'A right guid New Year to ein and a' . . .'

Tears blinded her as she picked up her skirts and hurried away in the direction of Grey Street which led to Camphill Road and home. She had turned the corner before the door of the cottage opened and the middle-aged man with the grey beard and head of curly hair stood on the step looking about him in despair.

'Kate!' he called after her. 'Where are you, Kate lass? Don't go . . . Please don't go!'

But Kate had already gone. She had disappeared into the night and insistent hands were pulling him back into the room. 'Leave her, Davey lad. Let her be. She's no' one o' us. Let her go.'

And so he did as they implored him, sitting back down in the chair by the fire and falling immediately into a drunken stupor as the party continued on all around him.

Chapter Thirty-four

The ball in full swing in the Royal Hotel in the centre of town came to a momentary halt as the hand on the clock above the door ticked slowly round to twelve. All eyes were turned to it, and you could have heard a pin drop as the dancers held their breath. Then from the Auld Kirk came the sound they were all waiting for as the steeple bells began ringing out the old year and in the new.

As the traditional cheer went up, Ewan grabbed his partner and swung her off her feet. He whirled round twice with her in the middle of the floor. 'Happy New Year, Emma!' he shouted, trying to make himself heard above the din as bonnets were thrown in the air and the hugging and kissing began all around them. Friend was greeting friend with shouts of 'Happy New Year!' and hearty back-slapping, and even old enemies were putting the past behind them and shaking hands for this one night of the year.

From the main door could be heard the skirl of the pipes as, with kilts swinging and drums beating, the local police pipe-band marched in to the strains of 'Auld Lang Syne'.

An almighty cheer greeted their arrival and it was then, in the middle of all the pandemonium, that Ewan gave Emma her first real kiss. Until that moment he had been the perfect gentleman throughout their stolen moments together. But there in the middle of the crowded dance-floor, to the strains of Robert Burns's most famous song, it seemed as if the whole city was doing the same, as neighbour kissed neighbour and the spirit of the new year suffused them all with its good cheer. Ewan lifted her off the floor to swing her round once more and, as glowing-faced and laughing they came to a dizzying halt, with her arms still clinging tightly around his neck, it seemed like the most natural thing in the world when their lips met.

When it was over and she clung on to him, her eyes shining, he thought his heart would burst with pride. With her long fair hair done up with blue ribbons, and her blue velvet ballgown, without a doubt she was the bonniest lassie in the place, and the fact that she had chosen to spend the evening with him was almost too much to keep to himself. He longed to race home to tell his mother that, no matter what she or anyone else said, they were determined to be together. They were in love and that was all that mattered. One day he would have the courage to do that, and she too would confess the truth to her father. 'Daddy's very protective of me with Mummy being dead and him being my only living parent and all that,' she had told him. 'But once he meets you and realizes how right we are for each other, I'm sure he'll let bygones be bygones and welcome you as a son.' He just prayed to God every night that that was true.

The band was in the centre of the floor and the dancers were all joining hands around it now to sing 'Auld Lang Syne'. Ewan winked his eye at Emma as they joined in the singing. 'Happy?' he asked needlessly when they had time to draw breath.

'Ecstatically!' she laughed, speaking for them both as his fingers tightened around hers.

In keeping with tradition, the ball ended shortly after the bells and the departure of the pipers, so the dancers could begin their first-footing of friends and neighbours. This was the part of the evening looked forward to by many of the revellers, but not by the young man and woman who stood hand in hand by the door.

'I wish I could go home with you and first-foot The Eyrie,' Ewan sighed as they said a lingering farewell to one another on the front steps of the hotel.

'Soon, Ewan, soon,' Emma told him softly. 'Have patience. It will be worth it.'

As he assisted her into her carriage and closed the door behind her, she wound the window down to lean out and make the most of their last few moments together. As she did so, he became aware of several older people looking at them curiously as they waited for their own transport to arrive. Emma noticed it too and commented on the nosy-parkers in their midst, but Ewan was quick to reassure her. 'They're just jealous,' he told her. 'They're jealous they're past it and we're still young and in love.'

She seemed mollified by that, and passed a kiss on the tips of her fingers from her lips to his. 'Till Thursday,' she whispered as her carriage wheels began to roll.

'Till Thursday,' he called after her. That was the day he hoped to slip away in the afternoon and they could meet 'accidentally' in the street outside the Exchange Coffee House. Right now it seemed a lifetime away.

He could see his breath forming a white cloud as he called, 'Goodbye!' after the disappearing coach, and for the first time he noticed the icy nip in the air. He shivered and dug his hands into his jacket pockets. It was as if her leaving had taken the very warmth from his body. He watched until her carriage was totally lost from sight amidst the dozens of others that were braving the snow-packed roads to take the dancers home to all areas of the city and surrounding villages. He was relieved he had decided to spend the night in the hotel for, although he had tried to disguise it from Emma, he had had one too many in the bar earlier on, and now as he stood in the freezing cold of the night air, he felt distinctly the worse for wear.

'I think I'll give first-footing a miss tonight, lads, and go on up to bed,' he told a group of old schoolfriends of his who stood inside the door, bottles at the ready, discussing the plans for the night ahead.

'Your bonnie blonde Cinderella of a kissing-cousin

has gone home then and left you all alone?' Hamish MacKinnon, the fattest of the group, asked with a knowing smirk to the rest of them. 'Is that it, Prince Charming?'

Ewan had deliberately avoided introducing Emma to any of 'the mob' as he liked to refer to them, and a momentary frown creased his brow as he gave the obligatory grin in return. 'Something like that,' he replied enigmatically, wondering how the devil they knew who she was or that there was a family connection.

Hamish's comment disconcerted him as he made his way upstairs to his room. How many other people had noticed that they had spent the whole evening in each other's company, he wondered? Somehow, in the middle of all that crowd, it was easy to believe oneself to be invisible, but that had obviously not been the case as they spent dance after dance in each other's arms. But what of it? Hamish and the lads were his friends, he told himself. It was only natural for them to take notice of whatever female any of their group had taken a fancy to. He did the very same when the opportunity arose.

'Ewan, old boy, you're becoming as nervous as an auld wifie!' he chastised himself aloud as he shut the bedroom door behind him. 'This has been the best night of your life. Be grateful for it!'

With that he lit the lamp and flung himself down on the bed and closed his eyes. His head was swimming, but in the centre of the merry-go-round he could see her face and hear her excited laughter as they danced round the floor once more. 'Emma . . . My Emma . . .' Surely her very name was the prettiest ever invented? His mouth broke into a contented smile as he felt the effects of love, drink and lack of sleep wash over him in a great tidal-wave that brought oblivion within seconds.

He was still lying there fast asleep over an hour later when there was an insistent banging on the bedroom door. The sound made absolutely no impression on his dream, and he continued to snore peacefully on top of the quilt.

'Open up, man! Are you stone deaf?'

The combination of banging, rattling of the handle and shouting eventually had its effect and, shaking his head to confirm where exactly he was, bleary-eyed and still only half-conscious, Ewan pulled himself up on the bed. For a moment he imagined he was in his room back home, and his heart sank as his eyes focused on the unfamiliar furnishings of the hotel bedroom.

'Open the door, for Christ's sake! Open it, damn you, before I break it down. I know you're in there!'

'What is it?' Ewan mumbled, as he attempted to get down off the bed. 'What do you want?' Was there a fire or something? Whoever was out there was obviously demented to be yelling his head off like that at this time of night. It was probably some poor devil even drunker than himself. 'I'm coming! I'm coming! Hold your horses, will you?'

He stumbled to the door to pull it open, and stood staring at the man in the passage outside. 'Jesus Christ!'

'No, it's not him – and he'll not help you now!' the stout, middle-aged man told him. 'It's far too late to go calling on any deity for assistance.'

Willie Falconer pushed past the dazed Ewan and strode into the room.

'Hey, wait a minute! You can't just barge in here like this!' Ewan protested, his heart sinking as at last he recognized Emma's father. The same height as himself but several stones heavier, he made an imposing figure in his bulky, fur-collared coat. 'You can't just push your way into other folk's bedrooms!'

'I just have, lad, and there's damn all you can do about it.' Willie's voice was gruff as he looked around him, as if for signs of his daughter, but there were none to be seen.

'She's not here if that's what you're thinking. She left for home ages ago.' He had not the faintest idea how long he had been asleep or what the time was now.

'And it's a bloody good job for you she did.' Willie was

421

well aware that Emma had come home and gone straight to bed at around twelve-thirty; it had only been minutes afterwards that his neighbour had arrived to put the cat among the pigeons. 'Aye, it's a bloody good job indeed!'

'Wh – what exactly do you mean by that?' Ewan did his best to stand on his dignity, but it was taking him all his time just to keep his balance. The very last thing he wanted in a state like this was a showdown with Emma's father, a man with whom he had never even exchanged the time of day before now.

He backed towards the bed and sat down heavily on the edge of the mattress. His head was pounding and the bed seemed to be rocking beneath him. He could not remember feeling this bad since he had first got drunk on a bottle of his mother's best whisky at the age of fifteen. But drunk he was, bloody drunk, and all he needed now was to bring up his supper at Willie Falconer's feet. 'What do you want with me? Coming here at this time o' night, for Christ's sake, it's not human!'

'It's human all right,' Willie said through gritted teeth. 'And I'm doing no more than any father would do in my position to protect his daughter.' His hazel eyes glinted in the lamplight as he glared at the dishevelled sight of the young man sitting on the bed. What a beautiful intelligent lassie like Emma saw in a pathetic drunk like this he could not imagine. 'You keep away from her, do you hear me? You're nothing more than a drink-sodden little worm, not fit to clean her boots. You stay away from my Emma or you'll have me to deal with.'

'You to deal with!' Ewan laughed out loud at the very idea as he looked up at the corpulent grey-haired figure before him. 'Don't make me laugh, Willie Falconer! You might have got away with saying that thirty years ago, but not now. Man, I'd make mincemeat out o' you!'

'Try it, lad. Just try it!'

The invitation was too good to resist. No young man, no matter how drunk, liked to have an old codger like that

422

insult his manhood. If Willie Falconer was testing him, trying to see what he was made of, then he would show him all right. He could feel his fists begin to clench as he sat there on the mattress glaring back at him.

'Go on, lad, what's the matter with you? Yellow, are you? Is that it?'

Ewan tensed even more. He was doing his best to restrain himself, but nobody was going to speak to him like that! 'Get out o' here, you auld bugger! Just clear off, will you?'

'Make me!' Willie goaded. 'Just try and make me!'

With that Ewan lurched from the bed towards the older man and tried to manhandle him towards the door, but the bulk of Willie's overcoat made it almost impossible to get a grip. 'Away wi' you, d'ye hear me? Get out o' my sight! I'll see Emma when and where I like, and there's not a damned thing you can do about it!'

'Is that so?' They stood grappling in the middle of the floor. Ewan's extravagant boast brought out the worst in Willie, who shrugged off the younger man with little difficulty, then aimed a perfect right hook to his midriff.

'Aaaahhhh!' Clutching his stomach, Ewan buckled at the knees and let out a roar like a stuck pig as he struggled to keep his feet. This was the way of it, was it? So be it! He made another lunge at his aggressor, who stepped deftly aside then planted another well-aimed blow to the side of Ewan's head.

Stumbling awkwardly, Ewan fell to the floor, making a grab for Willie's feet as he did so. He brought the older man down on top of him like a ton of bricks. It was the worst possible move, for Willie's sixteen stones completely knocked the breath out of him. As he lay there gasping on the polished floorboards, the older man began to lay into him with both his fists.

'I'll teach you to meddle with my lassie, you young whelp!' Willie shouted at the hapless Ewan. 'I'll teach you a lesson you'll never forget, my lad!'

Sweat was standing out on Willie's brow, and his bald head glinted in the lamplight as he let loose all the anger within him. It had been the worst moment of his life when his next-door neighbour had stopped by to first-foot him tonight and had lost no time in informing him that Kate Falconer's lad had been openly romancing Emma at the Hogmanay Ball he had just come from.

Kate Falconer . . . Even after all this time the very name was still a red rag to a bull. For a quarter of a century that woman had remained the devil-incarnate as far as he was concerned. Not only had she done him out of his birthright, but she had gone on to do her level best to thwart him at every turn since his return to Dundee. Dirty tricks such as the building of that mill on his own mother's land in Lochee were more than thorns in his flesh, they were direct insults to the true Falconer family. She was not one of them, but an evil, gold-digging interloper, who had wheedled her way into his father's affections, intending to deprive him of what was his by right – and succeeding. Three generations of Falconer industry and pride had been wiped out in one fell swoop when she had got that ring on her finger. The Falconer Mills belonged to himself and Ian, his own son, not to that Irish whore and this young drunken lout of hers.

All the anger and hurt he had kept inside him for a generation he now let loose on the son of the woman he hated with such a passion. Unable to move beneath the sheer weight of the older man, Ewan lay trapped beneath him as Willie continued to pummel into him with both fists. 'Bastard!' he cried. 'You're nothing but an Irish whore's bastard and I'll teach you to put your filthy hands anywhere near my lass!' As his fists moved like pistons, punching Ewan's face to a bloody pulp, he was totally unaware of the tears that were now streaming down his own whiskered cheeks. 'I'll teach you!' he cried, as he took hold of Ewan's head and began to bang it against the bare wood of the floor. 'I'll teach you a lesson you'll never forget!'

Finally, when his energy was all spent, he staggered to his feet and looked down at the bloodied features of the young man lying on the floor. Ewan was almost unrecognizable, for both his eyes were almost closed, and blood was oozing from his nose and mouth to mingle with the dark-red hair of his beard. 'Bastard!' Willie hissed once more. Then, clearing his throat, he spat straight down into Ewan's face. 'Your bitch of a mother stole all that was mine. You robbed me of all that I held dear in this life. I'll see you in your grave before you rob me of my own daughter!'

He was shaking with barely controllable passion now, and his breath was coming painfully from his heaving chest. As he stared down with real hatred in his eyes at the young man on the floor beneath him, he knew he had it in his power to do much more than just give him a bloody nose. All it would take would be to pick up that poker from the grate. Nobody would ever know who had done it. The hotel was full of drunks tonight. They would never find the body till morning, and Willie would be safely back in his own bed in West Ferry long before then. Nobody would have a clue.

As the idea took shape, sweat poured from him. It ran in rivulets from his brow and lay in small droplets on the thick grey hair of his moustache. The devil was on his shoulder, urging him to finish the job. It would be easy, so very easy.

A shudder ran through him and he let out a guttural animal roar, half of rage, half of frustration, as the torment raged within him. 'God help me!' he groaned. Had it come to this? Had it really come to this? Had that woman and her drunken bastard of a son actually driven him to contemplate murder?

His chest was heaving beneath the thick worsted of the overcoat as tears flooded his eyes. Impatiently, he wiped them away with the back of his hand, then he jerked round and half ran from the room. The door rattled on its hinges behind him.

When he had gone, Ewan lay there on the floor. The ceiling of the room span in a giddy carousel with the furniture. He could feel the warm cloying taste of blood on his tongue and could barely see out of his eyes. His whole head was throbbing and there was not a part of him that was not aching, but there was no way on earth he could begin to get up off the floor to help himself.

Slowly and painfully he rolled over on to his side and rested his throbbing cheek against the cold wood of the floorboards as a voice in the passageway outside shouted, 'Happy New Year!' to a retiring friend as a door banged in the distance.

'Happy New Year!' Ewan managed to mumble in an ironic response, and a bitter ghost of a smile hovered around his swollen lips before oblivion overcame him and he slipped into welcome unconsciousness.

Chapter Thirty-five

Since that one unexpected, wanton hour of desire spent with Samit in her husband's office, life had not been the same for Laura. Every romantic dream she had ever dreamt had become reality, and suddenly life was worth living again.

He had taken her into Blair's own office and locked the door. And there, on the smooth pile of the Bakhtiari carpet beneath the portrait of Queen Victoria, they had made love. With her husband, lovemaking had never been more than a few minutes' groping in the dark that had left her feeling used and abused, but with Sam it had been so very different. His passion for her was combined with a gentleness that she had never known before. It was like two halves at last finding each other and becoming whole. To leave him that night and return home alone to the bungalow she shared with her husband was the greatest torture she had ever endured.

From that night, Samit had filled her thoughts. They had met in secret and made love on every possible occasion since then, and life had taken on a whole new meaning. She lived for their stolen moments together. They were not hard to find, for at least two evenings a week Blair would stay behind after dinner at a friend's house to play cards.

To her surprise, he had noticed the change in her, commenting on how much more cheerful she seemed these days, and she had merely smiled and hugged her secret to herself. Perhaps their marriage had even profited by her falling in love with someone else, she told herself. It was not simply a case of paying him back for his betrayal. In a funny way perhaps she understood better now what it was that her husband felt for that woman down on Wellington Road. Craving to be with Samit every waking moment as she did, she could well imagine Blair being besotted in the same way with a woman like that, who was not only beautiful but was practised in all the secret erotic arts of lovemaking. They seemed to make a speciality of the sexual act out here, even carving copulating couples on the walls of their sacred temples. Lovemaking was regarded by the Indians as one of the highest of all art forms. They were a strange race all right. But to be in love with an Indian was no longer a strange phenomenon to her. Since falling in love with Samit, she knew there was something about those dark lustrous eyes and that smooth honey-coloured skin that could seem so much more desirable than the pale eyes and flaccid pink flesh of the European.

In the weeks and months that followed that first embrace, she lived only for those few moments alone with the man she loved. They never discussed the future, for things were happening around them in this particular part of India that made looking ahead too difficult. But Laura knew in her heart that she did not want to return to Scotland as Blair's wife. Somehow, some day, she had no idea how or when, her dream was for her and Samit to be together for ever. All she longed for was that the secrecy and deceit would soon be over. She hated the hole-in-the-corner life they were forced to live in order to avoid detection. She wanted to shout from the rooftops that she loved this man; one day, she promised herself, one day it would happen.

Just occasionally the waiting got too much, and on the few times she tentatively attempted to discuss the outcome of their love for each other, Samit would silence her by pressing his finger to her lips and saying gently, 'The future is not in our hands, my love. We must wait and see what happens. This is a trying time for everyone.'

And he was right. They were all waiting to see what was going to happen these days; the whole of North India was holding its breath.

British rule was going through its most testing period. It was now May, and since before Christmas the whole of the northern provinces had been trembling with unease as rumours of rebellion within the ranks of the army grew. Not only had the British East India Company, which had ruled the country since Clive's victory at Plassey in 1757, succeeded in antagonizing almost all sectors of society, but the Indian army that had helped conquer India for the British was now in ferment.

Run by British officers, the Indian army was mainly composed of Hindu and Muslim soldiers – sepoys – who were becoming increasingly agitated by the rumours that the British, tired of the restrictions brought about by the Indian caste system, were intending making life easier for themselves by turning them into Christians. Rumour had it that this would be accomplished in an underhand manner, by a new method of greasing the cartridges of the Enfield, the latest breech-loading rifle, that had just been introduced. The substance the soldiers would be given would be an amalgam of cow fat, the cow being a sacred animal to the Hindus, and pig fat, the use of which would be equally abhorrent to the Muslims. To be forced into contact with these substances would condemn the Indian soldiers to certain damnation and, having so sinned against their own religions, it was claimed that the British hoped they would be forced to turn to Christianity. An Indian army composed of Christian soldiers, with no caste restrictions to bother about, would be much easier to run, and it was firmly believed that this state of affairs was to be brought about as soon as possible.

The rumours began in January in the headquarters of the Bengali army at the Dum-Dum barracks, just outside Calcutta, and in February, Bengali soldiers in Berhampur refused to accept the contentious new cartridges, and so it had continued throughout the northern provinces. Mutiny was in the air.

By April the Punjab was affected, then, on the third of May, to the alarm of Laura and everyone else, Sir Henry Lawrence, the newly appointed resident governor in the palace at Lucknow, had to muster all available resources to avert a mutiny amongst the soldiers stationed within the walls of the compound itself. No one could quite believe it was happening. Their own native soldiers mutinying! It was unthinkable. A bunch of hot-heads, people said as the authorities were spurred into action. Shortly afterwards they consoled themselves with the news that it had all been put down with appropriate haste and that the perpetrators were now under lock and key and would be duly punished.

After the aborted mutiny on their own doorstep, Laura was convinced that the rumours of a deep-seated anti-British feeling were true, and it was now just a matter of time before things really got out of hand. Whilst the issue of the greased cartridges was undoubtedly the catalyst for the mutinies that had already taken place, it did not account for the deep unrest and sense of grievance amongst the non-Anglo population of Oudh. Since the deposing of the King the previous year, Samit had confided in her about the great disquiet amongst the native people. 'Promises have been broken,' he told her. 'Their patience has run out. People have lost their faith in the British.'

When she had diplomatically raised the matter with Blair, and pointed out that perhaps the brewing trouble had more to it than greased cartridges, her husband, like most of his colleagues, was adamant the continuing unrest had nothing to do with maladministration on their part. He was firmly convinced that the attempted mutiny they had experienced was simply the work of a few local hot-heads fired up by news of the disturbances elsewhere. 'This is one of the best-governed provinces in the country,' he assured his wife. 'Since we got rid of that debauched young pup, Wajid Ali, things have never been better.'

Laura listened as a dutiful wife should, but was not convinced.

But although her husband would not hear a word against their administration of the province, not everyone amongst the British authorities was so blind. She was soon to learn from Samit that Sir Henry Lawrence himself, on his arrival two months earlier as resident commissioner, had been shocked by the evidence of misgovernment he had found. The British had been high-handed in the extreme; the terms of annexation had been largely ignored, with local chiefs deposed, pensions withheld, and large numbers of other loyal Indian personnel summarily dismissed.

'Sir Henry is not stupid,' Samit told Laura, as they met in his office one evening a few days after the attempted mutiny. 'He knows the people have a grievance and realizes the danger, but he is a clever man and does not want to start people panicking. He is going about his business as normal and putting on a brave face, but he is preparing for the worst.' And then he had shocked her by telling her that very few on the compound realized the new governor was already laying in extra stores of grain and supplies, as well as organizing a spare water-supply, while carrying on the ordinary duties of his office. 'He is laying in supplies for a siege and it will come,' Samit warned.

The very word struck terror into Laura's heart. As someone so used to her husband pooh-poohing all talk of trouble, she had almost convinced herself that much of the danger was exaggerated. This was alarming in the extreme, though. One did not go to the bother of laying in stores and spare water-supplies unless one was expecting some sort of a prolonged attack. 'Do you really think that's possible?' she asked Samit. 'Could it really come to that?' Quite ridiculously, she had been more worried at the thought of their secret meetings being interrupted by another attempted mutiny than at facing an armed attack from outside.

Sensing her fear, Sam had been quick to reassure her. 'You have no need to worry about living here. We are lucky that the residential compound is one of the easiest to defend in the whole country, and Sir Henry is a wise and prudent man. He will make sure that nothing occurs that he can't cope with.'

'It's all nonsense, of course,' Blair declared when the subject came up over the supper table the following evening. 'I thought better of Sir Henry, I must admit. The man hasn't been here five minutes and is panicking already.'

But despite the brave words, in her heart Laura now knew different. As an Anglo-Indian, Samit saw and heard things that passed by those as elevated as her husband. She knew that terrible injustices had been done, and that hopes were now high in native Indian hearts that the day of reckoning was nigh. Well away from British ears, the talk was all about recapturing their country for themselves. India for the Indians. Their own Bengal army could do it, they said. And she believed it. The army was mainly recruited from Oudh province and their sepoys were brave, proud men with stout, patriotic hearts who loved Oudh and India with a passion. She also knew for a fact that the majority of their English officers were nothing but stupid, self-important boys in men's uniforms who preferred drinking, gambling and beating their men to real soldiering. As the days passed, she had little doubt that Sir Henry was right and that Oudh, like India itself, was ripe for revolution.

Despite the fears, however, life had to go on, and most people still refused to believe anything could go seriously wrong within the Residency compound itself. Rising tensions between the Indians and their white overlords were put down to 'native jitters'. But by the time the weekend came, previously faithful servants were beginning to desert their white masters and everyone's nerves were distinctly on edge.

Their dhobi-wallah was refusing to come on to the compound to do the laundry, and one of the punkah-wallahs disappeared overnight. 'Something's going to happen, I can feel it,' Laura told her husband as they dressed for dinner on the Saturday night of 9 May. 'Servants wouldn't just disappear and forgo their wages like this. Something terrible is going to happen – and soon.'

'Tosh, old girl!' Blair declared as he wrestled with his necktie. 'You're becoming as much of an old woman as Sir Henry! The Empire wasn't won by being faint-hearted, you know. Tensions do arise from time to time with the natives. It's up to the likes of us to ignore such nonsense and not be intimidated by it – show what we're made of.'

'Stiff upper lip and all that?' she murmured, giving a weary smile as she buttoned her evening shoes.

'Exactly!' Blair agreed, totally unaware of the irony in her voice.

Determined to put their worries behind them, they set off for dinner at the home of Martin Gubbins, Sir Henry's second in command and Blair's immediate boss. It proved to be a jolly evening, with the subject that was filling all their thoughts rarely mentioned, except in a jocular fashion.

By the time they got home at just after midnight, Laura was actually beginning to believe that perhaps it was all scaremongering on the part of a few malcontents, as most people at the dinner had declared.

She went to bed with a much easier mind, but the following night, unbeknownst to the British residents of the Lucknow Residency and all other colonial outposts, all hell was being let loose at the military station of Meerut, forty miles north of Delhi. British India's worst nightmare was already coming true.

The sepoys stationed at Meerut broke out in open rebellion, massacring not only their British officers, but the officers' entire families, before setting off on horseback for Delhi, with no one left alive brave enough to stop them.

The dreadful news reached Lucknow a few days later and it threw the whole compound into a state of panic. Meerut was supposed to be even safer from attack than Lucknow. It was the largest military station in the north-west provinces, with the highest proportion of British to Indian troops, which was supposed to guarantee its safety.

Blair was at his post in the palace when the news came in; at first he did not believe it. It very soon became clear, however, that it was true; the unthinkable had happened, and in a far more horrific fashion than anyone had ever imagined. Unable to leave his desk, he immediately sent Samit to tell Laura who was at home alone. 'I don't want her running up here panicking after hearing it from anyone else,' he said. 'I can trust you to play this wretched thing down so she doesn't go hysterical and add to my problems.'

But Samit had already read all the dispatches from Meerut, and had actually spoken to two of the eye-witnesses who had escaped the slaughter. There was no point in lying any more. Laura, like everyone else here, deserved to know the truth. It affected them all equally. His face was ashen as he set off to tell the news to the woman he loved.

Laura could not believe it as she opened the door to him. He had never stepped over their threshold before. But immediately she sensed something must be wrong. There was a look on his face she had never seen before.

'Your husband sent me,' he said.

Her hand flew to her throat. 'Then it must be bad news.'

He made no reply, but followed her into the drawing room and insisted she sit down.

'It *is* bad news!' she cried. 'It has to be!'

'Please, Laura . . .' He looked at the face he loved so much. The strain of the past few weeks was showing in the lines of tension around the eyes that fixed themselves on his as he wondered how to begin.

'Tell me the truth, Sam,' she said softly. 'Whatever is happening, tell me the truth. I have to know.'

She listened white-faced as he began to recount the horror that had taken place in Meerut that terrible Sabbath night. And, as he talked, she kept shaking her head. 'But Meerut was meant to be the most secure of all our stations. Innocent men, women and children – all dead! No . . . it's not possible.'

She could not begin to comprehend how all their own British officers out there could have been rendered so completely impotent; how hundreds of sepoys had been free to go on the rampage, shooting and hacking to pieces every white face they saw. Were all the British there cowards, or drunk, or what? And what of the sepoys? Surely many had been friends and acquaintances of long-standing of the British officers and their families? Did friendship and loyalty count for nothing? None of it seemed to make any sense, and Samit was almost as perplexed as she was at the sheer naked brutality of it all.

By the time he had finished his story, tears were rolling down Laura's cheeks, and for once there was nothing that Samit could say to console her. Nothing anyone could say could possibly lessen the utter horror of what had actually occurred on Sunday night. A grey dawn had revealed a scene far worse than anyone's worst nightmare as rows of gutted bungalows, their white inhabitants hacked to pieces, were left in mute testimony to the fact that the unthinkable had actually happened. Mutilated and burned British bodies, of men, women and children, lay strewn around the station in silent, bloody protest over an atrocity that should never have been allowed to occur. 'They must hate us so much,' was all Laura could say or think as visions of that bloody carnage filled her mind.

Samit held her hands in both of his and they looked at each other, their eyes and hearts full of fear for the future.

'It could be us next, my darling,' Laura whispered through her tears. 'It could be us.'

Samit squeezed more tightly on the slim fingers clutching his. She was pleading for words of comfort, but he had none to give.

Chapter Thirty-six

Broughty Ferry
1 January, 1857

Ewan's injuries at the hands of Willie Falconer were so severe that they merited a doctor accompanying him on the four-mile journey from the centre of the city to his home in Broughty Ferry.

Having fallen unconscious after the fight, he lay undetected in his hotel room until the maid came in with the breakfast tray at eight o'clock on New Year's Day. By the time a doctor was called he had regained consciousness, but was in no fit state to travel. It was not until his injuries had been attended to and he had been given a generous dose of laudanum to kill the pain that he was carried into a carriage and, with the elderly physician in attendance, made the precarious journey home through the snow to Falcon Ridge.

Although he had not returned home by midday, Kate was not unduly concerned about her son's absence. A too-energetic celebration of Hogmanay was a well-known cause of many a young man's disappearance at this time of year. They would usually turn up again within twenty-four hours to nurse their sore heads, and she knew better than to play the over-protective mother and go rushing into town to find him. In any case, she was still far too upset over Davey's behaviour the night before to worry too much about whether Ewan had remained sober or not. Finding that party in progress in her friend's cottage on the foreshore, with him obviously not giving a tuppenny damn about how she was spending the festival, was not a happy experience. She had taken it for granted she would be the one he would want to be with on that most special of nights 'for the sake o' auld lang syne', and to find that was not the case had brought the old year to the most dismal and depressing end.

She did not even bother with a drink after hurrying back up the hill in the snow, with the sound of kirk bells still ringing in her ears. After all, what was there to celebrate?

And now it was 1857. She had slept little last night and, as usual, there was not a soul to be seen on New Year's morning. It had snowed heavily overnight, and a flawless white blanket covered the whole village as she ate her lunch of bacon and eggs alone in the dining room and looked wistfully out through the bay-window. In the silence, the house seemed to echo with the voices of those long dead. Perhaps it was her disappointment over Davey last night that made her mind turn to Augustus and remember how he had loved this time of year above all. 'It's the time for family,' he once told her. 'The time to look back and give thanks for what has gone and to place your trust in the Lord for what may lie ahead.' What would he think if he could see her now, she wondered? Would he be happy that a quarter of a century on she was still alone and was still in her widow's weeds, despite the casting off of her deepest black gowns?

There were many in this town who had wondered why she had never remarried. Even her old friend Bertie Mooney had remarked on the fact on more than one occasion. 'You're still an attractive young woman, Kate,' he had told her. 'Your family will not stay bairns for ever. One day they will up and leave you for families of their own, then where will you be?'

Just where was she, she now wondered, as she picked listlessly at her food? Laura had already gone and Ewan was at an age where he would soon be following her. That would leave her alone in the big house, with nothing but her memories for company. Her memories and Davey, for her old friend was not half a mile away, so near in distance but still so far away in so many other respects.

With a sigh, she pushed the half-eaten meal from her and rose to gaze out over the village and the river beyond. There was nothing festive about the scene. Nothing stirred, neither man nor beast. Small ice-floes were visible along the shoreline of the Tay, and snow clung to the branches of the trees that stood like white sentinels along the bottom of the garden. Lovely though it might be to look at in all its bleak beauty, she found herself remembering another time in another place at this time of year, and her heart went out to those not so fortunate, in their freezing-cold tenements on the other side of town. She shivered inwardly and thanked God for the good fortune that had brought her to this warm room that was so different from her old home in the Hawkhill.

She was still standing there a few minutes later when the quietude was broken by a strange carriage rolling into the drive.

Puzzled, she watched as the horses slithered their way up the gentle slope to trundle the wheels of the Victoria to a stop outside the front door.

Curious as to who it could be, she did not wait for the maid to come and tell her, but hurried out into the hall herself, waving away the white-aproned girl who came running up from downstairs. 'It's all right, Helen, I'll see to it.'

At first she thought the black-coated elderly man who alighted was a minister of the kirk, but when he introduced himself as a Dr Donald Gould from the Overgate area of the city, her anxiety was evident as she queried, 'Did someone from the house call you?'

'Indeed they did not, ma'm. I'm here accompanying your son.'

'Ewan?' Kate's heart gave a lurch. 'Is anything wrong?'

Oblivious to the snow-covered steps, she rushed down to the carriage to push her way past the doctor to look inside.

'Oh, my God!' The sight that met her eyes had her leaning against the carriage door to steady herself.

Ewan was stretched out across one of the seats, a grey blanket covering his body. His face was still visible, but barely recognizable.

'Dear God, what's happened?' She scrambled up the steps and got in the carriage beside him. 'Ewan, son, what happened?' Had he been in some sort of accident? It must have been serious to cause this sort of damage. She looked out at the doctor for an explanation.

Dr Gould, who was standing at the door of the carriage, could only shrug his shoulders. 'I was called to the hotel about an hour or so ago. He's in a bad way.'

Kate could hardly bear to look at the swollen, bloodied mass that was her son's face, and she could feel the hot sting of tears in her eyes as she tenderly brushed the hair back from his brow and asked softly, 'What happened, son? What happened? Was it an accident?' She could just imagine him being knocked down in the road if he had one too many after the dance last night.

But to her surprise he shook his head. She turned and looked at the doctor who was none the wiser as to the cause of the injuries, but volunteered, 'It must have been a fight.'

'A fight?' Kate's shock was obvious. Ewan had never been one to get into fights, not even as a wee lad. Some drunk must have picked on him. That was the only explanation. She leant over and asked softly, 'Who was it? Who did this to you, son?'

Ewan's swollen, red-veined eyes were full as he looked at her for a moment then managed to whisper, 'Emma's . . . It was Emma's da . . .'

'Emma's da?' Kate sat bolt upright on the opposite seat. For a second the answer stunned her. 'You mean Willie Falconer is responsible for this?' She almost shouted the words at him.

Ewan closed his eyes and gave an imperceptible nod of the head.

'Holy Mother of God!' Kate looked askance at the swollen, bloodstained face and began to shake. 'Go into the house and get hold of the gardener and one of the younger coachmen to carry him inside,' she told the doctor. Then, turning back to her son, she shook her head and her voice was thick with emotion as she promised, 'He'll not get away with it, Ewan lad. Don't you worry, he'll not get away with it.'

She was still promising herself that five minutes later as she sat by the side of the bed holding his hand. He was no longer recognizable as the handsome, fun-loving young man who had set off in such high spirits for the celebrations the previous night.

The laudanum the doctor had administered had made him drowsy, and he had difficulty focusing his eyes as she leant over and stroked his brow with a damp cloth. There were tears hovering beneath the dark auburn lashes as he murmured, 'Why, Mam? Why?'

'Don't try to speak, Ewan lad,' she told him. 'Now is the time to rest and recover, not to ask questions.' Questions to which she had no answers to give, she thought bitterly. Her heart quailed at the knowledge he must have still been seeing Emma for Willie to have done such a thing. To tell him the real truth behind this vicious assault would be more than either of them could bear. And the terrible thing was that even Willie Falconer himself did not know the whole story.

A cold anger welled within her that that man could do this to his own son. The fact he believed himself to be only Ewan's half-brother was no excuse. It was an inhuman act he had carried out, and he must not be allowed to get away with it. For too long he had used his bullying tactics to get what he wanted in this town. He had tried it with the Falcon Mills before now. She ought to have tackled him personally before that case ever came to court over the land. But she had not had the guts. She could admit it to herself now, but could not have done so then. She had

441

made excuse after excuse. She would not stoop to his level. She would not soil her tongue by speaking to him. Excuses, that's what they were. Nothing but excuses. She would make no more. Like the devil himself, bullies like her stepson had to be faced down. 'Sleep now,' she said softly, bending to place a kiss on her son's brow. 'Sleep away the pain and I'll be in to see you again when you wake up.'

Slowly she stood up, grimacing slightly at the twinge of rheumatism in her left knee. The bitter weather of the past week had done nothing to ease the aches and pains that were a constant reminder of the passing years. She nodded to the newly arrived nurse to take over and left the room. There was business to be done on this first day of the new year and she was determined to get on with it.

A gentle snow was falling as her carriage made its way south on the mile-and-a-half's journey to West Ferry where Willie's mansion, The Eyrie, was situated. It was a long time since she had confronted him face to face, but she felt no fear. She was no longer the inexperienced young woman he had once known. For a quarter of a century she had run the Falcon Mills almost single-handed, and had made them into one of the most profitable businesses this city had ever seen. No longer was she a source of mild amusement amongst the city fathers. They now listened to her with respect at social gatherings when she gave her opinion on anything from the state of the government to the public water-supply.

She had put on her best purple velvet cape and matching muff for the journey. It was odd how clothes seemed to affect your mood. There was nothing like the right outfit to give one confidence, and she knew she made an impressive figure as she left her carriage at The Eyrie's gates, giving the coachman instructions to wait, before making her way up to the oak double-doors with the brass eagle knocker and bell-pull.

In answer to her ring, the door was opened by a frock-coated butler who bowed deeply at the sight of her.

'Is the Master at home?' Kate enquired before the elderly man had a chance to speak.

'Indeed he is, ma'm.'

'Then tell him his stepmother wishes to see him, will you?' That will put the cat amongst the pigeons, she thought to herself as the butler's white brows rose.

'Indeed I will, ma'm.' He bowed again and stepped back to allow her to enter. 'May I take your cape?'

Kate shook her head. 'No, thanks, I won't be staying long.'

'As you wish, ma'm. Will you kindly come this way?'

She followed him through a marble-tiled hall and was shown into the main drawing room, the two bay-windows of which faced south-east over the river. It was an impressive room, divided by a large arch. It contained the very best examples of French furniture Kate had ever seen. Several years ago she had got rid of the original furniture from her own drawing room and refurnished it with new mahogany pieces which she had never been quite happy with, and looking around her now she knew for certain she had made a mistake. This room had class. It was not often these days she was so pointedly reminded of her origins, but as her gaze lingered on the carefully chosen pieces, each in its own special place, she could not help feeling a pang of envy towards the likes of Helen Falconer, Willie's late wife, who had never had to learn such things the hard way.

On the walls were numerous oil paintings in ornate gilt frames. Most were of famous Scottish beauty spots; she recognized Loch Lomond and Glencoe immediately, and then her eyes travelled to the fireplace above which was a portrait of Helen herself. She was seated at a window, with an open book on her lap and, with her fair hair and delicate features, Kate was instantly struck by how like both her children she was. Ian and Emma had inherited very little from the Falconer side of the family and, by the looks of it, were all the better for it.

A large gilt harp stood at one side of the fireplace, with an intricately worked tapestry chair beside it. Obviously someone in the family played, most probably Emma she mused. In the bookcase behind it stood row after row of leather-bound volumes of all the best in world literature. It was a strange feeling standing here in the midst of all these personal effects. It was the home of a sensitive, cultured family, a fact she found hard to equate with the man who had caused so much misery in her life, and it made the coming confrontation that much harder.

For the first time since resolving to tackle Willie over Ewan's injuries, she felt nervous. Perhaps it had not been such a good idea coming here after all. She was no longer on her own ground, and that mattered.

She caught sight of herself in a nearby wall-mirror. Her face looked drawn and anxious, not at all how she intended to appear. She walked towards the glass and stood in front of it, contorting the muscles to relieve the tension lines around her eyes and mouth.

She was still standing there grimacing at herself when the door opened and in the mirror she caught the reflection of someone standing in the doorway looking at her.

'Willie!' She whirled round to stare straight into those hazel eyes she had once known so well. He had put on weight since she had last seen him on the steps of the Court House and again she was immediately struck by how like Augustus he was. The older he got, the more he resembled her late husband in both looks and mannerisms. It was not a comforting observation.

'You had no right coming here uninvited,' he told her in a cold voice, closing the door behind him. There was no need to ask why she had come, but he hadn't expected it. He hadn't believed she would have the nerve.

'If I'd waited for an invitation, I'd have waited a long time.'

A tall, stout figure, with the ruddy complexion and excess weight of a lifetime's over-indulgence, he walked to the centre of the room and lit a cigar from a box of Havanas on a side-table. Every gesture oozed confidence as he blew out the match and tossed it into the ashtray. 'If you've come for an apology you'll be disappointed,' he told her, exhaling a stream of tobacco smoke in her direction. 'You'll get none from me.'

'I expect nothing from you,' Kate replied stiffly, holding herself as erect as possible and looking him straight in the eye. 'In the years you have lived here I have kept my distance and allowed you to live your life as you thought fit, Willie Falconer. It is only when you overstep the mark and invade my life and that of my family that I would even consider acknowledging your existence. It was a despicable act you carried out on my son last night. A despicable act that says everything about the perpetrator.'

The frown that had been gradually forming on Willie's face deepened. 'Balls!' he said, with a dismissive wave of the hand. 'It was no more than the young whelp deserved.'

'No one deserves to be beaten senseless like that. You could have killed him.'

Willie coughed on the smoke and cleared his throat noisily as he stabbed the cigar in her direction. 'It would have been no more than he deserved if I had done! I swear to God when I heard he'd been trifling with my lassie it took me all my time not to go straight down there and strangle the young bugger!'

He flicked a column of ash in the general direction of the ashtray and glared at her. 'Good God, woman, you know as well as I do there's a blood tie! Quite apart from the fact that no bairn o' mine will be allowed within spitting distance of your dirty offspring, to have allowed them to carry on would have been to risk a bloody imbecile being born!'

'I dare say one of them in the family's enough!' Kate retorted angrily.

'Are you suggesting I'm an idiot?'

445

'Suggesting nothing! I'm telling you! You've always had a bitter, twisted way of looking at the world. I know, for I've suffered from it more than most since you came into my life . . . '

'Just hang on a minute there!' Willie interrupted, stabbing the air again. 'To hell with that! *I* never came into *your* life, remember. You bloody well thrust yourself into mine by seducing my father.'

'Seducing your father! Don't you talk to me about seducing! Who was it who raped me just weeks before my wedding, tell me that?'

He stared at her, his rheumy eyes registering shock.

'Oh, don't tell me you've forgotten! For I haven't. Not for a single minute has the sickening memory of that episode left me.'

He gave a cynical grunt and his eyes narrowed as he looked at her. 'Don't come the poor little virgin with me, Kate McMahon. Don't forget I grew up with hundreds of your type in my father's employ. Pure as the driven slush you were, and no better than you ought to be. But you were cleverer than most, I'll grant you that. You knew you had no chance with the likes o' me, so you set your sights on a helpless old man.'

'Your father was never a helpless old man!' Kate retorted angrily. 'He was twice the man you will ever be – in every way!'

'Oh, is that so?'

'Aye, it is. You were nothing but a gundiguts then, Willie Falconer, and you're no better now. You're a greedy, bloated caricature of the man that I married and buried twenty-five years ago. And worse than that, you're a bully. You're a bully who would half kill a young man whose boots you're not fit to black.'

Willie's face was frozen as he walked over to the fire and flicked his cigar ash into the flames. He was silent for a moment or two, then said in a quiet voice that had the unmistakable undertone of menace to it, 'I can't quite fathom what brought you here today, Kate, but I promise you this: that son of yours will have no future in this town from now on. I want him out of my city. Out of Dundee and as far away from my lassie as possible.'

'And if he won't go?'

'If he won't go, then I'll make him. It's as simple as that.'

'Just who do you think you are? God Almighty?'

'You can scoff as much as you like, but I'm telling you the truth. I'm warning you and I'm warning him. Dundee's a small city, Kate, and there is no room for young bastards like him here.'

'Young bastards like him?' Kate thought she would choke on the words.

'Aye, he's a young bastard all right, for I'll never recognize him as my father's son. Never.'

'Then perhaps it's just as well, for Ewan isn't and never has been Augustus's bairn.' Her heart stood still as the words left her lips. But once out they could not be called back. She could feel herself begin to sweat.

He stared at her from his stance at the fireplace and slowly a look of triumph came into his eyes. This was what he had waited almost a lifetime to hear. 'So you admit it at last,' he said quietly. 'Your brat is not my father's son.'

Kate took a deep breath to try to calm her shaking innards. 'That's right, Willie,' she replied, meeting his eyes with every ounce of control she could muster. 'Augustus never was Ewan's father . . . You are.'

Chapter Thirty-seven

Kate read in the local newspaper that William Falconer, Esquire, the eminent Dundee mill-owner, was leaving the following week for Paris. There his daughter Emma would be enrolled in a *lycée* for young ladies, where she would concentrate on her music with a view to giving several concerts after her return to her native city in a year's time. The article went on to give a profile of the young lady's family, calling her father 'the city's most important employer of labour' and stating he was from a branch of a family long associated with the mill trade. His son Ian, it read, was being groomed to one day take over the business, but Emma, it was hoped, would go on to be 'one of the brightest stars in not only Dundee's but Scotland's musical firmament'.

Wryly amused that Willie had now been given the accolade he craved, to be regarded as Dundee's most successful mill-owner, Kate was nevertheless relieved to learn that Emma was to be taken out of the country for a sufficient length of time to allow the relationship with Ewan to cool down. She deliberately kept the news from her son who, one week later, had still not recovered sufficiently from his battering to get out of bed. As well as his facial injuries, it had been discovered by their own family doctor that he had broken several ribs during the fight with Willie, and had fractured the femur in his left leg. Kate knew that reading about Emma's imminent departure was the last thing he needed, so she made sure she took the newspaper with her as she made her way down the village to see Davey.

The sky hung low and heavy with the snow that would undoubtedly come before nightfall, and Grey Street was rutted with the cartwheels and carriages that trundled through the half-light carrying on the business of the day. After the celebrations of the new year, the villagers now had a pale, drawn look to their faces as they scurried about their daily tasks, trying to get as much done as possible before the darkness that descended by mid-afternoon made any outdoor work impossible.

When she reached the shore it came as a relief to find her old friend was in, and Davey actually looked pleased to see her as he ushered her into the small living-room-cum-kitchen.

'I was just having a cup o' tea, Kate lass. You'll join me, I hope?' He was unshaven and his hair was tousled from an obviously restless night, and she noticed a button missing from his waistcoat. Her motherly instincts were instantly aroused. She took a jar of homemade jam from her basket and placed it on the table. 'A cup of tea would go down a treat,' she told him, divesting herself of her cape and hanging it on the back of the door before sitting herself down at the side of the fire.

As she toasted her hands at the crackling flames, she looked around her with satisfaction. It felt good to be with him again in his own place. The pungent smell of his favourite pipe tobacco hung in the air, and open books and writing material were scattered over the tabletop where he had been sitting making notes by the light of an oil-lamp at his elbow. 'I see your festive season is well and truly over by the looks of it,' she said, eyeing the sheets of paper covered in his familiar scrawl.

'Aye, well, it's not Hogmanay every day,' he sighed, avoiding her eyes. 'And it's maybe just as well, the way some folk behave.'

And no more was said on that particular subject. She had stayed away from his cottage for over a week, and knew from his demeanour and evident delight at seeing her again he had got the message that she had not been best pleased with his behaviour that night.

'I came to ask your advice,' she told him, accepting a cup of strong tea from the pot on the table. 'It's about Ewan.'

'Forget it, Kate,' he told her. 'Just forget it.'

'But you don't know what I'm going to say.'

'Whatever it is, the lad is a grown man now. You can't live his life for him.'

She glanced at the newspaper in the bag at her feet. 'Have you seen today's *Advertiser*?' she asked. 'That bit about Willie taking his daughter to Paris?'

'Aye, as a matter of fact I have, and if you ask my opinion it's the best thing that could happen to the lass. Those two have to be kept apart. And, anyway, she'll be all the better for it. Paris is a grand place for the young.'

Kate's face was pensive as Davey sighed and sat back in his chair, arms akimbo, his cup balanced on one knee. 'Aye, Paris is a grand place all right.'

He glanced at the pile of papers on the table. Amongst them lay an envelope containing enough money in French francs to keep him going for the best part of the coming year. It had been a bit of a struggle of late, for the income from his writings and speeches was barely enough to get by on, but his late father-in-law had made over a generous part of his estate to him personally in order to 'keep the people's flag flying' and the periodic windfalls that now arrived at the cottage door not only brought greater peace of mind, but meant food on the table every day. 'If it wasn't for the French and their quest for justice for the common man, the world would be in a much sorrier state,' he said with feeling. 'And, in fact, if it wasn't for the big-heartedness of a certain Frenchman, I wouldn't be sitting here talking to you now. I'd be back in that ships' chandler's place down by the docks, bending over a pile o' dusty old ledgers for a living.'

The last thing Kate wanted was to reawaken nostalgic memories of his life in France, so before he got any further she interjected, a trifle apprehensively, 'You're not thinking of going back there, are you?'

450

'Would you mind?'

She took a deep breath and let it out slowly as she stared down at the cup in her lap. 'Aye, I dare say I would.'

'Then I'll stay.'

She looked up and they both laughed. 'You're busy writing though, I see . . . Are they speeches?'

'Speeches? That's maybe a wee bit flattering, but one or two bits will go into some addresses I may be called upon to make. The rest of the stuff is an article I'm putting together for the Communist League's journal . . . The rights of workers and all that.' His eyes twinkled as he looked across at her. 'Man against the mill-owner, you know the sort of thing.'

She gave a strained smile. 'I'm thinking of building a new jute mill on some spare land we've got in Lochee to cope with a new order we've just landed for the Admiralty. I'll be looking for advice.'

'From me?' He could not contain his amusement as he looked at her quizzically and took a gulp of his tea.

'And who else would I ask?'

'Och, I'll happily give it, Kate, you know that, but I doubt very much if that lad o' yours would approve.'

Kate murmured her agreement. 'I'm afraid Ewan has had a bit of an accident,' she confided.

'I'm sorry to hear that.'

'Och, it could be worse, I suppose,' she shrugged, deliberately playing down the incident, having just been told to keep out of things on that score. 'He'll be confined to bed for another week yet, and out of action for a week or so after that. He'll not be able to venture downstairs, so you can come up the brae some night and we'll go over what plans there are to date and you can give your comments.'

'On one condition.'

'And what might that be?'

'That you come to my next major meeting; the one I'm preparing this stuff for. It's in London next month.'

'London!' She had never been to England's capital

before, and the thought of seeing it for the first time with him appealed greatly. 'I'll think about it,' she told him. There was still enough of the young woman in her not to want to appear too keen, but her mind was already made up.

Five days later, Davey visited Kate in her drawing room at Falcon Ridge, and the two of them had an enjoyable evening going over the plans for the next Falcon mill.

Against strong competition from Baxter Brothers, one of their main rivals, Falcon Mills had just secured a lucrative contract to supply the Admiralty through Her Majesty's Victualling Stores at Deptford and Gosport, with fabrics ranging from heavy sail canvas to biscuit bagging. To meet these increased demands, the proposed new power-loom mill would be built using 150 horsepower for its 6,700 spindles, and would employ 510 new hands. The whole town was talking about it, for it would mean the difference between destitution and bread on the table for a great many more families.

'You'll go down in this town's history as one of its people's great benefactresses once that mill's up and running, Kate my dear,' Davey told her, for even he was excited at the proposed project that would benefit so many.

She beamed back her pleasure at him from the other side of the table. His compliments were rare and meant a lot.

He had brought a facsimile of one of Robert Owen's – the great reformist's – mills and, with all the drawings spread out before them on the dining-room table, they spent a good hour comparing the two, with Kate making copious notes as to what improvements could be made to her own plans. She drew the line, however, at the special hall where the young ladies of the workforce could be taught the finer points of dance and deportment when their day's work was done. 'I somehow think such a luxury could be kept for a wee while in the future, Davey lad,' she told him. Knowing the local female population as she did, dance and deportment would not be that high on their list of profitable ways of spending what little leisure time they had.

So with the plans for the new mill well and truly laid, and Ewan well on the mend, it was with a much lighter heart the following month that she travelled down to London by train with him to hear him speak to a rally of almost a thousand Communists in Lambeth.

Although she could have afforded to stay at the very best hotel in the city she booked into a modest guest-house off the Old Kent Road, in the same row of houses as the German exile friends who were giving him lodgings. They very kindly offered to put her up too, but she politely declined, telling them she felt it better to avoid the scandal of the Dundee papers getting hold of the fact they had shared a house, albeit someone else's. In reality she did not want them to stretch their meagre resources any further on her behalf; she no longer gave a second thought to what other people might say about her friendship with Scotland's most active Communist, or anything else.

The day she left for London, Ewan began his first full week back at work. She knew he had heard from one of his friends that Emma had been whisked off to Paris by her father, and he had taken the news badly. He had withdrawn into himself and she had barely got a word out of him for several days. Then one evening over supper, he could contain himself no longer. 'If you've been hiding it from me, I might as well tell you that I know what's happened!' he suddenly blurted out.

Her heart had given a sudden jolt as she looked up from her apple-tart. 'Wh – what's happened?'

'About that bugger Falconer taking Emma off like that, I mean.' His teeth had been clenched as he spoke and Kate could feel her stomach churning at what was coming next.

453

'He won't win, you know. Separating us by distance won't make one iota of difference to our feelings for each other.' Then his voice had dropped. 'I spoke to Jim about it this morning.'

'Jim?' He could only mean his former classmate from the high school, whose own family, the Carmichaels, were in the jute business.

'Aye, he reckons it's a bit o' bloody bad luck having Willie Falconer as a cousin, but even first cousins marry each other these days, never mind second.'

Kate concentrated on her plate and offered up a silent prayer of thanks as she pushed a morsel of pie-crust around with her fork. Obviously even Jim thought the relationship with Willie was far more distant than it actually was, and this had reinforced Ewan's own belief that Emma was merely a second cousin. Oh that it were true . . .

She had concluded the conversation by murmuring something about having patience and everything working out well in the end, which had seemed to satisfy Ewan who had made no more of it and had gone off to bed shortly afterwards. His strength was still far below par and, even if he had felt like it emotionally, he was in no fit state yet to carry on the carousing lifestyle he had enjoyed before the fight with Willie.

But, despite her continuing worries over her son, the days Kate spent in London proved to be some of the happiest of her life. The people Davey so proudly introduced her to included many political exiles from the Continent who, despite their formidable reputations, were a lot of fun once the speeches were over and they had retired back to someone's house for a supper of ale and bread and cheese.

On the last evening she decided to do something special to show her thanks for their warm acceptance of her into their midst, so she hired the largest room in the guesthouse where she was staying, and had the landlord lay on a cooked supper of mutton stew and a cask of ale for around thirty of Davey's closest friends in the movement. The evening proved a huge success. She drank far too much, as they all did and, to her horror, was reliably informed next morning that she had sung a duet of 'Ye Banks and Braes' with Davey, which had received the loudest applause of the night. The fact that she protested that neither of them could carry a tune in a bucket did not seem to matter one whit. 'They say we were so good we could make a living at it, Kate lass,' he told her proudly on their way to the station the following day. 'Aye, if we're willing to live on bread and water for the rest of our days!' she had laughingly retorted.

On the train back she admitted to him that she had never experienced such comradeship in a group of human beings before. 'At all the social gatherings I've had to attend over the years in Dundee, if we're not trying to outdo each other, we're seeing what we can get out of somebody.'

'Aye well, at the risk of beginning to preach again and becoming even more of an old bore than I already am, that's what Capitalism's all about,' he told her. 'It's all take with very little give.'

'But I am what I am, Davey. I can't get out of it. I'm a mill-owner. It's how I make my living. I inherited the Falcon Mills and along with Ewan am responsible for the livings of hundreds of human beings. I'm one of those very folk you detest so much, but what can I do but carry on? What choice do I have?'

Even Davey had to admit there was no easy answer to that one. 'Maybe it will come to us,' he grinned. 'Maybe one fine day, before too long, like Moses coming down from the mountain, I will come up the brae and tell you I have the solution . . . Of course, failing that, you could always retire early and just hand over the lot to Ewan.'

'Ewan?' She gave a hollow laugh at the very thought. 'I doubt if the poor lad is in any fit state to run *himself* right now, never mind the mill,' she told him. 'In a wee while maybe. But at least with Emma safely on the other side of the Channel, we seem to be getting along not too badly.'

'He's accepted her absence then?'

'Accepted it like a dose of the toothache. But there's nothing he can do about it. Willie will never let that poor lassie set foot in Scotland again if he thinks there's the slightest chance of them getting back together.'

'What do you really think of him?'

'Willie?' She looked surprised by the question, but wanted to be fair. 'I think he's a talented man, just like his father was, but he's got a determined, even ruthless streak to him that Augustus never had. To tell you the truth I'm surprised that lass Helen Munro ever married him. She looked a gentle, cultivated soul.'

'Aye, well, there have been a few unlikely matches in this world,' Davey mused. 'And even one or two not a million miles from this very carriage.'

She could feel the colour rising in her cheeks as she glanced round at him and caught his eye. 'That's certainly true,' she laughed. 'But I vouch there would be an even more unlikely one in most folk's eyes if thee and me were ever to tie the knot!'

He joined in her laughter, then his face became serious again. 'Would you accept if I were ever to ask?'

She turned abruptly in her seat, thanking God they were alone in the carriage. 'Why, Wee Davey, that wouldn't be a proposal by any chance?'

To her amusement he blushed to the roots of his greying hair. 'It might be.'

'Ever the romantic Scot!'

'Well, would you accept?'

'Och sure, and if the right man were ever to ask me in the proper fashion I might very well consider the matter.'

And at that she sat back in her seat with just the vestige of a smug smile on her face. If she was ever to be proposed to by him, then she would make sure that he brought some of that Gallic charm and romance she had heard so much about into play. She had not waited this long to jump at any half-hearted suggestion put forward in a draughty railway carriage.

Then, seeing the chastened look on his face, she reached over and gave his hand a reassuring squeeze. 'Put it this way, if I ever did decide to discard my widow's weeds, you'd be the first to know.'

'Well, thanks for that, anyway,' he said, with a puzzled look on his face. What exactly did she mean? Funny creatures, women were . . .

Chapter Thirty-eight

Lucknow, India.
June, 1857

'I'm sorry, Laura, I realize it was for better or worse, but I didn't promise you this in those vows we made.' Blair Baxter's face was haggard from too many nights without sleep as he sank into a chair and looked bleakly at his wife.

Laura's own face was expressionless as she lay on the settee beneath the motionless drawing-room punkah with an unread book on her lap. It was the first time in their marriage he had ever apologized to her for anything. But now unfaithfulness, second wives and children; all these were as nothing. The past and future had no relevance. There was only now. Tomorrow they could all be dead.

Mutinies and massacres of British residents had been taking place at military barracks all around them in this part of North India. White men, women and children had been put to the sword, the innocent as well as the guilty. But what exactly was the guilt laid at the feet of the British officers? Was it all really about the grease they insisted be used to smooth the cartridges into the new Enfield rifles the Indian army had been issued with? Even Blair was now having second thoughts on that matter, and was far more inclined to agree with his wife that the problems that had brought about this terrible state of affairs went much much deeper than that. He had even gone so far as to admit that he, amongst others, might in some way have been unwittingly to blame. These were changed days indeed.

To add to the misery, this summer was proving to be one of the hottest in living memory. No matter how much water the *bhisti* poured on to the tatties, or how hard the two new punkah-wallahs worked to keep the fans moving, there was no escaping the relentless heat that scorched the lungs and burned the skin as the residents of the compound spent their days and nights living out a hell on earth they had not imagined in their wildest dreams.

As the news of the continuing massacres at other camps reached Lucknow, Sir Henry Lawrence had doubled his efforts to lay in provisions and defences against the coming horror that haunted all their minds night and day. The once-beautiful lawns, where tigers and panthers had lazed, tethered on chains of gold, were levelled, and the surrounding flower gardens cleared of all vegetation. Magnificent old trees that had for generations provided beauty and shade were cut down overnight; even the church where the residents gave thanks every Sunday was given over to storing grain for the dark days they all knew lay ahead. Time was running out and everyone knew it.

Laura watched it all as if in a dream – a living nightmare. She prayed that, God willing, she would one day soon wake up to discover she was still at home in Scotland, where such things could never happen.

For the past month she had rarely seen Samit, and that had only added to her misery. He, like most of the clerical staff, had been assigned to other duties deemed more relevant to the dire situation in which they all found themselves. She thought about him constantly and missed his calming presence in her life so much that it physically hurt. Blair, of whom she saw almost as little, she hardly missed at all. But in a funny way she no longer felt as bitter towards him as she had once done. No longer was he the hail-fellow-well-met individual riding the crest of the wave that had brought him to the top of his profession at such an early age. Now she saw another side of him, a quieter, more reflective part to his character that for the first time in his life made him question why such a thing should be happening to their well-ordered world.

The latest news to reach them was that Cawnpore, a military station forty-eight miles away on the Ganges, had been attacked with the inevitable slaughter; the remaining men and around four hundred women and children were now under siege. In the Residency compound at Lucknow they felt both grief and impotence at what was happening to their own people within a mere day or so's ride away. Tales almost too awful to hear continued to pour in; terrible tales of the suffering being endured by their fellow British, many of whom were old friends of Blair and the other, older Indian hands on the station. They all knew now it was just a matter of time before they themselves would become part of the hell that was engulfing India. Laura even found herself getting rid of the hour-glass in the kitchen: those grains of sand trickling down seemed an awful reminder of how time was running out for them all.

Then, on the evening of 28 June, their own fears were multiplied when news reached them that there was a large contingent of mutinous sepoys centred on Nawabganj only twenty miles away to the north. Panic set in, but those in charge did their best to maintain calm. Blair was in full agreement with his boss, Sir Henry Lawrence, that their own compound would be the next target. They could expect the attack within forty-eight hours.

The decision was made to move as many of the women and children as possible out of their bungalows and into the palace itself. 'You'll be better off in there,' Blair told his wife, still trying his best to downplay the danger. 'The rooms are so much larger and cooler. The heat won't affect you half as much, and, not only that, you'll have the other women to keep you company. There's safety in numbers.'

Laura listened to what he had to say but would make no decision. Much as she had hated it over the past year or so, she felt strangely reluctant to give up her home. She had reached the stage when she hardly cared what happened to her any more. The fierce heat was making her positively unwell. Hardly a day had gone by without her finding herself on the verge of a faint. It was too hot even to eat, and on the few occasions she was forced to attempt a proper meal, she invariably brought it up again, so that now she was a mere shadow of the young woman she had once been. To make matters worse, smallpox had broken out in the compound, with several of the women and children affected. One or two of the youngest infants had died from it, and Laura wondered how on earth those mothers stopped themselves from going completely mad with grief and fear for the future. Often she found her spirits so low that she wondered if it would not be a blessed relief to simply succumb to the dreaded disease herself so she would no longer have to endure this long wait for the death and destruction they now felt to be inevitable.

Like most of the wives, she had become a virtual prisoner inside her own home over the past few months. Outside all was dirt, dust and confusion as hundreds of coolies and inmates from the jail were working in shifts, night and day, on the fortifications to the compound. The noise was incredible as horses, donkeys, camels, bullocks and even majestic elephants were harnessed to the task of hauling the countless carts required in the digging of deep ditches and the erecting of palisades to deter the expected attack.

The news on the evening of 28 June about the massing of mutineers only twenty miles away had brought an unexpected influx of British families seeking shelter from outside the compound, which only added to the chaos. The hospital was already overflowing with dreadfully wounded soldiers and civilians who had arrived from other areas, as well as the most severe of the smallpox cases. Even as the barricades were being thrown up and the cannons being dragged into position, the injured survivors from other hells were still trickling in. Amputations to severely wounded limbs were being performed around the clock by a small team of doctors and nurses already on the point of exhaustion.

Some of the wounded had been moved into the palace itself, which was already bursting at the seams with refugees and compound families who, unlike Laura, had taken their husbands' advice and moved out of their own homes. But despite both Blair's and Samit's entreaties, she remained firmly in her bungalow, reasoning that if she was going to die, she might as well do it in the relative comfort of her own home rather than crowded with hundreds of others like rats in one of the Residency cellars.

For the first time in her life she began to pray every day. She had never been particularly religiously-minded but when even the almighty British crown could not save you, what was the alternative? She was thankful that Blair was now living almost full-time in his office, so he was not there to mock as she knelt by her bed every night and lit a special candle. Such flummery as candles were frowned upon by her own Presbyterian kirk, but she knew that, in deference to her Irish origins, her mother had occasionally resorted to lighting one when things got too much for one soul to bear.

Sometimes she thought her head and her heart would burst with the tension that was building up. As well as death they were waiting for the rains. They were there somewhere over the horizon, causing a sultriness that turned milk sour, caused heads to throb and made everything dank to the touch. Tempers were short, women wept and children fretted and cried constantly.

Then, on the last day of June, as the native workers toiled outside, the British administration sweated in their offices, and the women and children not in the Residency cellars kept fearfully to their homes, it all began to happen. Somehow Laura knew it would begin that morning. There was something in the air; something in the very marrow of her bones that turned her skin to gooseflesh from the moment she rose from her bed at daybreak and walked out on to the veranda to gaze up at the heavens.

She had not seen Blair for forty-eight hours. So dire

had the situation become that Sir Henry wanted him constantly by his side. But, to Laura's relief, that morning shortly after breakfast and before she had even had time to do her hair, he had sent Samit to see how she was coping.

They had not met for almost a week, and both were aghast at the change in the other's appearance.

Laura thought her heart would break as she gazed at his beloved face in the doorway for a moment or two before flinging herself into his arms. Even his body felt different. They had both lost far more weight than they could afford. 'I can feel all your bones,' she whispered as she clung on to him.

'It's just as well the sepoys are not cannibals, for neither of us would make much of a meal, would we?' His joke was well-intentioned but did nothing to lighten the mood.

'Where is everyone?' he asked, as he followed her into the drawing room. The first thing he had noticed was that all the servants were missing.

'They left before daybreak,' Laura said simply. Her words hung in the air.

'Rats leaving the sinking ship,' he said quietly.

She shrugged. 'You can't blame them. Who wants to stay here with us and be slaughtered?'

They sat down side by side on the rattan settee, and she listened in silence as he told her of the situation to date. A considerable number of the mutineers from Nawabganj had reached the village of Chinhat only six miles from Lucknow, and an expeditionary force of their own soldiers had been sent out at sunrise to try to disperse them, but had been heavily defeated. The dead included their commanding officer, Colonel Case, whom Samit knew was well liked by Laura. She drew in her breath at the news, but her face remained expressionless as he told of how the few square miles of plain between Lucknow and Chinhat was now a moving, seething mass of armed men heading towards them.

'How many are there?' she whispered, dreading the answer.

There was no point in lying. 'Around five thousand infantry, eight hundred horse, and they've got their thieving hands on at least a dozen decent pieces of artillery.'

'My God!' She shuddered and her hand flew to her mouth. This was no renegade band of mutineers. This was a whole army in rebellion. They did not stand a chance against numbers like that. She could feel the blood begin to drain from her face as she sat back on the settee and closed her eyes. Despite her resolve to remain calm, she could feel herself beginning to shake, and hot tears forming beneath her eyelids.

'Please, my love, be brave,' Samit pleaded, taking her hands in his. 'Help will come. To give up in your heart is to lose the battle before it begins.'

Laura opened her eyes and looked at him in despair. She had not come here to take part in any battle. She had come out as an army wife to what was supposed to be a life of leisure and pleasure. Samit's dark eyes were full of pain as they looked into hers. 'When it's all over,' she found herself saying softly. 'When it's all over, if we are still here, then we will leave this place of misery and death and nothing will ever part us again.'

He forced a tired smile to his lips but said nothing. Then he took his watch from his pocket. 'I must go back,' he said, raising her fingers and pressing them to his lips. 'Have courage, my love. Courage is all.'

She watched him go, then remained sitting quite still for a long time. Inwardly she was screaming, but no one would ever hear. If a friend or neighbour were to walk in right now they would remark on how calmly she was taking it all, on how she was a credit to her country. The stiff upper lip must remain intact, despite all provocation. She sighed a sigh that shuddered up from the depths of her very soul. It was funny how the niceties of everyday life out here were observed regardless . . .

Outside the city had become deathly quiet. Her servants were not the only ones to desert their posts. The exodus of native Indians had gone on all night. All eyes were on the Residency. The bridges over the river that divided the compound from the town were fortified by British guns, many manned by sepoys still loyal despite the danger, but these were pathetically few in number compared to the hordes about to descend upon them.

Already mutineers were taking possession of the buildings surrounding the compound and, as Laura remained sitting motionless in her drawing room, the first battery opened up from the other side of the river. The sound struck terror into every heart. The sustained enemy barrage that followed sent the Residency defenders on the bridge fleeing back behind the barricades as shell after shell began crashing through their meagre defences and the compound buildings behind them.

As soon as the attack began, Blair, who had remained constantly at Sir Henry's side throughout the past few days, left the Residency with his chief to begin a tour of the compound. Around them shells were crashing into the masonry and casualties were already being inflicted. The palace itself seemed to be the main target, so when Sir Henry asked, 'How about your wife, Baxter? Is she safe?' he could, thankfully, reply, 'As safe as possible, sir.' She had been right to choose to remain at home, at least for the time being whilst this barrage continued.

Because of the danger of shelling, Blair and Sir Henry and their staff had abandoned their offices on the ground floor and, for safety, moved to the top of the building, but as day turned to night and the relentless barrage continued unabated, even that move seemed doomed, for holes were being blown all over the masonry by the eight-inch howitzer aimed at it.

'I rather think we'd be better off on the ground floor once more, don't you, sir?' Blair remarked, and was not contradicted.

There was no sleep for anyone that night. In the darkness screams could be heard coming from outside, and terrible stories were emanating from the hospital which could no longer cope.

'God help us if the buggers actually storm the place,' Blair commented to Samit who, like him, had worked on and off for most of the night. 'We'll have to die where we fall, for the doctors certainly won't be able to help us. In fact, if a shell were to burst in here this minute, I wouldn't give tuppence for our chances if we had to wait our turn to be attended to!'

His words were to prove all too prophetic, for the following afternoon as the two of them were attending to dispatches with Sir Henry and his civilian secretary, Mr Coupar, a howitzer shell burst through the wall, straight into their office, sending chunks of masonry and dust flying everywhere. It left them all severely shocked but more determined than ever to carry on. It was decided, however, that they would be better off back downstairs, after all, so arrangements were put in hand to carry all essential files back to the ground floor.

Blair assigned Samit and two others to this work and, whilst it was in progress, he took ten minutes off to make his way back to the bungalow to see how Laura was coping.

He found her lying ashen-faced on her bed. She had been sick during the night. 'It's probably something in the water,' he told her. 'Even if we boil the bloody stuff, it's still not fit for man nor beast.' But in his heart he knew it was not the water. It was either the fear that was gripping them all and was making even grown men such as himself find it difficult to keep food down, or, heaven forbid, it might even be the dreaded smallpox which so many had succumbed to over the past few weeks.

Pulling back the mosquito netting, he sat down on the edge of the bed and took her hand, something he had not done for over a year. Her normally clear skin was grey-

466

looking and drawn tightly across the high cheekbones, her brown hair lank, with lifeless curls plastered to her damp brow as she lay on the pillow looking up at him. 'I'm sorry, Laura,' he said in a voice charged with emotion, for he had never been so near to tears before. 'You didn't deserve this.'

'Nobody did,' she whispered back. She did not blame him. It had not taken her long out here to realize that life was not fair, and what was happening now was simply a gross distortion of a situation that had always existed. Life here was cheap. People died before their time every day. Why should they be any different?

They had little else to say to each other. They were both too grown-up to pretend a sudden blossoming of love in the face of impending death. Instead he took her hand and kissed it, as one would the hand of an honoured friend. 'I'll come back as soon as I can,' he told her. 'Keep your head down; you know where to find me if you need me.'

He left her lying on the bed and returned to the Residency, where all was still chaos, with gaping holes throughout the building and dust and rubble everywhere. Most of the women and children were cowering in the cellars, which themselves were becoming an airless hell-hole.

He found Samit had located a relatively intact room on the ground floor to set up as Sir Henry's headquarters, and Blair joined him in there. The compound was full of wounded soldiers from other camps, all with their own particular tales of horror to tell. While some seemed to find relief in spilling out every gruesome detail of their experience, many more sat hollow-eyed and silent, staring into space. Blair gave his clerk the job of interviewing as many as possible and making notes on anything he thought might be relevant to their own predicament and, near exhaustion himself, Samit set to with his notebook in hand.

By nightfall they were all exhausted, but sleep was impossible as the relentless shelling continued unabated. In the stifling heat and darkness, cries could be heard from all parts of the compound, and terrified horses and other animals ran amok, adding to the mayhem. By morning none of them had had a wink of sleep, although those in the office had bedded down for the odd cat-nap every so often. It was another blisteringly hot day. 'More so inside than bloody well outside, as usual,' Sir Henry complained from the makeshift bed he occupied opposite the window.

Blair sat on the edge of his own mattress, silently smoking. He had already got through a dozen cigarettes that morning and the day had barely begun. His mind was on Laura alone in their bungalow. He had been wrong to marry her and bring her out to die in this foreign place, so far from all she had known and loved. What had he needed a wife for, anyway? He had already had Jaya and the children. Perhaps like so many men in his position he had wanted to have his cake and eat it. But it had proved a poisoned portion.

'The sepoys are as loyal as the day is long,' he had always claimed. He had never been one to look down as others had done on the Indians. God knows, he had had a family by one, hadn't he? But even he had been wrong. The sepoys who made up the 'poor bloody infantry' and other ranks of the Bengali army, were no longer the 'loyal unto death' creatures he had once believed them to be. He gave a bitter smile and corrected himself as he sat there and watched the smoke rise from his cigarette and curl up to the ceiling. He was wrong. They were 'loyal unto death' all right, but it was their white masters' deaths, not their own that were at hand. 'Strange bloody world,' he mused aloud, to no one in particular. 'It's a strange bloody world, all right.'

Sir Henry's nephew, George Lawrence, was lying on his bed a few feet away with his eyes closed, and a Captain Wilson had arrived to draw up a memorandum on how that day's rations should be shared out. He nodded to Blair, seated on the bed across from him, next to the punkah-wallah, who was slumped in a corner, still tugging on the cords in a futile attempt to bring air to the fetid atmosphere of the room. 'Morning, Major . . . Sleep well?'

'Sleep? What's that?'

They both gave rueful grins at the banality of the remark.

As Blair watched, the younger officer took a sheaf of papers from under his arm and positioned himself at the foot of Sir Henry's bed. 'With your permission, I'll just begin reading through my list for the day, sir,' he began.

'Fire away, Captain!' Sir Henry yawned and nodded, feigning an interest he did not feel after yet another long night with barely a wink of sleep.

The captain began to read from the list in a dull monotone, and had got no further than the second page when there was a terrific explosion, quickly followed by another, and a searing sheet of flame shot into the space between the beds. There was a high-pitched scream from somewhere in the room, and then for a few seconds there was nothing but darkness, groaning, and a choking dust-cloud.

Captain Wilson was the first to struggle to his feet and gather his thoughts as smoke and dust particles made vision impossible. The safety of his commanding officer was his main preoccupation. 'Sir Henry!' he shouted through the swirling dust and rubble. 'Sir Henry, are you all right?'

There was no reply. Particles of shattered mortar and thick grey dust clung to his eyelashes and moustache. He coughed and spluttered and tried again, louder this time. 'Sir Henry, you're not hurt, are you?'

Blindly he waved his hands in an attempt to disperse the dust-clouds as he battled his way round the foot of the bed.

He had got as far as he believed to be the other end when out of the smoke and debris a faint voice replied simply, 'I am killed . . .'

As the dust began to settle, Captain Wilson looked down at the bloodsoaked bed. To his horror, amid the debris and powdered plaster, it looked as if the upper part of Sir Henry's thigh had been blown away.

'Jesus!' Shocked, he looked around him to see how the others had fared. George Lawrence was still lying on his bed, covered with rubble, and although he was groaning slightly, he seemed relatively unscathed. Next to him, he could hear groaning coming from the corner by the window. Sir Henry's faithful punkah-wallah was sprawled amid the rubble, whimpering softly. His right foot had been blown off.

'Jesus!' The captain took one look at the bloodied stump and turned away. Who did that leave? Sickened, he coughed once more and looked round to where Blair's bed was situated. 'Major Baxter, sir, are you all right?'

There was no reply.

'Major Baxter?' Wiping the dust from his mouth and eyes, he stumbled across the rubble to where he knew his senior officer's bed was, but there was no sign of the occupant. 'Major Baxter, sir, are you all right?' he shouted.

'Major *sahib* here!'

At the sound of the punkah-wallah's cry, the captain looked round once more in the servant's direction. There, beside him, lying beneath a pile of dust and masonry, lay the body of Blair Baxter.

'Lord, no!' Holding a handkerchief over his mouth and nose to make breathing a little easier, he clambered over the ruins to reach his superior.

Blair Baxter was lying face down, sprawled across the floor next to where the punkah-wallah was sitting nursing his injured leg. The old man made a gesture with his bloodied hands to indicate that the major had shoved him away out of the line of fire, then he held his hands together in a gesture of prayer and bowed his head. Great silent tears were running down his dust-streaked cheeks. The captain frowned. What exactly was he trying to tell him? Was he saying that the major had lost his life saving him? 'Christ Almighty!'

Clumsily he scrabbled at the debris covering Blair's back, then stopped abruptly and groaned aloud at the sight that met his eyes. 'Holy Christ!' he breathed. The second shell must have landed a direct hit; just below the major's shoulder-blades was a massive hole that dripped red life-blood into a gathering pool beneath. He did not need to look at the face pressed against the floor. This told him all he needed to know.

'He's dead!' he shouted into the polluted atmosphere. 'The bastards have bloody killed him! Baxter's dead!'

Chapter Thirty-nine

Samit broke the news of her husband's death to Laura about an hour after it happened. At first he did not realize that the major had been killed. He was downstairs in one of the basement rooms of the Residency, attending to the dealing-out of stores for the day ahead, when the barely-conscious Sir Henry Lawrence was carried in and laid on a table hastily cleared for the purpose.

Dr Fayrer, the commissioner's personal physician, was called from the hospital immediately. While they waited, those already in the room did what they could to make Sir Henry comfortable. He was obviously in acute pain and had lost a great deal of blood. Orders went out to bring boiling water and clean towels as there was no doubt some kind of operation was called for, but when the doctor arrived and the bloodied clothing was cut away, it was clear to all present that the wound was fatal.

The room fell silent; all eyes were on the figure laid out on the table before them. 'How long have I got?' Sir Henry was heard to ask as the doctor, sleeves rolled up to the elbows, did his best to attend to the gaping wound.

'About three days,' was the truthful answer, as a makeshift tourniquet was hastily tied above the bloodied mass of flesh to stem the flow of blood. There was no point in lying or attempting an amputation, the injury was far too severe. The upper part of the thigh up to the groin had been torn apart with the shot, exposing the raw flesh and splintered bone.

'Three days . . . ?' A sigh came from the lips of the elderly man on the table. 'As much as that? I doubt I shall last that long . . .'

Samit and the clerk who had been helping him with the rationing exchanged worried glances.

'We'll be like a bleedin' headless chicken with him gone,' the other young man said under his breath. 'With the gov'nor out of it, we'll have no one left to lead us.'

'There's always Major Baxter,' Samit replied, still loyal to his boss, whose administrative abilities he had never doubted. 'He can take over. He knows the ropes better than anyone.'

'What d'you mean Major Baxter can do it?' one of the soldiers who had helped carry the commissioner down to the basement broke in. 'Ain't you been upstairs yet? He copped it at the same time as Sir Henry.'

Samit turned to stare at the young man. 'Copped it? You – you mean the major is . . .' he could barely bring himself to say the word. 'Is dead?'

'As a doornail,' the reply came back. 'Had half his chest blown away saving a bleedin' punkah-wallah.'

Samit looked askance at the bearer of the news. Major Baxter – Laura's husband – dead? Killed saving a punkah-wallah? For some unknown reason, punkah-wallahs had been the bane of the major's life for as long as Samit had known him. He was for ever making jokes at their expense. 'What kind of bloody job is that, pulling on a cord attached to your big toe all day long?' he would declare as he fired paper pellets in their direction if one happened to nod off. Now he was dead, saving the life of one. It was a grotesque joke. All of a sudden Samit felt quite sick.

Immediately he ran upstairs to investigate for himself; he arrived as they were carrying the major's body out of the wrecked office. The punkah-wallah in question was still lying in his corner whimpering as he nursed the bloody stump where his foot had been. No doubt he would be the last to be attended to.

Samit said a few words of comfort to the man, who seemed barely aware of his presence. Then he went out into the corridor and was physically sick.

He had seen injuries and death a-plenty over the past few weeks, but this was different. This had happened to people he knew, with whom he had worked closely every day. The cold hand of the grim reaper was reaching out and almost touching him now.

He was in the process of composing himself when Captain Wilson, still covered in dust and plaster from the blast, came out of an adjoining room. 'I say, Chaudri, you were the major's personal clerk, weren't you?'

Samit nodded and attempted to stand up straight. 'Yes, *sahib* sir, I was Major Baxter's clerk.'

'That's what I thought . . . Then you'd better do the decent thing and go and give his widow the bad news. Damned shame really, he was a fine man.'

Twenty minutes after that exchange, Samit found himself sitting in Laura's neat drawing room gazing at her worried face and wondering how on earth to tell her she would never see her husband again. He could still hardly believe it himself, even though he had seen the body. Blair Baxter had played such an important role in his adult life. Ever since he first left school to take a clerical post at the palace, Major Baxter had been his boss. It seemed unthinkable that he would never see him again.

For her part Laura knew nothing of the tragic nature of Samit's mission, or of the turmoil in his mind when he appeared at her door. She was simply glad to see him again so unexpectedly. She thought at first this was one of those stolen interludes where he had managed to slip away for a moment or two in the general mayhem, but when he had been in the house several minutes and had still not uttered a word, she began to realize something was wrong – terribly wrong. His face was pale, too pale, and his eyes had a haunted look to them. Slowly realization began to dawn. 'It's Blair, isn't it?' As soon as the words were uttered she could see from his face that she was right. This was no lovers' tryst. He was here for a reason – a terrible reason. 'What's happened, Sam? Has Blair been badly injured?'

Somehow she had had little fear for her husband as long as he was with Sir Henry.

Samit cleared his throat and took a deep breath to calm himself. His head was pounding and a nerve flickered in his right eyelid. He rubbed it with the back of his hand and passed his tongue over his parched lips. 'He was with the commissioner in his office when a shell-burst hit it,' he said in a hoarse voice. 'Sir Henry was mortally wounded in the leg . . .'

'And Blair? Was he wounded too?'

'He's dead, Laura,' he told her softly. There was no easier way of putting it. 'He was killed helping someone else . . . I'm sorry. So very sorry.'

'Dead?' She stared at him, as if she could not quite comprehend the meaning of the word, then she slumped in her seat. How could he be dead? Blair was one of the strongest, most capable men she had ever known. Along with Sir Henry, he ran this whole place. Everyone relied on him. How could he be dead? He was needed here too much. They all needed him to get them through this hell on earth. She shook her head as if to negate what she had just heard. 'No,' she said weakly. 'No, not Blair. It's not possible.'

Samit looked at her distraught face and longed to take her in his arms, but somehow at this moment he could not bring himself to do so. Shame overwhelmed him. Shame for the trust he had betrayed in the past by falling in love with her, by making love to the major's wife. But one could not apologize to the dead. It was too late for that. He had worked for the major all his adult life, and in a funny way he had respected and even liked the man, despite knowing all about Jaya and the double life he had been leading and the pain he had caused his wife. In so many ways Major Baxter had been an honest and decent man who, on the whole, had treated his native servants well. He had shown little of the contempt so many British officers showed to those of another race. He could feel a lump coming into his throat just thinking about him. 'Don't cry, Laura. Please don't cry,' he said automatically.

But Laura was not crying. She had no intention of crying as she sat there allowing the news to sink in. Blair was dead and she was sorry, desperately sorry, but after the initial shock a sort of elation was now gripping her. 'He is free,' she said in an awed voice. 'Nothing can touch him now. Those murdering sepoys – they can no longer harm him. He is far beyond this hell that we are still living. He is with the angels.'

She got up from the settee and began to pace the room. She felt she was standing on the edge of a precipice but was no longer afraid. The die was already cast. Some would die, like Blair, and some would live. What would be would be.

She began to laugh; wild, hysterical laughter that brought Samit rushing to her side to take her in his arms. They stood there together, swaying gently backwards and forwards in the middle of the floor, until her laughter subsided into quiet sobs, then he led her gently through to the bedroom.

He made her lie down and sip from a small glass of laudanum he poured, telling her it was best she get some rest and he would return as soon as possible. Then he sat with her until she fell asleep.

When he made his way back through the rubble and gunfire to the Residency to find a building shocked to its foundations by the news of the fatal injury to their leader and the death of his second in command, he felt devoid of all emotion. There was only so much a body and soul could take.

Blair was buried with the rest of the day's dead that same evening, as soon as darkness fell. It was impossible to keep the bodies above ground any longer because of the intense heat. The simple five-minute ceremony consisted of Mr Harris, the chaplain, saying a few prayers over the long trench that had been dug for the victims of the fighting who were being laid to rest along with two children who had passed away that morning through smallpox.

Laura attended the service, bare-headed and pale-faced, her senses still numbed by the laudanum she had been given by Samit earlier in the day. They stood side by side with one or two others from her husband's personal staff. One of them read out a poem, written on the wall of Blair's old office by one of the soldiers who had served under him, after hearing of his death.

'All honour to those,
Who, encompassed by foes,
Grew stronger in courage and might:
All honour to them,
Who, like brave Englishmen,
Are ready, aye ready, to fight!

All hail to the dead,
Who by treachery fled
From husbands, from parents, from friends.
There are brave hearts still here
Who your memory revere,
And will trample the heads of the fiends!

You wretches without,
Who go sneaking about,
A terror to none but the weak,
Beware of the wrath
Which your acts have brought forth –
'Tis the vengeance of Britons you seek!'

At the end of the ceremony, after throwing a handful of dry earth into the open trench where the body of her husband lay wrapped in a cotton sheet, Laura turned to Samit and said quietly, 'I am not going back to the bungalow. I shall go straight to the hospital. I dare say they have need of an extra pair of hands.' It was as if her life had turned a corner and there was to be no going back.

'Do you want me to come with you?' he asked. It was dark, after all, and the compound was a dangerous place these days. The attacking guns were as lethal by night as by day.

She shook her head. 'If I'm to stand on my own feet, I might as well start now.'

They buried Sir Henry Lawrence in the same trench two days later, along with several others who had fallen in the latest barrage. And when that trench was full up they dug another and another . . . Death walked with them day and night. There was no hiding place, for no one could tell where the next shell would fall.

At the hospital, where they welcomed Laura with open arms, they continued to do their best by the wounded, whose terrible injuries were little helped by the meagre resources at their command. Most of the staff were male army orderlies, but gradually one or two of the married women came to offer their services and, although suspicious at first of their staying-power, the resident medical staff soon came to regard them as an indispensable part of the team.

As the weeks went on and the siege continued, it became obvious that the mutineers' tactics were not to launch a full-scale assault on the Residency, but to starve those left inside into submission. Then the compound could be overrun with little or no resistance, and the poor weakened creatures that were still alive inside would be put to the sword. It was a terrifying thought for those still spared the death and disease that surrounded them, but they expected no mercy, for none had been given elsewhere. Why should they be spared when their friends in other outposts were slaughtered so mercilessly?

Rumour had it that their compound was surrounded by at least ten thousand armed mutineers. It was an awesome number, when they were so few in comparison, with more dying by the day. They knew that many of those lying in wait belonged to the personal army of the deposed King Wajid Ali, and these troops, in particular, were impatient for their chance to exact revenge for the humiliation of both them and their master. But the bulk of the rebels were regular soldiers of the Bengali army; in their carrying-out of the bombardment and the siege of the Residency, they were adhering to all the training and tactics instilled in them by their missing British officers.

Although each day that passed was a living hell for those inside the compound, Laura found night-time the worst of all, for just as they were at the point of exhaustion, the mutineers' regimental bands would strike up and they would march backwards and forwards in strict formation in front of the compound, incongruously playing all the best-loved British tunes. It was obviously meant to un-nerve those left inside. 'I swear if I hear, "The Girl I Left Behind Me" once more I shall scream,' Laura declared to a fellow nurse one night, and her neighbour heartily concurred. All their nerves were rapidly reaching breaking point.

They slept in shifts, for it was at night that the most difficult tasks were carried out. Not only was it slightly cooler then, but the enemy had less chance of seeing what was going on behind the barricades. The day's dead, both human and animal, were always buried under cover of darkness, and it was then too that the wounded were carried on litters from the various posts around the compound to the hospital. To be performing these distressing tasks to the sound of the brightest, most familiar tunes from home was disconcerting for all concerned.

What Laura found particularly hard to deal with was that many seemingly hardy individuals appeared to just give up the ghost: there were several fatal heart-attacks and people she knew and liked expired from quite trivial illnesses. Others, on the other hand, who had been re-garded in the past as rather ineffectual individuals, seemed to come into their own, totally disregarding their own health or safety to care for those in greater need.

For the first time since arriving in India, she had discovered a camaraderie that was quite new to her. And, gradually, as the death toll mounted and more and more women were widowed, she found she was joined by other females who wanted to help. These were mainly childless, like herself, who felt it better to make themselves of some use than to remain below ground all day and night along with the other wives and children whose basement quarters were now little more than a squalid dungeon. Without servants to perform the menial tasks, most of the wives had no idea how to care for themselves or their children, and carrying out even the most basic chores was beyond them. Others had to show them how to cook their own food, draw their own water and wash their own clothes.

Laura, who had never cooked before, but had watched meals being prepared often enough in the kitchen at Falcon Ridge, volunteered to do most of the cooking for their small team of hospital orderlies. The rations were meagre in the extreme, and consisted mainly of a little suspect meat, some fly-blown flour, 'attah' (a roughly-ground wheat-flour) and 'dal' (a sort of lentil). By the end of her first week in charge of the stove, she found she could produce a fairly edible chapatti which she served with lentils and a stew made with whatever meat or vegetables she could beg, borrow or steal from around the compound.

The nurses' room was on the south side of the hospital, straight in the line of fire, and was often the recipient of a direct hit. Consequently, what little glass was left in the windows was quickly removed to prevent further injury to the occupants. For Laura and the other female nurses, sleeping under fire quickly became a fact of life, and the month of July passed in a daze of exploding shells and back-breaking toil, with the badly injured being carried in at a far quicker rate than they could possibly care for them. By the end of the month, cholera as well as smallpox had broken out in the garrison, and it was decided to keep the affected soldiers apart from the wounded in the hospital, so the nurses took it in turns to go out to tend to these poor unfortunates billeted around the compound. Often at the end of a long, gruelling day, Laura found it was all she could do to crawl into bed, where she lay in an unconscious state until awoken next morning to resume her duties.

Samit watched it all with growing dismay. Every couple of days or so he found some excuse to visit the hospital, and they usually managed a few private words together. Although she professed to be fine, Laura seemed to be fading away before his very eyes. It alarmed him to see how little rest she was getting, and he told her so.

'Don't worry about me,' she told him. 'All I care about is that you are safe.' And it was true. She could cope with the bouts of occasional sickness and extreme fatigue she herself suffered from, as long as she knew he was in no immediate danger. The only way to survive, she decided, was to live within herself. As she fought to stop herself fainting from the stench of changing a festering wound, or gripped a young man's hand as a limb was amputated with only a glass of whisky to blur the pain, her mind would take flight. In her imagination she was no longer part of this hell on earth, but was walking with her beloved Samit on the golden sands of the beach at Broughty Ferry. She knew her mother and brother would learn to love him as much as she did and, as for the others – well, if they suspected, which she was sure many of them did, they could gossip amongst themselves as much as they liked. This was the man she had chosen, the man she loved, the man she would marry now that she was free, and there was nothing anyone could do about it.

'You are a born romantic,' Samit would tell her, and whenever she brought up the future, in their few stolen moments together, he would merely smile at her and murmur, 'Laura . . . Laura . . . Let us have done with the present first . . .'

She knew he was not as optimistic by nature as she was, and she put up with it. He was a sensitive man, and found it more difficult than she did to cope with the terrible suffering and stench of death all around them. It was not only in the hospital but in the grounds as well, where the corpses of rotting animals lay unburied by soldiers too exhausted or too drunk to attend to the task. It was hard enough digging holes to bury the human corpses, let alone finding the time or energy required for burying dead animals.

As the summer wore on, the smell in the compound became unbearable. The death toll was still rising, leaving fewer and fewer men fit enough to dig the graves, so that the corpses were often barely covered over and thereafter emitted the most unbearable stench. Black flies were everywhere, covering the dead, be they animal or human, in a seething black mass, even before the soul had fled.

By the end of August, even amongst the most long-suffering, tempers had frayed to breaking point as the terrible truth began to sink in that they could be here for weeks yet before either the final assault came from the mutineers that would finish them all off, or the relief they were all hoping for at last arrived in the shape of reinforcements from the British army.

Laura knew from Samit that, even with the strictest rationing, provisions could only hold out for a few weeks more at the most. As a consequence, by the time September came, everyone was put on half-rations and, considerably weakened by a diet that barely kept body and soul together, they limped on into autumn, praying constantly for the relief that seemed as far away as ever.

One of the worst aspects of the siege was that they were completely cut off from all news of the outside world. It was months since Laura had heard from her family back home in Scotland, which was a constant source of anxiety in itself. Did they even know of the horror she was going through, she wondered? Did anyone know? It often seemed that no one in the outside world either knew or cared.

Throughout there had been the faint hearts amongst them who had advocated surrender, but even that was now no longer an option. Towards the end of September, news came of the fate of relatives and friends at Cawnpore and Delhi. The whole compound listened in horror as a messenger told of how, after their leader General Wheeler's surrender to the mutineers, the men, women and children, including the sick and wounded, were all savagely massacred and their bodies thrown down a well.

On hearing this, and quite out of character, Laura found herself berating Samit at their next meeting for being half-Indian. 'I used to have some sympathy for the natives,' she told him as they walked around the perimeter of the hospital under cover of darkness. 'But not now. Not after hearing that. Now I see them for what they are — savages who murder innocent children. I hate this country and its people!'

'And me?' he asked softly. 'Do you also hate me?'

She turned to him. She could just make out the outline of his features in the darkness, but could not see the sadness in his eyes. 'I wish I could,' she said in a broken voice. 'Sometimes I really wish I could.'

It was the day after that exchange that Dr Fayrer passed a remark that had her looking at him in confusion and then considerable embarrassment. She had just assisted in the fourth amputation of the day, and had been sitting, exhausted, on the windowsill of the operating ante-room, when she was aware of him looking at her more intently than usual. Eventually he came across and, as he puffed on his first pipe of tobacco since breakfast, he asked outright, 'You wouldn't be pregnant by any chance, would you, my dear?'

Laura felt her stomach lurch. 'Pregnant? You mean am I expecting a baby?'

'That's usually what the word means.'

Embarrassment overcame her. 'Whatever makes you say that?'

'Oh, call it an old physician's instinct if you like. I've been watching you over the past few weeks, just as I watch all my staff. You've been displaying the classic symptoms, that's all.'

Classic symptoms? Laura had absolutely no idea what they were. Certainly she had not been feeling at all well for the past few months, since well before the siege, in fact, and was still occasionally bringing up her food. But was that surprising, given the ghastliness of it? But curiously, despite that, she now seemed to be gaining weight, which was certainly a strange thing indeed.

'Have your monthlies stopped?'

'You – you mean . . . ?' Her face was now burning crimson.

He gave a weary smile. 'Exactly.'

She shook her head in confusion. 'I – I . . .'

'You haven't had them for a few months, is that right?'

She nodded dumbly, then burst out, 'But is that surprising with all this to worry about?'

'That most certainly can have an effect.' Then, seeing how upset she was becoming, he sought to pacify her by saying quietly, 'Come and see me first thing tomorrow morning. It should set both our minds at rest.'

Chapter Forty

Laura was at Dr Fayrer's door at eight o'clock next morning. She hadn't slept all night and had hardly been able to think of anything other than the possibility she might be expecting a child. She had no doubt it was Samit's. She had not slept with her husband since finding out about his Indian family. But how would Sam react? Of all times to discover she was pregnant, this surely had to be the worst, from all angles. Her emotions were in turmoil as she was shown into the sparsely furnished office.

It took the elderly physician less than ten minutes to declare himself satisfied that his suspicions were correct. He took off his spectacles and placed them in his waistcoat pocket as he gave a sympathetic smile. 'Well, my dear, I'd say your baby is due some time around the end of February, beginning of March . . . I wish I could say congratulations, but I realize, being so recently widowed, this must be something of a bitter-sweet moment for you.'

Laura, who was now sitting up on the leather examination couch, avoided his eyes and managed to murmur, 'Yes . . . yes, it certainly is.'

'At least you will have the privilege of being able to tell the child that its father died a hero. I hear there's talk of honouring your husband posthumously for his gallantry in saving that servant's life at the expense of his own.'

'So they say.' Laura gave a wan smile. She had heard that, too, but the fact that Blair had died a hero was small consolation. She knew it would never enter the doctor's head that this was not her late husband's child. The thought of having to deal with all the sympathy she would receive made her quail. Only she and the baby's real father

485

would know the truth. That there would be whispers and sidelong glances as well as sympathy she did not doubt, for this child would have its father's Indian blood as well as her own coursing through its veins. But that was a hurdle she would have to cross when she came to it. Now was not the time to dwell on problems that had not yet arisen. She had quite enough real ones on her plate right now.

'You're not saying very much. I expect you're more than a little apprehensive about the future. I can understand that. We all are. But you'll make sure you come and see me regularly just to check everything's going well, won't you? I want to see you delivered of the healthiest little one possible under these trying circumstances.'

Buttoning up the bodice of her dress and pinning her cameo brooch into position at the neck, Laura slipped down from the couch and held out her hand. 'Thank you so much for all your concern, Dr Fayrer, but I must admit it does seem a little premature to be even thinking about the baby's birth when none of us know if we'll be alive tomorrow, never mind next spring.'

As she left the surgery, a young soldier of the 32nd was being carried into the next room on a bloodstained litter; he was only half-conscious and moaning. Part of his shoulder had been blown away.

'I'll be right there,' she heard Dr Fayrer say from the doorway behind her. 'Oh, by the way, Mrs Baxter!'

She turned in the narrow passageway. 'Yes?'

'You do realize this means the end of your nursing career?'

She looked at him blankly. The thought had never occurred to her. 'But I . . .'

'No buts. Your health and that of the baby is the most important thing for you now.' He gave a weary smile. 'It's taken us enough heart-searching to allow you wonderful women into the hospital wards at all. We couldn't even consider having a pregnant lady working in our midst.'

He patted her shoulder in a fatherly fashion as he made his way past her, hurriedly following the injured soldier into the makeshift operating theatre next door.

Laura leant against the passage wall and sighed. What was she expected to do all day from now on, sit and wait for death or the birth of the baby, whichever came sooner?

Rain was washing against the window as it had done all week, and a gale-force wind was blowing, causing the glass panes to rattle in their wooden frames. In the distance she could hear the dull boom of cannon-fire. It no longer had the power to frighten her; it was simply a part of everyday life. She had become quite fatalistic about it all. You could not experience death every day, as she had done for weeks now, and feel any other way about things.

She made her way over to the Residency later that morning to enquire about obtaining a bed there now that her services were no longer required in the hospital and, as she entered the main door, she was surprised to run straight into Samit.

He looked as if he had been up all night again, and was in dire need of a shave, but, as usual, his face lit up at the sight of her. He had no inkling as to the reason for the confused expression on her own face as he took her arm and led her into an empty ante-room off what used to be his office. 'This is a piece of good luck seeing you already. I was hoping to get over to see you some time today,' he said in a hushed voice as he dug into his pocket. 'Here – take a look at this.'

He seemed agitated as he handed her a piece of paper and kept glancing towards the door in case someone walked in. 'It's a copy I made of a letter that arrived in the commissioner's office late last night. For God's sake don't let on you've seen it. They're keeping quiet about it for the moment to see what transpires.'

She looked down at the hastily scrawled lines and read:

North Side of the River,
20 September, 1857

To Colonel Inglis,
The army crossed the river yesterday and, all the materiel being over now, marches towards you tomorrow, and

487

under the blessing of God will now relieve you. The rebels, we hear, intend making one desperate assault on you as we approach the city, and will be on the watch in expectation of your weakening your garrison to make a diversion in our favour as we attack the city. I beg to warn you against being enticed to venture far from your works. When you see us engaged in your vicinity, such diversion as you could make without in any way risking your position should only be attempted.

Yours sincerely,
J. Outram.

'It's from General Sir James Outram,' Samit told her excitedly. 'It looks as if help is on the way at last!'

Laura read then reread the words and handed the paper back with shaking fingers. Could it be true? Could it really be true? For once she was speechless.

Samit's eyes were shining and there was real excitement in his voice. 'Isn't that wonderful news, my love? We're not going to die after all . . . The British army is on its way!'

They clung to each other for a moment, then he slipped the paper back into his pocket. 'We're going to live, Laura. We've got a future at last!'

Nursing their secret, he took her arm as they walked back out into the corridor. A young corporal of the 32nd came out of a room further down the passage, and Samit immediately let her arm drop. 'I've got to go now,' he said quietly. 'I'm wanted in the operations room. All hell has been let loose since this was received, but I had to let you see a copy as soon as possible . . . Give me a smile. We're going to live, Laura. We're going to live!'

She forced her lips into the appropriate shape, but was still much too bemused to take it all in.

'I'll try and see you later tonight.'

'Tonight,' she repeated, and watched him hurry off in the direction of the operational headquarters. With information like that to preoccupy them, she decided her own news could wait.

Although an attempt was made to keep it under wraps, within an hour or so it became common knowledge that relief was at last on its way and this resulted in a growing state of near hysteria within the compound. Out of 1,720 soldiers at the beginning of the siege, over half had already been killed in defence of the Residency; out of the 270 children within the compound, 64 were now dead, and 14 out of the 240 women were dead. The hospital was filled to overflowing with many terminal cases amongst the patients, and those that had been fortunate enough to survive without real injury were little more than living skeletons; almost all had lost at least a third to a half of their normal body weight. But now that sense of dull apathy that had characterized their lives over the past weeks seemed to lift like an autumn rain cloud as friend greeted friend with genuine smiles, and laughter – albeit semi-hysterical – was again heard around the place.

'There's going to be hell to pay before the Jocks get here,' one of the clerical staff warned Laura as she sat in the housing office early that afternoon. 'Those rebels out there won't let our lads through without a real fight.'

'Let them do their worst,' she told him. 'We've survived up till now. We're not going to give up at the very last moment.'

But even she was not prepared for the bombardment that preceded the eventual arrival of the British Generals Havelock and Outram and the soldiers of the 78th Highland regiment, along with a contingent of loyal Sikhs. It was far worse than any of them had imagined. The relieving troops had to fight their way through the rebels laying siege to the Residency compound, and this meant a bitter battle that began in the early afternoon and seemed to go on for hours. It had the buildings of the compound shaking to their foundations as the enemy let loose with their cannons; all afternoon the whole area was obliterated by clouds of acrid black smoke. Casualties ran high and, amid the smoke and shell-fire, petrified animals ran amok, many wounded, and corpses of men and beasts soon littered the ground. Everyone knew that the cost in human lives was soaring, but so were the hopes of those within the barricaded walls as neighbour encouraged neighbour to carry on. Their own boys were out there, fighting their way inch by bloody inch towards them, and, here inside, as one by one their own defenders were killed or wounded, others would rush to take their places at the barricades. Tales of great acts of heroism abounded, especially concerning those loyal sepoys still guarding the Baillie Guard Gate, the main entrance into the compound and the major focus of enemy fire.

Despite Dr Fayrer's warnings, Laura spent most of the afternoon tending the wounded as they were brought into the hospital, which was now so crowded that the latest arrivals had to be stacked against the corridor walls and in the courtyard outside.

It was late in the afternoon, as she was bending over to staunch the blood of a young bandsman who had been caught in the temple by flying masonry, when she first heard the sound that made the hairs stand out on the back of her neck. She straightened up immediately and said in an awed voice, 'Can you hear it too?'

The young man looked puzzled, but listened, holding the swab to the side of his head.

'It's the pipes,' she breathed. 'Can't you hear it? It's the sound of bagpipes. The Highland laddies have come!'

Wrapping her patient's head as quickly as decency would allow, she ran from the corridor and made her way towards the main entrance to the Residency. Hundreds of others were there before her, lining the road into the compound and clambering on to every vantage point for a better view as, to the skirling sound of bagpipes, the kilted Highlanders, accompanied by their turbaned cohorts, marched through the battered and shell-holed Baillie Guard Gate.

They had waited eighty-seven days for this, and many wept openly as they embraced their saviours in a growing twilight thick with the smoke of gunfire and the smouldering ruins of what had once been stately buildings.

Laura stood on the edge of the cheering crowd with tears of joy running down her cheeks at the sight of her compatriots scooping siege-wan children into their brawny arms. Against a background of cannon-smoke and confusion, never had the soft burr of Scottish voices sounded so sweet.

Like everyone else, she believed that salvation was at hand, and she joined the other women who volunteered to prepare and cook the precious stocks of carefully hoarded food and drink that were brought out in celebration.

For the first time since the siege began, young soldiers could be heard whistling, and the women sang as they prepared the food for the celebratory meal ahead. And later that evening, as they shared their feast with their kilted saviours, they listened eagerly to news from the outside world. It seemed that two days before their own gallant Highlanders had fought their way into Lucknow, Delhi had been taken by the British, and the Punjab, the homeland of their comrades-in-arms, the Sikhs, was now safe. Other news was not quite so good, however, as atrocities committed against innocent women and children in other stations were confirmed and often described in graphic detail.

By the following day, however, once the euphoria had subsided and the barrage from the enemy began again in earnest, it became very quickly apparent that it was not yet over. Despite the reinforcements, the rebel troops besieging the Residency had not given up. Their cannons and mortars continued to pound the Residency walls, and they too would be reinforced with rebel troops in far greater numbers than the British could ever summon. The siege would continue, and with the numbers inside now vastly increased, food would be even more at a premium, despite extra rations brought in by the Highlanders.

Laura remained in the kitchens and, over the next few days, Dr Fayrer, who had always prided himself as a crack shot, began bringing bagfuls of dead sparrows in to supplement their meagre diet. Sparrow pie became a regular feature of the menu, although Laura herself could not be persuaded to try it.

As September gave way to October, she could both feel and see her stomach begin to swell even more, and she began to wonder just how long she could keep her secret from the father of her child. Preoccupied with his own increased workload, they had seen much less of each other than before. Samit had not queried her transition from hospital to kitchen work: she had merely told him her services were more urgently needed there. She took to wearing a long, loose smock for her kitchen duties, and made sure she still had it on whenever they managed a few moments together at night.

Every day that passed there seemed to be renewed rumours about a second major relief force and, reluctantly, she decided to wait to see what actually happened in this regard before having a heart-to-heart with Sam.

At long last, just as she was about to give up hope, on 17 November, it happened. Sir Colin Campbell and a force of 4,700 men and 32 guns arrived, blasting their way through the enemy to take the Residency and make it clear to all that they intended to hold it.

By midnight two days later the evacuation they had all prayed for was to begin. They were told that the remaining four hundred women and children, plus a thousand sick and wounded, would be conveyed first to Dilkoosha, then on to Cawnpore, and finally to Calcutta, from where those who wished to leave India would begin the long journey back to Britain.

Laura had seen nothing of Samit during the traumatic

days of fighting that preceded Sir Colin's entry into Lucknow, but once the gunfire had died down, it became clear very quickly that this was really the end. On the evening of 18 November, the day after the breakthrough and the night before she was due to leave the compound, she made a special visit to the operations rooms where she knew she would find him.

She waited anxiously in an ante-room for his arrival. It had all happened so quickly. After all the waiting and frustration she could barely comprehend she was due to leave the following night. They had plans to make – important plans concerning their future together. She would tell him about the baby . . . Her stomach churned with nerves. The room was lit only by a single candle and the night air was chill as she sat shivering in her shawl listening for his footsteps.

He looked drawn and haggard when finally he came into the room, closing the door behind him. 'Laura – it had to be you!'

She rushed into his arms and they stood hugging one another for a minute or two, both unwilling to be the one to let go.

But he knew he had no more than a few moments with her before he would be missed. 'I'm so sorry I haven't seen you,' he whispered into her hair. 'It has been hell in there since Sir Colin and his men arrived.'

'I know. I know,' she told him. 'But I had to come tonight. I had no choice. I heard this afternoon for certain – they're evacuating us tomorrow, Sam, all the women, the children and the wounded . . . I'll be heading for Calcutta and back to Scotland. You must come with me.'

Slowly he released his grip on her, his hands falling by his sides as he took a faltering step back. 'Come with you?'

'Yes. Yes . . .' she told him, her eyes dark and luminous in the pale glow of the candle. 'We love each other. There is no way I can go back to Scotland without you.'

But to her astonishment he made no response as

he stood there looking at her with the most strange expression on his face.

'You – you do love me, don't you?' There was something about the look in his eyes that made her heart turn over. 'You do love me, Sammy?'

'Of course I love you. You know how much I love you.'

She breathed an audible sigh of relief. 'Thank God for that! For one awful moment I was beginning to think you'd changed your mind about marrying me!'

'Marrying you?' He sounded genuinely taken aback.

'Well, that's what people in love do, isn't it? And there's nothing stopping us now that Blair is dead.' He was frightened, that was all, she decided. Nervous about leaving India and going all the way back to Scotland with her, to a strange land where people might not accept him as her husband. 'You mustn't be afraid,' she told him gently. 'I have a wonderful family who will accept you as a son.'

But he was shaking his head and, in the dim light of the candle, she could swear she could see tears in his eyes.

'What is it, Sammy?' she asked, her voice rising as anxiety took over. 'You do want to marry me, don't you? You don't want me to leave here for ever without you?'

'Yes, my love,' he answered her huskily. 'I do love you and I want to marry you with all my heart . . . But I can't.'

'You – you can't?'

'I can't, Laura . . . Please try to understand . . .'

But what was there to understand? 'Why can't you marry me?' she asked in a hushed voice. 'What are you trying to tell me, Sam?'

There was a long silence, then the answer came so quietly she had to strain to hear. 'I can't marry you, my love, because I already have a wife and family.'

'*What?*' She staggered backwards and almost collapsed against the wall. 'Married with a family?' she repeated dumbfounded as she steadied herself against the wood panelling. 'No . . . No . . . I don't believe it. You can't be married. You wouldn't have lied to me like that.'

'But I never lied, my love . . . It just never came up.'

'Never came up!' she exploded. 'What do you mean, it never came up?'

He lifted his hands and let them drop in a gesture of helplessness. This was the moment he had dreaded for months. The moment he had hoped would never come. 'I became betrothed to a cousin of mine at nine years old,' he told her in a voice devoid of all emotion. 'We married at fourteen and had our children before we were twenty . . . It was not of my doing, Laura. It is how things are here, that's all.'

'But – but you deceived me! How could you deceive me like that?'

'I did not deceive you,' he told her wearily. 'I fell in love with you, that's all. Just as you did with me. We were both married to other people at the time. I knew about your husband because I worked for him . . .'

'But I never knew about your wife.'

He shook his head. 'It did not seem so important when the major was still alive and there was no way we could ever begin to think of making a life together. But when he died . . . Well, when he died it was different. I realized I had been stupid in not telling you about Kali . . .'

'Stop it!' Laura covered her ears with her hands. She had no wish to know the name of the woman who was maried to the man she loved. 'Don't tell me any more, I can't bear it!'

He made a move towards her, but she backed away, leaving his outstretched hand in mid-air. 'I wish with all my heart it was different,' he told her.

'You could leave her.' She could hardly believe she had said the words.

But he merely shook his head. 'She lives with the children and my mother in a village twenty miles from here. I am their only means of support.'

'You could support them from Scotland,' she told him, throwing all dignity to the winds now. 'My family in

Dundee is wealthy. They could have more money than they ever dreamt of.'

His eyes were troubled as they looked into hers. 'What sort of a man would I be to walk out on my own children?' he asked her. 'Honour is all to the Indian.'

'And you are an Indian before you are a human being?'

'No,' he said patiently. 'I am what I am – an Indian *and* a human being.'

'Then you won't come with me,' she said softly. 'You are telling me you will not leave your wife and children for the woman you love . . . Or perhaps do not love enough?'

'No. What I am saying is that I love you with all my heart, Laura. I have never loved another as I love you and I know I never will. But we met ten years too late. I have a wife and children. My honour will not allow me to sacrifice them for my own happiness . . . I can only ask your forgiveness for loving you so much that I could not bring myself to be more honest with you before now.'

'So that is it, is it? We say goodbye and I leave with the others tomorrow – for ever. We will never see each other again.' She was unable to disguise the bitterness in her voice.

'You take with you my heart,' he said simply.

Laura gave a mirthless smile. She was taking with her much more than that. But he would never know. This man of honour would never be tortured with the knowledge that he had another child in faraway Scotland; a child who would never know his name.

'Goodbye, Samit,' she said softly. 'And may your God go with you.'

Samit's eyes were brimming as they looked into hers. 'I loved you, Laura,' he told her in a voice choked with emotion. 'I will always love you. I want you to know that.'

'I know it,' she answered. And she did. That was what made it all the harder to bear.

Chapter Forty-one

While Laura was coming to terms with the fact she would travel back to Scotland alone, leaving the man she loved in Lucknow, Kate still had no inkling about the terrible times her daughter had been going through. The last mail they had received had been a batch of letters written in early June, and, although they knew things were far from settled in the northern provinces of India at the moment, they were not unduly worried. There had been more than enough happening at home to occupy their thoughts.

The past six months had seen great progress in the fortunes of the Falcon Mills. New machines had been introduced during the summer that meant a competent worker could now reel 520 spindles of yarn in a working week of 60 hours. This amounted to 7,488,000 yards of yarn per person each shift, and meant a great increase in output. The installation of the new frames had caused quite a stir in the local press, and they were not surprised to hear shortly afterwards that identical looms were being installed in most of Willie Falconer's Eagle Mills. Willie had been particularly incensed just before that over the building of a new Falcon Mill housing the latest machinery, in the same part of Lochee in which there had been the bitter dispute over ownership of the land.

That mill was now due to go into production on 1 December and, out of a sense of devilment, Kate had decided to make this the most celebrated opening yet, with a large party organized at Falcon Ridge to celebrate the event. 'Having it at home will make sure that rogue Willie Falconer can't turn up to put a damper on things,' she told Davey. 'He'd rather die than set foot in his old family home, and I thank God for that, for I doubt if poor Ewan could bear to set eyes on the man without coming to blows.'

It had taken Ewan much longer to get over Emma's exile from Dundee than Kate had ever anticipated. For weeks after the young woman left for Paris he would moon around the house at weekends, refusing all coaxing by his friends to join them on the town. And even now, almost one year later, there were still times when he became strangely silent and that haunted look would come back into his eyes. 'Love-sick' was the only word his mother had to describe him, and she just prayed that time would prove the great healer to his mind that it had to his body.

It had been decided to move many of their best workers into the new mill, and for some weeks before the machinery was installed, Ewan had been busy designing the very latest in offices for himself. 'I plan on basing myself in Lochee,' he told his mother. 'It's far too tiring moving from office to office in different mills every day of the week.'

Kate thought that an admirable idea, and she was glad he seemed to have something other than Emma to occupy his thoughts. When he suggested after tea on the day before the scheduled opening that he might take a last run through to Lochee and just check everything was in place before the ceremony the following afternoon, she was enthusiastic at the idea. Anything that got him out of the house in the evening these days was to be encouraged. 'Do you want me to come with you?' she asked as he rose from the tea table.

'No, thanks all the same, Ma. I'm taking some of my files with me to put into the new office, and I'll probably call into the Royal for a drink when I finish there.'

Kate's heartbeat quickened. It had been so long since he had done that. 'You might see some of the lads,' she said as nonchalantly as possible as she screwed up her napkin and pushed it to one side. 'And it's certainly far too dreich a night for doing much else.' It had been dull and overcast all day, and with darkness falling by mid-afternoon at this time of year, there was little else to do during the evening but socialize or curl up in front of the fire with a good book, and the latter certainly wasn't Ewan's style.

When he had gone she contemplated taking a walk down the village to see Davey but decided against it. The roaring fire in the drawing room proved far too great a temptation simply to stay put and write some long-overdue letters. She still had her regular twice-weekly note to pen to Laura, and that always took the best part of an evening. There seemed to be so much news to tell these days.

In many ways she felt more settled now than she had done in a long time. With Laura happily married in India and the mills going from strength to strength again after quite a lean period, and Davey back in Dundee for two weeks out of three at least, she only had Ewan to worry about. But now, at long last, her son seemed to be returning to his old self again. As well as involving himself in the new mill, he was still looking into the idea of going into shipbuilding, and had made several trips to various ports around the country, investigating the methods used by the most up-to-date yards. Watching him gradually come back to life meant everything to Kate. It was as if her own ship of fate was running safely into port on a fair wind after a long period of being buffeted hither and thither.

It was funny how, even when they were grown up, you still worried more about the happiness of your children than your own. One of these days, God willing, she prayed he would meet another young lass every bit as pretty and talented as Emma and, before she knew it, there would be grandchildren about the place . . . Yes, that's what the old house needed, she thought to herself.

She heard the front door bang as Ewan set off for Lochee, and she snuggled down in the depths of her favourite armchair to contemplate the thought.

Grandchildren . . . She could see them now bringing life and love to the empty shell her beloved home so often seemed to have become. Young voices and happy laughter around the place would do more to guarantee her an enjoyable old age than all the new mills and the latest machinery that money could buy.

But giving his mother grandchildren was the last thing on Ewan's mind as he dismounted his horse and tethered it to a hitching-post in the courtyard at the rear of the new Lochee mill almost an hour later. He had brought a lantern with him and could feel his blood pulsating excitedly as he lit it and held it high outside the back door. This was an entrance he had had put in primarily for himself. The narrow stairs inside led up the six storeys to the very top of the building, where he had designed and furnished the suite of offices for his personal use. Having his own entrance and exit meant he could come and go as he pleased without the whole workforce knowing if he was on the premises. That would certainly help to keep them on their toes. And having his rooms at the very top of the building meant that, not only would he have the peace to work undisturbed, but he would also have one of the best views in the city. Yes, he was certainly looking forward to working here, he mused happily as, gripping the bag with his files in one hand, and holding the lantern aloft in the other, he pushed open the door with his shoulder and began the long ascent to the top storey.

He was out of breath and perspiring by the time he finished the climb and turned the key in the main door to his suite. The rooms were just as he had left them the previous day, except for a collection of potted plants which seemed to have arrived in abundance, for large jardinières stood on almost every available surface, sprouting green aspidistras and mother-in-law's-tongues, as well as a variety of ferns. That was his mother's doing, no doubt, for all things green and growing had become something of a passion with her as she had grown older.

Apart from the plants, he had chosen most of the furnishings himself, and in pride of place on the wall above his desk stood a mezzotint of his father, taken from his favourite oil painting of the old man. Ewan grinned happily up at him. 'You'd be a proud man tomorrow if you could only be here with us to celebrate,' he told him. 'Aye,' he sighed, catching his breath, 'we've carried the torch you passed us and it has never blazed more brightly than it will do the morn. The Falcon Mills will make headlines in every newspaper in the land, never mind the local press . . . Think of that, Pa. And just let that old bugger Willie Falconer try to better it!'

'Speaking of torches, it's bloody freezing in here!' He shivered as he looked down at the neatly set fire in the gleaming new grate. 'To hell, I'm the boss, aren't I?' he muttered, taking a spill from the brass holder on the mantelpiece and kneeling down with the lantern. 'There's no use risking pneumonia for the sake of a lassie cleaning it out and laying a new fire in the morning!'

Within minutes he had the fire blazing merrily. He walked to the walnut drinks cabinet by the window and, opening it, extracted a bottle of the best Scotch malt whisky. 'We'll toast tomorrow!' he said proudly, still addressing his father's picture, as he made for the desk beneath it.

With a happy sigh, he sat down in the leather chair, swivelling it round to place his booted feet on the polished surface of the desk as he leant back and unscrewed the top of the bottle before lighting a cigarette. 'Here's tae us!' he declared, holding high the bottle in his father's direction. 'Wha's like us, eh, Da? . . . Damn few. And they're a' deid!'

And with that he took a generous swig of the drink. 'Aaah, by God, that's better!'

The files he had brought with him were in the bag he had placed on top of the desk, and he lifted them out and stacked them into a neat pile at his elbow. He still had a bit of work to do on his speech for tomorrow so what more could he ask than to be seated here at his new desk, with a bottle of best Scotch at hand, a nearly full case of rolled cigarettes in his breast-pocket, and a warm fire to toast his frozen fingers and toes? For the first time in many a long day he felt a happy man indeed.

The whisky brought a warm glow to his whole being as it made its way to his stomach and, as he sat there over the next hour enjoying swig after swig, the world suddenly seemed a much kinder, more mellow place. The more effect the spirit had, the more easily and more mellifluently the words seemed to come to his pen as he paid tribute in his speech to the spirit of endeavour he had inherited from both his father and mother. Normally by this time he would have filled at least one wicker basket with discarded notes, but the one on the floor behind him was little more than half full. I'm getting better, he thought to himself as he emptied his overflowing ashtray into it and lit another cigarette. He was far too comfortable to get up and walk to the fireplace.

He drew deeply on the burning tobacco and leant back in the chair as he rested his eyes on the picture of his father. This time he had trouble focusing and his speech was slightly less coherent as he gave a heartfelt sigh and lifted the half-empty bottle to toast the old man yet one more time. 'If I live to be half the man you were, I'll be doing not so badly, Da! Here's tae ye! I wish to God I'd known ye . . .'

In his mind's eye he could vaguely recall leaning over the old man's coffin in his mother's arms as she said softly, 'Say goodbye to Daddy.' The quiet, almost holy atmosphere and the distinctive smell of the room that day had remained with him. It had smelt of old leather and his father's own favourite tobacco leaf, and it was that same brand that was contained in the specially rolled cigarettes in the case on the desk beside him now. When he had first begun to smoke several years ago, there had never been any question about which shag he would choose.

That same pungent smell now filled this, his own office, and, as he leant back in his chair and watched a smoke-ring drift lazily to the ornate ceiling, to his surprise, large tears began to form in his eyes. They hovered on his lower lashes for a moment or two, then began to trickle slowly down his cheeks. 'Jesus!' Embarrassed, he wiped them away with the back of his hand. What in heaven's name was he greetin' about? A right jessie he was becoming and no mistake! It was just as well that the lads were not here to see him now.

The lads! He had meant to head on to the Royal and have a dram or two with them before heading back to Broughty Ferry.

'Bugger it!' Annoyed with himself, he tossed his ciga-rette into the waste basket and reached for his pocket-watch. Leaning over to the pool of yellow light shed by the lantern, he saw it was reading just after ten. If he hurried they would probably still be there.

He attempted to get to his feet, only to stumble against the desk, knocking over the whisky bottle and spilling what little remained on to the new Indian carpet and down the side of the waste basket. He swore under his breath. Three-quarters of a bottle in just under an hour had taken its toll.

Blinking hard in an effort to focus his eyes, he sat back down in his chair and looked down at the floor. He could see two of everything; the tree-of-life pattern on the carpet seemed to be moving in a most disturbing fashion. Then he felt his eyes begin to smart. 'What the . . . !' Never mind the carpet – the bloody wastepaper basket was on fire! Flames were leaping up the wicker sides from the mass of burning paper inside.

'Jesus!' He staggered to his feet once more and lurched towards it. He attempted to pick it up to toss it into the grate, but let it drop immediately with a pained yell as the burning wickerwork of the sides scorched the skin of his fingers.

Horrified, he watched the mass of burning waste paper spill out on to the rug, sending tall sheaves of blue flame up from the carpet where the whisky had been spilled.

Panic-stricken now, he knew he needed something to douse the flames. Water! He needed water! Frantically he looked around him. There was none. Any liquid would do, his befuddled brain decided, as he raced to the drinks cupboard and began opening bottles and pouring alcohol into the growing inferno.

His eyes were streaming from the smoke and he had difficulty keeping his feet. For the life of him he could not understand why the flames were not going out. On the contrary, the bloody fire was raging more than ever now. In fact, the whole of the side of the room behind him was becoming one huge sheet of flame. He could not even see the door.

'Holy Christ!'

He staggered towards the window, only to discover it had a security grille of iron bars outside the glass.

A small bronze bust of Lord Aberdeen sat on the bookcase to the side. More in frustration than anything else, he picked it up and hurled it through a pane. The glass smashed into a thousand slivers, but the statuette merely bounced off the bars beyond and landed back at his feet.

He was coughing fit to burst now and could barely see through the black, billowing smoke as he turned around and tried to get his bearings. 'Help me! Someone – for Christ's sake, help me!'

But there was no one to hear his anguished plea, and no one to see as he staggered forwards to stand swaying in the middle of the room as the flames leapt waist-high around him.

The whole of the rear of the office was engulfed in a sea of searing orange and blue flames, and he could not see more than a foot in front of him for the lung-choking smoke. The door to the passage outside was somewhere behind that inferno.

But wait! There was another door! His heart leapt as he turned and made his way to the wall to the right of the fireplace and clutched in desperation at the brass door-knob. *'Nooo!'* he screamed. The bloody thing was locked and the keys were still in the other door.

Tears streamed from his eyes as he slumped against the locked door. All he could make out was the smoke, the black, breath-denying smoke and the flames which seemed to be everywhere.

Summoning up what little air he could he began to scream, 'Mam! Mam!... Help me, MAMMY... *PLEASE...!'*

Chapter Forty-two

'I cannot, cannot say,
Out of my bruised and breaking heart,
Storm-driven along a thorn-set way,
While blood-drops start
From every pore, as I drag on,
"Thy will, O God, be done!"'

Davey stood alone, sheltering beneath the bare branches of a gnarled and ancient oak tree that grew next to the stone wall that surrounded the cemetery. The other mourners had long gone, and only he and Kate remained. She stood about fifty feet away, a veiled and solitary figure dressed from head to toe in black, in front of the family vault where not half an hour since they had placed what was left of the body of her only son.

Davey shivered, his face pinched and grave in the biting wind, and he pushed his hands deeper into the pockets of his overcoat. Painfully conscious he must not intrude on her private grief, he had left her there to say her personal farewell to the young man she had loved more than life itself. Now he could only watch and pray that the blow that had befallen her with Ewan's death would not lead to her own demise, for never had he known her so low both spiritually and physically. Scarcely a morsel of food or cup of tea had passed her lips over the past three days, neither had she slept a wink, and great dark circles shadowed her eyes. She had withdrawn into herself and he had respected her silence. The pain she was going through was too deep for words and went far beyond mere tears. As he watched her now he felt impotent. When she most needed him, there was nothing he could do or say that could ease that pain. His heart ached for her. No mother should have to endure the agony of burying her own child. It went against the whole meaning of life itself.

He had not heard about the fatal fire at the new Falcon Mill until the morning after it happened, and it was later still that day that he learned Ewan was missing. As soon as the news reached him at around teatime, he had raced straight up the brae to see Kate. She had been pacing the drawing room in a state that veered between near hysteria and total collapse. It was the not knowing that had been so awful. It was not until nightfall it was finally confirmed that her son had indeed perished in the blaze.

He had been with her when the news was finally relayed to her by the family doctor, accompanied by a member of the local constabulary. For a few desperate hours she had cherished the hope that Ewan had already left the premises to go on to meet his friends and was still recovering from a hangover somewhere in town, but as the day dragged on they had both known that this was becoming more and more unlikely. Then, as darkness fell, among the smouldering rubble of what had once been her son's beloved new office suite, they found the remnants of a human being alongside the charred and melted remains of his father's silver cigarette case. They had handed Kate the blackened and twisted lump of metal; the proud beak of the falcon engraved on the front of the case was still visible. It was all the evidence she needed to believe the worst: her son was dead, for the case was never out of his pocket.

Davey knew as long as he lived he would never forget the look that came into her eyes at that moment, and a great surge of love burst from his heart as he looked across at her now, alone with her grief. A soft snow was falling, but Kate's black umbrella remained furled, her erect figure as motionless as the marble angels that stood sentinel over the surrounding graves. The biting wind that whistled down from the Sidlaw Hills behind the city caused the flakes to swirl in white clouds around her head, but she seemed oblivious to everything but the pain within her. And, when at last she turned to walk slowly back down the path between the tombstones to her waiting carriage, she did not even acknowledge her old friend's presence as Davey came out of the shadows and gently took her arm in his.

They rode back to Broughty Ferry together in silence, to a house that itself seemed as quiet as the marble tomb where Ewan now lay next to his Falconer forebears. Unable to face a social gathering after the funeral, Kate had flown in the face of convention and was offering no drinks or refreshments in the family home. For those mourners who wished to partake there would be a meal laid on in the local hotel, but she had made it clear she would not be attending.

Davey got out of the carriage first as it rolled up at the front door of Falcon Ridge. He helped her down, clasping her hand in the crook of his arm as they ascended the stone steps up to the house.

'If you need me you know where to find me,' he said quietly, letting go of her arm as she opened the door.

She nodded but made no other response as she walked inside and closed the door behind her.

He stood looking at it for a moment or two, then, turning up his collar in the face of the icy wind, he made his way slowly down the road to his own cottage. He was not offended she had not asked him in or even acknowledged his presence, for more than anyone he knew the depth of her sorrow. Ewan had been not only her beloved son, he had been her past, her present and her future rolled into one. To be forced to go on now without him seemed almost too much to bear.

On closing the door, Kate took off her black cape and bonnet and handed them and her unused umbrella to the maid who had come hurrying up from downstairs at the sound of the carriage arriving.

'Is there anything I can get you, ma'm?'

Kate shook her head. 'No, thanks. I'll go into the drawing room and rest a while . . . And I won't be wanting a meal tonight.'

A fire was roaring in the hearth as she opened the door. Quite out of character, she made straight for the drinks cabinet to pour herself a large whisky. She did not usually drink the spirit, but most of all right now she wanted something – anything – strong enough to dull the terrible aching pain within her. All through the service at the graveside she had been silently screaming. She almost envied those women from lands other than this cold northern clime who could show their grief by keening and wailing and gnashing their teeth and throwing themselves on the beloved's coffin. But this was Scotland in the year 1857, and respectable British matrons did not act in such a way. So she had had to stand there silently screaming while they said prayers over what was left of the body of her dead son. And unknown to the world she was still screaming now that she was back home and attempting to carry on as normal.

Nursing the glass in her cold hands, she sat down in the chair next to the fire and closed her eyes. Even at a distance of several feet she could feel the heat of the flames on her skin and a shudder ran through her as she imagined the final agonies of her son. He would have called for her, she was certain of that. But she had not been there. 'Oh God . . .' She groaned aloud as guilt overwhelmed her once more. She should have gone with him to the mill that evening. She should never have let him go into that new building alone after dark. She was well aware he had had a cabinet full of his favourite spirits in the office, just as she knew he had been drinking far too much this past year. What sort of mother was she not to put two and two together? Had she accompanied him that night he would be alive today. She took a gulp of the whisky and grimaced as it made its way down her throat. She should have been there. She could have saved him. She had tortured herself with that thought ever since, and would until her dying day.

She had drunk more than half the whisky in the glass when there was a knock on the drawing-room door and the maid entered. 'Begging your pardon, ma'm, but there's a gentleman here to see you . . . I told him you might not want to be disturbed.'

Before Kate had a chance to ask who it was, the large, black-coated figure of Willie Falconer loomed behind the girl.

Startled, Kate jumped from her seat, spilling what was left of the drink as, with shaking fingers, she placed the glass on a side-table by the fire and gaped at the man in the doorway. He was the very last person she had expected to see today.

Willie's face was grave as solemnly he entered the room, hat in hand, and looked at her, as if waiting for her to be the first to speak.

Stunned, Kate indicated to the maid to leave, which she did, closing the door quietly behind her.

She knew she should observe the normal civilities and offer him a drink and a seat, but she could not bring herself to do so. With chin raised high, she looked Willie straight in the eye and held her peace. Let him be the first to break the silence, she thought. She had not invited him here, and she could feel resentment growing within her at this intrusion on her private grief.

When the silence between them grew too much to bear, Willie cleared his throat, his fingers nervously gripping the brim of his hat which he held defensively in front of him. 'I didn't attend the funeral today, Kate,' he said in a halting voice. 'It was a big turn-out so you may not have noticed. God knows there was no reason why you should. It's not that I meant any disrespect by not going, I want you to know that. It was simply that I didn't want to cause you any more upset by my presence at the graveside . . . But — God help us — I could not let this terrible day pass

510

altogether without coming to pay my final respects. Your lad and I . . . Well, we may have had our differences over the past year, but that's by the by. He was a young man in the prime of life and didn't deserve this. I can imagine what you must be going through.'

Kate's hands were clasped in front of her and she could feel her nails digging into her skin as she fought with her emotions. This was no longer the Willie she knew, neither in looks nor manner. To her surprise she realized she was looking at an elderly man who was having great difficulty finding the right words to express his feelings. He had very little hair left now, and what there was was pure white, as were his side-whiskers and moustaches. The skin of his nose and cheeks was far too ruddy to be healthy, and deep furrows lined his brow. He appeared older, so much older than when she had last seen him, and he looked more like his father than ever. Despite her natural animosity to-wards him, that very fact tugged at her heart-strings as he stood there fiddling with the brim of his hat. There was little left to be seen of the Willie of old. Long gone was the proud, womanizing young hot-head she had once known, and there was even little sign of the embittered mature man whose only wish was to take revenge on her for having what he would always regard as rightfully his. The man who now stood before her had come as a father who had a beloved son of his own. 'I appreciate you coming here today,' she said more stiffly than she intended. 'I know what it must have cost you.'

An awkward silence followed as they stood avoiding each other's eyes. 'Would – would you care for a drink?' Kate said at last.

But Willie shook his head. 'No, thanks all the same.' This was not a social call. He could not wait to leave, although just being in this room again was an experience he found profoundly moving. He had been born in this house and had presumed he would die in it. How often, as a small child, on a freezing winter's day such as this, had he knelt in front of that very fire and read his fortune in the sparks that clung to the chimney behind the dancing flames? His father had once told him the burning sparks were particles of magic dust left by the fire-fairies and if he looked hard enough he could see the future in the flames. He had told that same story to Ian, his own son.

His eyes moved to the oil painting of the old man above the mantelpiece. He had loved his father and, despite what had been done to disinherit him, that love was there still. It was a bond of blood that could not be broken. Death had no dominion over such a tie. It went far beyond the grave. And Ewan too had been his father's son. But he had not been Augustus's. He had been his own son . . .

It had taken the whole of the young man's lifetime and now his death for him to accept that fact. When Kate had told him a year ago that he was the father of her first-born, he had been sickened to his core. He had spent half a lifetime resenting the boy.

Shame had filled his soul when he heard of the young man's death. He should never have blamed the lad. Children were not to blame for the circumstances into which they were born.

'I – I just want you to know,' he found himself saying in a strained voice, 'that, despite all that's been said and done in the past, I want you to know that I recognize that Ewan was a Falconer, and I am sorry, so very sorry for what has happened.'

Kate drew in her breath and let it out slowly. She was shaking inside but was determined not to let it show. She knew what it must be costing him to tell her that. What exactly he was sorry about, she could not be sure. Was it their son's death or his attitude towards the boy throughout his young life? Somehow it scarcely mattered any more. 'A lot of water has passed under a great many bridges since you were last in this house,' she said quietly. 'And a great deal of hurt has been caused – often need-lessly – on both sides, I have no doubt. But we are older now and, I hope, a great deal wiser. Our wounds must not be inflicted on the generation to come.' As she said the words she realized that it was already too late for her son and her eyes began to brim.

Biting her lip in an attempt to stem the flow of tears, she turned from the man in front of her and walked quickly to the window. The curtains were not yet closed. It was dark outside and still snowing; she could see flakes, the size of silver threepenny bits, drifting down in the pale glow of the oil-lamp on the curve of the drive outside. The old oak box containing the Falconer family Bible lay on a side-table beside her, and she rested her fingers on it as she fought to compose herself. Ewan's birth was recorded in there, and tonight she would record his funeral. Unable to write an untruth in the Lord's book, she had deliberately omitted the name of his father when writing in details of his birth. But now as she stood there in this room that held so many ghosts from the past, she knew that the time for lies was over.

Slowly she turned to the man only a few feet away. 'I buried my son today,' she said, choosing her words carefully, 'and he went to his death believing Augustus to be his father. I confess I would never have had the courage to tell him the truth had he lived – perhaps I loved him too much for that . . . But your coming here today has meant a lot to me.' She spoke haltingly and paused, closing her eyes as she struggled to keep her emotions in check. What she had to say would not be easy, but in a strange way she knew it had to be said if her son's soul was to rest in peace.

She turned to face the man she had been at odds with for the whole of their son's lifetime. 'Ewan is dead,' she said to him in a voice husky with emotion. 'Neither the truth nor all the lies in the world can hurt him now. And we the living must carry on. Let it be in a spirit of recon-ciliation.' She paused and sighed. 'We are neither of us young any more; perhaps we owe it to the living as well as the dead to admit the truth. Ewan was your son; in coming here today you have accepted that truth, and I thank you for it. I feel our son can rest in peace now.'

Willie's pale eyes were fixed on her face as her words found their mark, and Kate's eyes were brimming as she looked at this nervous old man who, as a young Jack-the-lad, had taken her virginity in lust, not love, and in doing so had fathered her beloved son. For that reason alone she could never bring herself to hate him. 'Ewan was as much a Falconer as any that lie in the chill of that great marble tomb,' she told him. 'But he is dead, and all my wishing in the world is not going to bring him back. And all my tears will never wash his name from that granite block. If there is such a place as heaven, then he is with the Lord and the truth can no longer hurt him.'

'So he . . .? So he didn't . . . ?'

'Know you were his father?' She finished the question for him and shook her head. 'No, he didn't know, and he would never have known had he lived, for I would have taken the secret to the grave with me rather than hurt him in that way.'

'Then why did you tell me, Kate?'

'Because I was angry. Angry at what you had done to your own flesh and blood. And maybe I was tired of living a lie. Tired of all the bitterness and hurt that has been caused over the years. Tired of looking at that picture of your father up there and feeling guilty about the hate that has grown within the Falconer family since his death. It has been like a cancer eating away at my very soul.'

Willie shook his head. Suddenly his collar felt far too tight and he could feel the sweat running in rivulets down his back beneath the fine linen of his shirt. 'I – I don't know what to say,' he said, totally at a loss for words. He was aware of the eyes of the old man in the portrait looking down at him.

'Then don't say anything,' Kate told him in a voice of surprising gentleness. 'Let what has passed between us this day be for our ears alone . . . Go back to your family,

Willie. Cherish those two youngsters of yours. And, God willing, help them grow into fine adults, without the hatred and bitterness in their hearts that there has been in ours.'

Willie was silent for a moment or two. He could cope better with her anger than her compassion. He could feel a choking sensation in his throat as he walked towards her a trifle shakily, and held out his hand. 'I'm glad I came,' he said simply.

'So am I.'

She watched him walk from the room with tears streaming down her face. Exactly why she was crying she could not be sure. Was it for Ewan? For his father – the man who was now leaving? Or for herself? Perhaps it was for all three, she told herself as she wiped her eyes and walked to the window to watch the tall, stout figure shamble down the frozen steps and climb into the waiting carriage.

The snow had turned to rain. And, in a strange way, a great burden had been lifted from her soul.

Falling upon the frozen world . . .
I hear the slow beat of the winter rain –
Poor foolish drops, down dripping all in vain;
The ice-bound Earth but mocked their puny might,
Far better had the fixedness of white
And uncomplaining snows – which make no sign,
But coldly smile, when pitying moonbeams shine –
Concealed its sorrow from all human sight.
Long, long ago, in blurred and burdened years,
I learned the uselessness of uttered woe.
Though sinewy Fate deals her most skilful blow,
I do not waste now the gall of my tears,
But feel my pride upon its bitter, while
I look straight in the world's bold eyes, and smile.

515

Chapter Forty-three

Davey could not account for the change in Kate when he called to see her the week after Ewan's funeral. She seemed so much more relaxed and at peace with herself and the world as they sat in the breakfast room, enjoying the pale beams of winter sunshine that filtered through the sash-windows. She had been in the conservatory when he arrived, making plans for planting out in the coming spring, and that in itself had been a revelation to him. She was actually beginning to look ahead. Life was going to go on.

On his arrival she had ordered tea and cake to be sent up for them, and now as they took their ease in the comfortable Windsor chairs, the maid placed the tray with the tea things on the table and Kate rose herself to attend to the cutting of the freshly baked Dundee fruitcake. 'I'll see to this,' she told the girl, who backed from the room, aiming a shy smile and a 'Good-day to you, Mr Lorimer,' in Davey's direction.

'My, but that looks tasty!' Davey took the proffered teaplate piled high with two thick slices of fruitcake and sat it on the windowsill beside him as he reached across for his cup of tea.

Kate sat down at the table. She looked better slept than she had in a long time, and even in her black mourning dress she seemed to have more colour in her cheeks as she poured herself a cup of tea from the china pot. 'It was good of you to come,' she told him. 'I was afraid I might have given offence. I wasn't the best of company the last time I saw you.'

He looked surprised. If she couldn't be herself with him

516

at a time like that it was a rum do indeed. 'Och, you've no need to worry about that. I'm just relieved to see you looking more like your old self today . . . You won't have gone back to work yet, though?'

'No, I thought I'd give it a few days more.' She longed to tell him of Willie's visit, but couldn't. He had no idea of the true relationship between Augustus's son and Ewan and never would. That particular secret would go with her to the grave, for she knew Willie himself would never breathe a word. 'How about yourself? Have you any speeches lined up before Christmas?'

He looked down at the cup in his hands. 'I've been asked to give the odd one or two – Glasgow and Edinburgh, that sort of thing. But I don't suppose . . .'

'That I'd come with you?'

He gave an awkward half-smile. 'I realize it's early days yet,' he said quickly. 'I'd quite understand . . .'

'I'd love to come.'

His grey brows rose in surprise as he looked across at her. 'Really? You really mean that?'

'Yes, really.' She took another sip of her tea and nodded in confirmation. 'There's only me now to bother about, remember. If Ewan's death has taught me anything it's that life is too short to put things off any more. The Falcon Mills don't need me there every single day. I have good managers and the best workers in the world who are quite capable of carrying on their daily tasks without me looking over their shoulders all the time.'

Davey took a deep breath and let it out slowly. This was a new Kate indeed. 'And you don't mind us travelling together and booking into the same hotel as Mr Lorimer and Mrs Falconer?'

'Do I have a choice?'

Her question, so innocently put, took him aback. She was looking straight at him, without a smile on her face. He placed his cup and saucer on the windowsill and cleared his throat. 'I – I'm not quite sure what exactly you mean by that, Kate.'

She looked surprised. 'Oh really? I merely asked if I had a choice in whether to travel as Mrs Falconer or not.'

There was a total silence, broken only by the ticking of the black marble clock on the mantelpiece some feet away. Davey could feel himself colouring as a hot flush of embarrassment crept up from his collar to suffuse the skin beneath the grey whiskers of his cheeks. 'You wouldn't be asking me to marry you, by any chance?' He almost choked on the words and they came out far more clumsy than he'd intended.

'Most certainly not! It's hardly a woman's place, is it now?' She deliberately avoided his eyes as she broke a piece off her slice of cake and popped it into her mouth. She chewed on it thoughtfully as she brushed some imaginary crumbs from her lap.

Davey shifted uneasily in his seat. Was she teasing him or not? This was the last sort of conversation he had expected when he called up here today. Marriage had been the only great taboo in all their conversations over the years. At least on his part. On the few occasions the subject had arisen it had been in a lighthearted fashion to save the other any possible embarrassment. Even when he was alone he had seldom allowed himself the luxury of even contemplating such an event. What on earth did he have to offer her? She was not only the richest woman in her own right in the whole of the city, but was the most successful as well. Since Augustus's death she had done the unthinkable and succeeded in a man's world, while to most in this town he himself was no more than a radical rabble-rouser, a political agitator who would be better off locked up in the tolbooth than going round the country inciting insurrection against the factory and landowners.

Deeply conscious of his silence, he could now feel her eyes on him as he concentrated on adding more sugar to what was already a perfect cup of tea. His armpits were uncomfortably damp beneath the blue worsted of his shirt as he stirred the spoon for far longer than was necessary.

'You're not saying very much.'

The teaspoon stopped in mid-stir. 'Aye . . . No . . . Well, I was just remembering I've got a meeting lined up for this morning I'd quite forgotten about.' Whatever made him tell such a lie he could not imagine.

'Oh.'

Thoroughly ashamed of himself for this quite blatant untruth, he half rose from his seat, gulping down the last of the tea before placing the empty cup on the table. The cloying sweetness in the bottom of the cup set his teeth on edge as he wiped his moustache with the back of his hand.

'You'll have to be off in a rush then.' Kate found it hard to disguise the disappointment in her voice or face as she watched him straighten his jacket ready to take his leave. Quite obviously she had gone too far, much too far, in her teasing of him.

'I thank you for the tea and cake, Kate. It made a braw change from my usual dry bannock wi' my morning cuppie,' he said, placing a restraining hand on her shoulder as she made to rise to see him out. 'I think I ken the way out by now. There's no need for you to disturb yourself.'

She listened to his booted feet echoing down the corridor outside. When he had gone the room seemed empty without him. As she finished her tea she wondered at the stupidity that had come into her to tease him about such a thing. It really was unforgivable. But had she been teasing? Or was there something in her that made such a question more important now than it had ever been? While Ewan was alive she had known in her heart there could never be any question of her marrying Davey, for her son would never have come to terms with it. To him Davey would always have been the enemy, both in terms of his mother's affections and as a committed opponent of what was conceived as the Capitalist class.

But now all that had changed, and changed dramatically. Ewan was dead and she was alone in the world. Laura was thousands of miles away and would probably never return to her native city in years, and Falcon Ridge was nothing but a big empty barn of a place full of memories and ghosts of the past. When Augustus died she had had the children to occupy her time, but now there was no one; apart from the servants she was quite alone here, and it was not a good feeling. She needed someone on whom to bestow the care and affection that were still within her. And not just a part-time love; she wanted to be whole again, both in mind and body.

It came as quite a surprise to her, after his hasty exit that morning, when Davey reappeared just as she was finishing lunch early that same afternoon. He had hired a carriage from the village and informed her it was waiting at the front door. 'I'm being charged by the quarter-hour so you'll do me the favour of getting a move on and fetching your cape and bonnet so the auld devil that's driving it doesn't take me for everything I've got.'

'What on earth is all this about?' she asked as, only minutes after his arrival at the door, she found herself seated beside him in the cab as it rattled its way along the frozen road towards Dundee. She could only imagine that someone he had met this morning, when he had rushed off in such unseemly haste, had expressed a desire to see her. She knew that as his 'pet mill-owner', as she liked to put it, she was something of an object of curiosity amongst his Communist comrades. 'Is it one of your political pals we're going to see?'

He gave an infuriatingly enigmatic smile. 'You'll find out soon enough.'

To her surprise, on reaching the city, they did not head for the Overgate or the Perth Road or any of the other main thoroughfares, but the carriage made straight for the Hawkhill. Apart from her regular visits to her own mills which stood at the foot of the hill, it was years since she had been in this part of town, and Kate craned her neck to look curiously about her as they passed by familiar landmarks that filled her heart with a strange mixture of bitter-sweet emotions. 'Our old stomping ground,' she murmured as they passed closes where they had tussled together as children, or fought the good fight against neighbouring gangs from the Overgate and beyond.

'Whoa there, lasses!' The cab-driver's voice instructing the two horses to come to a stop could be heard through the half-open windows as the carriage trundled to a grinding halt outside Granny Mutch's sweet-shop on the corner of the block where they were both brought up.

'It looks like we're here,' Davey said, leaning over to open the carriage door.

He clambered down and leant back into the cab, holding out his hand to help her out.

'You've brought me all the way here to Granny Mutch's?' Kate said, now completely perplexed. 'Did you think a wee bag o' sweeties or a sherbet-dab would cheer me up?'

'Aye,' he said, in all seriousness. 'That's exactly what I thought.'

He crooked his left arm and she placed her right hand in it as they bent their heads and went down a step to enter the dark interior of the shop.

It smelt the very same: the stuff childhood dreams had been made of and, despite over thirty years of high living, Kate found it could still make her mouth water to see all the halfpenny trays laid out on the counter and the gleaming glass bottles standing in rows behind. To her astonishment, the old lady herself, now in her late seventies at least, was still serving.

'Davey lad!' Granny Mutch's face lit up at the sight of one of her favourite customers. 'What can I get for you this fine day?'

'A bag of your very best bull's-eyes for my old friend here, if you please, Granny,' he told her. 'It's been a fair while since she's had the pleasure of such a treat.'

521

'Well, that's certainly true!' Kate laughed at the absurdity of it all as the old lady lifted a glass jar containing the delicacies from a shelf behind her. 'Dear me, but these bring back memories . . .'

As the sweets were measured out, Kate gazed around her at the plethora of mouth-watering confections that she had craved so desperately as a small child, but had never had the money for. Sherbet-dabs, lucky tatties, granny-sookers, barley-sugar twists, licorice roots, they were all there and, to her embarrassment, she could feel her eyes begin to mist as she turned back to Davey who was now proudly holding the bag of bull's-eyes.

He gave a wink to the old lady behind the counter, and led Kate back out to the waiting carriage. 'It's a wee bit chilly to be hanging about in the cold,' he told her. 'I reckon we should have a seat inside to enjoy our treat.'

Still somewhat perplexed at the meaning of this trip down memory lane, she followed him into the cab and sat down beside him as he concealed the paper bag behind his back.

> 'Nievie nievie nick-nack
> Which hand will ye tak?
> Gin ye're richt or gin ye're wrang
> I'll beguile ye if I can.'

Kate burst out laughing. She had not heard that bit of nonsense in donkey's years. It was as if they really were bairns again, coming here like this and sharing a special treat. Suddenly, as she looked at him, his grey hair and grizzled beard had vanished in the twinkling of an eye with that one small poem; he was her Wee Davey again, the lad with the cheeky grin and permanently grazed knees.

'Come on – choose!' he urged her. 'She who hesitates is lost and I'll scoff the lot myself!'

She swithered for a minute then pointed to his right hand. 'I'll have that one!'

'You win the first prize!' he declared, holding up the grey sugar-paper twist full of sweeties in triumph before handing them to her. 'Ooh, thank you!' Delighted, she opened the bag and was about to put her fingers in to pull out one of the coveted black and white balls when something else claimed her attention. Something that looked nothing whatsoever like a bull's-eye. She poked her finger into the bag then, puzzled, she looked up at him. Davey was sitting there beside her with a grin from ear to ear.

'I don't believe it!' She gazed into the bag once more as her heart began to race.

'Go on, don't just leave it there.'

She shook her head in complete disbelief as she dipped her thumb and forefinger into the bag and pulled out the prettiest gold ring she had ever seen. It was in the shape of two clasped hands and her own hand shook as she laid it in her palm and gazed down at it.

Gently he took it from her and reached for her left hand which he held in both of his. 'Will you marry me, Kate?' he asked in a quiet voice. 'I can be a cantankerous auld bugger at times and probably nobody knows that better than you. But you know I love you. I've always loved you since we first shared suck-about of one of these very sweeties from auld Granny Mutch's jar. God knows, I have little more to offer you now than I had in those far-off days, but I loved you then and I love you still . . .'

His voice tailed off as he looked at the girl he had loved for a lifetime. 'We've come a long way since then, Katie McMahon, but, God willing, we still have some way to go on our journey through this life. It seems sense to me that we make that journey together. I know I have the cheek of the devil in making such a request, but you can only say No . . . Will you do me the inestimable honour of becoming my wife?'

Tears swam in Kate's eyes as he slipped the ring on her finger. She did not have to answer the question, for they had both known all their lives what the answer would be.

Chapter Forty-four

'This is my country, the land that begat me,
These windy spaces are surely my own,
And those who here toil,
In the sweat of their faces,
Are flesh of my flesh and bone of my bone.'

Laura stood on the ship's deck, her infant daughter clasped in her arms, as the vessel made its way through the foaming white horses into the Firth of Tay. The brisk breeze had made the sea more choppy than usual for this time of year, and a fierce groundswell came off the perilous sands of the Abertay that skirted the village of Monifieth.

To the left, gently undulating against the pale blue of the sky, were the green hills of Fife and the grey harbour of Newport-on-Tay. On the opposite bank lay the rich farmlands of Angus, where fat cattle grazed in lush green meadows. It was a beautiful and ancient land; a land at peace with itself, and a far cry from what she had left behind just four short months ago.

They were now passing the stone fortress of Broughty Castle on its craggy promontory, jutting into the grey expanse of river. Behind that was the village of Broughty Ferry itself, with its whitewashed fisher cottages snuggled around the harbour; and along the brow of the hill behind them, the great mansions of the mill-owners, such as her own family – the folk who lived on the hill whom the villagers called the jute barons. From her stance at the rail she could quite easily make out the stone turrets of Falcon Ridge, next to Carbet Castle, the Grimonds' Gothic mansion at the top of Grey Street. Her heart leapt at the sight of it. It was not so long ago she had given up all hope of ever seeing her old home again.

As they rounded the slight bend in the river, the whole city of Dundee came into sight, its ancient streets rising in layers of grey stone up to the green summit of the Law Hill, where in times past they would mete out a savage justice to any felon who threatened the peace of this hardworking port.

Despite the pale spring sunshine, a grey mist hung like a veil over the middle stratum of the city, and above it the tall mill chimney stacks were still belching their smoke heavenwards into the early April sky.

'Home . . .' she whispered into the soft down of dark hair as she held her two-month-old daughter up to her cheek and together they looked shorewards. 'We're coming home, India, my love . . .'

The child whimpered as the gusting wind blew the sea-spray into their faces, and as Laura cradled her daughter in her arms once more, murmuring words of comfort as she wiped the droplets from the smooth skin of the baby's cheeks. Large dark eyes gazed back into hers. His eyes. But Samit would never know this child. She had left Lucknow without talking to him or even setting eyes on him again after that terrible day she had found out about his wife and family; the night he had rejected her.

Did she blame him? It was a question she had asked herself a million times over the long weeks of the voyage home. All she knew for certain was that she had loved him with all her heart and would have asked for nothing more than to live at peace with him in her native land with their daughter. But to do that he would have had to do the unthinkable: walk out on his responsibilities in his own homeland. There a man's honour was worth more than a maharaja's riches – more even than life itself – so there had been no real choice to make.

The baby had been born at sea, after a long labour lasting thirty-six hours, during a particularly bad squall as they rounded the Cape of Good Hope. Laura had called her India: it had seemed the only name possible.

Since her daughter's birth her life had changed dramatically. She had assumed a totally different outlook on life. She was now responsible for another human being. It was an awesome thought, and it made her appreciate all the more how well her own mother had coped over the years, bringing up herself and Ewan, after having been widowed so tragically young. Had she ever thought of remarrying, Laura wondered? Her mother was a strong and attractive woman, but maybe it was that very strength which made remarriage not the easy option it might otherwise have been. It would need someone very secure in his own strengths to take on such a partner and, as she now knew to her cost, such men were few and far between.

So many men seemed to die young, leaving women to struggle on raising families alone. The ship out of Calcutta had been full of survivors of the siege, and of the terrible massacres that had taken place at other stations throughout the north of India. Many were young women like herself, returning home as widows to face a lonely and uncertain future bringing up fatherless children alone. No one had talked much about their experiences on the voyage home; they had simply been glad to be leaving. Most had disembarked at ports in the south of England, and now there were mainly military personnel left and several of her mother's own employees, as well as those of other local mill-owners, coming back to Scotland for their well-earned leave after a long stint in the jute mills on the Hooghly River.

Laura had been informed that word would already have reached her family of her circumstances, and that she would be returning on this ship, so she presumed they would be there waiting on the shore to meet her, but she was still in a highly nervous state at the thought of seeing her mother for the first time since Blair's death. Her feelings towards her late husband had mellowed over the intervening months, and she could almost understand now what had driven him to retain contact with his Indian family after their marriage. Hard though it was at first, she now accepted he must really have loved that young woman and, as she now knew to her cost, you could not turn your emotions on and off at will.

The authorities had told her before she left that she would be receiving Blair's posthumous gallantry medal in person from the Queen some time in the autumn when the royal family was in residence at Balmoral, and she knew she would display it with pride. She might even present it to his old regiment, the Black Watch, for Highland soldiers had been their saviours in Lucknow. Never could the sound of the pipes or the swing of tartan kilts have been so welcomed by so many people as on that glorious day when Sir Colin Campbell's men finally liberated the compound.

It all seemed a whole world away from her now as she stood on deck and feasted her eyes on her native shores. She had been a young girl when she had first sailed down this firth a few short years ago, but she was returning both a widow and a mother. Of course they would presume the child in her arms was Blair's, but one look would give the lie to that deception. India was a beautiful baby, but with her dark eyes and mop of thick dark hair, she was nothing like the sandy-haired Baxters, or even her own side of the family, although much would be made of the fact that the child's dark-brown locks were a throw-back from the purely Celtic strain of her Irish grandparents.

The deck was now crowded with passengers straining at the rail in the hope of catching a first glimpse of waiting loved ones on the dockside. And for those waiting on the shore the anticipation was every bit as acute.

Kate stood at Davey's side, every so often throwing decorum to the winds as she jumped up to try to see above the heads of those crowding in front of her as the gangplank was lowered and the great ship's bell rang out its greeting to all and sundry.

News of what had happened out there in India had only reached them a few weeks ago, and they had been appalled at what they had read. Then Laura's own letter had arrived, telling them of her husband's death, to be followed shortly afterwards by one telling them she was expecting a baby. Kate had clung tightly to Davey on reading that over a cup of tea in the morning room one blustery March morning. 'She will need us more than ever now,' she had told him, and he had murmured his agreement. 'We'll be here,' he had said. 'We'll be here for as long as she needs us – as long as they both need us.'

And now that moment was almost here.

Kate shaded her eyes with her gloved hand as she peered at the crowd of passengers leaning over the ship's rail as the din of shouting relatives and the clanging bell made even coherent thought an impossibility.

Then she saw her. 'There she is!' she shouted, clutching excitedly at Davey's arm. 'Look! Just to the right of the gangplank!'

A slim figure, dressed in a dark blue two-piece and hat, and carrying an infant wrapped in a shawl, was waving frantically at them.

Within minutes Laura was down the gangplank and hurrying towards them.

'Mother!'

Both were in tears as Kate wrapped her arms around her daughter and new grandchild. For several minutes they just stood there, comforting each other with their embrace. Then, prising herself away, Kate gazed down into the face of the tiny child in her daughter's arms.

'May I?'

'Of course.'

Leaving the new mother, she took the child and, cradling it in her own arms, she walked the few yards to where Davey was standing with a quiet smile on his face. 'Our first grandchild,' she said softly, handing over the baby to him.

The gesture touched him almost more than the words, as for the first time he held his own flesh and blood in his arms.

Kate beckoned to Laura who came towards them, looking slightly puzzled at the sight of her new daughter in the arms of her mother's old friend. 'How nice to see you again, Mr Lorimer,' she said, holding out her hand.

Handing the child back to Kate, Davey doffed his hat and took Laura's hand in both of his. 'Welcome home, lass,' he said with feeling. 'I can't tell you how glad we are to have you safely home.'

It was not until an hour or so later, after the baby had been put to sleep in the old nursery, and the three of them were sitting together in the drawing room at Falcon Ridge, that Laura once again voiced the question that had been puzzling her since her arrival. 'Isn't Ewan in town at the moment, then?' She could only imagine that he must be through in Edinburgh on business or something, otherwise he would surely have been at the dock to meet her. An earlier dockside query as to his whereabouts had been met with a rather embarrassed, 'Oh, we'll talk about that later.'

Kate and Davey, who were sitting across from her on either side of the fireplace, exchanged glances. Then, seeing the look that came into Kate's face, it was Davey who took on the awful task of explaining to Laura about the fire and her brother's death.

He spoke quietly and with feeling for almost five minutes. Laura listened with a stunned look on her face. On coming home to Scotland she had imagined she had done with tragedy. She had experienced more heartbreak this past year than most people would know in a lifetime. And in a way, on a very personal level, this was more terrible than anything that had gone before. When he had finished she could only shake her head at the awful waste and futility of it all. 'Poor Ewan . . .' she said softly. 'Poor, poor Ewan. He didn't deserve that.'

For months last year she had lived with death as a constant companion, and before it was all over she had buried her own husband and been rejected by the man she loved, but somehow her brother's death touched a chord that went far deeper than that. Ewan had been an integral part of her life since the very beginning. Not having a father, she had looked to him to be the male protector she had never known. Right up until she had left here as a married woman, he had meant more to her than any other human being, more almost than her own mother, who now looked at her with eyes brimming with the pain she herself still felt for the young man who was no longer with them.

'It is a hard homecoming for you, Laura my dear,' Kate said. 'First your husband and now your brother.'

Laura sat quite still, and only an almost imperceptible nod as her mother spoke indicated she had heard. Suddenly she felt much older than her years. She had been a child when she left these shores, but she had returned a mature woman who now knew what it must have been like for her own mother all those years ago. 'It was no easier for you,' she said in a quiet voice. 'I know better than anyone what Ewan meant to you. And you too were widowed far too young. You have spent a lifetime alone. It can't have been easy. You had a business to run as well as two small children to bring up.' She gave a wistful smile. 'When I was little I used to pray you would get married again so I could have a father like other wee girls.'

'I never knew that!'

'How could you have known?' Laura sighed. 'You were far too busy being both mother and father to us . . . But it would have been nice all the same. And it would have been lovely now for India to have a grandpa, seeing as she has no father or uncle to turn to any more.'

Kate nervously twisted the gold engagement ring on her finger and glanced across at Davey.

He rose from his seat and walked to where she was sitting, to pause by her chair and rest his hand protectively on her shoulder. He cleared his throat, something he only did when he was particularly nervous, and he looked across at the young woman on the settee. 'We weren't going to say anything to you today, Laura lass,' he said in a quiet voice. 'Seeing as you've only just learned of Ewan's death and all. But maybe this is as good a time as any to let you know there has been a wee bit of good news amongst the bad . . . Aye, you could say a candle has been lit in the terrible darkness of these past few months . . . I have had the gross cheek to ask this fine woman here – your dear mother – to be my wife and, God help me, she has been foolish enough to say Yes.'

'No!' Laura looked at them both in astonishment. Her mother was sitting there with the blush of a young girl burning her cheeks, and Davey himself was a picture of embarrassment. Laura shook her head in incredulity. 'How stupid of me!' she breathed. She ought to have known there was something of the kind going on from the mere fact that the two of them were there to meet her and had been sitting here on either side of the fireplace ever since like two Staffordshire Wally Dugs. Then a wide smile replaced the dumbfounded look on her face. 'But that's wonderful!'

She jumped from the chair to rush across to envelop Davey in a heartfelt hug. 'I'll have a father at last!' she cried. 'I can't tell you what that means to me right now!'

Davey had tears in his eyes as he hugged his daughter in return and glanced down at the woman he loved on the chair beside him. 'I think I know, lass,' he said huskily. 'I think both your mam and I know very well.'

Slowly Kate stood up and reached out to touch the whiskered cheek of the man she had loved for so long as he stood there with their daughter in his arms. In all the years she had known him she had never seen him cry, but now there were tears running freely down his cheeks to mingle with the grey hairs of his beard as his eyes met hers. 'We're home at last, Wee Davey,' she said softly. 'It's been a long, long journey, but we've all come safe to port at last . . .'

A Woman Under Suspicion

Naomi Ragen

'A strong story of a strong young woman. I truly
enjoyed *A Woman Under Suspicion*. Read it!'
BELVA PLAIN

Beautiful and sweet-natured, Dina is the most dutiful of
Faigie Reich's three lovely daughters. Living in the heart
of orthodox Jerusalem, the Reichs are a loving, happy
family, but Dina feels the dangerous call of her own
passions, which frighten and excite her.

In artistic Judah, Dina thinks she has met the man to
share these feelings, but, although he loves her deeply, he
cannot understand her yearnings. Lonely and frustrated,
she makes one, last, desperate bid for fulfilment... but her
innocence is cruelly betrayed and she finds herself accused
of a sin so great she fears she will be banished forever.

'A compelling glimpse into a world few of us
ever see, and of a courageous woman's battle for
freedom from that world'
JULIE ELLIS

0 00 647285 0

£4.99

Noble Beginnings

Christine Marion Fraser

Despite a traumatic childhood, young Anna McIntyre's indomitable spirit has won her many friends in the Argyllshire village where she lives. She is liked by everyone, especially by Lady Pandora of the Big House, who sees her young self in this lively girl, and by her nephew Peter who falls deeply in love with Anna. However, the person who should be closest to her resents her deeply, for reasons she cannot understand . . .

Roderick McIntyre, her father, is a tyrant with an insatiable taste for women and a determination to crush Anna's spirit. And when a surprise offer promises her the freedom she's yearned for, Roderick, too, sees his chance – to fulfil an enduring passion – and to shatter Anna's dreams forever. But Roderick has not counted on the courage of his only daughter, nor on the enemies he has made in Leannachoran, enemies waiting for revenge . . .

0 00 649013 1

Profit and Loss
Nicola Thorne

WHEN POWER AND PLEASURE
TURN POUNDS INTO PENNIES

The Binghams and Townsends are attractive, privileged, fulfilled. They live in Rushington, a charming and prosperous town whose inhabitants are enjoying the best of the boom. Natalie and Hilary are best friends. They each exude kindness and generosity, traits mutually admired. Their anxieties concern which evening class to attend, where to take the next holiday. Happiness is state-of-the-art Rushington. Or so it would seem. Then into their smug and smooth lives erupts a new couple – a thrusting bank manager and his socially ambitious wife. And before you could say 'Black Wednesday', that taboo word recession begins to have a meaning.

This story of contemporary life, of love, ambition, success and failure, will strike a chord with anyone who has survived the good times and the bad. Moving and relevant, it is also totally enthralling.

ISBN: 0 586 21171 3

Frank Delaney
A Stranger in Their Midst

INNOCENCE IS NO DEFENCE . . .

In village Ireland of the 1950s, Thomas and Ellen Kane's daughters, Helena and Grace, are gullible young women. Then, into their lives slinks Dennis Sykes, a brilliant and driven man, with a secret history of emotional mayhem and scandal. The Kane girls, lovingly close in fear of their disturbed father, have no defences against this sexual terrorist. As the decades roll forward, the outside world comes to Deanstown. Rural electrification, intended to illuminate the land, brings instead a tragedy as dark as Thomas Kane's moods.

Using great dramatic themes – the drowning of traditional houses in an ancient valley to build a dam, the destruction of a family's inner life – Delaney draws you in deep, into a time, and place, and family, in a novel that will keep you thinking long after you've finished reading.

'*A Stranger in Their Midst* is a dramatic novel. Written in clear, dry prose, it seldom loses its conviction.'   *The Times*

'Blast Frank Delaney. With his devious, seductive writing he keeps story addicts from their sleep.'   *OK!*

'Frank Delaney's *A Stranger in Their Midst* is excellent.'
     Woman and Home

'A powerful story vividly told.'   *Choice*

'A good old-fashioned tale of simple Irish folk doing battle with the future.'   *Evening Standard*

ISBN: 0 00 649318 1
(Published in paperback in May 1996)

Everything to Gain

Barbara Taylor Bradford

Mallory Keswick is a woman with the world at her feet. Then out of the blue, that world is shattered by violent tragedy and she loses all that she holds dear.

Torn by grief, Mal knows that she must rebuild her life. She flees to a village on the Yorkshire moors where she learns to draw on the deepest reserves of her spirit, and to look life in the eye once more.

Returning to Connecticut, Mal opens a café and shop selling gourmet food and kitchenware and turns it into a highly successful venture. But there remains in her life an aching void, a grief that no individual, nor her new-found business acumen, can assuage. Then she meets Richard Markson, and once more, Mal's life has come to a crossroads. It is he who shows her that she has everything to gain – but only if she has the courage to take it.

Totally absorbing and heartrendingly real, *Everything to Gain* lays bare Mallory's life to expose powerful feelings that are startlingly familiar, because they are our own.

'Heart-rending stuff . . . *Everything to Gain* is truly uplifting'
Today

ISBN: 0 586 21740 1